The
Nantucket
Reader

The
Nantucket
Reader

Edited and with an Introduction by
Susan F. Beegel

Mill Hill Press
Distinctive Nantucket Books
Nantucket, Massachusetts
MMIX

Published by Mill Hill Press
An affiliate of the
Egan Maritime Institute
4 Winter Street
Nantucket, Massachusetts 02554

www.eganmaritime.org

Cover art from a mural in Mitchell's Book Corner, Nantucket.
Reproduced courtesy of the artist, Kevin Paulsen
www.kevinpaulsen.com

Book design by Cecile Kaufman, X-Height Studio

ISBN 978-0-9822668-0-9

Library of Congress Control Number 2008922323

First Mill Hill Press printing 2009
Second Mill Hill Press printing 2010

Printed in the United States of America

In Loving Memory
of Wesley N. Tiffney, Jr.
1940-2003

Contents

VI. Refuge of the Free

VII. Distressing Calamities

VIII. Humor

IX. Contemporary Voices

X. Shipwrecks

XI. Finale

Introduction

FIRST AND FOREMOST, *The Nantucket Reader* is intended to supply a rollick-ing good read. Here you will find a selection of all the sorts of adventures we've come to expect from an island with Nantucket's illustrious whaling history—men hunting dinosaur-sized beasts from small boats, whales sinking ships, mutineers hacking up officers, and even an old-fashioned spot of drawing lots and cannibalism. You'll find samples, too, of all the pleasures a grand old summer resort can supply—swimming, sailing, sunbathing—and some vacation adven-tures as well—escaped pet canaries on the ferry, a creepy rented cottage, melt-down in a hotel lobby on a rainy day. And there are some less-expected adventures—a ghost in the attic, a great white shark terrorizing beach-goers, a kayak trip across Nantucket Sound—and wait until you learn what Tom Congdon found on a chimney ledge in his old house. . . .

But if, like Captain Ahab's first mate, Starbuck, "thou requirest a little lower layer," this anthology can supply that, too. More than a quaint backwater of charming regional writing, Nantucket has made major contributions to American literature, inspiring novels by Herman Melville and Edgar Allan Poe, journal entries by Henry David Thoreau and Ralph Waldo Emerson, a poem by Robert Lowell, a short story by John Cheever, essays by Paul Theroux and David Halberstam. Strong writers touched by the Nantucket experience have taken up their pens to change the life of the nation. The rhetoric of Edmund Burke, Thomas Jefferson, Frederick Douglass, William Lloyd Garrison, Stephen

Symonds Foster, Lucretia Mott, and Edward Pompey helped craft a vision of America as a global superpower commanding the commerce of two oceans, a nation with woman suffrage and without slavery, a nation with integrated schools, where literacy is the right of all and not a privilege of the few.

With choices ranging from certified masterpieces to light entertainment, *The Nantucket Reader* includes fifty selections loosely grouped according to broad themes. It's up to you to decide whether you'd rather explore the island or go whaling in the far Pacific, whether you're in the mood for comedy or calamity, whether you'd prefer the incendiary rhetoric of abolitionist days or cooler contemporary voices, whether you're interested in the words and deeds of the island's famously strong women or in one of the shipwrecks that have made Nantucket's shoals notorious. There's more than enough reading material here for the longest crossing by ferry, and plenty of selections short enough for a twenty-minute hop by airplane across Nantucket Sound. The book can be read from cover to cover if you're the ambitious sort, or by the section if a particular theme interests you—but it's primarily designed to allow readers to dip in and out as time and whimsy dictate. To facilitate "dipping," each selection has a brief introduction explaining the author's relationship to Nantucket.

This longer general introduction has a different purpose—to offer an overview of Nantucket's literary history, to shake the kaleidoscope of selections included here and drop them into the patterns of the past, surrounded by the colorful events that give them context. Now, if your favorite armchair or porch hammock is calling, and you are in a hurry to rush off and begin reading what John Greenleaf Whittier or Sena Jeter Naslund or Russell Baker or Nancy Thayer or J. Hector St. Jean de Crèvecoeur or Nathaniel Philbrick has had to say about Nantucket—go in peace. This is a Nantucket anthology after all, and what is Nantucket about if not the leisure to wander in and out as you please, whether in a dripping bathing suit or dripping oilskins. But if you find yourself curious about what these writers have in common, or about how the selections in *The Nantucket Reader* fit together from a historical perspective—linger now, or come back later. From a harpooneer who wrote the Great American Novel, to skinny-dipping, hard-drinking Nobel Prize winners, Nantucket's literary history is rich, illustrious, and a story in itself.

The first island author to make a lasting contribution to American literary history—Peter Folger—arrived in 1663, just four years after Nantucket's first English settler, Thomas Macy. Folger, in the words of Cotton Mather, was "a godly learned Englishman." Believing in education and literacy for others, Folger learned to read, write, and speak the Massachusett language in order to serve as an interpreter, schoolmaster, and evangelist to the Indians on both Martha's Vineyard and Nantucket. A Baptist who had removed to Nantucket to escape persecution by the Puritans on Martha's Vineyard, Folger was also something of a political firebrand, leading Nantucket's half-share men in a revolt against the island's proprietors when he was in his sixties.

Folger's best-known contribution to American literature was a lengthy poem, *A Looking Glass for the Times; or, The Former Spirit of New England Revived in this Generation,* published in 1676. Folger's grandson, Benjamin Franklin, described the poem—written during King Phillip's War—as "in favour of Liberty of Conscience, and in behalf of the Baptists, Quakers, and other Sectaries, that had been under Persecution; ascribing the Indian Wars and other Distresses, that had befallen the Country to that Persecution, as so many Judgments of God, to punish so heinous an Offence; and exhorting a Repeal of those uncharitable laws."

A Looking Glass for the Times sounds an important theme that will echo in much of the Nantucket literature to come—a tradition of dissent, of intellectual freedom, of standing apart from the mainland's most oppressive ideas. And it's significant because in the poem, the man who helped set off Nantucket's half-share revolt would unwittingly model some of the principles of the American Revolution for his more famous grandson. But Folger's writing, in the words of one critic, is "without one sparkle of poetry." *The Cambridge History of English and American Literature* opines that "its four hundred lines in ballad quatrains are very bad verse." Even Benjamin Franklin, while admiring the poem's "Decent Plainness and manly Freedom," had to admit that his grandfather's style was at best "homespun." The conclusion of *A Looking Glass* is an example:

> I am for Peace, and not for War,
>   And that's the reason why,
> I write more plain than some Men do,
>   That use to daub and lie;
> But I shall cease and set my Name
>   To what I here insert,
> Because to be a Libeller,
>   I hate it with my Heart.
> From Sherburne Town where now I dwell,
>   My name I do put here,
> Without Offence, your real Friend,
>   It is Peter Folgier.

Four hundred lines of this sort of thing might be a bit much for today's reader, so you won't find *A Looking Glass* in this collection. But those interested in Folger's influence—which extends beyond Franklin—should turn to Henry David Thoreau's journal entries about his Nantucket visit. There, Thoreau quotes some of Folger's most powerful remarks on intolerance and the war with the Indians.

It would take more than a century for the next author of note to arrive on Nantucket. J. Hector St. John de Crèvecoeur, whose classic *Letters from an American Farmer* (1782) is well represented in this volume, visited the island in 1773. There he found the inhabitants far too busy with the demanding occupations of farming, fishing, and whaling to have much time for literary endeavor. "I found very few books among these people, who have very little time for reading"; Crèvecoeur observed, "the Bible and a few school tracts, both in the Nattic and English languages, constituted their most numerous libraries."

But Crèvecoeur did note two curious exceptions: "I saw indeed several copies of Hudibras and Josephus, but no one knows who first imported them." Crèvecoeur, who was French, was positively baffled by Nantucket's affection for *Hudibras,* a long, satiric epic by English poet Samuel Butler. "It is something extraordinary to see this people, professedly so grave and strangers to every branch of literature, reading [*Hudibras*] with pleasure. . . . They all read it much and can by memory repeat many passages." Full of bawdy, Rabelaisian humor and modeled on Miguel de Cervantes's 1605 comic adventure *Don Quixote,* *Hudibras* mocks the hypocrisy and self-seeking of the English Puritans. Crèvecoeur didn't get it, but it's not hard to guess why Nantucketers, whose Baptist ancestors came to the island to escape Puritanism's iron grip on the Massachusetts Bay Colony, and who were predominantly Quaker by 1773, may have found *Hudibras* hilarious. Nantucket's interest in the works of first-century Jewish historian Flavius Josephus (Yosef Ben Matityahu), providing an eyewitness account of early Christianity, was more understandable to Crèvecoeur, "as it describes the history of a people from whom we receive the prophecies which we believe and the religious laws which we follow." Still, he wondered, "Is it not a little singular to see these books in the hands of fishermen, who are perfect strangers almost to any other?"

During the years surrounding the American Revolution, Nantucket's principal contribution to our soon-to-be national literature was to become a kind of metaphor for the American experience, or, in Nathaniel Philbrick's words, "an American icon." "What then is the American, this new man?" Crèvecoeur asked in *Letters from an American Farmer,* and believed he had found the answer on Nantucket—"[T]hough it is barren in its soil, insignificant in its extent, inconvenient in its situation, deprived of materials for building, it seems to have been inhabited merely to prove what mankind can do when happily governed!" Indeed, between 1762 and 1770, Nantucket's whaling fleet grew from seventy-five to a hundred and twenty-five vessels as this little island—Melville's "mere hillock and elbow of sand"—launched "a navy of great ships on the sea."

Nantucket understandably became a metaphor for America's aggressive entrepreneurship and pioneering spirit. By 1775, according to Edouard Stackpole, she would have a hundred and fifty sloops, schooners, and brigs hunting whales in the North and South Atlantic. That same year, when Edmund Burke stood up in Parliament and tried to persuade Great Britain not to go to war with the rebellious American colonies, Nantucket was his example of how much the mother country had to lose:

> No sea but what is vexed by their fisheries; no climate that is not witness to their toils. Neither the perseverance of Holland, nor the activity of France, nor the dexterous and firm sagacity of English enterprise ever carried this most perilous mode of hardy industry to the extent to which it has been pushed by this recent people; a people who are still, as it were, but in the gristle, and not yet hardened into the bone of manhood. When I contemplate these things; . . . when I see how profitable they have been to us, I feel all the pride of power sink. . . .

Parliament failed to heed Burke's warning, and the years of the American Revolution would be years of blockade, famine, and capture for Nantucket whalemen. But there is no finer testimony to their persistence and vitality than the fact that in 1783, with the Revolution just ended, the Nantucket whaleship *Bedford* became the first American vessel to fly the Stars and Stripes in British waters.

By 1788, the year the U.S. Constitution was ratified, Nantucket had become Thomas Jefferson's example of how much the new nation had to lose if the island's prime seamen, with their expertise in whaling, succumbed to British and French blandishments to leave the island for foreign shores. In "Observations on the Whale Fishery," Nantucket became for Jefferson what it had been for Burke—an icon of America's potential maritime and economic power. Seven years before George Washington signed the Armament Act, creating the U.S. Navy, Jefferson "saw the danger of permitting five or six thousand of the best seamen existing to be transferred by a single stroke to the marine strength of their enemy, and to carry over with them an art which they possessed almost exclusively."

No less a writer than James Fenimore Cooper took this view of Nantucket to heart when, in 1823, he published the book widely proclaimed to be the first sea novel—a fiction in which the sea and a ship are the principal settings—*The Pilot*. The novel follows the cruise of two Continental vessels during the American Revolution and is largely set in the English Channel, so we've reluctantly chosen not to represent it in this collection. But *The Pilot* does feature perhaps the first Nantucket character in American fiction, Long Tom Coffin, who in a pitched battle with a British cutter uses his harpoon to pin the British commander to the mast of his own ship. "In such a business as this," says the novel's American Captain Barnstable, "I would sooner trust Tom Coffin and his harpoon to back me, than the best broadside that ever rattled out of the three decks of a ninety-gun ship." Coffin is the embodiment of that dangerously vigorous Nantucket species of *Homo americanus* hinted at by Crèvecoeur, Burke, and Jefferson.

As stocks of whales in the Atlantic became exhausted, Nantucket seamen like Long Tom would play a crucial role in opening the vast and largely unexplored wilderness of the Pacific Ocean to exploitation. For a time, as Jefferson feared, it remained uncertain whether the young American nation or older European powers would benefit most from Nantucket expertise. In 1789, as mobs in France stormed the Bastille, Nantucketer Archaelus Hammond became the first white man to strike and kill a sperm whale in the Pacific Ocean—an act performed for the British whaleship *Emelia*. By 1792, there would be nine whaleships in the Pacific—four from France, two from Nantucket, two from England, and one from New Bedford—all but one of them commanded by a Nantucketer. Years of global warfare—the French Revolution, the Napoleonic Wars, the War of 1812, the Tripolitan Wars—took their toll on maritime enterprise worldwide, including Nantucket whaling. But by 1815, with these wars fading in their wake, Nantucketers were poised to turn the Pacific into an American ocean, and by 1820, the Golden Age of Nantucket whaling had begun—with around twenty-five ships a year setting sail from the island for the Pacific grounds.

The result was a sea change in Nantucket literature, as the island became synonymous not only with American enterprise, but with high adventure. It's difficult to recapture how distant and exotic, dangerous and enticing, the Pacific seemed to readers in the early nineteenth century. Suffice it to say that in 1969 it took Apollo 11 astronauts just three days to reach the moon, while in 1819 it took the men of the whaleship *Essex* three and half months to sail from Nantucket to Cape Horn, at the tip of South America, and, once at the Cape, another month to battle their way around into the Pacific through contrary winds and mountainous seas. The Pacific, then, was forty-five times more distant than the moon. And while there is no life on the moon, the Pacific's tens of thousands of islands teemed with flora and fauna and aboriginal peoples unknown to nineteenth-century science.

Small wonder that contemporary readers craved true stories from the brave Nantucket whalemen who had penetrated and explored this extreme environment. Especially, nineteenth-century readers thrilled to disaster narratives—a ship stove by a whale, cannibalism in open boats, mutiny, massacre, and marooning. Two Nantucket narratives from the 1820s—Owen Chase's *Narrative of the Most Extraordinary and Distressing Shipwreck of the Whaleship Essex of Nantucket* (1821) and William Lay and Cyrus Hussey's *Mutiny on Board the*

Whaleship Globe (1828) made a lasting impact on American literature, and are still in print today.

A relatively new genre when the century began, the novel would become the dominant literary form of the nineteenth century. By the 1830s, there was widespread recognition that the Nantucket experience might be the stuff of bestselling fiction. Edgar Allan Poe, capitalizing on the rage for disaster narratives, produced a satire of the genre, *The Narrative of Arthur Gordon Pym of Nantucket* (1838), a wild romp through every conceivable sort of maritime mishap. The magazine grew in popularity alongside of the novel (Poe's *Pym* was originally serialized in the *Southern Literary Messenger),* creating a market for short fiction. In an 1839 issue of the New York *Knickerbocker,* explorer Jeremiah N. Reynolds—who had circumnavigated the globe earlier in the decade—published a salty yarn ostensibly collected from a Nantucket whaleman: "Mocha-Dick; Or, the White Whale of the Pacific."

As the Golden Age of Nantucket whaling approached its zenith, the island's more than ten thousand residents began to look with pride on their illustrious history, and Nantucket literature changed accordingly. In 1834, the same year that Edward Bulwer-Lytton's historical novel *The Last Days of Pompeii* was a smash hit, Joseph Coleman Hart won equivalent success in America with *Miriam Coffin, or The Whale Fishermen,* set both on Nantucket and on the Pacific whaling grounds during the Revolution. Perhaps inspired by Hart's success, Obed Macy produced his nonfiction *History of Nantucket* in 1835, understanding that on the island, many a truth is stranger than fiction. Macy would begin the insatiable demand for Nantucket history that continues to this day.

Literacy on Nantucket was no longer the perquisite of a privileged few. In 1825, the island opened the doors of its first public elementary schools. These schools were segregated, however, and because whaling provided jobs for free black men, with opportunities for responsibility and promotion, the island possessed a large and relatively prosperous black community interested in securing the blessings of education for their children. Black sea captain and businessman Absalom Boston, whose cruise in the schooner *Industry* with an all-black crew is memorialized in this volume, took action, funding construction of the island's African school. By 1838, Nantucket was ready to open its first public high school. But again, black students were excluded, and when political agitation on the island failed to resolve the problem, another black mariner took the helm. Captain Edward J. Pompey, together with a hundred and four other black citizens of Nantucket, petitioned the state legislature for redress in 1845, and the result was Massachusetts House Bill Number 45, An Act Concerning Public Schools, thought to be the first civil rights bill in the United States guaranteeing equal access to education.

Many island shipowners began to recognize the benefits of an educated work force, and provided lending libraries on board their vessels so that crew members could enjoy reading during long and tedious hours at sea. The Nantucket Historical Association's Research Library possesses the book list for the 1840–45 voyage of the whaleship *Charles and Henry*. That list tells us something about what Nantucket's whaling barons expected a shipboard library to accomplish. Whaleship literature was above all morally uplifting (*Young Christian, Moral Tales, Fireside Piety, Are You a Christian?*). It encouraged young men to work hard and save their money (*Strive and Thrive, Victims of Gaming, A History of Banking*), and to follow a lifestyle including temperance, chastity, cold showers, fresh air, loose clothing, exercise, and whole-wheat bread (*Graham's Lectures on the Science of Human Life*). Whalemen were expected to take a serious interest in history (*Washington, The American Revolution, Readings in History*) and contemporary politics (*Harrison versus Van Buren*), and to savor just a smattering of adventure (*Shipwrecked on a Desert Island, Jack Halyard*). They were not all expected to be able to read very well, as evidenced by *A Child's Robinson Crusoe*.

One foremast hand on that voyage of the *Charles and Henry*, a ragged harpooneer picked up off the beach in Tahiti, was doubtless grateful to discover anything at all to read on board, although he would have preferred Dante or Shakespeare. Herman Melville, who found the *Charles and Henry* a "comfortable craft" with a "free-hearted captain," nevertheless poked fun at its library in *Moby-Dick*, gently mocking Quaker shipowners for plying their crews with religious tracts and for placing hymnals in the seamen's bunks to curb "profane singing."

Melville's misgiving notwithstanding, nineteenth-century Nantucket readers had come a long way from the rude fishermen Crèvecoeur had observed handing around a few threadbare books. A seafaring people whose business now girdled the globe, islanders were among the most cosmopolitan of Americans. Sarah Orne Jewett's nostalgic character Captain Littlepage, looking back on the Age of Sail in her lovely novel *The Country of the Pointed Firs* (1896), might have been describing the island during this period when he says:

> In the old days, a good part o' the best men here knew a hundred ports and something of the way folks lived in them. They saw the world for themselves. . . . They may not have had the best of knowledge to carry with 'em sight-seein', but they were some acquainted with foreign lands an' their laws, an' could see outside the battle for town clerk here in Dunnet; they got some sense o' proportion. Yes, they lived more dignified, and their houses were better within an' without.

The "best men" on Nantucket were understandably ambitious to be among the most literate of Americans as well. As Captain Littlepage puts it, "A shipmaster was apt to get the habit of reading . . . for company's sake in the dull days and nights he turns to his book. Most of us old shipmasters came to know 'most everything about something. . . .'" "Literature thrives well in Nantucket," wrote Theodore Parker. "There is a deal of reading."

As the magnificent Federal and Greek Revival mansions of Main Street—built in the 1830s and 1840s—so eloquently demonstrate, whaling brought immense wealth to the island. Wealth, in its turn, brought education, culture, and leisure for pursuing the arts and sciences. And so the year 1834 saw a momentous occasion for island readers, the incorporation of the Nantucket Atheneum. The library was the brainchild of two men—David Joy, a self-educated "mechanic" and amateur chemist who grew rich when he invented a process for manufacturing spermaceti candles, and Charles G. Coffin, wealthy shipowner and eldest son of whaling baron Zenas Coffin. Together, Joy and Coffin combined the collections of the Nantucket Mechanics Social Library Association and the Columbian Library Society, and purchased a disused Universalist church at the corner of Federal and Pearl (now India) streets to house the books. They sold ten-dollar shares to civic-minded men and women who would become their fellow proprietors, and used the funds to endow and operate the library. "This humble beginning," quoth the Reverend Adin Ballou, speaking at Joy's memorial service in 1875, "culminated at length in the Nantucket Atheneum, the literary glory of your town—now replete with the treasures of art and knowledge to bless thousands yet unborn."

Astronomer Maria Mitchell, who would be catapulted to international fame by her discovery of a comet in 1847, served as the Atheneum's librarian from 1836 until 1856. Mitchell, with a fervent belief in the value of higher education (she would eventually become the first Professor of Astronomy at Vassar College and President of the Association for the Advancement of Women), selected books for the community throughout her tenure at the Atheneum, and did a great deal to shape the values of Nantucket readers. "[T]here are persons," she wrote, "hungry for the food of the mind, the wants of which are as imperious as those of the body. . . . So I steadily advocate in purchasing books for the Atheneum, the *lifting* of the people. 'Let us buy, not such books as the people want, but books just above their wants, and they will reach up to take what is put out for them.' We may in this way, form on Nantucket, a taste for the refined and elevated. . . . " Mitchell crammed the Atheneum's shelves with volumes that could, in themselves, comprise a fine college education—the latest scientific books and journals, a carefully developed history collection, the classic works of Milton and Shakespeare, and the finest contemporary literature, such as Harriet Beecher Stowe's bestselling anti-slavery novel, *Uncle Tom's Cabin* (1852) or Elizabeth Barrett Browning's epic feminist poem, *Aurora Leigh* (1856).

More than a library, the Nantucket Atheneum in the mid-nineteenth century was also the scene of an ongoing series of lectures that brought some of the most distinguished minds of the age to the island. This phenomenon was part of the era's nationwide Lyceum Movement. Named for the Greek Lyceum, a school near Athens where the philosopher Aristotle lectured to students, the movement was intended to promote adult education by bringing inspiring speakers and college-style lecture courses directly to communities. During this period, a few of the luminaries gracing the Atheneum's stage included artist and ornithologist John James Audubon, Harvard biology professor Louis Agassiz, educational reformer Horace Mann, Unitarian minister Theodore Parker, editor of the *New York Tribune,* Horace Greeley, and pioneering female journalist Sarah Josepha Hale. But Nantucket readers must especially rejoice in visits by two towering figures of the American literary renaissance—Ralph Waldo Emerson and Henry David Thoreau—and the impressions of the island they left in their journals.

During the 1840s, Nantucket was swept up in the anti-slavery agitation gripping the nation. Abolitionist sentiment burned fiercely in Massachusetts, and in a poem titled "The Exiles" (1840), the immensely popular John Greenleaf Whittier used an episode from island history—Thomas Macy's harboring of a Quaker fleeing Puritan persecution—to suggest how citizens of a free state ought to receive fugitive slaves. Whittier called Nantucket a "refuge of the free"—and in the 1840s that title was hard-fought and hard-won, with consequent gains for American literature. In 1841, a shareholder revolt forced the Atheneum to open its doors to political debate and to "persons of color" just in time for a fugitive slave named Frederick Douglass to make his first-ever speech to an anti-slavery meeting. Douglass electrified Nantucket, and his success at the Atheneum began his career as the pre-eminent African-American author, editor, orator, and diplomat of the nineteenth century. Abolitionist William Lloyd Garrison, editor of *The Liberator*, also thundered from the Nantucket stage, and wrote about the advent of Douglass. Yet another anti-slavery convention sparked a riot that saw library windows smashed and audiences driven from the Atheneum by angry mobs. This too was a literary event, as Stephen Symonds Foster, the speaker who had roused such wrath, chose to explain himself in another important publication of the abolitionist movement, *The Brotherhood of Thieves, or A True Picture of the American Church and Clergy; A Letter to Nathaniel Barney of Nantucket* (1843).

Nantucket women of the whaling era were made literate by a Quaker belief in equality of education and made self-reliant by their husbands' long absences at sea. Island-born Lucretia Coffin Mott would use her Nantucket heritage and her skill at writing and oratory to create the American movement for woman suffrage. Mott was an architect of the nation's first Women's Rights Convention, held in 1848 at Seneca Falls, New York. In 1854, Mott would return to the island in triumph to speak from the stage of the Atheneum, an institution whose fine collections and lyceum lectures, in an era when women could not attend college, had special significance for her Nantucket sisters. Mott's efforts would have some unintended consequences for island women. While prior to 1848 it was considered unthinkable for women to accompany their whaling husbands to sea, after Seneca Falls a new consciousness of women's capacities made such voyages not only permissible but common-place—giving to the Nantucket reader treasures such as Eliza Spencer Brock's journal of her cruise on the whaleship *Lexington* (1853–56) and Martha Ford's "Nantucket Girls' Song" (1855).

"Like a billow that's all one crested comb," the glory days of Nantucket literature would peak with the 1851 publication of Herman Melville's *Moby-Dick*. "It is surely Melville's greatest book," wrote critic Carl Van Vechten, and, echoing the sentiments of many readers, "surely the greatest book that has yet been written in America, surely one of the great books of the world." "Who is this rough 'sailor before the mast,' in jacket and tarpaulin, with rolling gait and tarry aspect, who intrudes so unceremoniously upon the grave and black-coated fraternity of American Authors, and boldly elbows his way to a front seat among the best of them?" asked an anonymous contemporary reviewer about Herman Melville. The question seems to echo Crèvecoeur's "What, then, is the American, this new man?" We might answer that Herman Melville was a kind of literary Long Tom Coffin, ready to pin the best authors in the English language to the mast with his harpoon.

Moby-Dick owes its very existence to the Nantucket experience, to Melville's four years at sea (1841–45) as a whaleman. As Melville's authorial character Ishmael acknowledges, "A whale ship was my Yale College and my Harvard." The curriculum of that college included an extensive course in Nantucket literature—*Moby-Dick* is openly indebted not only to Dante, Milton, and Shakespeare, but to almost all of the Nantucket authors who preceded Melville—Edmund Burke, Thomas Jefferson, James Fenimore Cooper, Owen Chase, William Lay and Cyrus Hussey, Joseph C. Hart, and Obed Macy, as well as to the island's Indian legends, shipboard folklore, and sea chanteys. Many scholars believe the novel is also indebted to Jeremiah N. Reynolds and to Edgar Allan Poe.

Moby-Dick is, however, a romantic and nostalgic book. Nantucket's supremacy as a whaling port had ended well before the novel's 1851 appearance. The island's drifting harbor bar; its lack of access to mainland railroad facilities;

the Great Fire of 1846, which destroyed the warehouses and factories that were an essential part of Nantucket's whaling infrastructure; and the 1849 departure of her whaling fleet to carry passengers to the California Gold Rush were in part responsible. Whaling itself was a dying industry. Nantucketers knew that whales, hunted to the brink of extinction, could not continue to supply oil for a burgeoning Industrial Revolution, and the quest was on for alternative sources of energy. The first commercial uses of petroleum had begun a decade before *Moby-Dick* appeared, and 1852, the year after the novel's publication, saw the patenting of kerosene, the fuel that would make whale oil obsolete. Then, too, the Age of Sail was drawing to a close. While Ishmael in *Moby-Dick* travels to Nantucket on a sailing packet, Melville in 1852 arrived on the steamship *Massachusetts*—then a ten-year-old vessel in the island's twenty-year-old steamship service.

To those with a literary turn of mind, nothing is more tragic than the destruction of an historic library. The Great Fire of 1846 also claimed the original Nantucket Atheneum. Gone was a collection of some three thousand books, including such cherished volumes as a first edition of Melville's first novel, *Typee: A Peep at Polynesian Life,* and an invaluable copy of John James Audubon's elephant folio, a collection of ornithological prints carried to Nantucket by Audubon himself. Gone, too, was an unequaled collection of Polynesian artifacts brought home from the South Seas by the island's whalemen. Yet despite the fact that seven-eighths of the island's working people had lost their shops, stock, and tools in the fire, and although hundreds of Nantucketers were homeless, the community rallied to rebuild the focal point of its intellectual life. Within six months, the magnificent Greek Revival building that houses the Atheneum today rose from the blackened wasteland of Nantucket's burnt-out business district.

Up until Maria Mitchell's departure as librarian in 1856, the Atheneum continued to supply islanders with well-chosen literature and lively lyceum lectures by famous figures. But the Nantucket community was withering away. In the words of Richard Miller and Robert Mooney, "The island of Nantucket in 1860 was in a condition of economic and social depression. The population had fallen to 6,094, representing a forty percent decline during the previous decade. ...As the new decade opened, Nantucket's once proud fleet had dwindled to six ships and was at the point of extinction." The coming of the Civil War in 1861 continued the exodus from the island, and would end Nantucket whaling—and Nantucket's nineteenth-century prosperity—permanently. So worthless had the island's aging whaleships become that a number of them were taken south, filled with stones, and sunk in the entrance of Charleston Harbor to assist with the blockade of this important Confederate port. Even this endeavor proved fruitless, as shifting currents reopened the channel. Yet these vessels would serve the cause of literature. Herman Melville wrote their epitaph in a poem, "The Stone Fleet: An Old Sailor's Lament" (1861), which opens:

> I have a feeling for these ships,
>   Each worn and ancient one,
> With great bluff bows, and broad in the beam:
>   Ay, it was unkindly done.
>   But so they serve the Obsolete—
>   Even so, Stone Fleet!

By the end of the Civil War in 1865, Nantucket's year-round population had dropped to 4,830, and in 1870 it hit a temporary bottom of 4,123—a sixty percent decline from the heyday of whaling. Not only was whaling over, but the war had destroyed the possibility of other maritime business as well. Before the war began, the American merchant fleet, much of it centered in New England, had carried two-thirds of the nation's foreign commerce. But during the war, fear of Confederate raiders sent insurance rates so high that there was a "flight from the flag," as Northern merchants shifted to British ships and British ports to save money and protect their cargoes and Northern shipowners sold their vessels abroad. At war's end, American vessels carried less than one-third of foreign commerce, and by the end of the century, less than ten percent. Nantucket's era as a maritime community was firmly and irrevocably over, and with this sea change, the literary tide went out as well.

It didn't take the remaining islanders long, however, to decide that the tourist trade might make Nantucket rich again. They swiftly took stock of their assets—the handsome historic architecture of Nantucket town, the quaint village of 'Sconset, the eighty miles of pristine beaches, the cool sea breezes, the rolling moors, the fascinating history. The Massachusetts Old Colony Railroad entered into the scheme, deciding in the 1870s that it too might thrive by promoting the vacation trade on Cape Cod and the islands. The railroad began service from Boston to Hyannis and Woods Hole, where tourists could connect with steamboats to Martha's Vineyard and Nantucket. As American cities became ever more crowded and unwholesome in an era before air conditioning, refrigeration, concern about air pollution, or widespread vaccination against epidemic disease, more and more urbanites found the wisdom of summering on then-uncrowded Nantucket, with its clean air, clean water, fresh seafood, and farm produce. Slowly, the island began to work its way back towards prosperity. And slowly the literary tide—a very different kind of literary tide—began to creep back in.

During the month of September 1910, a matron from the Chicago suburb of Oak Park decided to take her eleven-year-old son to Nantucket to enjoy the sort of vacation she herself had enjoyed when her parents had taken her to the island as a child during the 1870s and early 1880s. They stayed at Miss Annie Ayers's boarding house on Pearl Street, a traditional Nantucket home over a hundred years old, and enjoyed such amusements as visiting a whaling exhibition at the Fair Street Museum, created by the Nantucket Historical Association, recently founded in 1894. They toured the still-active Surfside Lifesaving Station, hiked across the moors, and best of all, chartered a catboat to take them fishing and sailing to Great Point. They picnicked and collected seashells. The boy caught a mackerel and the boarding house cook prepared it for dinner. He went for his first swim in the ocean—a bit unnerved by the kelp and the horseshoe crabs— while his mother, attired in a floppy, broad-brimmed hat, a long-sleeved bathing dress featuring a skirt over bloomers, black stockings, and canvas bathing shoes, decorously dunked herself in heated salt water at Hayden's Salt Water Baths.

The eleven-year-old boy was Ernest Hemingway, and perhaps the highlight of the trip for him was meeting an old fisherman on the docks who sold him the bill of an immense swordfish. Young Ernest thought the old man's name was "Judas," but the late Edouard Stackpole and J. Clinton Andrews have both identified the fisherman as Judah Nickerson. Interestingly enough, the *Inquirer and Mirror* reported in July 1887 that Judah had caught a "noble swordfish," an exceptionally large specimen that might have weighed over a thousand pounds to earn such mention. It may have been the bill of this swordfish, almost certainly captured by harpooning, that Judah gave to the boy. Hemingway never wrote about Nantucket directly, except to mention it affectionately in letters to his mother, but something of his island experience seems to have crept into *The Old Man and the Sea* (1952), which climaxes with the harpooning of a giant marlin:

> The old man dropped the line and put his foot on it and lifted the harpoon as high as he could and drove it down with all his strength, and more strength he had just summoned, into the fish's side just behind the great chest fin that rose high in the air to the altitude of the man's chest. He felt the iron go in and he leaned on it and drove it further and then pushed all his weight after it. . . . Then the fish came alive, with his death in him, and rose high out of the water showing all his great length and width and all his power and his beauty.

Hemingway's boyhood visit to Nantucket echoes most strongly of all, however, in the novel's tender final moments when the boy, Manolin, asks for and receives the spear of the old Cuban fisherman Santiago's great catch. The triumphant success of *The Old Man and the Sea* would be instrumental in Hemingway's receipt of the 1954 Nobel Prize for Literature.

When the Hemingways vacationed on Nantucket in 1910, they found an island with fewer than three thousand year-round residents that nevertheless possessed a vibrant cultural life. Ernest's mother, Grace Hall Hemingway, a music professional with an opera-quality contralto voice, gave two recitals while on-island, attended woman suffrage meetings in the Atheneum's Great Hall, and was inspired, in time, to write a collection of short stories about strong island women, "Tales of Old Nantucket." In part because of the strong ties between the village of 'Sconset and New York's theater community, Nantucket at the turn of the twentieth century was a place where visitors could meet artists, musicians, and writers. Between 1895 and the outbreak of World War I, 'Sconset was home to a flourishing summer colony for actors affiliated with the Lambs of New York—the first club for theater professionals in America. William O. Stevens notes that at its peak there could be as many as fifty Lambs actors on Nantucket at one time, and that virtually "all the head-liners of the stage" summered on the island during this period. Naturally, the actors' colony attracted producers and playwrights, too. The Hemingways, for instance, were excited to meet playwright Austin Strong, soon-to-be author of New York theater hits *Three Wise Fools* (1918) and *Seventh Heaven* (1922). Robert Louis Stevenson's step-grandson, Strong told his thrilled guests stories of life with Stevenson on Samoa.

After an especially grim hiatus for World War I, when German submarines stalked the channels through Nantucket's shoals, torpedoed passing ships, and even shelled fishing boats on Georges Bank—Americans were ready once again for carefree summer days on the island. Frank B. Gilbreth, Jr. and Ernestine Gilbert Carey's exuberant memoir, *Cheaper by the Dozen* (1945), captures the sheer joy of summering on Nantucket during the Roaring Twenties. The Gilbreth family—with twelve children—began vacationing on the island in 1921, in the era when automobiles were still banned. Today's summer residents might be surprised to know how much fun a large family can have living in a ramshackle cottage and two small "bug-lights" (once range-finding light-houses for the harbor channel), with one lavatory, no hot water, and no shower or bath. For the Gilbreth children, summer was about sailing, swimming, and "quality time" with their otherwise busy professional parents.

The year 1922 saw a momentous occasion for Nantucket readers—the creation of the 'Sconset School of Opinion. Economist and liberal political reformer Frederic C. Howe purchased an old barn near the 'Sconset firehouse, and transformed it into an auditorium called the Tavern on the Moors, with housing for participants in primitive cottages and even tents nearby. Harking back, in a way, to the nineteenth-century Lyceum Movement, the School of Opinion was to be an adult summer school for discussion among intellectuals, modeled on Emerson's School of Philosophy at Concord, and hosting as many as one hundred attendees at a time. "Great days are dawning for that village which the gods call Siasconset and men call 'Sconset," trumpeted *The New York Times*. "Many liberal thinkers of high eminence will lecture or conduct round-table conferences. . . . There are to be discussions as well as lectures; two or more of these in the morning, followed by an hour on the beach, with the afternoon free for tennis, golf, tramping parties and conferences; and the evenings will be filled with lectures and discussions."

The 'Sconset School lasted for just nine seasons, but would do much to convince the literary world of Nantucket's desirability as a place to escape from the pressures of urban civilization and find the peace for writing undisturbed. Sinclair Lewis, who would win the Nobel Prize for Literature in 1930, is a case in point. Lewis took part in a literary roundtable at the 'Sconset School in 1924, spending his hours away from the seminars working on his novel *Arrowsmith* (1925) and driving across the moors to go skinny-dipping off the south shore. *Arrowsmith* is not about Nantucket, but rather the career of a physician who finds his ideals tested by the greed and opportunism he encounters in the practice of medicine and research. Nevertheless, Dr. Arrowsmith faces his greatest challenges during an outbreak of plague on a Caribbean island—and Lewis's time on Nantucket may have helped him to imagine what an island would be like during an epidemic.

The Roaring Twenties was also the era of Prohibition—and Nantucket was an ideal spot for bootlegging. European vessels loaded with Scotch whisky and French champagne moored in the Sound, and small boats went out under cover of darkness to bring their illicit cargo ashore. Crime syndicates from both Boston and New York operated around the island—one Brooklyn gang alone had a fleet of twenty boats stationed at Nantucket—and alcohol flowed freely on the island. What has this got to do with literature? Well, to quote Sinclair Lewis, himself an alcoholic—"Can you name five American writers since Poe who did not die of alcoholism?" The question is not entirely facetious—five out of eight American writers who have won the Nobel Prize for literature have been alcoholic. During Prohibition, easy access to good liquor, as well as to good times, was definitely one attraction Nantucket possessed for writers such as Eugene O'Neill, another 'Sconset School participant and future Nobelist. O'Neill spent the summer of 1925 writing in a rented cottage at 5 Mill Street and also got roaring drunk aboard a friend's yacht and fell into the harbor fully clothed. Not surprisingly, it wasn't an especially productive visit.

The 'Sconset School of Opinion and the village actors' colony were also responsible for bringing theater critic, screenwriter, actor, raconteur, and bon vivant Robert Benchley to Nantucket in 1922. Benchley was an especially valuable addition to Nantucket literature because he would become part of the life of the island, returning again and again to stay at the Underhill Cottages, performing at the 'Sconset Casino, founding a literary dynasty of Nantucket writers including his son Nathaniel Benchley and grandson Peter, and finally purchasing the first family property on the island—a burial plot in Prospect Hill Cemetery. And Robert Benchley was loyal to Nantucket, writing humorous essays about *la dolce vita* and the summer scene even during the dark years of the Great Depression.

In the 1930s, Nantucket, like the rest of the nation, fell on hard times. The tourist trade dried up, and the Nantucket Savings Bank foreclosed on three of the island's largest hotels, the Sea Cliff (demolished in 1968), the Point Breeze (renovated and opened as a private club with the same name in 2008), and the Ocean House (today the Jared Coffin House). By the middle of the decade, there was almost universal unemployment on Nantucket. Hundreds of men lined up for jobs with a public works project improving the island's dirt roads. In the summers of 1935 and 1936, prices were so depressed that a boy just starting college, Robert Lowell, could afford to rent a cottage at Madaket and try his hand at writing poetry. Some old-time natives remember not having enough money for food, and eating seagulls to make ends meet. Some summer people who had lost everything in the Crash of 1929 gave up their mainland homes and retreated to their island cottages year-round, adding a new dimension to Nantucket society. And yet islanders—year-round and summer residents alike—conducted themselves with determined cheer—perhaps best exemplified by the giant inflatable sea monster launched in the harbor by Tony Sarg in 1937. Robert Benchley's comedic repertoire, which takes its satirical thrust from finding extreme hardship in the midst of luxury (the terrible difficulty of finding a comfortable position for sunbathing, for instance), brought smiles to people experiencing the real thing.

And then came World War II. The island advertised itself as "An Oasis of Peace in a World at War," but even so, restrictions on travel, gasoline rationing, and the coastal "dim-out" took their toll on the tourist trade. The Army took over Crest Hall Hotel (now the Harbor House); the Navy took over the airport. Ferries were painted battleship gray, and passengers were forbidden to use cameras. The *Naushon* was taken by the government to become a hospital ship, and the *New Bedford* became a freight carrier. The beaches were closed at sunset. The shoreline was littered with wreckage and slicked with oil from the many ships sunk by German U-boats in the Battle of the Atlantic. Nantucket men and women signed up to do their part. The war was not a time for literary endeavor, yet it made two important contributions. Robert Mooney notes that "Mysterious sightings of submarines, flashing lights off-shore, and actual landings of U-boats to pick up supplies were part of the rumor mill." Nathaniel Benchley, who served in the U. S. Naval Reserve during the war, took note, and would later translate this material into his novel of Cold War comedy, *The Off-Islanders* (1961). World War II would also give American literature its first Nantucket masterpiece since *Moby-Dick,* Robert Lowell's great poem about the tragedy and brutality of war, "The Quaker Graveyard in Nantucket" (1945).

When World War II ended, the summer people came flooding back, and with them came the writers. Tennessee Williams and Carson McCullers spent the summer of 1946 in a cottage at 31 Pine Street. He worked on his play *Summer and Smoke* (1948); McCullers on revising her newly published novel, *A Member of the Wedding* (1946), for the stage. They found time for some summer hijinks, too, visiting the farm of an annoying neighbor, filling her pigs' trough with whisky, and watching the animals get drunk. The summer of 1947 brought Truman Capote and Christopher Isherwood. When he wasn't bicycling to 'Sconset or tanning on the deck, the twenty-two-year-old Capote worked on *Other Voices, Other Rooms* (1948), his breakout bestseller.

Alerted to the special virtues of the island by New York neighbors Nathaniel and Marge Benchley, John Steinbeck took his new bride and two young sons from a previous marriage to 'Sconset in the summer of 1951, and wrote much of *East of Eden* (1952) in a cottage called "Footlight," next to the Sankaty Lighthouse. "This is a beautiful place," he wrote to his editor, Pascal Covici, "and the most peaceful I have ever seen.... I have a little room to work in and it is mine exclusively and I can look at the ocean out of my window. It has a desk to work on.... The work day will be like this.... To work at 8:30. Elaine and the boys will go to the beach mostly taking their lunch. I will work until I have finished. Then we will go to other beaches, go fishing, swimming, sailing or what have you. To bed very early after dining.... " 'Sconset posed just one problem for a writer. "As this mss. [*sic*] will tell you, it is very damp here," Steinbeck complained. "Stamps stick together. I am glad I am spraying the paper now. Even the pencils seem softer in the dampness. But the air is cool and lovely and the sun is warm."

The 1960s and 1970s would be the last decades when young writers like Russell Baker, David Halberstam, and Frank Conroy could purchase summer homes on the island and still find Nantucket a peaceful place for writing in the summer months, as Steinbeck had done. Slowly and inexorably the tourist trade was growing and island real estate was being devoured by off-islanders hungry for a slice of paradise. Wisely, Nantucketers sought protection against the changes in the wind. In 1963, the Nantucket Conservation Foundation was created to acquire and protect as many of the island's unique and beautiful natural areas as possible. And in 1966, the entire island of Nantucket was designated a National Historic Landmark, the largest conventional historic district in the United States. In 1972, Senator Edward Kennedy introduced the "Nantucket Sound and Islands Trust Bill" in an attempt to limit building and place federal protections on Nantucket's remaining undeveloped land. But fiercely independent islanders, with a new sense of their home's national significance, voted against participation. "Nation of Nantucket makes its own war & peace," Emerson had observed in 1847. It was true again in 1977, when the island lost its representative in the state legislature and Nantucket made a serious attempt to secede from Massachusetts, even going so far as to devise its own flag, with a seagull rampant. The secession movement would give Nantucket readers a splendid comic novel about this period, Nathaniel Benchley's *Sweet Anarchy* (1979).

In the final decades of the twentieth century and the early years of the twenty-first, the development of Nantucket accelerated like a rocket leaving earth's atmosphere. In the forty years between 1930 and 1970, the island's year-round population had remained steady at around thirty-five hundred. But in the same period of time between 1980 and 2006, the island grew from five thousand to more than ten thousand year-round residents. For the first time, off-islanders including young professionals and wealthy retirees outnumbered Nantucket natives in the year-round population. The island also grew a community of between fifty and sixty thousand summer residents. With real estate prices and summer rentals grown astronomically expensive, the island was no longer a place for writers—always somewhat impecunious—on vacation. Instead, artists seeking solitude for their work began to come in winter. Alice Koller's *An Unknown Woman: A Journey to Self-Discovery* (1982), the product of an off-season sojourn and existential crisis in 'Sconset, is perhaps the best-known product of this phenomenon. More and more, literary endeavor on Nantucket became the province of the year-round community, now back to the strength of the whaling era, as writers including Elin Hilderbrand and Tom Congdon, Nat Philbrick and Nancy Thayer cast eyes of affectionate objectivity on island life.

Preservation of Nantucket's natural and historic beauty had, ironically, made the island ever more desirable—placing ever more pressure on the very things that made it desirable in the first place. For Philip Caputo, writing for the Nature Conservancy in "No Space to Waste" (1994), the fate of Nantucket and her sister island, Martha's Vineyard, with their finite spaces and conservation lands hemmed in by the homes of the privileged, would serve as a cautionary tale for those seeking to preserve far larger continental spaces, a sneak peek at what the nation as a whole could look like in the not too distant future.

Nantucket's late-twentieth-century literature is, pre-eminently, haunted. Because the entire island has more than eight hundred houses built before the Civil War, many present-day Nantucketers reside in homes where the lives of previous residents are still mysteriously palpable. In *Spirit Lost* (1988), novelist Nancy Thayer translates this phenomenon into Gothic romance, when a modern wife must fight to save her husband from the lonely, sex-starved ghost of a captain's widow who haunts the attic of their old house. Tom Congdon's comic essay, "Mrs. Coffin's Consolation" (1997), offers a literal encounter with unseemly relics of an earlier occupant of his own historic home. "'My God,' I thought. 'They were people, too,'" writes Congdon in a lovely expression of a Nantucketer's intimacy with the past.

Nor are Nantucket hauntings restricted to historic houses. Summer renters also share the sometimes disturbing experience of living in cottages haunted by those who have gone before. John Cheever's masterful short story, "The Seaside Houses" (1961), explores this premise: "You unfasten the lock and step into a dark or light hallway, about to begin a vacation—a month that promises to have no worries of any kind. But as strong as or stronger than this pleasant sense of beginnings is the sense of having stepped into the midst of someone else's life. All my dealings are with agents, and I have never known the people from whom we have rented, but their ability to leave behind them a sense of physical and emotional presences is amazing." In the course of Cheever's tale, the narrator will find himself possessed.

Recent Nantucket literature is haunted as well by the island's rich history. And no incident from Nantucket history has so intrigued writers as the catastrophic 1820 wreck of the whaleship *Essex,* stove by a whale in mid-Pacific, and the subsequent suffering of her crew in open boats, their drawing lots, and their cannibalism. In the nineteenth century, the story of the *Essex* inspired portions of Edgar Allan Poe's *Pym* and gave Melville's *Moby-Dick* its climactic final chapter. In the twentieth century, the *Essex* disaster has given us Henry Carlisle's novel, *The Jonah Man* (1984), the fictionalized narrative of Captain George Pollard, and Nathaniel Philbrick's bestselling nonfiction account, *In the Heart of the Sea: The Tragedy of the Whaleship Essex* (2000). Dust-jacket copy for *The Jonah Man* sums up our fascination: "[T]he true story of the *Essex* . . . has never ceased to provoke the imagination wherever men speak of ships. . . . [A] lottery of death that will haunt . . . the reader forever."

Twentieth-century Nantucket literature is also haunted—and magnificently so—by "one grand hooded phantom, like a snow hill in the air"—*Moby-Dick.* Critic Harold Bloom has written compellingly of the "anxiety of influence," an impulse that compels strong writers, major figures, "to wrestle with their strong precursors, even to the death." Literature thus becomes, in Bloom's view, a "battle between strong equals, father and son as mighty opposites, Laius and Oedipus at the cross-roads." It is impossible for a strong writer to visit Nantucket without feeling anxious about Melville—or inspired by him. Pulitzer Prize-winning poet Robert Lowell is a case in point. "Sailor, can you hear/ The *Pequod's* sea wings, beating landward, fall/ Headlong and break on our Atlantic wall/ Off 'Sconset [?]" he writes in his beautiful poem "The Quaker Graveyard in Nantucket" (1945).

Writing *The Old Man and the Sea* in 1951, as the nation celebrated the centennial of *Moby-Dick's* publication, Ernest Hemingway certainly heard those sea wings. Shortly before his suicide in 1961, Hemingway wrote to a Mrs. Jenson who had asked him whether Melville had influenced *The Old Man and the Sea* that his childhood visit to Nantucket had left him "specially equipped to appreciate *Moby-Dick* at an early age." Peter Benchley, in his 1974 thriller *Jaws,* transformed Captain Ahab's monomaniacal hunt for a great white whale into Captain Quint's monomaniacal hunt for a great white shark terrorizing a summer community—a concept that in the hands of movie director Steven Spielberg would shatter all previous box office records. And sometimes, in the struggle with Melville, Bloom's "battle between strong equals, father and son," is a battle between father and daughter. Sena Jeter Naslund's 1999 novel, *Ahab's Wife; or, The Star-Gazer,* is a chapter-by-chapter feminist revision of *Moby-Dick,* with many excursions into Nantucket history.

Nantucket in the twentieth century has inspired not only high literature, but genre fiction as well—especially murder mysteries. Ever since Agatha Christie's 1939 classic, *And Then There Were None* (originally titled *Ten Little Indians*), mystery fans have understood the special possibilities of islands. Hard to reach and difficult to leave in a fog or a storm, an island offers to the mystery writer a larger, geographic equivalent of the locked room. And an unknown killer stalking a small, isolated community of people who *think* they know one another well and seldom lock their doors inspires the special terror suggested by another Christie title, *Cat Among the Pigeons.* So while Christie herself never visited Nantucket, the island has, over the years, excited many descendants of this grande dame of crime. Nantucket mysteries include Martha Reed's *The Nature of the Grave* (2005), Peter Clayton's *Near Death on Nantucket* (2005), Elin Hilderbrand's *Nantucket Nights* (2002), Jeannine Kadow's *Dead Tide* (2002), Larry Maness's *Nantucket Revenge* (1995), Francine Matthews's *Death in the Off-Season* (1994), and Virginia Rich's *The Nantucket Diet Murders* (1986). To represent the genre, we've chosen an excerpt from one of the earliest and best, Jane Langton's *Dark Nantucket Noon* (1975).

In June 2005, a front-page article for a *New York Times* special section titled "Class Matters," notoriously announced what Nantucketers already knew: "that over the past decade or so this fifty-square-mile, fishhook-shaped island off the Cape Cod coast has come to be dominated by a new class: the hyper-rich. They emerged in the 1980s and 1990s, when tectonic shifts in the economy created mountains of wealth. They resemble the arrivistes of the Gilded Age, which began in the 1880s when industrial capitalists amassed staggering fortunes. . . ." Nantucket has become an island of $16-million waterfront homes, personal transcontinental jets, $250,000 golf club memberships, two-hundred-foot yachts, and $300,000 yacht club memberships. And its literature has become correspondingly class-conscious.

Sometimes, that class-consciousness takes the form of comedy, as in Russell Baker's essays "Quaintness" and "The Taint of Quaint" (1982–84) which lampoon year-round Nantucket's unseemly haste to market its history to the wealthy newcomers. Baker's island character, Crowley, goes shopping for a Pilgrim suit and enrolls in the Moby Dick Academy of Antique Auctioneering and Public Candle Dipping in order to earn $500 tips from "Texans, who see nothing remarkable about buying the Taj Mahal if Italy is not for sale." In *The Beach Club* (2000), island novelist Elin Hilderbrand finds edgy humor in the plight of a hotel clerk at a posh resort, overwhelmed by wealthy, whiny guests who cannot cope with a rainy day. And sometimes that class-consciousness takes the form of a serious concern for the loss of civility and of a quieter, more modest way of life on Nantucket, as in David Halberstam's essay, "Nantucket on My Mind" (1999) or Frank Conroy's memoir, *Time and Tide: A Walk Through Nantucket* (2004).

In the three hundred and fifty years since its first settlement, Nantucket has undergone tremendous change. But one thing about the island has remained constant—the sea. "An old, old sight," cries Melville's Ahab, "and yet somehow so young; aye, and not changed a wink since I first saw it, a boy, from the sand-hills of Nantucket! The same—the same!—the same to Noah as to me." Melville's grizzled whale-hunter clearly hadn't imagined the possibility of a hundred and thirty wind turbines covering twenty-four square miles of Nantucket Sound in a world whose quest for energy has not diminished in manic intensity—or violence—since his time. But until that comes to pass, his point remains well taken. To locate something more timeless and essential about the island than fine dining and boutique shopping, the Nantucket reader—or writer—has only to turn to the sea. Paul Theroux's "Dead Reckoning to Nantucket" (1989) provides an example. How radically Theroux transforms today's Nantucket experience into a rare, solitary adventure simply by picking up a paddle and traveling to the island by kayak rather than joining the throngs crowding the steamship terminals and airports.

The sea around Nantucket remains a vast narrative engine, rolling and booming out stories. The shifting sands, extreme weather, and dense fogs of Nantucket's shoals have made the waters around the island a true graveyard of the Atlantic, with more than seven hundred wrecks since Nantucket's settlement, and thousands of lives lost. Whether shipwrecks are caused by bad luck or carelessness, whether they end in tragedy or triumph, each is a compelling story of human courage and ingenuity tested by sudden disaster and the occasional Old Testament wrath of the sea. Dozens, if not hundreds, of Nantucket shipwreck stories have taken form on the printed page. We've provided two fine examples by two fine twentieth-century island writers—Edouard Stackpole on the 1886 wreck of the *T. B. Witherspoon* (1972) and Robert F. Mooney on the 1851 wreck of the *British Queen* (1988). Modern navigation technologies and search-and-rescue methods may have diminished the number of wrecks and, thankfully, the loss of life seen in earlier days—but writing like Ron Winslow's *Hard Aground: The Story of the Argo Merchant Oil Spill* (1978) reminds us that the risks have never gone away, and that the stakes are higher than ever. Melville predicted it: "[A] moment's consideration will teach, that however baby man may brag of his science and skill, and however much, in a flattering future, that science and skill may augment; yet for ever and for ever, to the crack of doom, the sea will insult and murder him. . . . "

What does the future hold for Nantucket literature? The sea will almost certainly write the island's closing chapter, as rapidly rising sea level, more powerful storms, and coastal erosion caused by global warming eat away at Melville's "ant hill in the sea." Scientists give Nantucket anywhere between four hundred and eight thousand years before it slips beneath the waves. The island's last literature will surely record Nantucket's struggle with the sea, and her final gift to future readers may be the mythology of a New England Lost Atlantis.

In the meantime, Nantucket readers—this book is for you. For lazy summer days, for long winter nights, for warding off mental scurvy on the ferry, for perusing in a Windsor chair at the Atheneum. Enjoy.

Susan F. Beegel
November 2008

Editor's Note

WITH THREE AND A HALF CENTURIES of literature to choose from, the greatest difficulty for me in compiling *The Nantucket Reader* has been deciding what to include and what to leave out. Quite simply, this volume is intended to supply a sampling of fine writing about the Nantucket experience—but defining what makes a Nantucket experience is not so simple. Obviously, many Nantucket experiences take place on or near the island—whether it's attempting to rescue passengers from a vessel breaking up in freezing surf, gorging on quahogs and melted butter at a sheep-shearing festival, growing increasingly enraged over rudeness in the supermarket checkout line, or discovering you've left six pounds of bay scallops in the airport waiting area. But many other distinctly Nantucket experiences have taken place on the far side of the world.

"[T]wo thirds of this terraqueous globe are the Nantucketer's," wrote Herman Melville. "For the sea is his; he owns it, as Emperors own empires." A seafaring people engaged in the global enterprise of whaling for much of their history, Nantucketers were cosmopolitan in their interests and enjoyed a wide sphere of influence. And so, the Nantucket experience may range from Georges Bank in the Atlantic to New Zealand's Bay of Islands in the Pacific, from the halls of Britain's Parliament in London to the first women's rights convention in Seneca Falls, New York.

Almost without exception, those writers best able to deliver the Nantucket experience have lived on the island year-round, summered there for many years, or made one or more notable visits. There are, however, famous exceptions that prove the rule. Herman Melville, for instance, did not visit the island until after

Moby-Dick was published. Instead, he based his novel not only on copious reading but on a true Nantucket experience as a harpooneer on the island-owned whaleship *Charles and Henry*. So far as we know, Edgar Allan Poe never set foot on Nantucket, but the wild adventures (and writings) of the island's world-wandering whalemen inspired his only novel—*The Narrative of Arthur Gordon Pym of Nantucket*.

Because the Nantucket experience has primacy in our criteria for selection, this collection does *not* include work by the many literary lions who *have* visited the island and found it a congenial place for writing, but who, alas, chose other subjects for their work. Tennessee Williams, who wrote much of his play *Summer and Smoke* at 31 Pine Street, is one example. Because the entire action of *Summer and Smoke* takes place in Glorious Hill, Mississippi, the play is not included here. Eugene O'Neill, Carson McCullers, Sinclair Lewis, and John Steinbeck are examples of other famous writers who visited the island but did not write about the Nantucket experience.

That experience has found its way into a wide variety of literary genres, both humorous and serious, formal and informal. In *The Nantucket Reader* you will find poetry and sea chanteys, a short story; selections from novels, including classics; a murder mystery; a horror story; and a Gothic romance, among other subgenres. There are also excerpts from sea narratives and other book-length nonfiction, as well as essays, oratory, diaries, journals, and lectures.

What's missing here? Making only a few exceptions for works with a larger literary significance, we've tried to exclude most researched, nonfiction writing about Nantucket history. Nantucket's endlessly fascinating history has occasioned so much exploration that an anthology of the very best writing about it would probably rival the *Encyclopedia Britannica* in length. The nearly two-hundred-year run of the island's newspaper, the *Inquirer and Mirror*, along with its many rivals and the island's array of vibrant magazines, have frightened us away from trying to include a fair or manageable selection of Nantucket journalism. Also missing because of space constraints are selections from the island's rich tradition of children's literature. The work of Jan Brett, Tony Sarg, Nat Benchley, Joan Aiken, and many others springs to mind.

The Nantucket Reader makes no pretense of supplying a definitive text (in the academic sense) of any of the works represented here. Rather, every effort has been made to supply reasonably accurate texts for reading enjoyment free of scholarly and editorial apparatus. I have made no additions to the original texts, and when excerpting a selection has required an editorial omission, it is indicated by bracketed ellipses [. . . .] Ellipses not in brackets are the authors' own.

A literary work designed to show how different writers have imagined the Nantucket experience, this book is not meant to be historically precise, so I haven't endeavored to correct errors of fact in the original texts. Only obvious typographical errors, as originally published, have been silently corrected.

I have tried to conserve original punctuation (Melville's mad dashes, Emerson's ampersands, Eliza Brock's apparent allergy to end punctuation). I have also endeavored to conserve the authors' original spellings—if only for the sadistic pleasure of watching orthographers down the ages struggle with the island's Indian place-names: Coitou/Coatue, Shèmah/Shimmo, Mardiket/Madaket, Palpus/Polpis, Croskaty/Coskata, and, my favorite, Suffakatchè/Sesachacha.

Finally, to all of those Nantucket readers out there who haven't been able to locate their personal favorites in this volume, and to all of those fine writers who aren't represented this time—heartfelt apologies! Nantucket literature is a phenomenally abundant subject—far more has been left out than we had space to put in. Perhaps someday there will be a *Nantucket Reader II*. We'd welcome your suggestions.

—SB

I

Overture

Herman Melville

Nantucket and its whaling history have the honor and glory of having inspired Herman Melville's masterpiece, Moby-Dick *(1851), a book that must top any list of the greatest American novels ever written. Ironically, Melville (1819–91) visited Nantucket only once, for just two days in July 1852, one year after Moby-Dick was published. His knowledge of the island's culture came instead from his experience of whaling, especially his 1842–43 cruise as a harpooneer on board the Nantucket whaleship* Charles and Henry, *captained by John B. Coleman. Melville served before the mast not only with Nantucket shipmates but with seamen of many races and nationalities. He knew firsthand what it was like to stand up in a pitching whaleboat and heave a harpoon at a sperm whale. Melville also experienced Nantucket through his voracious reading. Many of the writers represented in this book—Edmund Burke, Thomas Jefferson, Owen Chase, William Lay and Cyrus Hussey, Obed Macy, Joseph Hart, and Jeremiah Reynolds—provided him with raw material for* Moby-Dick.

Readers who love both the island and Moby-Dick *anticipate Melville's "Nantucket" chapter as opera fans anticipate a favorite aria. With pulse-pounding prose and extravagant exaggeration, Melville gives the island's history from the legend of its discovery by Indians to the aggressive thrust of Nantucket's bold whalemen into the Pacific, making their enterprise an epic metaphor for young America's expansionist character. The chapter seems a perfect overture—or curtain-raiser—for* The Nantucket Reader. *— SB*

From "Nantucket," Chapter 14 of *Moby-Dick; or, The Whale*

[....] Nantucket! Take out your map and look at it. See what a real corner of the world it occupies; how it stands there, away off shore, more lonely than the Eddystone lighthouse. Look at it—a mere hillock and elbow of sand; all beach, without a background. There is more sand there than you would use in twenty years as a substitute for blotting paper. Some gamesome wights will tell you that they have to plant weeds there, they don't grow naturally; that they import Canada thistles; that they have to send beyond seas for a spile to stop a leak in an oil cask; that pieces of wood in Nantucket are carried about like bits of the true cross in Rome; that people there plant toadstools before their houses, to get under the shade in summertime; that one blade of grass makes an oasis, three blades in a day's walk a prairie; that they wear quicksand shoes, something like Laplander snowshoes; that they are so shut up, belted about, every way inclosed, surrounded, and made an utter island of by the ocean, that to their very chairs and tables small clams will sometimes be found adhering, as to the backs of sea turtles. But these extravaganzas only show that Nantucket is no Illinois.

Look now at the wondrous traditional story of how this island was settled by the red men. Thus goes the legend. In olden times an eagle swooped down upon the New England coast, and carried off an infant Indian in his talons. With loud lament the parents saw their child borne out of sight over the wide waters. They resolved to follow in the same direction. Setting out in their canoes, after a perilous passage they discovered the island, and there they found an empty ivory casket,—the poor little Indian's skeleton.

What wonder, then, that these Nantucketers, born on a beach, should take to the sea for a livelihood! They first caught crabs and quahogs in the sand; grown bolder, they waded out with nets for mackerel; more experienced, they pushed off in boats and captured cod; and at last, launching a navy of great ships on the sea, explored this watery world; put an incessant belt of circumnavigations round it; peeped in at Bhering's Straits; and in all seasons and all oceans declared everlasting war with the mightiest animated mass that has survived the flood; most monstrous and most mountainous! That Himalehan, salt-sea Mastodon, clothed with such portentousness of unconscious power, that his very panics are more to be dreaded than his most fearful and malicious assaults!

And thus have these naked Nantucketers, these sea hermits, issuing from their ant-hill in the sea, overrun and conquered the watery world like so many Alexanders; parcelling out among them the Atlantic, Pacific, and Indian oceans, as the three pirate powers did Poland. Let America add Mexico to Texas, and pile Cuba upon Canada; let the English overswarm all India, and hang out their blazing banner from the sun; two-thirds of this terraqueous globe are the Nantucketer's. For the sea is his; he owns it, as Emperors own empires; other seamen having but a right of way through it. Merchant ships are but extension bridges; armed ones but floating forts; even pirates and privateers, though following the sea as highwaymen the road, they but plunder other ships, other fragments of the land like themselves, without seeking to draw their living from the bottomless deep itself. The Nantucketer, he alone resides and rests on the sea; he alone, in Bible language, goes down to it in ships; to and fro ploughing it as his own special plantation. *There* is his home; *there* lies his business, which a Noah's flood would not interrupt, though it overwhelmed all the millions in China. He lives on the sea, as prairie cocks in the prairie; he hides among the waves, he climbs them as chamois hunters climb the Alps. For years he knows not the land; so that when he comes to it at last, it smells like another world, more strangely than the moon would to an Earthsman. With the landless gull, that at sunset folds her wings and is rocked to sleep between billows; so at nightfall, the Nantucketer, out of sight of land, furls his sails, and lays him to his rest, while under his very pillow rush herds of walruses and whales.

II

Crossings

John Greenleaf Whittier

Today, Quaker poet and fervent abolitionist John Greenleaf Whittier (1807–92) is best remembered as the author of such chestnuts as "Snow-Bound" ("The sun that brief December day, / Rose cheerless over hills of gray"), "Barbara Freitchie" ("Shoot, if you must, this old gray head, / But spare your country's flag," she said), and "The Barefoot Boy" ("Blessings on thee, little man, / Barefoot boy with cheeks of tan."). To contemporary readers, Whittier's rhymes and meters, as well as his sentiments, can seem more than a bit conventional. During his own lifetime, however, Whittier enjoyed immense popularity, and was perhaps America's best-known and best-loved poet after Henry Wadsworth Longfellow. Nineteenth-century Nantucketers would have been proud to see their island featured in a poem by Whittier.

Whittier's "The Exiles" (1840) tells how Nantucket's first English settler, Thomas Macy, came to the island in 1659. As Whittier recounts the story, Macy was in trouble with Puritan authorities for harboring Quakers in his home, and fled to Nantucket to escape harsh punishment—flogging or worse. First published by the Female Anti-Slavery Society of Philadelphia in a little gift book titled The North Star: The Poetry of Freedom, by her Friends, *"The Exiles" was intended to hearten opponents of slavery and encourage abolitionists to follow Macy's historic example by defying the law and taking fugitive slaves into their homes. Whittier exaggerated Macy's heroism to serve his poem's political purpose. According to Whittier's biographer, Roland Woodwell, the actual Thomas Macy purchased land on Nantucket well before the incident with the fugitive Quakers. He did not leave his mainland home in Amesbury, Massachusetts immediately, and before his departure he wrote a letter of apology to the Puritan court. Yet Whittier's poem constructs one of Nantucket's foundation myths—the idea of the island as a "refuge of the free," settled by a founding father seeking religious and civic freedom.—SB*

"The Exiles"

The goodman sat beside his door,
One sultry afternoon,
With his young wife singing at his side
An old and goodly tune.

A glimmer of heat was in the air,—
The dark green woods were still;
And the skirts of a heavy thunder-cloud
Hung over the western hill.

At times the solemn thunder pealed,
And all was still again,
Save a low murmur in the air
Of coming wind and rain.

Just as the first big rain-drop fell,
A weary stranger came,
And stood before the farmer's door,
With travel soiled and lame.

Sad seemed he, yet sustaining hope
Was in his quiet glance,
And peace, like autumn's moonlight, clothed
His tranquil countenance,—

A look, like that his Master wore
In Pilate's council-hall:
It told of wrongs, but of a love
Meekly forgiving all.

"Friend! wilt thou give me shelter here?"
The stranger meekly said;
And leaning on his oaken staff,
The goodman's features read.

"My life is hunted,—evil men
Are following in my track;
The traces of the torturer's whip
Are on my aged back;

"And much, I fear, 't will peril thee
Within thy doors to take
A hunted seeker of the Truth,
Oppressed for conscience' sake."

Oh, kindly spoke the goodman's wife,
"Come in, old man!" quoth she,
"We will not leave thee to the storm,
Whoever thou mayst be."

Then came the aged wanderer in,
And silent sat him down;
While all within grew dark as night
Beneath the storm-cloud's frown.

But while the sudden lightning's blaze
Filled every cottage nook,
And with the jarring thunder-roll
The loosened casements shook,

A heavy tramp of horses' feet
Came sounding up the lane,
And half a score of horse, or more,
Came plunging through the rain.

"Now, Goodman Macy, ope thy door,—
We would not be house-breakers;
A rueful deed thou'st done this day,
In harbouring banished Quakers."

Out looked the cautious goodman then,
With much of fear and awe,
For there, with broad wig drenched with rain,
The parish priest he saw.

"Open thy door, thou wicked man,
And let thy pastor in,
And give God thanks, if forty stripes
Repay thy wicked sin."

"What seek ye?" quoth the goodman;
The stranger is my guest;
He is worn with toil and grievous wrong,—
Pray let the old man rest."

"Now, out upon thee, canting knave!"
And strong hands shook the door.
"Believe me, Macy," quoth the priest,
"Thou'lt rue thy conduct sore."

Then kindled Macy's eye of fire:
"No priest who walks the earth,
Shall pluck away the stranger-guest
Made welcome to my hearth."

Down from his cottage wall he caught
The match-lock, hotly tried
At Preston-pans and Marston-moor,
By fiery Ireton's side;

Where Puritan, and Cavalier,
With shout and psalm contended;
And Rupert's oath, and Cromwell's prayer,
With battle-thunder blended.

Up rose the ancient stranger then:
"My spirit is not free
To bring the wrath and violence
Of evil men on thee."

"And for thyself, I pray forbear,
Bethink thee of thy Lord,
Who healed again the smitten ear,
And sheathed His follower's sword.

"I go, as to the slaughter led.
Friends of the poor, farewell!"
Beneath his hand the oaken door
Back on its hinges fell.

"Come forth old graybeard, yea and nay,"
The reckless scoffers cried,
As to a horseman's saddle-bow
The old man's arms were tied.

And of his bondage hard and long
In Boston's crowded jail,
Where suffering woman's prayer was heard,
With sickening childhood's wail,

It suits not with our tale to tell;
Those scenes have passed away;
Let the dim shadows of the past
Brood o'er that evil day.

"Ho, sheriff!" quoth the ardent priest,
Take Goodman Macy too;
The sin of this day's heresy
His back or purse shall rue."

"Now, goodwife, haste thee!" Macy cried.
She caught his manly arm;
Behind, the parson urged pursuit,
With outcry and alarm.

Ho! speed the Macys, neck or naught,—
The river-course was near;
The plashing on its pebbled shore
Was music to their ear.

A gray rock, tasselled o'er with birch,
Above the waters hung,
And at its base, with every wave,
A small light wherry swung.

A leap—they gain the boat—and there
The goodman wields his oar;
"Ill luck betide them all," he cried,
"The laggards on the shore."

Down through the crashing underwood,
The burly sheriff came:—
"Stand, Goodman Macy, yield thyself;
Yield in the King's own name."

"Now out upon thy hangman's face!"
Bold Macy answered then,—
"Whip women on the village green,
But meddle not with men."

The priest came panting to the shore,
His grave cocked hat was gone;
Behind him, like some owl's nest, hung
His wig upon a thorn.

"Come back! come back!" the parson cried,
"The church's curse beware."
"Curse, an thou wilt," said Macy, "but
Thy blessing prithee spare."

"Vile scoffer!" cried the baffled priest,
"Thou'lt yet the gallows see."
"Who's born to hang will not be drowned,"
Quoth Macy, merrily;

"And so, sir sheriff and priest, good-by!"
He bent him to his oar,
And the small boat glided quietly
From the twain upon the shore.

Now in the west, the heavy clouds
Scattered and fell asunder,
While feebler came the rush of rain,
And fainter growled the thunder.

And through the broken clouds, the sun
Looked out serene and warm,
Painting its holy symbol-light
Upon the passing storm.

Oh, beautiful! that rainbow span,
O'er dim Crane-neck was bended;
One bright foot touched the eastern hills,
And one with ocean blended.

By green Pentucket's southern slope
The small boat glided fast;
The watchers of the Block-house saw
The strangers as they passed.

That night a stalwart garrison
Sat shaking in their shoes,
To hear the dip of Indian oars,
The glide of birch canoes.

The fisher-wives of Salisbury—
The men were all away—
Looked out to see the stranger oar
Upon their waters play.

Deer Island's rocks and fir-trees threw
Their sunset-shadows o'er them,
And Newbury's spire and weathercock
Peered o'er the pines before them.

Around the Black Rocks, on their left,
The marsh lay broad and green;
And on their right with dwarf shrubs crowned,
Plum Island's hills were seen.

With skilful hand and wary eye
The harbor bar was crossed;
A plaything of the restless wave,
The boat on ocean tossed.

The glory of the sunset heaven
On land and water lay;
On the steep hills of Agawam,
On cape, and bluff, and bay.

They passed the gray rocks of Cape Ann,
And Gloucester's harbor-bar;
The watch-fire of the garrison
Shone like a setting star.

How brightly broke the morning
On Massachusetts Bay!
Blue wave, and bright green island,
Rejoicing in the day.

On passed the bark in safety
Round isle and headland steep;
No tempest broke above them,
No fog-cloud veiled the deep.

Far round the bleak and stormy Cape
The venturous Macy passed,
And on Nantucket's naked isle
Drew up his boat at last.

And how, in log-built cabin,
They braved the rough sea-weather;
And there, in peace and quietness,
Went down life's vale together;

How others drew around them,
And how their fishing sped,
Until to every wind of heaven
Nantucket's sails were spread

How pale Want alternated
With Plenty's golden smile;
Behold, is it not written
In the annals of the isle?

And yet that isle remaineth
A refuge of the free,
As when true-hearted Macy
Beheld it from the sea.

Free as the winds that winnow
Her shrubless hills of sand,
Free as the waves that batter
Along her yielding land.

Than hers, at duty's summons,
No loftier spirit stirs,
Nor falls o'er human suffering
A readier tear than hers.

God bless the sea-beat island!
And grant forevermore,
That charity and freedom dwell
As now upon her shore!

Paul Theroux

John Greenleaf Whittier's Thomas Macy rows all the way from Amesbury to Nantucket in a wherry, a small, light, racing rowboat (in reality, the historic Macy probably chose a more substantial sailing craft). Today's visitor to the island is more likely to crowd into a crammed commuter aircraft for a flight measured in minutes, rather than hours or days, or lounge across Nantucket Sound in a capacious ferry, with television, restroom, and snack bar close at hand. With hundreds of thousands of tourists and island residents making such voyages each year, it's hard to find novelty or adventure in crossing to Nantucket these days.

That is, unless you happen to be master travel writer Paul Theroux (b. 1941), part-time Cape Cod resident and author of such travel classics as The Great Railway Bazaar *(1975),* The Old Patagonian Express *(1979),* Riding the Iron Rooster *(1988), and* The Happy Isles of Oceania: Paddling the Pacific *(1992). The following selection recounts Theroux's solo voyage to Nantucket in a sea kayak, braving miles of open water and the notoriously dangerous winds, tides, and currents of Nantucket Sound. The result is a fresh perspective on the island's distance and uniqueness, as Theroux finds himself arriving at a Nantucket very different from the Nantucket of the ferry passenger. "Dead Reckoning to Nantucket" first appeared as "Small-craft Warnings" in the August 1989* Condé Nast Traveler *and was revised by Theroux for inclusion in* Fresh Air Fiend *(2000), a collection of his travel writing. Our text is taken from the later edition. —SB*

"Dead Reckoning to Nantucket"

I SET OUT ONE MORNING in my kayak, facing the open sea, intending to paddle thirty-five miles or so from Falmouth on Cape Cod to the island of Nantucket, stopping at Martha's Vineyard on the way. I felt waterproof, buoyant, and portable, with a sleeping bag and food for four days. It was a lovely morning, but I was already in a sunny frame of mind knowing that in order to paddle to Nantucket and camp on the way I would have to trespass and break the law.

For me the best sort of travel always involves a degree of trespass. The risk is both a challenge and an invitation. Selling adventure seems to be a theme in the travel industry, and trips have become trophies. Wealthy people pay big money to be dragged up Everest on ropes, or go whitewater rafting down the Ganges, or risk death for photo opportunities with gorillas in war-ravaged Rwanda.

Adventure travel seems to imply a far-off destination, but a nearby destination can be scarier, for no place is more frightening than one near home that everybody has warned you against. You can dismiss ignorant opinions—"Africa's dangerous!" or "India's dirty!" or "China's crowded!"—but when someone you know well, speaking of someplace near home, says, "Don't go there," it sounds like the voice of experience. This does not usually deter me, however. The idea is to devise a way of going, as when in 1853 Sir Richard Burton learned colloquial Arabic, grew a beard, darkened his skin, and gave his name as Mirza Abdullah and his occupation as "dervish," in order to take the haj as a born Muslim to the holy city of Mecca, closed to infidels. When the Chinese told me a place was forbidden—a word they love and use often—I merely smiled and thought of ways to disobey.

Warnings applied to the ocean around Cape Cod sound especially dire. But if you took all advice and heeded all warnings and obeyed the opinion of scare mongers, you would never go anywhere. Most people who hand out advice are incapable of putting themselves in your shoes: they fear for their own safety, and impose this fear on you; and when they are speaking of a place with a bad reputation near home, they can be bullies. There is no terror like the terror of what is nearby. The vaguely familiar can be worse than the unknown, because any number of witnesses have supplied spurious detail, the hideous certainty of specific fatal features, and the lurking idea that if you go, you will either die or be horribly disappointed.

Such opposition can be stimulating, perversely inspiring. Everybody and his oceangoing brother told me not to try to paddle to Nantucket. I listened to them and then, that morning, I rose before dawn, got the latest weather report for Cape Cod and the islands, and prepared my kayak for the trip I was determined to make.

Cape Cod is not one little jigjog of land. It is vast, composed of all the seas around it, the sounds, the channels, the fetch and chop of the tide races, the sandbars, the islands so small they appear only once a day at low tide and have scarcely enough room to serve as a platform for a sea gull's feet.

The sea is a place, too, and it is not empty either. It contains distinct locations, shoals, rocks, buoys, cans, and nuns—and wrecks that stick up with the prominent authority of church steeples or bare ruined choirs. The angler facing south from the jetty at Hyannisport sees just an expanse of blue water, yet there are nearly as many features on the nautical chart of Nantucket Sound as there are on the adjacent map of Hyannis. These are not only the sites of nameless wrecks and gongs and bells, but memorable and resonant names. Crossing to the Vineyard from Falmouth, you pass L'Hommedieu Shoal, Hedge Fence (a long narrow shoal), and Squash Meadow, and if you cross from there to Edgartown, you pass many named rocks. The current—its changing speed and direction—is another serious consideration, and the water depths range from a few inches to more than a hundred feet. But it is misleading to think that because the sea is a place, it is safe and hospitable. In his book *Cape Cod*, Thoreau wrote, "The ocean is a wilderness," and he went on to say that it is "wilder than a Bengal jungle, and fuller of monsters."

In bad weather you can't see the Vineyard from the Cape shore, and even on the clearest day you can't see Nantucket. The challenge to the paddler is more than open water; it is also a swift and changeable current, a strong prevailing wind, and scattered shoals that send up a steep chop of confused waves. Nantucket Sound has a long history of being a ship swallower, one of the most crowded graveyards of any stretch of ocean. It was not uncommon in the nineteenth century for a whaling ship to leave Nantucket and spend two years sailing around the world, crossing to the southern ocean, going around the Horn and through the Roaring Forties, only to be smashed to bits on the rocks or shallows at Nantucket, within sight of the harbor.

Nonetheless, I was thrilled by the warnings. For a number of years I had wanted to cross the sound, head for Nantucket through open water, and get there in one piece, in my own craft, by using dead reckoning—a chart, a compass, and vectoring on the incoming tide by my estimated speed. I knew it wasn't simple. Nantucket lies far below the horizon, and only its "lume"—the flaring halo of its harbor light—shows at night from the nearest part of the Vineyard.

Whenever I spoke about paddling there, people tried to put me off. They were sailors with boats that drew five feet of water, or else fellows with speedboats who had never been out of sight of land, or tourists and partygoers who knew the route only from the long, cold ferry ride from Hyannis.

My dream of paddling through the wilderness of open water was the dream of an Eagle Scout (I was in Troop 24). It was also the dream of someone who had had enough of foreign travel for a while, of places that were crowded and thoroughly tame, of the tedium and sleep deprivation of a long plane journey, and of the yappy turbulence of other travelers. I had recently been to Tibet, Polynesia, northern Scotland, and the southern island of New Zealand; I had not been alone. Tourists have penetrated to the farthest, wildest parts of the world. An article I would prefer not to write, about the spread of tourists, might be titled "They're Everywhere."

They are not in the Muskeget Channel. I knew I would not run into anyone on the way. I had never heard of anyone making this crossing, or even wanting to. Small craft warnings are frequent. The *Eldridge Tide and Pilot Table* shows a four-and-a-half-knot current running in some places in the Muskeget Channel, and with a strong wind and tide it would be much greater than that. To cap it all, it is illegal to camp on any of the outer islands. It was dangerous, it was unlawful, it was foolhardy, it was forbidden.

Catnip, I thought. Who wouldn't want to paddle a kayak to Nantucket?

I left Green Pond Harbor in East Falmouth, paddling my folding Klepper kayak, the nearest thing there is to an Inuit kayak.

An Asian man and woman were fishing from the breakwater. Perhaps to amuse the woman, the man shrieked at me, "You'll never make it!"

I considered this remark and kept paddling into the slop of the sound. Among the Klepper's many virtues are its seaworthiness and stability, its lightness, its ample storage space, and its portability—it can be taken apart in about fifteen minutes and stuffed into two bags. It can't be rolled over easily, and if you fall out, you can climb back in, which is almost impossible to do in other kayaks.

It was one of those beautiful mornings in early September, after Labor Day, when the Cape has a bright, vacant look—no traffic, no pedestrians, no swimmers, and only fishing boats on the water. The sky was clear, the wind was light; a low dusting of haze prevented me from seeing the Vineyard distinctly. My plan was to head for the East Chop Lighthouse, continue on that shore for a few miles, and have lunch on the beach below Oak Bluffs. My afternoon plan would have to depend on the wind and the weather, but the outlook was good.

Crossing Nantucket Sound is the Cape sailor's first psychological barrier. I had rowed and sailed across it before I paddled it, but paddling was the simplest of the three. The sound can be dangerous to vessels of any size. On August 20, 1992, I was crossing from Green Pond to Oak Bluffs and saw a passenger liner anchored off East Chop. I paddled toward it, and the rising tide, flowing east, gave the illusion that the ship was moving slowly west. In fact, I was being tugged away from the anchored liner. Approaching it, I saw that its main deck was as tall as a twelve-story building, and rounding its stern I saw QUEEN ELIZABETH II—SOUTHAMPTON. Passengers were being taken ashore to Oak Bluffs, a mile and a half away, in whale boats. I paddled to the gangway and struck up a conversation with the mate.

"I've never seen the *QE II* here."

"We call here every few years."

"Where are you headed?"

"New York City. We're sailing tonight."

"I just paddled from the Cape and crossed several shoals. I know there are plenty up ahead. How does a big ship like this manage?"

"No problem. We come through here all the time."

That night, the *Queen Elizabeth II* ran into an uncharted rock at the western edge of the sound, near Sow and Pig rocks, causing millions of dollars' worth of damage to the hull. The passengers were taken off the ship and ferried to New Bedford, where they were transported by bus to New York City. It was a whole year before the ship was repaired and put back into service.

The tide can also be a problem. On the morning of my dead-reckoning departure it was against me—I knew it would be, because I needed it in my favor that afternoon. The tidal current creates the strangest effects. A mile off Green Pond there was a tide rip, a mass of spiky white waves drawing me toward them from my patch of clear water. The thing to do was stay upright. I paddled through them, and after awhile I saw that I was way off course, nearer West Chop than East Chop (these are the separate arms of Vineyard Haven, and each indicates a patch of rough water). I struggled against the current, feeling that I was paddling upstream, and about an hour and a half after leaving the Cape I was at the Vineyard shore. Thirty minutes later I was lying on the beach at Oak Bluffs, drinking Chinese tea and eating a cheese sandwich.

Here, as postprandial reading, I looked at the *Tide and Pilot Table* and saw that everything was in my favor: the tide had just turned, and I would have a cooperative current to lead me to Edgartown and Katama Bay. And if I eluded the ranger and camped on the beach at the southern point of Chappaquiddick Island, I would have a merciful current tomorrow on the way to Nantucket—that is, it would carry me safely northeast. But it was not endlessly merciful. If I was delayed, or if I didn't paddle fast enough, I would be carried into the Atlantic Ocean when the current reversed in midmorning.

The great fear that everyone had expressed to me was the Muskeget Channel, which is a sort of teeming drain capable of sluicing any craft into the Atlantic. No boats dared enter it. How could they? If the currents didn't get you, the sandbars or the rocks would. But a kayak draws only a few inches of water. And anyone could see that the dangers of the channel had to be set against its advantages—it was only an eight-mile crossing to the nearest piece of land, uninhabited Muskeget Island, where I could trespass if the weather happened to deteriorate. What tempted me most to cross the channel was that no one I had met or spoken to, and no one I had heard of, had ever done it. It meant that I might be the first non-Indian to do it alone in a self-propelled boat. I might even discover that it was not dangerous at all.

The traveler is essentially an optimist, and in that hopeful mood I paddled all afternoon, south to Edgartown. This is one of the loveliest and snuggest harbors anywhere, a tidy town of brilliant white, slightly haughty houses and brick walls and shady streets. Just across the harbor is Chappaquiddick, with low woods and sandbanks and expensive, hunkered, furtive-looking houses, mostly the seasonal haunts of fleeing New Yorkers.

I pulled my kayak onto a public landing and walked into Edgartown to buy some beer and verify tomorrow's weather report (sunny, scattered clouds, light winds, ten to fifteen knots). I considered staying the night at a hotel, but that would have complicated my trip. I needed the earliest possible start from an advantageous position on the coast, and thus I had designated as my campground: Wasque Point, on the southeastern corner of the island.

So, although I had been paddling for more than seven hours, I crawled back into my kayak and paddled another hour across Katama Bay. The sun was setting and the air was turning cool; it was twilight and chilly by the time I got to the sand spit. I was so tired I could not pull my loaded kayak over it. I sat and rested among some nervously bleeping oystercatchers, and then I gathered armfuls of slimy seaweed, spread it on the sand, and pulled my kayak up this slippery track into the dunes.

A few four-wheel-drive vehicles—fishermen—were leaving the beach, and there was a tawny Bronco with RANGER lettered on its door. I ambled around the beach until sunset, then tipped my kayak on its side and spread out my ground sheet and sleeping bag. I drank a beer and had dinner in the starry, moonless dark as the waves monotonously dumped and broke on the sand with the sound of someone sighing. I wanted to be invisible, so I did not build a fire. Just before I turned in, I walked to the edge of the beach and looked east-southeast with my binoculars and saw the lume of Nantucket—no land but a definite light, like the dim flash of a thunderstorm or the glow of a distant fire in the sea.

> Then I lay down in my sleeping bag and murmured,
> Oh, God, make small
> The old star-eaten blanket of the sky,
> That I may fold it round me and in comfort lie.

I woke often in the night—listened to the waves, listened to the wind in the sea grass and the drizzling sand grains—and I felt like a savage, just as portable, just as naked and vulnerable to attack. I lay there like a dog on a rug. I was exposed, but I was in an out-of-the-way place. No one came here except fishermen, and they wouldn't return until after sunup. By then I would be gone.

With good food, tucked in my expensive sleeping bag, lying alongside my unsinkable kayak, as an early September dawn was breaking, I did not feel that I was roughing it. This merely seemed an eccentric form of luxury: I was comfortable, I was alone, and I was successfully trespassing.

Sunrise was a messy reddened eruption out of the sea, and it kept spilling garish light everywhere, draining the redness into the water as the sun rose like a squeezed blood orange. A cloud the shape of a huddled animal soon smothered the brightness, and the sea turned the blue-white color of skim milk.

By then there was no sign of Nantucket, which lay below the horizon. The wind was light, though the sea swell was pronounced, and the waves were still dumping steadily. I ate a banana, drank the last of my tea, took a bearing with my compass, and headed east-southeast into a wave that broke over my deck and into my face. There were no other people on the beach, no other boats on the water. The sea was clear, the sky was empty. The Chappaquiddick shore was just a sandbank, a bluff with a whiffle of sea grass on top. Light and water and sand: it was a minimalist landscape, three bands of light, dawn pouring over it, and all of it looking just like a just-emerged corner of a continent, bobbing at the surface of a watery planet without a soul in it, a sort of prologue to Paradise.

The rest was oceanic, endless and eternal. I was paddling into nothingness. Behind me, Chappaquiddick had begun to drop into the sea. I was nervous, because I am not much of a navigator and I could see rough water ahead, and beyond it only more water. But it was not even seven o'clock in the morning. I had a whole day to get where I was going. If something went wrong, I had twelve hours of daylight in which to save myself.

The rough water looked like a river flowing swiftly through the sea. This jumble of steep breaking waves was the result of the tidal stream being pushed upward by a shoal. The vertical current produced an "overfall" of turbulent surface water. The waves broke over me and drenched me as the current pulled me sideways. I braced myself with my paddle and didn't fight the current. I had included it in my crude calculations. That is what dead reckoning is—getting to a hidden destination by figuring your average speed and true course after leaving a known point of land. I was counting on the current taking me northeast as I paddled four knots an hour east-southeast, and I assumed I would get a glimpse of Muskeget Island after an hour or so. Traveling hopefully into the unknown with a little information: dead reckoning is the way most people live their lives, and the phrase itself seems to sum up human existence.

I had not known that Muskeget Island was so flat and hard to spot. On all charts certain prominent landscape features are indicated—a dome, a water tower, a radio antenna, a steeple. There was nothing shown on the chart for Muskeget Island. From my boat I thought I saw a smudge, which could have been an island, but I kept losing it as my boat slid from the crest of a wave into the trough. Then it was like sitting in a box, unable to see over the sides. What might have been obvious from the deck of a sailboat was impossible to see from my kayak, so low in the water.

And what water. Now I understood why larger boats never crossed this channel. There were waves, breaking in the middle of nowhere, indicating a sandbar or some rocks. I crossed at least three more overfalls—one was fifty yards wide and had the look of a maelstrom. In the distance I saw more waves breaking, and no land in sight. That seemed ominous—I might find myself surfing out to sea. But I was still paddling hard. I did not want to turn back. And the smudge in the distance was definitely a piece of land. Now it was off to the far right, which meant I was being carried faster by the current than I had calculated.

By midmorning I was paddling off Muskeget, the flat island that is one of the most remote and least visited pieces of land for hundreds of miles—just a low ledge in the sea. Shaped like an anvil lying on its side, it is about a mile long and half a mile wide. No trees grow on its windswept surface, only blowing grass and rose bushes. At its western end sits a single unoccupied house. I paddled to the back of the island, out of the wind, and went ashore. There was no need for me to shelter here. It was not even noon, and I could see Nantucket through the smoky haze, the western tip of it, Eel Point, the northern arm of Madaket Harbor; and ahead, as Robert Lowell writes in "The Quaker Graveyard in Nantucket," "a brackish reach of shoal off Madaket." That was about five miles away, beyond another island, Tuckernuck, beyond two ship-wrecks hulking out of the blue sea, ocherous with rust.

My nervousness about the open-water crossing was gone. Having gained confidence in my use of dead reckoning, I felt stronger. Now I could see where I was going. I paddled through the miles of shallows off Tuckernuck and onward to a beach where I lolled in the sand and had lunch. The tide had long since shifted: the current was against me; I battled it all the way to the long breakwater that guards Nantucket Harbor, and I glided past Brant Point to the landing.

I had been to Nantucket on the ferry many times. But because I had come this way—plowing the waves alone, seeing no one, not saying a word, only tres-passing on the beaches and on the notorious channels—the place seemed new. I now had some sense of its distance and its uniqueness, of how much of it there was, and how from the sea it seemed to stagger westward in a succession of sinking fragments.

Yachts bobbed in the harbor, and people strolled among the bright white houses, buying ice cream and T-shirts. Nantucket town is always in a state of high excitement, because so many of the visitors have come for the day and want to make the most of it before the ferry leaves. The place is full of fishermen and millionaires, Yankees and Ivy Leaguers. It is, as Melville wrote, "a mere hillock, an elbow of sand," and yet if you somehow delete all the Jeeps and sport utility vehicles, it has one of the most beautiful main streets in America. As for the rest of the island, it took Melville a whole chapter of *Moby-Dick* to describe it properly—its look, its meaning, and its moods.

I was salt-crusted and sunburned. No one noticed me beach my boat. I walked urgently, because I had hardly used my legs for two days. I bought an ice cream cone and a souvenir T-shirt and became part of the crowd. But I had a sense of having discovered Nantucket in my own way and, through dead reckoning, had discovered something in myself. That to me is the essence of the travel experience. Is there any point in going across the world to eat something or buy something or watch people squatting among their ruins? Travel is a state of mind. It has nothing to do with distance or the exotic. It is almost entirely an inner experience. My particular way of getting to Nantucket—alone, almost blindly over water—seemed to transform the destination. The Nantucket I had arrived at was a different place from the Nantucket of the ferry passenger, and I was different, too—happier, for one thing. The trip had done what all trips ought to do. It had given me heart.

First published in *Condé Nast Traveler,* August 1989 © 1989, permission of The Wylie Agency.

III

On-Island

Obed Macy

Obed Macy (1762–1844) has a special place in Nantucket literature as the island's first historian. His The History of Nantucket *(1835) is the original source from which all subsequent versions of island history flow, especially valuable as Macy himself was an eye-witness to Nantucket's late eighteenth and early nineteenth centuries, and able to draw on the memories of his parents' and grandparents' generations. His* History of Nantucket *is also important to American literature as the source for Herman Melville's vision of the island. As Howard P. Vincent wrote in* The Trying-Out of Moby-Dick, *Melville "extracted shimmering gold from Macy's . . . ore." In Chapter 35 of* Moby-Dick, *"The Masthead," Melville acknowledges his debt, referring to Macy as "Nantucket's sole historian," and affectionately calling him "the worthy Obed."*

Here we turn to Macy's History of Nantucket *for an account of the island's first inhabitants, who, sadly, left no written history of their own. Macy was a toddler during the 1764 "Indian sickness" that took the surviving remnant of Nantucket's Native Americans to the brink of extinction, and recorded the death of the island's last full-blooded Indian in 1822, his own sixtieth year. To the story of Nantucket's Native American tragedy, "the worthy Obed" brings special insight and a devout Quaker's well-developed sense of injustice.* —SB

From Chapter 3
of *The History of Nantucket*

T HE INDIANS LIVED scattered over the island in such parts as best suited themselves. Although the emigrants early purchased their land, they were still allowed to till and improve as much as was necessary for their subsistence. When any were about to go to sea, the whites ploughed as much for them as their squaws and children could cultivate.

The Indians, being with the whites much of their time, they became conversant together, and learned each other's language, which rendered the former very useful in the whaling business, as well as in many other respects; as they were often employed by the whites in various kinds of labor.

King Philip, sachem of Mount Hope, in the year 1665, very soon after the settlement of the island by the whites, came there with a number of canoes in pursuit of an Indian, to punish him for some heinous crime. There being but a small number of English at that time, they had everything to fear. Philip's hostile appearance and preparations made them apprehensive, that he would destroy them, if any measures were taken to arrest his progress in pursuit of the delinquent. On the other hand, if they assisted to search after him, they dreaded the revenge of the island natives. They therefore declined lending their aid in any respect. Philip then went with his party in pursuit of the criminal, and at length found him on the south-east part of the island. His name was John Gibbs; his crime was the mentioning of the name of Philip's dead father. Rehearsing the name of the dead, if it should be that of a very distinguished person, was decreed by the natives a very high crime, for which nothing but the life of the culprit could atone. Philip, having now the poor criminal in possession, made preparations to execute vengeance upon him, when the English spectators, commiserated his condition, and made offers of money to ransom his life. Philip listened to these offers and mentioned a sum which would satisfy him; but so much could not be collected. He was informed of this, but refused to lessen his demand. The whites, however, collected all they could in the short time allowed them, in hopes that he would be satisfied, when assured that more could not be found; but, instead of this, he persisted in his demand with threatening language, pronounced with an emphasis which foreboded no good. This very much provoked the English, so that they concluded among themselves to make no farther offers, but to try and frighten him away without giving him any more money. The sum raised, which was all that the inhabitants possessed, was eleven pounds; this had already been paid to him, and could not be required back again. Philip had surrounded and taken possession of one or two houses, to the great terror of the inmates; in this dilemma they concluded to put all to risk;—they told him, that, if he did not immediately leave the island, they would rally the inhabitants, and fall upon him and cut him off to a man. Not knowing their defenceless condition, he happily took the alarm, and left the island as soon as possible. The prisoner was then set at liberty.

The natives early acquired a propensity to strong drink. Some of the whites were wicked enough to furnish them with rum, so long as they could pay for it, although it was done in strict violation of the law, and against the wishes and endeavors of the sober part of the inhabitants. Intemperance prevailed amongst them, and soon reduced them to a station far below what they would otherwise have held, if they had abstained from ardent spirits. By the practice of excessive drinking, many were soon reduced to beggary and distress: they were regardless of the cares of their families: and owners of vessels, at the same time that they took the men into their employment, were compelled to furnish their families with the necessaries of life.

Although this was the character of many, it was not of all. Some were sober, steady people, and endeavored to cultivate religious principles among their brethren; when this disposition was manifest, it was encouraged by the whites. They were assisted by a translation of the New Testament into their language, and encouraged to meet together for divine worship. They at one time had four meeting-houses, one towards the east end of the island, at a place called Okorwaw, near the east end of Gibb's swamp, one at Myercommet, a little south from the town, one other near Podpis, and the fourth in Plainfield, situation not exactly known.

In these they held their religious meetings, under ministers of their own nation. Some of them patterned after the English in many respects; they built neat framed houses, kept cows, horses, and other domestic animals, and lived comfortably. But they did not long enjoy these privileges, for it was the will of Heaven to visit them with an epidemic which cut them off, except a few, and destroyed them as a nation forever. The disease was called by some the yellow fever, and by some the plague. It made its appearance among them on the 16th of the 8th month, 1763. Whether it originated with the natives, has not been ascertained. Some circumstances render it probable that the infection came out of a brig, from Ireland, which was cast ashore on the north side of the island. One of the crew appeared to have the same fever; he was brought on shore, and died at a house whither the Indians frequently resorted. Soon after the disorder broke out among them, and spread to an alarming degree in a short time. The sickness was so general and severe, and the deaths so numerous, that they could not contribute to their necessities. The whites, apprehensive that the disorder would spread among themselves, were at first cautious in approaching the sick, but they at length found that the natives only were affected by it, for how much soever they exposed themselves, not one was taken sick. This discovery emboldened the English to go among the Indians, and render such assistance as their distressing situation demanded. They visited them daily, furnished them with provisions and clothing, and assisted in burying their dead. This care was taken by the authority of the town. The kindness of individuals was at the same time liberally extended toward them.

The sickness continued until the 16th of the second month, 1764, at which time it ceased as suddenly as it commenced; for on the evening preceding the date just mentioned there was no apparent abatement of the disease, but on the following morning all the sick were convalescent throughout their different places of abode. The following will show the extent of the ravages of this disorder:

34 were sick and recovered.
36 living among the natives did not take the disease.
8 living by themselves at the west end of the island, escaped.
40 lived among the whites, not one of whom had the sickness.
18 were at sea at the time, and escaped.
222 died with the disorder.

_____

358 the whole number belonging to the island before the sickness.

The number of Indians having become so reduced, it is not worth our while to trace them in a very particular manner to their final extinction. It will be sufficient to add, that the few who survived the sickness continued in their wonted occupation, that of whaling; that, with few exceptions, they would drink to excess whenever they could have access to spirituous liquors; that many of them perished miserably, as is the lot of the intemperate, by sickness, or exposure, or accident; and that the last of the race died in 1822.

Thus the existence of a tribe of natives terminated, and thus their land went to strangers. In the simple charity of nature, they received our fathers. When fugitives from Christian prosecution, they opened to them their stores, bestowed on them their lands, treated them with unfailing kindness, acknowledged their superiority, tasted their poison, and died. Their only misfortune was their connection with Christians, and their only crime, the imitation of their manners.

J. Hector St. John de Crèvecoeur

The tongue-twisting moniker J. Hector St. John de Crèvecoeur is actually a nom de plume for the equally tongue-twisting Michel Guillaume Jean de Crèvecoeur (1735-1813). Born in Caen, France, Crèvecoeur came to North America at age twenty to serve in the wilderness campaigns of the Seven Year War pitting his native land against Great Britain. After being wounded at the Battle of Quebec (1759), he fled to the British colonies, and in 1769 married and settled down to raise a family on a farm in New York. In 1773, Crèvecoeur visited Nantucket, and, happily for us, recorded his impressions in Letters from an American Farmer *(1782), a classic of eighteenth-century American literature. Composed as a series of letters describing the American scene to a friend in England, Crèvecoeur's narrative has a Romantic sensibility akin to that of his great contemporaries Samuel Taylor Coleridge and Jean-Jacques Rousseau. His uniquely American project is "to prove what mankind can do when happily governed" and free of Old World tyrannies.*

Nantucket is his prime example. "Would you believe," Crèvecoeur enthuses, "that a sandy spot of about twenty-three thousand acres, affording neither stones nor timber, meadows nor arable, yet can boast of a handsome town consisting of more than 500 houses, should possess above 200 sail of vessels; constantly employ upwards of 2,000 seamen; feed more than 15,000 sheep, 500 cows, 200 horses; and has several citizens worth £20,000 sterling!" Here we offer a passage from Crèvecoeur's detailed description of Nantucket's environment. Much of what he observed in 1773 seems eerily familiar today. At a time when most of the North American continent was still a howling wilderness, Nantucketers already thought of land in terms of "subdivisions," and had to apply to a council of proprietors for permission to build a house. Crèvecoeur is thoroughly modern, too, in his understanding of coastal erosion. Without the benefit of satellite imaging, he understood that Nantucket's shoals absorb wave energies offshore that would "dissolve" the island's "foundations" if they struck directly on the beach without this natural mitigation. —SB

"Description of the Island of Nantucket" From Letter IV of *Letters from an American Farmer*

T HE ISLAND OF Nantucket lies in latitude 41° 10¹ 60 miles S. from Cape Cod; 27 S from Hyanes or Barnstable, a town on the most contiguous part of the great peninsula; 21 miles E. by S. from Cape Pog, on the vineyard; 50 E. by S. from Wood's Hole, on Elizabeth Island; 80 miles S. from Boston; 120 from Rhode Island; 800 N. from Bermudas. Sherborn is the only town on the island, which consists of about 530 houses, that have been framed on the main; they are lathed and plastered within, handsomely painted and boarded without; each has a cellar underneath, built with stones fetched also from the main: they are all of a similar construction and appearance; plain, and entirely devoid of exterior or interior ornament. I observed but one which was built of bricks, belonging to Mr. —, but like the rest it is unadorned. The town stands on a rising sandbank, on the west side of the harbour, which is very safe from all winds. There are two places of worship, one for the Society of Friends, the other for that of Presbyterians; and in the middle of the town, near the market-place, stands a simple building, which is the county court-house. The town regularly ascends toward the country, and in its vicinage they have several small fields and gardens yearly manured with the dung of their cows, and the soil of their streets. There are a good many cherry and peach trees planted in their streets and in many other places; the apple tree does not thrive well, they have therefore planted but few. The island contains no mountains, yet is very uneven, and the many rising grounds and eminences with which it is filled, have formed in the several valleys a great variety of swamps, where the Indian grass and the blue bent, peculiar to such soils, grow with tolerable luxuriancy. Some of the swamps abound with peat, which serves the poor instead of firewood. There are fourteen ponds on the island, all extremely useful, some lying transversely, almost across it, which greatly helps to divide it into partitions for the use of their cattle; others abound with peculiar fish and sea fowls. Their streets are not paved, but this is attended with little inconvenience, as it is never crowded with country carriages; and those they have in the town are seldom made use of but in the time of the coming in and before the sailing of their fleets. At my first landing I was much surprised at the disagreeable smell which struck me in many parts of the town; it is caused by the whale oil, and is unavoidable; the neatness peculiar to these people can neither remove nor prevent it. There are near the wharfs a great many storehouses, where their staple commodity is deposited, as well as the innumerable materials which are always wanted to repair and fit out so many whalemen. They have three docks, each three hundred feet long, and extremely convenient; at the head of which there are ten feet of water. These docks are built like those in Boston, of logs fetched from the continent, filled with stones, and covered with sand. Between these docks and the town, there is room sufficient for the landing of goods and for the passage of their numerous carts; for almost every man here has one: the wharfs to the north and south of the docks, are built of the same materials, and give a stranger, at his first landing, an high idea of the prosperity of these people; and there is room around these three docks for 300 sail of vessels. When their fleets have been successful, the bustle and hurry of business on this spot for some days after their arrival, would make you imagine, that Sherborn is the capital of a very opulent and large province. On that point of land, which forms the west side of the harbour, stands a very neat lighthouse; the opposite peninsula, called Coitou, secures it from the most dangerous winds. There are but few gardens and arable fields in the neighbourhood of the town, for nothing can be more sterile and sandy than this part of the island; they have, however, with unwearied perseverance, by bringing a variety of manure, and by cow-penning, enriched several spots where they raise Indian corn, potatoes, pumpkins, turnips, etc. On the highest part of this sandy eminence, four windmills grind the grain they raise or import; and contiguous to them their rope walk is to be seen, where full half of their cordage is manufactured. Between the shores of the harbour, the docks, and the town, there is a most excellent piece of meadow, inclosed and manured with such cost and pains as show how necessary and precious grass is at Nantucket. Towards the point of Shèmàh, the island is more level and the soil better; and there they have considerable lots well fenced and richly manured, where they diligently raise their yearly crops. There are but very few farms on this island, because there are but very few spots that will admit of cultivation without the assistance of dung and other manure; which is very expensive to fetch from the main. This island was patented in the year 1671, by twenty-seven proprietors, under the province of New York; which then claimed all the islands from the Neway Sink to Cape Cod. They found it so universally barren and so unfit for cultivation, that they mutually agreed not to divide it, as each could neither live on, nor improve that lot which might fall to his share. They then cast their eyes on the sea, and finding themselves obliged to become fishermen, they looked for a harbour, and having found one, they determined to build a town in its neighbourhood and to

dwell together. For that purpose they surveyed as much ground as would afford
to each what is commonly called here a home lot. Forty acres were thought
sufficient to answer this double purpose; for to what end should they covet
more land than they could improve, or even inclose; not being possessed of a
single tree, in the whole extent of their new dominion. This was all the territorial property they allotted; the rest they agreed to hold in common, and seeing
that the scanty grass of the island might feed sheep, they agreed that each proprietor should be entitled to feed on it if he pleased 560 sheep. By this agreement, the national flock was to consist of 15,210; that is the undivided part of
the island was by such means ideally divisible into as many parts or shares; to
which nevertheless no certain determinate quantity of land was affixed: for
they knew not how much the island contained, nor could the most judicious
surveyor fix this small quota as to quality and quantity. Further they agreed, in
case the grass should grow better by feeding, that then four sheep should represent a cow, and two cows a horse: such was the method this wise people took
to enjoy in common their new settlement; such was the mode of their first
establishment, which may be truly and literally called a pastoral one. Several
hundred of sheep-pasture titles have since been divided on those different
tracts, which are now cultivated; the rest by inheritance and intermarriages
have been so subdivided that it is very common for a girl to have no other portion but her outset and four sheep pastures or the privilege of feeding a cow.
But as this privilege is founded on an ideal, though real title to some unknown
piece of land, which one day or another may be ascertained; these sheep-
pasture titles should convey to your imagination, something more valuable and
of greater credit than the mere advantage arising from the benefit of a cow,
which in that case would be no more than a right of commonage. Whereas,
here as labour grows cheaper, as misfortunes from their sea adventures may
happen, each person possessed of a sufficient number of these sheep-pasture
titles may one day realise them on some peculiar spot, such as shall be adjudged
by the council of the proprietors to be adequate to their value; and this is the
reason that these people very unwillingly sell these small rights, and esteem
them more than you would imagine. They are the representation of a future
freehold, they cherish in the mind of the possessor a latent, though distant,
hope, that by his success in his next whale season, he may be able to pitch upon
some predilected spot, and there build himself a home, to which he may retire,
and spend the latter end of his days in peace. A council of proprietors always
exists in this island, who decide their territorial differences; their titles are
recorded in the books of the county, which this town represents, as well as
every conveyance of land and other sales.

This island furnishes the naturalist with few or no objects worthy of observation; it appears to be the uneven summit of a sandy submarine mountain,

covered here and there with sorrel, grass, a few cedar bushes, and scrubby oaks; their swamps are much more valuable for the peat they contain, than for the trifling pasture of their surface; those declining grounds which lead to the seashores abound with beach grass, a light fodder when cut and cured, but very good when fed green. On the east side of the island they have several tracts of salt grasses, which being carefully fenced, yield a considerable quantity of wholesome fodder. Among the many ponds or lakes with which this island abounds, there are some which have been made by the intrusion of the sea, such as Wiwidiah, the Long, the Narrow, and several others; consequently those are salt and the others fresh. The former answer two considerable purposes, first by enabling them to fence the island with greater facility; at peculiar high tides a large number of fish enter into them, where they feed and grow large, and at some known seasons of the year the inhabitants assemble and cut down the small bars which the waves always throw up. By these easy means the waters of the pond are let out, and as the fish follow their native element, the inhabitants with proper nets catch as many as they want, in their way out, without any other trouble. Those which are most common, are the streaked bass, the blue fish, the tom-cod, the mackerel, the tew-tag, the herring, the flounder, eel, etc. Fishing is one of the greatest diversions the island affords. At the west end lies the harbour of Mardiket, formed by Smith Point on the south-west, by Eel Point on the north, and Tuckernuck Island on the north-west; but it is neither so safe nor has it so good anchoring ground, as that near which the town stands. Three small creeks run into it, which yield the bitterest eels I have ever tasted. Between the lots of Palpus on the east, Barry's Valley and Miacomet pond on the south, and the narrow pond on the west, not far from Shèmàh Point, they have a considerable tract of even ground, being the least sandy, and the best on the island. It is divided into seven fields, one of which is planted by that part of the community which are entitled to it. This is called the common plantation, a simple but useful expedient, for was each holder of this track to fence his property, it would require a prodigious quantity of posts and rails, which you must remember are to be purchased and fetched from the mainland. Instead of those private subdivisions each man's allotment of land is thrown into the general field which is fenced at the expense of the parties; within it everyone does with his own portion of the ground whatever he pleases. This apparent community saves a very material expense, a great deal of labour, and perhaps raises a sort of emulation among them, which urges every one to fertilise his share with the greatest care and attention. Thus every seven years the whole of this tract is under cultivation, and enriched by manure and ploughing yields afterwards excellent pasture; to which the town cows, amounting to 500 are daily led by the town shepherds, and as regularly driven back in the evening. There each animal easily finds the house to which it belongs, where they are sure to be well-rewarded for the milk they give, by a present of bran, grain, or some farinaceous preparation; their economy being very great in that respect. These are commonly called Tètoukèmah lots. You must not imagine that every person on the island is either a landholder, or concerned in rural operations; no, the greater part are at sea; busily employed in their different fisheries; others are mere strangers, who come to settle as craftsmen, mechanics, etc., and even among the natives few are possessed of determinate shares of land: for engaged in sea affairs, or trade, they are satisfied with possessing a few sheep pastures, by means of which they may have perhaps one or two cows. Many have but one, for the great number of children they have, has caused such sub-divisions of the original proprietorship as is sometimes puzzling to trace; and several of the most fortunate at sea, have purchased and realised a great number of these pasture titles. The best land on the island is at Palpus, remarkable for nothing but a house of entertainment. Quayes is a small but valuable track, long since purchased by Mr. Coffin, where he has erected the best house on the island. By long attention, proximity of the sea, etc., this fertile spot has been well manured, and is now the garden of Nantucket. Adjoining to it on the west side there is a small stream, on which they have erected a fulling mill; on the east is the lot, known by the name of Squam, watered likewise by a small rivulet, on which stands another fulling mill. Here is fine loamy soil, producing excellent clover, which is mowed twice a year. These mills prepare all the cloth which is made here: you may easily suppose that having so large a flock of sheep they abound in wool; part of this they export, and the rest is spun by their industrious wives and converted into substantial garments. To the southeast is a great division of the island, fenced by itself, known by the name of Siasconcèt lot. It is a very uneven track of ground, abounding with swamps; here they turn in their winter's provisions. It is on the shores of this part of the island, near Pochick Rip, where they catch their best fish, such as sea bass, tewtag, or black fish, cod, smelt, perch, shadine, pike, etc. They have erected a few fishing houses on this shore, as well as at Sankate's Head, and Suffakatchè Beach, where the fishermen dwell in the fishing season. Many red cedar bushes and beach grass grow on the peninsula of Coitou; the soil is light and sandy, and serves as a receptacle for rabbits. It is here that their sheep find shelter in the snow storms of winter. At the north end of Nantucket, there is a long point of land, projecting far into the sea, called Sandy Point; nothing grows on it but plain grass; and this is the place from whence they often catch porpoises and sharks, by a very ingenious method. On this point they commonly drive their horses in the spring of the year, in order to feed on the grass it bears, which is useless when arrived at maturity. Between that point and the main island they have a valuable salt meadow, called Croskaty, with a pond of the same name famous for black ducks. Hence we must return to Squam, which abounds in clover and herds grass; those who possess it follow no maritime occupation, and therefore neglect nothing that can render it fertile and profitable. The rest of the undescribed part of the island is open, and serves as a common pasture for their sheep. To the west of the island is that of Tuckernut, where in the spring their young cattle are driven to feed; it has a few oak bushes and two fresh-water ponds, abounding with teals, brandts, and many other sea fowls, brought to this island by the proximity of their sand banks and shallows; where thousands are seen feeding at low water. Here they have neither wolves nor foxes; those inhabitants therefore who live out of town, raise with all security as much poultry as they want; their turkeys are very large and excellent. In summer this climate is extremely pleasant; they are not exposed to the scorching sun of the continent, the heats being tempered by the sea breezes, with which they are perpetually refreshed. In the winter, however, they pay severely for those advantages; it is extremely cold; the northwest wind, the tyrant of this country, after having escaped from our mountains and forests, free from all impediment in its short passage, blows with redoubled force and renders this island bleak and uncomfortable. On the other hand, the goodness of their houses, the social hospitality of their firesides, and their good cheer, make them ample amends for the severity of the season; nor are the snows so deep as on the main. The necessary and unavoidable activity of that season, combined with the vegetative rest of nature, force mankind to suspend their toils: often at this season more than half the island are at sea, fishing in milder latitudes.

This island, as has already been hinted, appears to be the summit of some huge sandy mountain, affording some acres of dry land for the habitation of man; other submarine ones lie to the southward of this, at different depths and different distances. This dangerous region is well known to the mariners by the name of Nantucket Shoals: these are the bulwarks which so powerfully defend this island from the impulse of the mighty ocean, and repel the force of its waves; which, but for the accumulated barriers, would ere now have dissolved its foundations, and torn it to pieces. These are the banks which afforded to the first inhabitants of Nantucket their daily subsistence, as it was from these shoals that they drew the origin of that wealth which they now possess; and it was the school where they first learned how to venture farther, as the fish of their coast receded. The shores of this island abound with the soft-shelled, the hard-shelled, and the great sea clams, a most nutritious shell-fish. Their sands, their shallows are covered with them; they multiply so fast, that they are a never-failing resource. These and the great variety of fish they catch, constitute the principal food of the inhabitants.

Joseph C. Hart

Joseph C. Hart (1798–1855) was a New York attorney and journalist whose middle name—Coleman—testifies to his Nantucket ancestry on his mother's side. Although little is known about Hart's life, it's possible that he made a whaling voyage as a young man, and probable that he had an extended stay on Nantucket in 1832, when a cholera epidemic swept New York City. Certainly Hart spent substantial amounts of time on the island, absorbing the particulars of its daily life and learning its rich history from elders who could still remember the American Revolution. The result was Miriam Coffin, or The Whale Fishermen *(1834), an historical novel based on the smuggling and war-profiteering career of Nantucket's notorious "she-merchant," Keziah Coffin (1723–98), and with many dramatic scenes of Pacific whaling. A bestseller in its time,* Miriam Coffin *went into a second printing almost immediately. The novel's success seems to have persuaded more than one writer that there was literary gold in the business of transforming Nantucket history into fiction.* Miriam Coffin *became an important source for Edgar Allan Poe's only novel,* The Narrative of Arthur Gordon Pym of Nantucket *(1838), and for Herman Melville's* Moby-Dick *(1851). It may even have precipitated Obed Macy's nonfiction* History of Nantucket *(1835), published the following year.*

"Short of a time machine," writes island historian Nathaniel Philbrick, Miriam Coffin *"is probably the best way to experience the sights, sounds, and even the smells of Old Nantucket." The selection that follows carries us back to an eighteenth-century sheep-shearing festival, when islanders banded together to round up their thousands of sheep, scrub the struggling animals in Miacomet Pond, and relieve them of their fleece. As with other forms of communal labor, such as barn raisings or husking bees, this annual three-day event was also a celebration—the occasion for a vast community potluck involving mountains of food, here described by Hart in mouth-watering detail. —SB*

From Chapter 4 of *Miriam Coffin or The Whale-Fisherman*

An EAGER IMPORTANCE sat enthroned upon the countenances of the islanders, on the morning of the "Shearing," which followed the arrival of the Leviathan. Hundreds of curious strangers from the continent had taken advantage of the recent sunshine and favourable breeze, in order to participate in the "doings." No one who has ever voyaged to Nantucket at this interesting period, has sojourned with regret, or gone away unamused or uninstructed. The Shearing, which lightens many thousands of sheep of their fleece, and adds proportionately to the wealth of the people, was celebrated with a "pomp and circumstance" before the Revolution that is, perhaps, not equalled by the parade of the present day. We are not among those who value the past at the expense of the present, and would fain assert that no unseemly innovation has been suffered to creep in upon this time-honoured festival,—nor to retrench the homely, but well ordered—nay, liberal provision, that of yore was furnished forth. It is not likely, however, that the festal day will ever be forgotten, though its splendours may be somewhat dimmed. At any rate, it is still kept sacred by the islanders, and the proper day of the month of June is regularly marked upon the calendar as the advent thereof.

It is remarkable that war, though it has more than once sensibly diminished the number of flocks annually submitted to trenchant instruments of the island shepherds—and terrible and overwhelming as it has always proved to Nantucket especially,—it is remarkable, we repeat, that it has never put its extinguisher upon the merry sheep shearing. Amidst sufferings the most intense, and privations the most appalling, it has been kept as a holyday season for more than a hundred years, and without the interregnum of a single year. Its undoubted antiquity thus carries it back to a period long prior to the existence of the Republic; while its observance, both ancient and modern, has been as regular as that of the national jubilee. It is a rational holyday of labour and recreation—of toil and profit—of enjoyment, unsullied by dissipation or excesses. Long may it endure—and long may it prove the source of happiness, and of increase of store to the worthy island dwellers!

By early cockcrowing, the plain, or common, which we have elsewhere spoken of, was ornamented with its yearly complement of camp tents and awnings of canvas, marshalled in approved array, and skirting the area in the

vicinage of the sheep-pens. The flocks scattered here and there since the shearing of the previous year, had been carefully collected, and after the inspection
of the marks of the owners, and the customary washing in the limpid waters of
Miacomet, had been folded in temporary enclosures. They were thus kept in
readiness for the operation of shearing. The poet Thomson gives a vivid
description of a sheep-washing in his own land, and has saved us the trouble of
entering into the same preliminary particulars—

> "They drive the troubled flocks
> To where the mazy running brook
> Forms a deep pool; this bank abrupt and high,
> And that fair spreading in a pebbled shore.
> Urged to the giddy brink, much is the toil,
> The clamour much, of men, and boys,
> Ere the soft fearful creatures to the flood
> Commit their woolly sides. And oft the swain,
> On some impatient seizing, hurls them in:
> Emboldened then, nor hesitating more,
> Fast, fast they plunge amid the flashing wave,
> And pant and labour to the farthest shore.
> At last, of snowy white, the gathered flocks
> Are in the wattled pen innumerous pressed
> Head above head: and, ranged in lusty rows,
> The shepherds sit and whet the sounding shears."

By sunrise the selectmen, or magnates of the town, dressed in their "best
bib-and-tucker," were seen moving towards the common in a body. The
solemn importance of the office, and the magnitude of their calling, were
observable in their prim and sedate carriage, while acting in their official
capacity of umpires or judges in the division of the fleece, or in determining
the ownership of the sheep whose marks had been obliterated or defaced. Next
came the inhabitants and their guests—staying not for precedence, or the order
of going forth—but bending their hasty steps to the common. These were
immediately followed by a train of carts and calêches, or those little two-
wheeled vehicles peculiar to Nantucket, and adapted, by their uncommon
lightness and small friction of the hub and axle to the sandy soil—if such may
be dignified by the name of soil which forms the super-stratum of the island.
The heavier and more capacious carriages were laden with the profusion of
good things, carefully provided against the great day by every family, and destined for the comfortable refreshment of the body during the progress of the
shearing. Each family had reared its own tent, and now garnished the suburban

board with its choicest provisions. With some, the savings of a whole year were liberally and anxiously appropriated to furnish the various appointments of tents and camp equipage, and the other paraphernalia of meats, bread stuffs, and vegetables. The rare teas of the East, so shortly destined to provoke a bloody quarrel between Great Britain and her stubborn daughter; the confectionery of the West Indies, and the substantial *et cetera* of their own island and adjacent coast; foreign wine, of generous vintage—seldom used except upon rare occasions by these people of simple habits; home-made fermentations and pleasant beverages; the freshest produce of the domestic dairy, in all its variety of rose-impregnated butter, yielded by means of the tender herbage of June; pot-cheese, curds and cream, and the venerable cheese, which in distant countries would pass current for "Parmesan;" pies of dried fruit, custards, and tarts of cranberry; cakes of flour, mixed up with ginger and treacle, and the more costly and ambitious pound cake, stuffed with raisins and frosted over with an incrustation of sugar, resembling ice; puddings of bread, of rice, and of Indian meal, enriched with eggs; pickles of cucumber, beans, beets, and onions;—these and all the other eatables and accompaniments, which a prudent and well instructed housewife can imagine, or put down upon a catalogue, after a week's thinking and preparation, were plentifully provided, and importunately—after the good old American fashion,—piled and pressed upon the pewter platters of the thronging guests, as long as the shearing lasted, or a hungry customer could be found.

While the tables beneath the tents were spread with snow-white linen, and decorated with the choicest and best provisions by the matrons, the sturdy and vigorous men were hard at work among the sheep. It was the pride and boast of these people, in that day, to rear the best sheep in the colonies;—and wool as fine, though without the Merino cross, and mutton as fat as any found in America, were the produce of the excellent breed possessed by the Nantucketers, whose flocks in the aggregate numbered some twenty thousand head. It was, therefore, no trifling job to shear the fleece from so many animals; and, although a day of leisure and pastime to most of the islanders, especially the females, it was to the men a busy and laborious season, and, at the same time, to strangers a curious and highly gratifying display.

"—The glad circle round them yield their souls
To festive mirth, and wit that knows no gall.
Meantime their joyous task goes on apace:
Some, mingling, stir the melted tar; and some,
Deep on the new-shorn vagrant's heaving side
To stamp the cipher, ready stand;—
Others th' unwilling wether drag along:

And glorying in his might, the sturdy boy
Holds by the twisted horns th' indignant ram.
Fear not, ye gentle tribes!—'tis not the knife
Of horrid slaughter that is o'er you waved;
No, 'tis the swain's well guided shears."

It was not, however, the congregation of the flocks, and the temptations for
the appetite, that solely constituted the interest of the scene. The shearing, as it
is called, is seized upon, also, as a fitting occasion for the free interchange of
those friendly courtesies that so signally distinguish and cement the families of
the island, whose pursuits and whose gains,—whether on land or on sea,—are
in a measure common to the whole. The success of one is sure to bring gain
and prosperity to his neighbour. Their sheep and their cattle fed and herd
together on the same unenclosed pasturage, which of itself is owned in common by the islanders, and denominated the property of the town. The success
of a whaling ship at sea brings joy and worldly store, not only to the owners,
but to the crew and their families in their due proportions. The people are thus
linked together by the strongest ties;—by a sort of community of interest. The
failure of pasturage, or blight in the flocks, curtails the enjoyments of all; and a
disastrous voyage affects, in the same degree, the property and happiness of all
the members of the little community [. . . .]

But there are other considerations that weigh with the inhabitants, and
mark the wisdom of the founders, if so they may be called, of this annual festival. Friends and relatives, long sundered and kept apart by a wide expanse of
water, now make it a point to cross the Sound which divides them; and a pretty
general assemblage upon the island at the shearing, though but for once in the
year, compensates in a considerable degree for the long separation, and for the
slender and unvarying amusements of the isolated settlement. The reunion is
not unlike that of the aged grandfather who assembles his children and grand-
children, during the Christmas holydays, at his own festive board; and, by promoting general hilarity and exciting the buoyant mirth of his youthful
descendants, adds thereby to his own happiness, while he contributes to that of
those who surround him.

The hour of eating approached, and was welcomed by the worshipful
Selectmen, "and all others in authority," as well as by the industrious clippers of
wool and the gadders after amusement; who all sat down, as they could find
places in the tents, and intermingled without ceremony. It may perhaps be a
work of supererogation to inform the reader that, thus circumstanced, they fell
to work upon a substantial and "glorious breakfast." To attack and demolish
huge mountains of toast, vast broiled slices of the unequalled salmon, caught by
the Indians and brought in cars from the waters of the wild region of the

Penobscot, cutlets of veal, slices of mutton, ham boiled and peppered in various dark spots, and garnished at intervals with cloves, beefsteaks swimming in butter, the finest flavored fish which but an hour before were sporting in the sea,—but which now appeared in the various garbs of "roasted, baked, and boiled, and brown:"—we say, to attack and demolish these comfortable appliances, and to wash them down with a strong mug of coffee or tea, was but the work of a few minutes; for the Americans are quick eaters, and the invigorating air, and the morning's exercise had whetted the appetite of the multitude. And yet there was enough for all, and many baskets to spare, without the imputation of a miracle.

The savoury and hearty meal was further supplied, or we may say "topped off," with amazing quantities of a species of animal called by the islanders the "*Pooquaw*," and sometimes by the other Indian name of "*Quohog.*" These are found in great numbers on the sandy shores of the island; and, but for their great plenty in the northern parts of America, they would be esteemed a delicious luxury.

Lest we may not be well understood while we speak of the inimitable quohog, and, by our obscurity, engender doubts of its inexhaustible abundance, it may be well to inform the gentle reader and enlighten his understanding. Its aboriginal name, and that which it still holds in the oldest parts of America, is just as we have written it down. Nevertheless, the "*quo-hog*" hath neither bristles nor tail, nor is it a quadruped, as its name would seem to import; but it is in truth a species of shell-fish, which naturalists, in the plenitude of their lore, denominate *bivalvular.* It is grievous further to say, in explanation, that its original and sonorous name, and that by which it is still known on Nantucket, has been made to yield, by the pestilent spirit of innovation in the middle states, to the flat, insipid and unsounding title of—the clam! Spirit of the erudite Barnes, the conchologist—spirits of Sir Joseph Banks, and Sir Humphrey Davy—Spirit of the learned Mitchell—could you not, in the course of your long and well-spent lives, hit upon a more euphonious jawcracker for the persecuted quohog, than the abominable name of "*clam?*"

The manner of cooking the quohog in the most palatable way at the "*Squantums*" of Nantucket, as oracularly given out by the knowing Peleg Folger, was resorted to on this occasion, to eke out the foregoing meal. Even unto this day, some of the eastern people adopt the same method, to "stap the vitals" of the quohog at their "roast-outs" or forest junketings. As to the peculiar mode of cooking, we adopt the argument of Peleg, even as he learnedly discussed the matter while arranging a bed of the aforesaid bivalvular shell-fish on the morning of the shearing. Imprimis—The quohogs were placed upon the bare ground, side by side, with their mouths biting the dust. The burning coals of the camp-fires, which had done the office of boiling and broiling, were removed from under the cross-trees, where hung the pot and tea-water kettle, and applied plentifully to the backs of the quohogs. In a few minutes after the application of the fire, the cooking was declared to be at an end, and the roasting of the quohogs complete. The steam of the savoury liquor, which escaped in part without putting out the fire, preserved the meat in a parboiled state, and prevented it from scorching, or drying to a cinder, and the whole virtue of the fish from being lost. The ashes of the fire were effectually excluded by the position in which the animal was placed at the beginning; and the heat as completely destroyed the tenacity of the hinge which covered the shells.

"And now," said Peleg, "take a few on thy platter; remove the upper shell, and apply a lump of fresh butter and a sprinkling of pepper and salt." Our blessings on thee, Peleg Folger. The morsel, if taken hot, might be envied by an eastern emperor, whose palate is pampered by bird-nest delicacies;—or by the exquisite gourmand of any nation. But in America, who eats a clam or a quohog? None but the wise—and that includes a majority of the people;—the fashionable, never—more's the pity. [. . . .]

Ralph Waldo Emerson

*When Ralph Waldo Emerson (1803-82) visited Nantucket in May 1847 to lecture at the Atheneum, newly rebuilt after the devastating fire of 1846, he was perhaps the most celebrated man of letters in America, the principal spokesman for the literary and philosophical movement known as Transcendentalism. Harvard-educated and an ordained Unitarian minister, Emerson at age forty-three had already published a volume of poetry, a collection of essays including such classics as "Self-Reliance" and "The Over-Soul," and two books limning his philosophy (*Nature, *1836, and* The American Scholar, *1837). Attracting thinkers such as Margaret Fuller, Bronson Alcott, Elizabeth Peabody, and Henry David Thoreau in addition to Emerson, Transcendentalism proclaimed the unity of God and the world, and the immanence of God both in nature and in the soul of the individual. Believing in the divine authority of the soul's own intuitions and impulses, Transcendentalists advocated a doctrine of self-reliance and individualism, and a disregard of external authority and tradition.*

Such ideas were understandably controversial among New England's established clergy. After giving an inflammatory address at the Harvard Divinity School in 1838, Emerson had been effectively banned from the pulpit, and had instead taken his ministry to the lecture circuit. Quaker Nantucketers, however, might have listened to his Transcendentalist ideas with special interest. Although Transcendentalism has many intellectual strands, from German philosophy to English Romanticism to Buddhist religious thought, one of them was the progressive New Light Quakerism advocated by Emerson's friend and mentor, island-born Mary Rotch (1777-1848). Emerson once told a young relative that he was "more of a Quaker than anything else," believing in "the 'still small voice' and that voice is Christ within us."

Over a period of two weeks on Nantucket, he gave a series of six lectures on "Representative Men"—Plato, Swedenborg, Montaigne, Shakespeare, Napoleon, and Goethe—each considered as an embodiment of the divine attributes in man. Six feet tall, loose-limbed, and with intense blue-grey eyes, Emerson was an electrifying public speaker, leaning out at an acute angle towards his audience and holding them rapt with the intensity of his thought. He would return to the island to lecture in 1855, 1856, and 1857.

Maria Mitchell found him "exceedingly captivating" as a speaker, his mind "like a meteor's beam of light moving in undulatory waves, with occasional meteors in its path."

In 1850, Emerson published Representative Men *in book form—there readers may learn in detail what he spoke about on the island. Here, we've chosen instead to reproduce Emerson's impressions of Nantucket, recorded in his journal. The entries are short, and there are all too few of them, but they are written vividly, and with a poetic economy of language. Only Emerson could, in just a few lines, offer a Transcendentalist vision of the sea as well as a scheme to use the surf for alternative energy, several astute observations on the "nation of Nantucket," a hair's breadth escape from a whale, and more. . . . —SB*

From Emerson's Journal, May 1847

On the seashore at Nantucket I saw the play of the Atlantic with the coast. Here was wealth: every wave reached a quarter of a mile along shore as it broke. There are no rich men, I said to compare with these. Every wave is a fortune. One thinks of Etzlers and great projectors who will yet turn this immense waste strength to account and save the limbs of human slaves. Ah what freedom & grace & beauty with all this might. The wind blew back the foam from the top of each billow as it rolled in, like the hair of a woman in the wind. The freedom makes the observer feel as a slave. Our expression is so slender, thin, & cramp; can we not here learn a generous eloquence? This was the lesson our starving poverty wanted. This was the disciplinary Pythagorean music which should be medicine.

Then the seeing so excellent a spectacle is a certificate that all imaginable good shall yet be realized. We should not have dared to believe that this existed: Well what does not the actual beholding of a hero or of a finished woman signify?

> *"Il faudrait pour bien faire que tout le monde fût millionnaire."*
>
> [Augustin Eugène] Scribe
> *Le Mariage d'Argent*

Nation of Nantucket makes its own war & peace. Place of winds bleak shelterless & when it blows a large part of the island is suspended in the air & comes into your face & eyes as if it was glad to see you. The moon comes here as if it was at home, but there is no shade. A strong national feeling. Very sensitive to everything that dishonours the island because it hurts the value of stock till the company are poorer.

50 persons own $\frac{5}{7}$ of all the property on the island. Calashes. At the fire they pilfered freely as if after a man was burnt out his things belonged to the fire & everybody might have them.

Before the Athenaeum is a huge jawbone of a sperm whale & at the corners of the streets I noticed (Chester street) the posts were of the same material. They say here that a northeaster never dies in debt to a southwester but pays all back with interest.

Capt. Isaac Hussey who goes out soon in the "Planter" had his boat stove in by a whale; he instantly swum to the whale and planted his lance in his side & killed him before he got in another boat. The same man being dragged under the water by the coil of his line got his knife out of his pocket & cut the line & released himself. Capt. Brayton was also dragged down but the whale stopped after a short distance & he came up.

I saw Captain Pollard.

The captains remember the quarter deck in their houses.

Fifty-five months are some voyages.

9500 people	80 ships
New Bedford	300 ships

I saw Capt. Isaac Hussey in the steamboat & asked him about that pocket knife. He said no he felt in his pocket for his knife but had none there; then he managed to let down his trowsers & get the line off from his leg & rose. At last he saw light overhead & instantly felt safe. When he broke water his men were a quarter mile off looking out for him. They soon discovered him & picked him up.

Capt. Brooks told me that the last whale he killed was 72 feet long, 52 feet in girth & he got 200 bbls of oil from him.

The young man sacrificed by lot in the boats of the ship Essex was named Coffin, nephew of Capt. Pollard & a schoolmate of Edw. Gardner.

"Grass widows" they call the wives of these people absent from home for 4 or 5 years.

Walter Folger has made a reflecting telescope and a clock which is now in his house & which measures hours, days, years, & *centuries*. In Wm. Mitchell's observatory I saw a nebula in Casseopeia, the double star at the Pole, the double star Zeta Ursi.

At Nantucket every blade of grass describes a circle on the sand.

Henry David Thoreau

Ironically, Henry David Thoreau (1817-72), the Transcendentalist bard of life lived in harmony with nature, traveled to Nantucket not on a sailing vessel running with the wind, but on a newfangled steamship making heavy work against rough seas. Not surprisingly, the experience disagreed with him. "I was obliged to pay the usual tribute to the sea," he wrote to a friend. Thoreau thought ruefully of his Harvard classmate, Richard Henry Dana, Jr., and Dana's voyage around Cape Horn as a working seaman, recorded in the popular narrative Two Years Before the Mast *(1840). "I went neither before nor behind the mast, since we hadn't any," Thoreau wrote about the Nantucket steamship. "I went with my head hanging over the side all the way."*

When Thoreau staggered ashore on 27 December 1854, he may have been green around the gills, but he was also the celebrated author of a new book, Walden *(1854). A classic of the American Renaissance,* Walden *records how Thoreau "lived alone, in the woods, a mile from any neighbor, in a house which I had built myself, on the shore of Walden Pond, in Concord, Massachusetts, and earned my living by the labor of my hands only." For two years and two months, Thoreau had pursued this experiment in self-reliance and material economy as the means to spiritual wealth.*

Thoreau had been invited to Nantucket to deliver a lecture at the Atheneum. He spoke on the evening of 28 December 1854, and the Nantucket Inquirer *reported: "Notwithstanding the damp, uncomfortable weather of Thursday evening, and the muddy streets, a large audience assembled to listen to the man who has rendered himself notorious by living, as his book asserts, in the woods, at an expense of about sixty dollars a year, in order that he might there hold free communion with Nature, and test for himself the happiness of a life without manual labor or conventional restraints."*

The third in a series of eleven lectures by such distinguished speakers as Horace Greeley and Ralph Waldo Emerson, Thoreau's Atheneum lecture was titled "What Shall It Profit?", later published as the essay "Life Without Principle" (1863). The speech was an attack on the moral and spiritual poverty of America's business culture. "I think that there is nothing, not even crime, more opposed to poetry, to philosophy, ay, to life itself," Thoreau opined. His arguments against development would seem familiar to

Nantucketers today: "If a man walk in the woods for love of them half of each day, he is in danger of being regarded as a loafer; but if he spends his whole day as a speculator, shearing off those woods and making earth bald before her time, he is esteemed an industrious and enterprising citizen. As if a town had no interest in its forests but to cut them down!"

In New Bedford just a few days previously, Thoreau's audience had not enjoyed "What Shall It Profit?" Whaling baron Charles W. Morgan was understandably not amused, and wrote in his journal: "[W]e had a lecture from the eccentric Henry J. [sic] Thoreau—The Hermit author very caustic against the usual avocations & employments of the world and a definition of what is true labour & true wages—audience very large & quiet—but I think he puzzled them a little." The Nantucket lecture was more successful. The Inquirer *reported that "his lecture may have been desultory and marked by simplicity of manner, but not paucity of ideas." And Thoreau wrote that "Nantucket people" were "the very audience for me."*

A dedicated diarist, Thoreau kept journals throughout his adult life. Here, we offer his impressions of Nantucket, recorded during his visit. Nantucket readers should also seek out Thoreau's Cape Cod, *his book-length account of walking the moors and beaches of the Cape. In it, as Paul Theroux has observed, Thoreau "seemed to raise beachcombing to a priesthood." —SB*

From Thoreau's Journal, December 1854

Dec 27th

To Nantucket via Hyannis in misty rain. On Cape Cod saw the hills through the mist covered with cladonias. A head wind & rather rough passage of 3 hours to Nantucket—the water being 30 miles over—Capt. Edward W. Gardiner (where I spent the evening) thought there was a beach at Barnegat similar to that at Cape Cod. Mr. Barney (formerly a Quaker minister there) who was at Gardiner's told of one Bunker of Nantucket in old times "who had 8 sons, & steered each in his turn to the killing of a whale." Gardiner said you must have been awhaling there before you could be married—& must have struck a whale before you could dance. They do not think much of crossing from Hyannis in a small boat in pleasant weather—i.e. but they can safely do it. A boy was drifted across thus in a storm in a row boat about two years ago—by luck he struck Nantucket.

The outline of the island is continually changing. The Whalers now go chiefly to Behring's straits & anywhere bet 35 N & S. lat. & catch several kinds of whales. It was Edmund Gardiner of N.B. (a relative of Edwards—) who was carried down by a whale—& Hussey of Nantucket who, I believe, was one to draw lots to see who should be eaten.

As for communication with the mainland being interrupted Gardiner remembers when 31 mails were landed at once—which taking out Sundays—made 5 weeks & one day.

The snow 10 days ago fell about 2 inches deep—but melted instantly.

At the Ocean House I copied from Wm. Coffin's map of the town 1834—this 30,590 acres including three isles beside 1,050 are fresh ponds—about 750 peat swamp. Clay in all parts— But only granite or gneiss boulders.

Dec 28th

A misty rain as yesterday—Capt. Gardiner carried me to Siasconset in his carriage. He has got from 40 to 45 or 50 bushels of corn to an acre from his land. Wished to know how to distinguish guinea cocks from Guinea hens— He is extensively engaged in raising pines on the island. There is not a tree to be seen—except such as are set out about houses— The land is worth commonly from 1 dollar to a dollar and a half. He showed me several lots of his—of different ages—one tract of 300 acres sewn in rows with a planter—where the young trees 2 yrs old are just beginning to green the ground—& I saw one of Norway pine & our Pitch—mixed 8 years old—which looked quite like a forest at a distance— The Norway pines had grown the fastest with a longer shoot & and had a bluer look at a distance more like the white pine. The com[mon] pitch pines have a reddish crisped look at the top. Some are sown in rows some broad-cast. At first he was alarmed to find that the ground moles had gone along in the furrows directly under the plants & so impared the roots as to kill many of the trees & he sowed over again. He was also discouraged to find that a sort of spindle-worm had killed the leading shoot of a great part of his neighbors older trees— These plantations must very soon change the aspect of the island. His com. P. pine seed obtained from the Cape cost him about 20 dollars a bushel at least about a dollar a quart with the wings—& they told him it took about 80 bushels of cones to make one such bushel of seeds.

I was surprised to hear that the Norway pine seed without the wings imported from France had cost not quite $200 a bushel delivered at New York or Philadelphia. He has ordered 8 hogsheads!!! Of the last clear wingless seeds at this rate—I *think* he said it took about a gallon to sow an acre. He had tried to get White pine seed, but in vain. The cones had not contained any of late (?).

This looks as if he meant to sow a good part of the island though he said he might sell some of the seed. It is an interesting enterprise.

Half way to Siasconset I saw the old corn hills where they had formerly cultivated—the authorities laying out a new tract for this purpose each year. This island must look exactly like a prairie except that the view in clear weather is bounded by the sea— Saw crows—saw & heard larks frequently—& saw robins—but most abundant running along the ruts or circling about just over the ground in small flocks— What the inhabitants call snow birds a grey bunting like bird about the size of the snow bunting—Can it be the Sea-side finch—? or the Savannah Sparrow?—or the shore lark?

Gardiner said that they had Pigeon—hen—& other hawks—but there are no places for them to breed—also owls, which must breed, for he had seen their young. A few years ago someone imported a dozen partridges from the mainland—but though some were seen for a year or 2 not one had been seen for some time & they were thought to be extinct. He thought the raccoons which had been very numerous, might have caught them. In Harrisons days some coons were imported and turned loose—& they multiplied very fast & became quite a pest killing hens etc.—& were killed in turn— Finally they turned out & hunted them with hounds—& killed 75 at one time since which he had not heard of any. There were foxes once but none now—& no indigenous animal bigger than a "ground mole." The nearest approach to woods that I saw was the swamps where the blueberries maples etc. are higher than one's head. I saw as I rode—High blueberry bushes & maple in the swamps—huckleberries—shrub-oaks—uva ursa (which he called mealy plum) gaultheria—beach plum—clethra—may-flower (well budded). Also withered poverty grass—golden-rods—asters— In the swamps are cranberries & I saw one carting the vines home to set out—which also many are doing. G. described what he made out to be "star-grass" as common. Saw at Siasconset perhaps 50 little houses but almost every one empty. Saw some peculiar horse carts for conveying fish up the bank—made like a wheel barrow—with a whole iron bound barrel for the wheel—a rude square box for the body resting on the shafts—& the horse to draw it after him— The barrel makes a good wheel in the sand. They may get sea weed in them. A man asked 37 cents for a horse cart load of sea weed carried ¼ mile from the shore. G. pointed out the house of a singular old hermit & genealogist Franklin Folger—over 70 years old and who for 30 years *at least* has lived alone & devoted his thoughts to genealogy— He knows the genealogy of the whole island & a relative supports him by making genealogical charts from his dictation for those who will pay for them. He at last lives in a very filthy manner—& G. helped clean his house when he was absent about 2 years ago. They took up 3 barrels of dirt in his room.

Ascended the light house at Sancoty head. The mist still prevented my seeing off—& around the island. I saw the eggs (?) of some creature in dry masses as big as my fist like the skins of so many beans—on the beach. G. told me of a boy who a few years since stole near to some wild geese which had alighted & rushing on them seized 2—before they could rise—& though he was obliged to let one go—secured the other.

Visited the museum at the Athenaeum various south sea implements—etc. etc. brought home by whalers.

The last Indian—not of pure blood—died this very month—& I saw his picture with a basket of huckleberries in his hand.

Dec 29ᵗʰ

Nantucket to Concord at 7½ AM—still in mist. The fog was so thick that we were lost on the water—stopped & sounded many times. The clerk said the depth varied from 3 to 8 fathoms bet the island & Cape. Whistled & listened for the locomotive's answer—but probably heard only the echo of our own whistle at first—but at last the locomotive's whistle & the life boat bell.

I forgot to say yesterday that there was at one place an almost imperceptible rise not far west of Siasconset—to a slight ridge or swell running from Tom Nevers Head northward to John Gibbs' Swamp— This conceals the town of Nantucket (John Gibbs was the name of the Ind. Philip came after) This seen a

mile off through the mist which concealed the relative distance of the base &
summit appeared like an abrupt hill—though an extremely gradual swell.

    At the end of Obed Macy's Hist. of Nantucket are some verses signed "Peter
Folger 1676" as for the sin which God would punish by the Indian war

> "Sure 'tis not chiefly for those sins
>   That magistrates do name,"

but for the sins of persecution & the like—the banishing & whipping of godly
men—

> "The cause of this their suffering
>   was not for any sin,
> But for the witness that they bare
>   against babes sprinkling."

X

X

X

> "The church may now go stay at home.
>   there's nothing for to do;
> Their work is all cut out by law,
>   and almost made up too."

X

X

> "'Tis like that some may think and say,
>   our war would not remain,
> If so be that a thousand more
>   of natives were but slain.
> Alas! these are but foolish thoughts;
>   God can make more arise.
> And if that there were none at all,
>   He can make war with flies."

Philip Caputo

*In 1991, the Nature Conservancy launched its "Last Great Places" campaign, desig-
nating forty ecosystems around the world, including the heaths and sandplain grasslands
of Nantucket and Martha's Vineyard, as among the planet's most threatened and unique.
As part of the campaign, the Nature Conservancy invited thirty-one prominent writers—voices for the environment including Barry Lopez, Peter Mattheissen, Terry
Tempest Williams, and Barbara Kingsolver—to visit the Last Great Places and contribute essays about them to an anthology titled* Heart of the Land *(1994).*

*To represent Nantucket and Martha's Vineyard, the Nature Conservancy chose
novelist and Pulitzer Prize-winning reporter Philip Caputo (b. 1941). A journalist who
has covered wars in Vietnam, Afghanistan, the Middle East, and Africa, Caputo is the
author of fourteen books as of this writing, best known for* A Rumor of War *(1977), a
memoir of his tour of duty with the U.S. Marines in Vietnam, and* Acts of Faith
*(2005), a novel about mercenaries, missionaries, and aid workers in the Sudan. The
Nature Conservancy was doubtless attracted by his penchant for adventure travel and his
writing about wild places from the Arctic Circle to Australia, from the American High
West to the grasslands of East Africa, as well as by his love of islands and the sea. Some
of Caputo's finest nature writing is collected in* In the Shadows of the Morning:
Essays on Wild Lands, Wild Waters, and a Few Untamed People *(2002).*

*Islanders may not appreciate his vision of Nantucket and the Vineyard's carefully
conserved "wild" places as the thoroughly domesticated products of human impact, requiring vigilant management and restricted use. Yet Caputo sees clearly the Nantucket environment that had already been "subdivided" by the time of Crèvecoeur's visit in 1773,
and intensely manipulated before Thoreau arrived in 1854. The limited and regulated
island landscapes described here hold important lessons for the fate of the untrammeled
continental wilds that Caputo prefers and also help explain the historic attraction of
islanders to the open freedom of the sea.*

"No Space to Waste"

Ever since the Pilgrims stood on Plymouth Rock face to face with a green new world commensurate with man's capacity for wonder (to borrow Fitzgerald's lovely phrase), a dichotomy has dwelled within the American soul. On the one hand, we are romantics awed and enchanted by vast, pristine wilderness; on the other, we are conquerors roused to possess and exploit it.

The Puritans peopled the New England forests with devils and witches; at the same time, the more adventurous among them shed their dour broadcloth for buckskins and pushed into those forests to build new lives. The North American wilderness thus became the province of wickedness, to be combatted for moral reasons, and yet the realm of freedom and beauty where a new race of humankind was born. It's been observed, by historian Frederick Jackson Turner and novelist Wallace Stegner, among others, that our national character was formed and periodically renewed by a confrontation with the uncharted and the unknown. And so the paradox was established at the very start: we had to devour that which nourished us and our boundless American dreams.

I was thinking about this contradiction as I sat, late one windy, overcast afternoon, atop a hill on Martha's Vineyard. I like islands. I lived on one—Key West—for eleven years. Islands are worlds unto themselves, where the larger dramas of nature and civilization can be observed in microcosm. Our North American islands, the inhabited ones, that is, are also places where the dichotomy in our collective soul becomes more apparent than it does in the immensity of the mainland. And they are the stages where the last act in the drama *between* nature and civilization, between our love of wilderness and our compulsion to own and tame it, may be holding its dress rehearsals. If you want a forecast of what might happen in, say, New Mexico, Montana, or Alaska fifty years from now, take a look at the Florida Keys, Martha's Vineyard, or Nantucket today.

The reason is simple enough: the fruitfulness and preciousness of land is far more obvious on an island. Even on a large one like Martha's Vineyard, the limiting shore is never more than a long hike or a short ride away.

Sitting on the hill in the island's Waskosims Rock Reservation, a nature preserve the size of a large farm, I recalled a horsepacking trip my wife and I took in New Mexico's Gila Wilderness in the summer of 1992. We rode for eight days through fenceless, unpeopled mountains, encountering only a handful of backpackers and few signs of man's intrusive hand. One day, resting our horses and ourselves on a mountaintop, we looked westward more than eighty miles into Arizona, southward for more than two hundred miles into Old Mexico, and saw nothing but more mountains and mesas and the red and brown expanse of the Rio Grande Basin. The Big Open.

The Gila rolls and soars over an area the size of some New England states. It's one of those places, which still can be found in the West, that nurtures one of our most cherished illusions: that we have, even in the late twentieth century, room and resources to spare, even to squander.

The belief, founded upon the sheer size of this country, that there is always someplace to go, someplace to which one can escape, is as fundamental to our national creed as the Declaration of Independence. The escape might be a two-week camping trip, or a flight to a new place where one can start life anew. The covered wagons of the Oregon Trail vanished in the 1860s, but the faith that things will be better beyond the horizon has not. We pursue that dream today in U-Hauls and Ryder trucks on paved trails called Interstates. And in that pursuit, we continue to gobble up what's left of our wild forests—those new starter homes, bigger second homes, and vacation homes need lumber. Our unspoiled coastlines have become picketed by summer getaways on stilts. In the deserts east of L.A., the concrete tide is washing over the last stands of Joshua trees while golf courses and retirement communities in Arizona suck the Colorado dry to feed these developments' insatiable need for water and power.

But what the hell, there are thousands of miles of coastline in America, millions of acres of forest, deserts the size of small countries, right?

As the century draws to a close, maintaining that illusion is getting harder and harder. There is a nervous recognition, just beneath the surface of our consciousness, of a truth that ought to have been obvious long ago: America is finite after all. And the fact that we are running out of room and resources flies into the face of another of our cherished beliefs: that growth and expansion can and should be unlimited.

The heightening awareness that the American pie is shrinking accounts, I think, for the Manichean nature of the debate between development interests and environmentalists, with each demonizing the other. Whether for the purposes of preservation or of exploitation, Americans seem desperate to grab what can be grabbed now. Sometimes, listening to radical environmentalists, I get the impression that they won't be happy until everything we've come to call progress is wiped away and we all go back to living in log cabins, maybe even in wigwams. Sometimes, listening to laissez-faire capitalists, I get the impression that *they* won't be happy until every hillside in the Northwest has been clear-cut and every open space transformed into a mall or a golf course.

Isn't there some sensible middle ground where the works of men and those of nature can coexist in harmony?

Look to our islands . . . .

Martha's Vineyard and Nantucket are good ones to choose; their European settlement dates back almost as far as the founding of Plymouth colony. They have known every kind of civilized activity except heavy industrialization; but the natural world still thrives there, although tenuously and in domesticated form.

The Waskosims Rock reserve, in the narrow, western half of the Vineyard, is owned by the island's Land Bank. It gets its name from a large granite boulder that crowns a hill dominating a range of smaller hills and an oak-covered basin created by receding glaciers some twenty thousand years ago—a tick on the geological clock. On the spring afternoon I sat musing, the scrub oak were not yet fully leafed, the Nantucket shadbush were just beginning to throw out their white blossoms, and the wind made the air hazy with blowing sand from the shoreline only a mile or so away, beyond the last line of hills. Off to the right, a house and pond peeked through the trees, while behind me an old stone fence walled off the reserve, which is open to the public, from the Frances Woods wildlife sanctuary, which is not. Clearly, it was no wilderness I was looking at, but the sort of tame, pastoral landscape that used to inspire romantic poets. Yet even this rustic scene was almost lost in the 1980s, that decade of greed gone amok. A developer planned to fill the woods near the reserve with townhouses, but Martha's Vineyard residents managed to block the project, forcing the developer to sell the property to the Land Bank.

Not all the residents were overjoyed at this turn of events. On Martha's Vineyard, as in other places where environmental and economic concerns clash, there is a class-warfare element to the debate about what shall be preserved and what shall not. Martha's Vineyard being rather genteel, the dispute wasn't as nasty as elsewhere, but it wasn't without bitterness. The fantasy that there is room for everyone cannot be sustained on an island that covers only one-third the area of New York City, yet everyone wants a piece of it, each for his or her own purposes. It has been a summer resort for decades, mostly for the well-to-do. The island's year-round inhabitants—shopkeepers, carpenters, contractors, and fishermen—have seen public access to shorelines severely limited by beachfront community associations, woods and wetlands where they once walked or hunted fenced off as sanctuaries. I've always found it difficult to wax righteous about conservation when it creates difficulties for ordinary people. Yet the truth is that prosperity, as we've come to know it, carries the well-known prices of pollution, overcrowding, cluttered landscapes, and the Kmart tawdriness of the concessions one sees at popular national parks.

To gain broad support, conservationists cannot ignore human material and economic needs, but can preservation be made compatible with social democracy and free enterprise? The predicament strikes me as fundamental.

A kind of truce has been called to the land wars on the Vineyard, an armistice that owes as much to the current recession as it does to hard-won compromises between the forces of economic development and those of conservation.

I toured an area where conservation brought about a happy ending. This was the 180-acre Katama Park, which has been an airport for the town of Edgartown since the 1920s, but also contains one of the last patches of sandplain grassland on the planet.

When Dutch and English settlers set foot on the New World in the early seventeenth century, sandplain grasslands covered hundreds of thousands of acres from Long Island to Cape Cod. These rare ecosystems came into being during the last ice age, when the glaciers reached the limit of their advance and melted. Countless tons of earth were released from the glaciers, creating flat outwashes of sandy, dry soils that became covered with grasses related to those of the short-grass prairies in the Midwest. The coastal plains flourished through all the millennia between glacial recession and the arrival of the first white people in America. In 1602, an explorer named Bartholomew Gosnold reported discovering vast prairies on the islands off present-day Massachusetts.

In contrast to their midwestern cousins, the prairies of the East weren't congenial to agriculture. The topsoil was too sandy and shallow to support large-scale farming; but the grasses proved ideal as sheep pasturage. Despite heavy grazing, the grasslands continued to thrive, and were prevented from natural succession by periodic floods, fires, and storms.

They have barely survived the twentieth century. Since the 1950s, relentless development has caused the sandplains to suffer ecological cataclysm. From Massachusetts to New York, the grasslands and related heathlands now cover approximately fifteen thousand acres on three islands. The designation of the Katama Plains on Martha's Vineyard as one of Nature Conservancy's "last great places" is literally true.

That phrase—last great place—suggests the breathtaking, a natural wonder like Mount McKinley or Big Sur or the Everglades. There is nothing awe-inspiring or charismatic about Katama Park. A townhouse development is clearly visible from it, and it is in the middle of an airport that services the private planes of visitors who fly in and out on weekends. The airport has its charms—its grass runways and small hangar and "terminal" recall the days of biplanes and barnstormers—but strolling through swales of false indigo, blue-eyed grass, and sandplain flax while Beechcrafts and Cessnas land and take off doesn't exactly make you feel you are in the wild.

Like a lot of people, I want to be stunned by natural grandeur. My guide introduced me to the quieter rewards of nature in miniature. The small purple flowers at my feet were bird's-foot violet, a food source for the regal fritillary butterfly, one of the rare creatures of sandplain habitat. The trilling coming from the huckleberry hummock nearby was the call of the grasshopper sparrow. Although the Katama grasslands are a little contrived—they're in the middle of an airport, after all—it was inspiring to see such small creatures surviving in such a civilized environment. It proved that we and our works can reach an accommodation with those of God.

The contrivance extends to the ways the Katama grasslands are maintained. To keep them healthy and free from succession by pitch pine, scrub oak, and huckleberry, biologists stage periodic controlled burns, replicating what nature used to do on her own.

But preservation brings costs of its own.

My guide is a descendant of settlers who came to Martha's Vineyard three hundred years ago, yet she has to struggle in an environment of soaring costs and real estate prices.

"I was priced out of this place the day I was born," she says.

But she's lucky. Many of her contemporaries have been forced to seek livelihoods on the mainland.

There are other costs . . . .

After leaving Katama, we hiked through what must pass for wilderness on a place like Martha's Vineyard: the Frances Woods wildlife sanctuary, 500 pristine acres of scrub oak savannah and wetlands adjacent to the 145-acre Waskosims reserve. I was enjoying a rare privilege. Access to the reserve is restricted; it is papered with No Trespassing signs. Given the lack of space on the island, wildlife does needs a refuge from human intrusion, even the benign intrusions of bird watchers and nature lovers; but putting myself into the shoes of a resident, barred from beaches where his or her grandfathers launched fishing boats, barred from pastures where his or her ancestors grazed sheep because those pastures are now filled with vacation homes, I could understand why the signs and fences must rankle residents.

We crossed into the Waskosims reserve by climbing over a low stone wall erected hundreds of years ago to divide the Vineyard's Indian lands from those set aside for white settlement. The Indians must have been as rankled by that wall as today's inhabitants are by the barriers of restrictions and regulations.

Later, I went back to the reserve to sit and think and explore some of its marshes and woods. It's a lovely spot, a sanctuary in which the soul can be renewed and the body exercised with a vigorous walk. But it is a tight little place on a tight little island, biologically managed, the trails well-marked and maintained, and, considering the crowds that must pass through it during the tourist season, exceptionally tidy. Signs ask visitors not to leave the trails because the reserve contains rare and endangered plants.

Again, such restrictions are necessary in a place where space is at a premium and human activities have to be controlled if wildlife and its habitat are to be spared. I realize that, yet as I walked through the scrub oak, pitch pine, and juniper, I found myself irritated by the little colored arrows telling me which trail I was on, by the marker posts that told me when I had come to the boundaries of the reserve. I began to feel claustrophobic, and, having something of the American anarch in my character, I ignored a boundary post and hiked into private property. The trespass was rewarded. I saw a wild turkey and couple of shy scarlet tanagers.

The next day, I visited the Miacomet Plains on Nantucket with Peter Dunwiddie, an Audubon Society biologist, and Elizabeth Bell, a land-acquisition specialist for the Nature Conservancy. Nearly a third of the island's thirty thousand acres have been set aside for conservation. As on Martha's Vineyard, they are carefully managed by controlled burns and with restricted access trails and roads. These protected areas were also threatened in the 1980s, when genealogist-entrepreneurs traced the descendants of the island's original European settlers, cleared up fragmented and legally clouded land titles, then bought the property cheap and began selling it to developers for up to $100,000 an acre.

Had this gone unchecked by conservation groups, the Miacomet Plains might well be townhouse and vacation homes today. Precious habitat for the endangered short-eared owl and the northern harrier hawk would have been lost. Now you can stand on a height in the plains and look over rolling, somber, windswept expanses that recall an English moor. If you are lucky, as we were that day, you'll get to see a harrier soaring on the thermals, diving with talons extended to capture a field mouse or sparrow.

Watching the hawk swoop toward a clump of bearberry, I was reminded once more that I was enjoying a privilege. Most of Nantucket's ordinary people have had to leave the island, except for those who cater to the tourist trade. The combination of high real estate prices and preservation efforts have turned the island into a complete resort, its economy almost entirely dependent on tourism and the trade of the "summer people."

"The last commercial fishing boat left here five years ago," Dunwiddie said.

Although some small-scale commercial fishing and scalloping operations continue, the big trawlers that used to sail from Nantucket are now almost as bygone as the whalers of Melville's day. And a Nantucket without working seamen seemed as strange as the West without cowboys. Biodiversity is being spared, but a kind of human monoculture seems to have been created.

Hiking past a pond, Dunwiddie told me that the future of conservation on Nantucket lies not in acquisition but in management. Is that another price we will have to pay to save our wild places and wild creatures from oblivion? Isn't a managed wilderness an oxymoron? Of course, true wilderness vanished from Nantucket and Martha's Vineyard long ago. Environmentalists seek to preserve biodiversity, not the wild.

Thinking of the wild places I had been in—the Gila in New Mexico, the Absaroka Wilderness in Montana, the Minnesota boundary waters, the Upper Peninsula of Michigan—I recalled hearing wolf howls and wildcat screeches, the sight of a grizzly's claw marks on a tall pine tree, and the time I waded a bonefish flat in the Florida Keys, near a spot where an eleven-year-old boy had been killed by an alligator only the week before. With the dangers came freedom, the freedom to wander more or less at will without bumping into a sign or fence every half-mile.

Much of New England is already that way, except for the northern reaches of Maine and New Hampshire. It's beginning to look a lot like old England, where the woods, streams, and heaths are the private preserves of the rich or the restricted refuges of conservation organizations. To put a literary spin on it, this is not nature as Jack London liked it, but as Wordsworth did: defanged and declawed.

I wondered if, some day in the not-too-distant future, much of the lower forty-eight will be like a gigantic Martha's Vineyard, an enormous Nantucket. I would hate like hell to ride up to the mountaintop in the Gila where my wife and I rested our horses and see subdivisions spreading across the Rio Grande basin. I would hate equally to run into a park ranger telling me that I can't enter a certain valley because it's habitat for some endangered butterfly or bird.

"Managed wilderness" may be the only way to resolve the dichotomy in our collective soul, but if all of our last great places become so managed and regulated, so fenced in and signposted that they are turned into outdoor zoos, we will lose something as valuable as the spotted owl, old-growth firs, and grizzly bears. A sense of adventure, the excitement of encountering the unexpected around the next bend, the awe that comes when standing face to face with nature in the raw, with all her teeth and claws and majesty. We will miss running into the interesting people who earn their livelihoods in remote places— cowboys and loggers and miners and backcountry eccentrics. No human surprises, just a lot of people like us, with predictable outlooks and opinions, predictably dressed in Land's End shirts and Timberland hiking boots. And we will lose the exultation of unrestricted space. The Big Open will be closed up and we'll all be required to stay on the marked trails, please, and turn back when we bump into a sign that warns No Trespassing—Wildlife Sanctuary.

Reprinted with the permission of the Aaron Priest Agency.

Russell Baker

Russell Baker (b. 1925), summered on Nantucket for more than thirty years, and is well-known to millions of television viewers as the host, from 1992 until 2004, of the PBS series Masterpiece Theatre. *The author or editor of seventeen books, Baker has won distinction as a journalist, essayist, humorist, and memoirist—in 1983, he received a Pulitzer Prize for his autobiography,* Growing Up *(1982). But he is perhaps best-known for the trenchant wit and biting commentary displayed in his syndicated newspaper column, "The Observer," which ran in* The New York Times *from 1962 until 1998. Baker wrote more than 4,600 columns for "The Observer," not only the longest-running column in* Times *history, but also the winner of a Pulitzer Prize for distinguished commentary. For Nantucket readers, an "Observer" column about the island was always cause for celebration and a mad dash to The Hub for the* Times. *Here, in a column first published in 1982, Baker offers a comic comparison of Nantucket and Martha's Vineyard as well as an affectionate look at what sets Nantucket apart. —SB*

Nantucket: Sufficient Unto Itself

Seventeen years ago, deciding to vacation in one of the watery parts of the world, we wrote to chambers of commerce of a dozen islands chosen at random off a road map of the northeastern United States and had an answer from Nantucket a week later. It contained full-page descriptions of two dozen houses available for summer rental. We're still waiting to hear from Martha's Vineyard.

First impressions are enduring. To me, Nantucket seemed warm and welcoming. To this day, despite friendships with many Vineyarders, I still think of their island as inhospitable and snooty, a place where people examine your stationery and, if the watermark is inferior, dismiss you as not worth the price of a postage stamp.

This is unjust. We have since visited the Vineyard—once—and were treated with exquisite courtesy. My old uneasiness was revived, though, upon learning that its propertied classes regarded island beaches as private possessions not to be touched without the owner's permission. In Nantucket there is scarcely a foot of beach not open to all of humanity that can get to the seashore.

Miami Beach hotel owners of course enforce claims to ownership of the shore. At least one hotel there even lays claim to the ocean, announcing daily at sundown that "the ocean is closed for the night." One expects this sort of megalomania from hotel syndicates, but what kind of human being wants to own the ocean? In Martha's Vineyard, apparently, there were such people.

Fear of being judged socially unfit, of being jugged for trespassing on the ocean, only partly explains why I haven't set foot on the Vineyard since, and probably explains nothing at all about why most Nantucket summer people have never set foot there at all. The broader explanation is that Nantucket is sufficient unto itself.

Having undergone the agonies always involved in getting to Nantucket, why would anyone want to leave for—horrors!—a trip to Cape Cod or—ho hum—a visit to the Vineyard? Every Nantucket fanatic knows that greed and real-estate speculation have turned Cape Cod into Calcutta-by-the-Sea, just as he knows that Martha's Vineyard is a nice place to visit if you like the Pennsylvania countryside.

"It's very pretty over there—sort of like the Pennsylvania Dutch country—but I could never find the ocean," a friend told me last summer on returning from the Vineyard after a two-day visit. Before my one and only visit, a native Nantucketer who went over every two years for the Vineyard–Nantucket football game told me, "It's an awesome big place—pretty poor excuse for an island."

If you're Nantucket-minded you're likely to smile a bit condescendingly about the Vineyard's claim to islandhood. Compared to Nantucket, the Vineyard is an island only in the sense that Australia is an island, except of course that the Vineyard is jammed smack up against the mainland.

You can see the thing with the naked eye from the Cape and get over there by ferry in 40 minutes. Call that an island? Raise a bridge from Woods Hole to one of those Chops they're always talking about on the Vineyard and it would be as easy as getting from Manhattan to Queens.

Nantucket's people pride themselves on being on a real island. Miles out of sight from the mainland, a tiny mound of sand in the angry Atlantic, assaulted by winds that have been gathering momentum all the way from Iceland—that's an island, folks, not Pennsylvania.

"The faraway island," some antique chamber of commerce type dubbed it years ago, and "faraway" explains a lot of Nantucket's allure. Just getting there is an adventure. There's a quixotic car ferry that comes in two or three times a day when it isn't broken down and everybody's in the mood to make the trip and the weather isn't acting up, but naturally they can never fit you on when you want to go.

And of course you can get in by airplane if you're canny about meteorology and cunning enough to squeeze yourself onto a flight scheduled to arrive between fogs.

I've often spent two days trying to get there from New York and once needed four days to succeed. When you finally arrive you feel faraway, you feel you've really gotten someplace, you feel you've survived an adventure. Nantucket evenings are spent listening to tales comic and hair-raising about getting there, and when we get there we are proud of ourselves. It must be the way the pioneers felt when they finally got to Oregon.

The Vineyard is a dull commuter's trip from the mainland. Vineyarders never know the triumph of getting there. Let us state it plainly: Vineyarders are soft. They have it easy. They do not know suffering. No, we Nantucketers are not much interested in that sort of life. We were not made to loll in bosky Pennsylvanian glades and amuse ourselves with tales of hoi polloi successfully routed from our private oceans. We are people of fiber and grit in whom the brotherhood of the ocean air has bred democratic tolerance. We answer our mail.

I speak of course only for "summer people," the heroes of many a well-driven traffic jam in Boston, New York, Philadelphia or Washington. Year-round Nantucketers must speak for themselves. The island they know is different from the "summer people's."

"What's it like here in the winter?" I once heard a tourist ask an old gentleman sitting on a wharf watching the tourists come and go. "I'll tell you," the old man said, "that wind'll blow your tongue right back down your throat."

He had it right. On a deep winter night with all the visitors gone, stars glittering above like diamonds against black velvet, wind howling through wires and naked trees, you can walk the streets and feel like a passenger on a great abandoned ocean liner far out in the North Atlantic, outward bound toward God knows where. That's some feeling. And you can hear majestic thunder from the beach as the ocean claws the land away, pounding and pounding, with nobody there to book it on charges of trespassing.

Reprinted with permission of *The New York Times*.

IV

The Whaleroad

Edmund Burke

Author, orator, statesman, and political philosopher, Edmund Burke (ca. 1729–97) served as a member of the British Parliament's House of Commons during twenty-nine exciting years (1765–94) that spanned both the American and the French Revolutions. The son of an Irish attorney, Burke was educated at a Quaker boarding school and at Dublin's Trinity College; he studied law for a time at London's Middle Temple before leaving to travel on the Continent and turn his attention to writing. Burke's early achievements include A Philosophical Enquiry into the Origin of Our Ideas of the Sublime and Beautiful *(1757) and the creation and editing of the* Annual Register, *a publication reviewing international political events. His career as a politician began in 1765 when he entered Parliament and became private secretary to the Marquis of Rockingham, First Lord of the Treasury. Published versions of Burke's powerful speeches to the House of Commons (some of them eight hours long!), and especially those opposing King George III's increasingly harsh taxation of the increasingly rebellious American colonies, made him well known. His* Reflections on the Revolution in France *(1790), read throughout Europe in his time, made him famous. In London, Burke rubbed elbows with many notable intellectuals of the eighteenth century—Samuel Johnson, David Garrick, Oliver Goldsmith, and Joshua Reynolds.*

Burke earned his place in Nantucket's literary history by becoming the first writer to use the island's whaling industry as a cultural metaphor for American entrepreneurship and global ambition. In his 1775 speech, On Conciliation with America, *Burke rose in Parliament to argue against passage of the Restraining Act, which was designed to punish the New England colonies by severely restricting both trade and fishing (whaling included) throughout the region. It was folly, Burke argued, to alienate colonies and trading partners whose vigor in the pursuit of wealth far surpassed that of their motherland. Nantucket was his case in point, and not without reason. By 1775, New England had at least 250 vessels employed in whaling, and of these as many as 150 sloops, schooners, and brigs came from Nantucket alone. Perhaps Benjamin Franklin, whose mother was a Nantucket Folger, had reminded Burke of these facts when the two men met a few days before the speech. Regardless, Burke would transform Nantucket into what Nathaniel*

Philbrick has called "an American icon," and the island's whaling industry into "an example of how [America] might conduct itself as an independent world power." Here is Burke's eloquent exaltation of Nantucket whaling, a characterization that will echo throughout the island's early literary tradition and reach its apotheosis in the Nantucket chapter of Moby-Dick *(1851). —SB*

From the speech *On Conciliation with America*

[. . . .] AS TO THE WEALTH which the Colonies have drawn from the sea by their fisheries, you had all that matter fully opened at your bar. You surely thought those acquisitions of value, for they seemed even to excite your envy; and yet the spirit by which that enterprising employment has been exercised ought rather, in my opinion, to have raised your esteem and admiration. And pray, Sir, what in the world is equal to it? Pass by the other parts, and look at the manner in which the people of New England have of late carried on the whale fishery. Whilst we follow them among the tumbling mountains of ice, and behold them penetrating into the deepest frozen recesses of Hudson's Bay and Davis's Straits, whilst we are looking for them beneath the Arctic Circle, we hear that they have pierced into the opposite region of polar cold, that they are at the antipodes, and engaged under the frozen Serpent of the south. Falkland Island, which seemed too remote and romantic an object for the grasp of national ambition, is but a stage and resting-place in the progress of their victorious industry. Nor is the equinoctial heat more discouraging to them than the accumulated winter of both the poles. We know that whilst some of them draw the line and strike the harpoon on the coast of Africa, others run the longitude and pursue their gigantic game along the coast of Brazil. No sea but what is vexed by their fisheries; no climate that is not witness to their toils. Neither the perseverance of Holland, nor the activity of France, nor the dexterous and firm sagacity of English enterprise ever carried this most perilous mode of hardy industry to the extent to which it has been pushed by this recent people; a people who are still, as it were, but in the gristle, and not yet hardened into the bone of manhood. When I contemplate these things; when I know that the Colonies in general owe little or nothing to any care of ours, and that they are not squeezed into this happy form by the constraints of watchful and suspicious government, but that, through a wise and salutary neglect, a generous nature has been suffered to take her own way to perfection; when I reflect upon these effects, when I see how profitable they have been to us, I feel all the pride of power sink, and all presumption in the wisdom of human contrivances melt and die away within me. My rigor relents. I pardon something to the spirit of liberty. [. . .]

Thomas Jefferson

As one of our nation's most influential Founding Fathers—Virginia's delegate to the Continental Congress, principal author of the Declaration of Independence, architect of the American Revolution—Thomas Jefferson (1743–1826) needs no introduction. Those who stayed awake in history class will also recall his efforts as American ambassador to France and as George Washington's Secretary of State, as well as his accomplishments as third President of the United States: the Louisiana Purchase, which more than doubled the size of the nation, and the Lewis and Clark expedition to explore the new territory and discover a route to the Pacific Ocean. Jefferson is remembered, too, as a founder of the University of Virginia and as a scholarly and scientific man, happy among his books and experiments at Monticello, the beautiful home of his own design.

His interest in Nantucket whaling is less well known, but should come as no surprise. The Jeffersonian vision for America was fundamentally a maritime vision—he saw how thirteen states strung along the eastern seaboard could become a continental nation stretching "from sea to shining sea," a maritime power controlling the commerce of two oceans. Nantucket whalemen, the first American mariners to penetrate, explore, and exploit the natural resources of the South Atlantic and the Pacific, played an integral part in that vision. If Edmund Burke, before the American Revolution, had warned Britain about the folly of alienating the industrious and adventurous Nantucketers, Jefferson, after the war, would warn his own countrymen about the dangers of losing the "Nantucketois" to the blandishments of the British and French. In his "Observations on the Whale-Fishery" (1788), Jefferson, like Burke before him, viewed Nantucket whaling as emblematic of America's national potential. A visionary politician, he saw that nothing less than a veritable navy of prime seamen and control of the world oil market was at stake in European efforts to co-opt the islanders. Unlike Burke, Jefferson, the natural historian and amateur scientist, also had a healthy curiosity about different species of whales and the properties of their oil—especially the spermaceti whales so important to Nantucket. Here are some specimens of his thought. —SB

From "Observations on the Whale-Fishery"

W HALE OIL ENTERS, as a raw material, into several branches of manufacture, as of wool, leather, soap: it is used also in painting, architecture and navigation. But its great consumption is in lighting houses and cities. For this last purpose however it has a powerful competitor in the vegetable oils. These do well in warm, still weather, but they fix with cold, they extinguish easily with the wind, their crop is precarious, depending on the seasons, and to yield the same light, a larger wick must be used, and greater quantity of oil consumed. Estimating all these articles of difference together, those employed in lighting cities find their account in giving about 25 per cent more for whale than for vegetable oils. But higher than this the whale oil, in its present form, cannot rise; because it then becomes more advantageous to the city-lighters to use others. This competition then limits its price, higher than which no encouragement can raise it, and becomes, as it were, a law of its nature, but, at this low price, the whale fishery is the poorest business into which a merchant or sailor can enter. If the sailor, instead of wages, has a part of what is taken, he finds that this, one year with another, yields him less than he could have got as wages in any other business. It is attended too with great risk, singular hardships, and long absences from his family. If the voyage is made solely at the expence of the merchant, he finds that, one year with another, it does not reimburse him his expences. As, for example, an English ship of 300 ton, and 42 hands brings home, communibus annis, after a four months voyage, 25 ton of oil, worth 437 l. 10s. sterl. but the wages of the officers and seamen will be 400 l. The Outfit then and the merchant's profit must be paid by the government. And it is accordingly on this idea that the British bounty is calculated. From the poverty of this business then it has happened that the nations, who have taken it up, have successively abandoned it. The Basques began it. But, tho' the most economical and enterprising of the inhabitants of France, they could not continue it; and it is said they never employed more than 30 ships a year. The Dutch and Hanse towns succeeded them. The latter gave it up long ago tho' they have continued to lend their name to British and Dutch oils. The English carried it on, in competition with the Dutch, during the last, and beginning of the present century. But it was too little profitable for them in comparison with other branches of commerce open to them. In the mean time too the inhabitants of the barren Island of Nantucket had taken up this fishery, invited to it by the whales presenting themselves on their own shore. To them therefore the

English relinquished it, continuing to them, as British subjects, the importation of their oils into England duty free, while foreigners were subject to a duty of 18 l. 5s. sterl. a ton. The Dutch were enabled to continue it long, because, 1. They are so near the northern fishing grounds, that a vessel begins her fishing very soon after she is out of port. 2. They navigate with more economy than the other nations of Europe. 3. Their seamen are content with lower wages: and 4. their merchants with a lower profit on their capital. Under all these favorable circumstances however, this branch of business, after long languishing, is at length nearly extinct with them. It is said they did not send above half a dozen ships in pursuit of the whale this present year. The Nantucketois then were the only people who exercised this fishery to any extent at the commencement of the late war. Their country, from its barrenness, yielding no subsistence, they were obliged to seek it in the sea which surrounded them. Their economy was more rigorous than that of the Dutch. Their seamen, instead of wages, had a share in what was taken. This induced them to fish with fewer hands, so that each had a greater dividend in the profit. It made them more vigilant in seeking game, bolder in pursuing it, and parcimonious in all their expences. London was their only market. When therefore, by the late revolution, they became aliens in Great Britain, they became subject to the alien duty of 18 l. 5s. the ton of oil, which being more than equal to the price of the common whale oil, they were obliged to abandon that fishery. So that this people, who before the war had employed upwards of 300 vessels a year in the whale fishery, (while Great Britain had herself never employed one hundred) have now almost ceased to exercise it. But they still had the seamen, the most important material for this fishery; and they still retained the spirit of fishing: so that at the reestablishment of peace they were capable in a very short time of reviving their fishery in all its splendor. The British government saw that the moment was critical. They knew that their own share in that fishery was as nothing. That the great mass of fishermen was left with a nation now separated from them: that these fishermen however had lost their ancient market, had no other resource within their country to which they could turn, and they hoped therefore they might, in the present moment of distress, be decoyed over to their establishments, and be added to the mass of their seamen. To effect this they offered extravagant advantages to all persons who should exercise the whale fishery from British establishments. But not counting with much confidence on a long connection with their remaining possessions on the continent of America, foreseeing that the Nantucketois would settle in them preferably, if put on an equal footing with those of Great Britain, and that thus they might have to purchase them a second time, they confined their high offers to settlers in Great Britain. The Nantucketois, left without resource by the loss of their market, began to think of removing to the British dominions: some to Nova Scotia, preferring smaller advantages, in the neighbourhood of their ancient country and friends; others to Great Britain postponing country and friends to high premiums. A vessel was already arrived from Halifax to Nantucket to take off some of those who proposed to remove; two families had gone on board and others were going, when a letter was received there, which had been written by Monsieur le Marquis de la Fayette to a gentleman in Boston, and transmitted by him to Nantucket. The purport of the letter was to dissuade their accepting the British proposals, and to assure them that their friends in France would endeavour to do something for them. This instantly suspended their design: not another went on board, and the vessel returned to Halifax with only the two families.

In fact the French Government had not been inattentive to the views of the British, nor insensible of the crisis. They saw the danger of permitting five or six thousand of the best seamen existing to be transferred by a single stroke to the marine strength of their enemy, and to carry over with them an art which they possessed almost exclusively. The counterplan which they set on foot was to tempt the Nantucketois by high offers to come and settle in France. This was in the year 1785. The British however had in their favour a sameness of language, religion, laws, habits and kindred. 9 families only, of 33 persons in the whole came to Dunkirk; so that this project was not likely to prevent their emigration to the English establishments, if nothing else had happened. . . .

The Refinery for whale oil lately established at Rouen, seems to be an object worthy of national attention. In order to judge of its importance, the different qualities of whale oil must be noted. Three qualities are known in the American and English markets. 1. That of the Spermaceti whale. 2. Of the Groenland whale. 3. Of the Brazil whale.

1. The Spermaceti whale found by the Nantucketmen in the neighbourhood of the western Islands, to which they had gone in pursuit of other whales, retired thence to the coast of Guinea, afterwards to that of Brazil, and begins now to be best found in the latitude of the Cape of Good Hope, and even of Cape Horn. He is an active, fierce animal and requires vast address and boldness in the fisherman. The inhabitants of Brazil make little expeditions from their coast, and take some of these fish. But the Americans are the only distant people who have been in the habit of seeking and attacking them in numbers. The British however, led by the Nantucketois whom they have decoyed into their service, have begun this fishery. . . . Still they take but a very small proportion of

their own demand. We furnish the rest. Theirs is the only market to which we carry that oil, because it is the only one where its properties are known. It is luminous, resists coagulation by cold to the 41st degree of Farenheit's thermometer, and 4th of Reaumur's, and yields no smell at all. It is used therefore within doors to lighten shops, and even in the richest houses for antichambers, stairs, galleries, &c. It sells at the London market for treble the price of common whale oil. This enables the adventurer to pay the duty of 18 l. 5s. sterl. the ton, and still to have a living profit. Besides the mass of oil produced from the whole body of the whale, his head yields 3 or 4 barrels of what is called headmatter, from which is made the solid Spermaceti used for medicine and candles. This sells by the pound at double the price of the oil. The disadvantage of this fishery is that the sailors are from 9 to 12 months absent on the voyage, of course they are not at hand on any sudden emergency, and are even liable to be taken before they know that a war is begun. It must be added on the subject of this whale, that he is rare, and shy, soon abandoning the grounds where he is hunted. This fishery being less losing than the other, and often profitable, will occasion it to be so thronged soon, as to bring it on a level with the other. It will then require the same expensive support, or to be abandoned.

2. The Groenland whale oil is next in quality. It resists coagulation by cold to 36 degrees of Farenheit and 2 degrees of Reaumur; but it has a smell insupportable within doors, and is not luminous. It sells therefore in London at about 16 l. the ton. This whale is clumsy and timid, he dives when struck, and comes up to breathe by the first cake of ice, where the fishermen need little address or courage to find and take him. This is the fishery mostly frequented by European nations; it is this fish which yields the fin in quantity, and the voyages last about 3 or 4 months.

3. The third quality is that of the small Brazil whale. He was originally found on the coast of Nantucket, and first led that people to this pursuit. He retired first to the banks of Newfoundland, then to the western islands; and is now found within soundings on the coast of Brazil, during the months of December, January, February and March. This oil chills at 50 degrees of Farenheit and 8 degrees of Reaumur, is black and offensive, worth therefore but 13 l. the ton in London. In warm summer nights however it burns better than the Groenland oil.

Owen Chase

In the early decades of the nineteenth century, the seventy-million square miles of the Pacific Ocean, together with its 20,000 to 30,000 islands (even today the exact number is unknown), was almost entirely uncharted—a supremely dangerous wilderness for Nantucket whalemen with at best a few inches of wooden plank between them and a watery grave. Pacific whaling was the stuff of true—and tragic—misadventures, and none was more strange or more influential than that of Nantucket-born Owen Chase (1796–1869), first mate of the ship Essex. *The title of his account says it all:* Narrative of the Most Extraordinary and Distressing Shipwreck of the Whale-Ship Essex of Nantucket; Which Was Attacked and Finally Destroyed by a Large Spermaceti Whale, in the Pacific Ocean; With an Account of the Unparalleled Sufferings of the Captain and Crew During a Space of Ninety-Three Days at Sea in Open Boats in the Years 1819 & 1820 *(1821).*

The Essex *disaster has a special place in maritime history. The 4,500-mile voyage of the surviving crew is one of the longest ever made in open boats, and the "unparalleled sufferings" of the men included drawing lots and cannibalism. The story of the Nantucket whaleship sunk by a whale in mid-ocean spawned an almost limitless number of period accounts, many of them found in compilations of disasters at sea such as* The Mariner's Chronicle *or in seamen's memoirs. Great writers including Ralph Waldo Emerson, Edgar Allan Poe, and Walt Whitman learned the* Essex *story from various sources and took an interest. But Owen Chase's firsthand narrative won a special place in American literature when a foremast hand named Herman Melville read it while on board the whaleship* Acushnet *of Fairhaven.*

It's easy to imagine young Melville devouring the narrative by lantern light in his forecastle berth, or out on deck in the tropical sun. Melville later recalled "The reading of that wondrous story upon the landless sea, & close to the very latitude of the shipwreck had a surprising effect on me." Of course the sinking of the Essex *by a whale inspired the climactic final chapter of* Moby-Dick. *Many years later, as Melville was finishing the novel, he would have his own personal copy of Chase's narrative at hand. What's more, Chase's persona, his courage, and unwavering faith in a wise Providence—even in*

the face of random misfortune and genuine horror—helped Melville to draw the charac-
ter of Starbuck, brave and pious first mate of the Pequod.

Yet Chase's Essex *narrative is a gripping survival story in its own right, probably writ-*
ten with the aid of Harvard-educated William Coffin Jr., also suspected of assisting Obed
Macy with his History of Nantucket, *as well as William Lay and Cyrus Hussey with*
their narrative of the Globe *mutiny. After his return from the* Essex *ordeal, Chase was at*
home for just six months before he returned once more to the sea—a very short time for
writing and seeing a book into press. The exact nature of the narrative's authorship didn't
matter much to Melville, and probably shouldn't to us: "Its whole air plainly evinces that it
was carefully & conscientiously written to Owen's dictation of the facts.—It is almost as
good as though Owen wrote it himself."

Here Chase records the encounter with the whale that started it all.—SB

From Chapter 2 of *Narrative of the Most Extraordinary and Distressing Shipwreck of the Whale-Ship Essex*

[. . . .] ON THE 20th of November, (cruising in latitude 0° 40' S. longitude 119° 0' W.) a shoal of whales was discovered off the lee-bow. The weather at this time was extremely fine and clear, and it was about 8 o' clock in the morning, that the man at the mast-head gave the usual cry of, "there she blows." The ship was immediately put away, and we ran down in the direction for them. When we got within half a mile of the place where they were observed, all our boats were lowered down, manned, and we started in pursuit of them. The ship, in the mean time, was brought into the wind, and the main-top-sail hove aback, to wait for us. I had the harpoon in the second boat; the captain preceded me in the first. When I arrived at the spot where we calculated they were, nothing was at first to be seen. We lay on our oars in anxious expectation of discovering them come up somewhere near us. Presently one rose, and spouted a short distance ahead of my boat; I made all speed towards it, came up with and struck it; feeling the harpoon in him, he threw himself, in an agony, over towards the boat, (which at that time was up alongside of him), and giving a severe blow with his tail, struck the boat near the edge of the water, amidships, and stove a hole in her. I immediately took up the boat hatchet, and cut the line, to disengage the boat from the whale, which was by this time running off with great velocity. I succeeded in getting clear of him, with the loss of the harpoon and line, and finding the water to pour fast in the boat, I hastily stuffed three or four of our jackets in the hole, ordered one man to keep constantly bailing, and the rest to pull immediately for the ship; we succeeded in keeping the boat free, and shortly gained the ship. The captain and the second mate, in the other two boats, kept up the pursuit, and soon struck another whale. They being at this time a considerable distance to leeward, I went forward, braced around the main-yard, and put the ship off in a direction for them; the boat which had been stove was immediately hoisted in, and after examining the hole, I found that I could, by nailing a piece of canvass over it, get her ready to join in a fresh pursuit, sooner than by lowering down the other remaining boat which belonged to the ship. I accordingly turned her over upon the quarter, and was in the act of nailing on the canvass, when I observed a very large spermaceti whale, as well as I could judge, about eighty-five feet in length; he broke water about twenty rods off our weather-bow, and was lying quietly, with his head in a direction for the ship. He spouted two or three times, and then disappeared. In less than two or three seconds he came up again, about the length of the ship off, and made directly for us, at the rate of about three knots. The ship was then going with about the same velocity. His appearance and attitude gave us at first no alarm, but while I stood watching his movements, and observing him but a ship's length off, coming down for us with great celerity, I involuntarily ordered the boy at the helm to put it hard up; intending to sheer off and avoid him. The words were scarcely out of my mouth, before he came down upon us with full speed, and struck the ship with his head, just forward of the fore-chains; he gave us such an appalling and tremendous jar, as nearly threw us all on our faces. The ship brought up as suddenly and violently as if she had struck a rock, and trembled for a few seconds like a leaf. We looked at each other with perfect amazement, deprived almost of the power of speech. Many minutes elapsed before we were able to realize the dreadful accident; during which time he passed under the ship, grazing her keel as he went along, came up alongside of her to leeward, and lay on top of the water, (apparently stunned with the violence of the blow,) for the space of a minute; he then suddenly started off, in a direction to leeward. After a few moments' reflection, and recovering, in some measure, from the sudden consternation that had seized us, I of course concluded that he had stove a hole in the ship, and that it would be necessary to set the pumps going. Accordingly they were rigged, but had not been in operation more than one minute, before I perceived the head of the ship to be gradually settling down in the water; I then ordered the signal to be set for the other boats, which, scarcely had I despatched, before I again discovered the whale, apparently in convulsions, on the top of the water, about one hundred yards to leeward. He was enveloped in the foam of the sea, that his continual and violent thrashing about in the water had created around him, and I could distinctly see him smite his jaws together, as if distracted with rage and fury. He remained a short time in this situation, and then started off with great velocity, across the bows of the ship, to windward. By this time the ship had settled down a considerable distance in the water, and I gave her up as lost. I however, ordered the pumps to be kept constantly going, and endeavoured to collect my thoughts for the occasion. I turned to the boats, two of which we had then with the ship, with an intention of clearing them away, and getting all things ready to embark in them, if there should be no other resource left; and while my attention was thus engaged for a moment, I was aroused with the cry of a man at the hatch-way, "here he is—he is making for us again." I turned around, and saw him about one hundred rods directly ahead of us, coming down apparently with twice his ordinary speed, and to me at this moment, it appeared with tenfold fury and vengeance in his aspect. The surf flew in all directions about him, and his course towards us was marked by a white foam of a rod in width, which he made with the continual violent thrashing of his tail; his head was about half out of water, and in that way he came upon, and again struck the ship. I was in hopes when I descried him making for us, that by a dexterous movement of putting the ship away immediately, I should be able to cross the line of his approach, before he could get up to us, and thus avoid, what I knew, if he should strike us again, would prove our inevitable destruction. I bawled out to the helmsman, "hard up!" but she had not fallen off more than a point, before we took the second shock. I should judge the speed of the ship to have been at this time about three knots, and that of the whale about six. He struck her to windward, directly under the cat-head, and completely stove in her bows. He passed under the ship again, went off to leeward, and we saw no more of him. Our situation at this juncture can be more readily imagined than described. The shock to our feelings was such, as I am sure none can have an adequate conception of, that were not there: the misfortune befel us at a moment when we least dreamt of any accident; and from the pleasing anticipations we had formed, of realizing the certain profits of our labour, we were dejected by a sudden, most mysterious, and overwhelming calamity. Not a moment, however, was to be lost in endeavouring to provide for the extremity to which it was now certain we were reduced. We were more than a thousand miles from the nearest land, and with nothing but a light open boat, as the resource of safety for myself and my companions. I ordered the men to cease pumping, and every one to provide for himself; seizing a hatchet at the same time, I cut away the lashings of the spare boat, which lay bottom up, across two spars directly over the quarter deck, and cried out to those near me, to take her as she came down. They did so accordingly, and bore her on their shoulders as far as the waist of the ship. The steward had in the mean time gone down into the cabin twice, and saved two quadrants, two practical navigators, and the captain's trunk and mine; all which were hastily thrown into the boat, as she lay on the deck, with the two compasses which I snatched from the binnacle. He attempted to descend again; but the water by this time had rushed in, and he returned without being able to effect his purpose. By the time we had got the boat to the waist, the ship had filled with water, and was going down on her beam-ends: we shoved our boat as quickly as possible from the plank-shear into the water, all hands jumping in her at the same time, and launched off clear of the ship. We were scarcely two boat's lengths distant from her, when she fell over to windward, and settled down in the water.

Amazement and despair now wholly took possession of us. We contemplated the frightful situation the ship lay in, and thought with horror upon the sudden and dreadful calamity that had overtaken us. We looked upon each other, as if to gather some consolatory sensation from an interchange of sentiments, but every countenance was marked with the paleness of despair. Not a word was spoken for several minutes by any of us; all appeared to be bound in a spell of stupid consternation; and from the time when we were first attacked by the whale, to the period of the fall of the ship, and of our leaving her in the boat, more than ten minutes could not certainly have elapsed! God only knows in what way, or by what means, we were enabled to accomplish in that short time what we did; the cutting away and transporting the boat from where she was deposited would of itself, in ordinary circumstances, have consumed as much time as that, if the whole ship's crew had been employed in it. My companions had not saved a single article but what they had on their backs; but to me it was a source of infinite satisfaction, if any such could be gathered from the horrors of our gloomy situation, that we had been fortunate enough to have preserved our compasses, navigators, and quadrants. After the first shock of my feelings was over, I enthusiastically contemplated them as the probable instruments of our salvation; without them all would have been dark and hopeless. Gracious God! what a picture of distress and suffering now presented itself to my imagination. The crew of the ship were saved, consisting of twenty human souls. All that remained to conduct these twenty beings through the stormy terrors of the ocean, perhaps many thousand miles, were three open light boats. The prospect of obtaining any provisions or water from the ship, to subsist upon during the time, was at least now doubtful. How many long and watchful nights, thought I, are to be passed? How many tedious days of partial starvation are to be endured, before the least relief or mitigation of our sufferings can be reasonably anticipated. We lay at this time in our boat, about two ship's lengths off from the wreck, in perfect silence, calmly contemplating her situation, and absorbed in our own melancholy reflections, when the other boats were discovered rowing up to us. They had but shortly before discovered that some accident had befallen us, but of the nature of which they were entirely ignorant. The sudden and mysterious disappearance of the ship was first discovered by the boat-steerer in the captain's boat, and with a horror-struck countenance and voice, he suddenly exclaimed, "Oh, my God! where is the ship?" Their operations upon this were instantly suspended, and a general cry of horror and despair burst from the lips of every man, as their looks were directed for her, in vain, over every part of the ocean. They immediately made all haste towards us. The captain's boat was the first that reached us. He stopped about a boat's length off, but had no power to utter a single syllable: he was so completely overpowered with the spectacle before him, that he sat down in his boat, pale and speechless. I could scarcely recognise his countenance, he appeared to be so much altered, awed, and overcome with the oppression of his feelings, and the dreadful reality that lay before him. He was in a short time however enabled to address the inquiry to me, "My God, Mr. Chase, what is the matter?" I answered, "We have been stove by a whale." I then briefly told him the story. After a few moments' reflection he observed, that we must cut away her masts, and endeavour to get something out of her to eat. Our thoughts were now all accordingly bent on endeavours to save from the wreck whatever we might possibly want, and for this purpose we rowed up and got on to her. Search was made for every means of gaining access to her hold; and for this purpose the lanyards were cut loose, and with our hatchets we commenced to cut away the masts, that she might right up again, and enable us to scuttle her decks. In doing which we were occupied about three quarters of an hour, owing to our having no axes, nor indeed any other instruments, but the small hatchets belonging to the boats. After her masts were gone she came up about two-thirds of the way upon an even keel. While we were employed about the masts the captain took his quadrant, shoved off from the ship, and got an observation. We found ourselves in latitude 0° 40¹ S. longitude 119° W. We now commenced to cut a hole through the planks, directly above two large casks of bread, which were most fortunately between decks, in the waist of the ship, and which being in the upper side, when she upset, we had strong hopes was not wet. It turned out according to our wishes, and from these casks we obtained six hundred pounds of hard bread. Other parts of the deck were then scuttled, and we got without difficulty as much fresh water as we dared to take in the boats, so that each was supplied with about 65 gallons; we got also from one of the lockers a musket, a small canister of powder, a couple of files, two rasps, about two pounds of boat nails, and a few turtle. In the afternoon the wind came on to blow a strong breeze; and having obtained every thing that occurred to us could then be got out, we began to make arrangements for our safety during the night. A boat's line was made fast to the ship, and to the other end of it one of the boats was moored, at about fifty fathoms to leeward; another boat was then attached to the first one, about eight fathoms astern; and the third boat, the like distance astern of her. Night came on just as we had finished our operations; and such a night it was to us! so full of feverish and distracting inquietude, that we were deprived entirely of rest. The wreck was constantly before my eyes. I could not, by any effort, chase away the horrors of the preceding day from my mind: they haunted me the live-long night. My companions—some of them were like sick women; they had no idea of the extent of their deplorable situation. One or two slept unconcernedly, while others wasted the night in unavailing murmurs. I now had full leisure to examine, with some degree of coolness, the dreadful circumstances of our disaster.

The scenes of yesterday passed in such quick succession in my mind that it was not until after many hours of severe reflection that I was able to discard the idea of the catastrophe as a dream. Alas! it was one from which there was no awaking; it was too certainly true, that but yesterday we had existed as it were, and in one short moment had been cut off from all the hopes and prospects of the living! I have no language to paint the horrors of our situation. To shed tears was indeed altogether unavailing, and withal unmanly; yet I was not able to deny myself the relief they served to afford me. After several hours of idle sorrow and repining I began to reflect upon the accident, and endeavoured to realize by what unaccountable destiny or design, (which I could not at first determine,) this sudden and most deadly attack had been made upon us: by an animal, too, never before suspected of premeditated violence, and proverbial for its insensibility and inoffensiveness. Every fact seemed to warrant me in concluding that it was anything but chance which directed his operations; he made two several attacks upon the ship, at a short interval between them, both of which, according to their direction, were calculated to do us the most injury, by being made ahead, and thereby combining the speed of the two objects for the shock; to effect which, the exact manoeuvres which he made were necessary. His aspect was most horrible, and such as indicated resentment and fury. He came directly from the shoal which we had just before entered, and in which we had struck three of his companions, as if fired with revenge for their sufferings. But to this it may be observed, that the mode of fighting which they always adopt is either with repeated strokes of their tails, or snapping of their jaws together; and that a case, precisely similar to this one, has never been heard of amongst the oldest and most experienced whalers. To this I would answer, that the structure and strength of the whale's head is admirably designed for this mode of attack; the most prominent part of which is almost as hard and as tough as iron; indeed, I can compare it to nothing else but the inside of a horse's hoof, upon which a lance or harpoon would not make the slightest impression. The eyes and ears are removed nearly one-third the length of the whole fish, from the front part of the head, and are not in the least degree endangered in this mode of attack. At all events, the whole circumstances taken together, all happening before my own eyes, and producing, at the time, impressions in my mind of decided, calculating mischief, on the part of the whale, (many of which impressions I cannot now recall,) induce me to be satisfied that I am correct in my opinion. It is certainly, in all its bearings, a hitherto unheard of circumstance, and constitutes, perhaps, the most extraordinary one in the annals of this fishery.

Jeremiah N. Reynolds

*Few careers better exemplify the mysterious nature of the unexplored lands and seas fre-
quented by early Nantucket whalemen than the life of newspaper editor, lecturer, explorer,
and author Jeremiah N. Reynolds (1799?–1858). In 1823, Reynolds embarked on a
path that would change maritime and literary history when he sold his interest in the*
Spectator, *a Wilmington, Ohio, newspaper, and joined a lecture tour with John Cleves
Symmes, an amateur geographer who theorized that the center of the earth was hollow,
and accessible by "holes at the poles." While today this idea sounds like the wildest science
fiction, in the 1820s Symmes's theory had the respect of many prominent scientists.
Reynolds was passionate about it, and became a tireless and vocal advocate for a national
expedition to the South Pole. He eventually won the approval of John Quincy Adams's
administration and was appointed a special envoy to the U.S. Navy. In 1828, Reynolds
visited Nantucket in that capacity to collect data about the South Seas from the island's
ship captains and owners. But when Andrew Jackson took office later that same year, plans
for the expedition were canceled.*

*Undaunted, Reynolds organized a privately funded expedition of discovery and
sealing, helping to outfit two vessels—the* Annawan, *commanded by Captain Nathaniel
Palmer, and the* Seraph, *under Captain Benjamin Pendleton. Together, they attempted
to explore the coast of the still unknown continent of Antarctica—until their crews
mutinied, driven to the brink by an absence of seals and by the misery and danger of
working in icy seas. Set ashore in Chile, Reynolds found himself a berth on the U.S.
Navy frigate* Potomac *as Commodore Downes's personal secretary, and returned home
after an adventure-packed circumnavigation of the globe, recorded in Reynolds's narrative,*
Voyage of the Potomac *(1833).*

*Back ashore, Reynolds returned with new commitment to the idea of a government-
sponsored expedition, where crews would have regular pay and be subject to naval disci-
pline. In 1836, he addressed Congress on the matter, and in 1837 none other than
Edgar Allan Poe reviewed a published version of Reynolds's speech—"Address on the
Subject of a Surveying and Exploring Expedition to the Pacific Ocean and the South
Seas"—for the* Southern Literary Messenger. *Sometime during this period, Poe*

almost certainly met Reynolds. Poe's fantasy novel The Narrative of Arthur Gordon Pym *of Nantucket (1838) owes a great deal to Reynolds's advocacy of Symmes's hollow-earth theory, and even includes some 1,500 words lifted verbatim from Reynolds's "Address." Reynolds was eventually successful in persuading Congress to launch the U. S. Exploring Expedition, which set sail in 1838 under the command of Lieutenant Charles Wilkes and not only discovered the continent of Antarctica, but dozens of uncharted islands in the Pacific and myriad species of flora and fauna unknown to science. Their voyage of discovery is recorded in Nantucket author Nathaniel Philbrick's* Sea of Glory *(2003).*

Sadly, Reynolds was left behind, denied a coveted position with the expedition by his political enemies. But his contribution to American, and Nantucket, literature was not yet over. In 1839, he took time from his new career as a lawyer to set down a wild sea yarn told to him by a Nantucket whaleman. Published in Knickerbocker Magazine, *Reynolds's "Mocha Dick; or The White Whale of the Pacific: A Leaf from a Manuscript Journal" (1839) is an acknowledged source for Herman Melville's* Moby-Dick *(1851), as well as a wonderful example of the kinds of tall tales Melville would hear as a foremast hand during his own years at sea. —SB*

From "Mocha Dick: Or The White Whale of the Pacific: A Leaf from a Manuscript Journal"

[. . . .] IT WAS LATE in the afternoon, when we left the schooner; and while we bore up for the north, she stood away for the southern extremity of the island. As evening was gathering around us, we fell in with a vessel, which proved to be the same whose boats, a day or two before, we had seen in the act of taking a whale. Aside from the romantic and stirring associations it awakened, there are few objects in themselves more picturesque or beautiful, than a whaleship, seen from a distance of three or four miles, on a pleasant evening, in the midst of the great Pacific. As she moves gracefully over the water, rising and falling on the gentle undulations peculiar to this sea; her sails glowing in the quivering light of the fires that flash from below, and a thick volume of smoke ascending from the midst, and curling away in dark masses upon the wind; it requires little effort of the fancy, to imagine one's self gazing upon a floating volcano.

As we were both standing to the north, under easy sail, at nine o'clock at night we had joined company with the stranger. Soon after, we were boarded by his whale-boat, the officer in command of which bore us the compliments of the captain, together with a friendly invitation to partake the hospitalities of his cabin. Accepting, without hesitation, a courtesy so frankly tendered, we proceeded, in company with Captain Palmer, on board [. . . .]

We found the whaler a large, well-appointed ship, owned in New-York, and commanded by such a man as one might expect to find in charge of a vessel of this character; plain, unassuming, intelligent, and well-informed upon all the subjects relating to his peculiar calling. But what shall we say of his first mate, or how describe him? To attempt his portrait by a comparison, would be vain, for we have never looked upon his like, and a detailed description, however accurate, would but faintly shadow forth the tout ensemble of his extraordinary figure. He had probably numbered about thirty-five years. We arrived at this conclusion, however, rather from the untamed brightness of his flashing eye, than the general appearance of his features, on which torrid sun and polar storm had left at once the furrows of more advanced age, and a tint swarthy as that of the Indian. His height, which was a little beneath the common standard, appeared almost dwarfish, from the immense breadth of his overhanging shoulders, while the unnatural length of the loose, dangling arms which hung from them, and which, when at rest, had least the appearance of ease, imparted to his uncouth and muscular frame an air of grotesque awkwardness, which defies description. He made few pretensions as a sailor, and had never aspired to the command of a ship. But he would not have exchanged the sensations which stirred his blood, when steering down upon a school of whales, for the privilege of treading, as master, the deck of the noblest liner that ever traversed the Atlantic. According to the admeasurement of his philosophy, whaling was the most dignified and manly of all sublunary pursuits. Of this he felt perfectly satisfied, having been engaged in the noble vocation for upward of twenty years, during which period, if his own assertions were to be received as evidence, no man in the American spermaceti fleet had made so many captures, or met with such wild adventures, in the exercise of his perilous profession. Indeed, so completely were all his propensities, thoughts, and feelings, identified with his occupation; so intimately did he seem acquainted with the habits and instincts of the objects of his pursuit, and so little conversant with the ordinary affairs of life; that one felt less inclined to class him in the genus homo, than as a sort of intermediate something between man and the cetaceous tribe.

Soon after the commencement of his nautical career, in order to prove that he was not afraid of a whale, a point which it is essential for the young whaleman to establish beyond question, he offered, upon a wager, to run his boat "bows on" against the side of an "old bull," leap from the "cuddy" to the back of the fish, sheet his lance home, and return on board in safety. This feat, daring as it may be considered, he undertook and accomplished; at least so it was chronicled in his log, and he was ready to bear witness, on oath, to the veracity of the record. But his conquest of the redoubtable MOCHA DICK, unquestionably formed the climax of his exploits.

Before we enter into the particulars of this triumph, which, through their valorous representative, conferred so much honor on the lancers of Nantucket, it may be proper to inform the reader who and what Mocha Dick was; and thus give him a posthumous introduction to one who was, in his day and generation, so emphatically among fish the "Stout Gentleman" of his latitudes. The introductory portion of his history we shall give, in a condensed form, from the relation of the mate. Substantially, however, it will be even as he rendered it; and as his subsequent narrative, though not deficient in rude eloquence, was coarse in style and language, as well as unnecessarily diffuse, we shall assume the liberty of altering the expression; of adapting the phraseology to the occasion; and of presenting the whole matter in a shape more succinct and connected. In this arrangement, however, we shall leave our adventurer to tell his own story although not always in his own words, and shall preserve the person of the original.

But to return to Mocha Dick—which, it may be observed, few were solicitous to do, who had once escaped from him. This renowned monster, who had come off victorious in a hundred fights with his pursuers, was an old bull

whale, of prodigious size and strength. From the effect of age, or more probably from a freak of nature, as exhibited in the case of the Ethiopian Albino, a
singular consequence had resulted—he was white as wool! Instead of projecting his spout obliquely forward, and puffing with a short, convulsive effort,
accompanied by a snorting noise, as usual with his species, he flung the water
from his nose in a lofty, perpendicular, expanded volume, at regular and somewhat distant intervals; its expulsion producing a continuous roar, like that of
vapor struggling from the safety-valve of a powerful steam engine. Viewed
from a distance, the practised eye of the sailor only could decide, that the moving mass, which constituted this enormous animal, was not a white cloud sailing along the horizon. On the spermaceti whale, barnacles are rarely
discovered; but upon the head of this lusus naturae, they had clustered, until it
became absolutely rugged with the shells. In short, regard him as you would, he
was a most extraordinary fish; or, in the vernacular of Nantucket, "a genuine
old sog", of the first water.

Opinions differ as to the time of his discovery. It is settled, however, that
previous to the year 1810, he had been seen and attacked near the island of
Mocha. Numerous boats are known to have been shattered by his immense
flukes, or ground to pieces in the crush of his powerful jaws; and, on one occasion, it is said that he came off victorious from a conflict with the crews of
three English whalers, striking fiercely at the last of the retreating boats, at the
moment it was rising from the water, in its hoist up to the ship's davits. It must
not be supposed, howbeit, that through all this desperate warfare, our leviathan
passed scathless. A back serried with irons, and from fifty to a hundred yards of
line trailing in his wake, sufficiently attested, that though unconquered, he had
not proved invulnerable. From the period of Dick's first appearance, his
celebrity continued to increase, until his name seemed naturally to mingle
with the salutations which whalemen were in the habit of exchanging, in
their encounters upon the broad Pacific; the customary interrogatories almost
always closing with, "Any news from Mocha Dick?" Indeed, nearly every
whaling captain who rounded Cape Horn, if he possessed any professional
ambition, or valued himself on his skill in subduing the monarch of the seas,
would lay his vessel along the coast, in the hope of having an opportunity to
try the muscle of this doughty champion, who was never known to shun his
assailants. It was remarked, nevertheless, that the old fellow seemed particularly
careful as to the portion of his body which he exposed to the approach of the
boat-steerer; generally presenting, by some well-timed manoeuvre, his back to
the harpooneer; and dexterously evading every attempt to plant an iron under
his fin, or a spade on his "small". Though naturally fierce, it was not customary with Dick, while unmolested, to betray a malicious disposition. On the

contrary, he would sometimes pass quietly round a vessel, and occasionally swim lazily and harmlessly among the boats, when armed with full craft, for the destruction of his race. But this forbearance gained him little credit, for if no other cause of accusation remained to them, his foes would swear they saw a lurking deviltry in the long, careless sweep of his flukes. Be this as it may, nothing is more certain, than that all indifference vanished with the first prick of the harpoon; while cutting the line, and a hasty retreat to their vessel, were frequently the only means of escape from destruction, left to his discomfited assaulters. [. . . .]

The whaler now resumed. [. . . .] "[L]ittle of interest occurred, until after we had doubled Cape Horn. We were now standing in upon the coast of Chili, before a gentle breeze from the south, that bore us along almost imperceptibly. It was a quiet and beautiful evening, and the sea glanced and glistened in the level rays of the descending sun, with a surface of waving gold. The western sky was flooded with amber light, in the midst of which, like so many islands, floated immense clouds, of every conceivable brilliant dye; while far to the northeast, looming darkly against a paler heaven, rose the conical peak of Mocha. The men were busily employed in sharpening their harpoons, spades, and lances, for the expected fight. The look-out at the mast-head, with cheek on his shoulder, was dreaming of the "dangers he had passed," instead of keeping watch for those which were to come; while the captain paced the quarter-deck with long and hasty stride, scanning the ocean in every direction, with a keen, expectant eye. All at once, he stopped, fixed his gaze intently for an instant on some object to leeward, that seemed to attract it, and then, in no very conciliating tone, hailed the mast-head:

"'Both ports shut?' he exclaimed, looking aloft, and pointing backward, where a long white bushy spout was rising, about a mile off the larboard bow, against the glowing horizon. 'Both ports shut? I say, you leaden-eyed lubber! Nice lazy son of a sea-cook you are, for a look-out! Come down, Sir!'

"'There she blows!—sperm whale—old sog, sir;' said the man, in a deprecatory tone, as he descended from his nest in the air. It was at once seen that the creature was companionless; but as a lone whale is generally an old bull, and of unusual size and ferocity, more than ordinary sport was anticipated, while unquestionably more than ordinary honor was to be won from its successful issue.

"The second mate and I were ordered to make ready for pursuit; and now commenced a scene of emulation and excitement, of which the most vivid description would convey but an imperfect outline, unless you have been a spectator or an actor on a similar occasion. Line-tubs, water-kegs, and waif-poles, were thrown hurriedly into the boats; the irons were placed in the racks, and the necessary evolutions of the ship gone through, with a quickness almost magical; and this too, amidst what to a landsman would have seemed inextricable confusion, with perfect regularity and precision; the commands of the officers being all but forestalled by the enthusiastic eagerness of the men. In a short time, we were as near the object of our chase, as it was considered prudent to approach.

"'Back the main-top-s'l!' shouted the captain. 'There she blows! there she blows!—there she blows!'—cried the look-out, who had taken the place of his sleepy shipmate, raising the pitch of his voice with each announcement, until it amounted to a downright yell: 'Right ahead, Sir!—spout as long an's thick as the mainyard!'

"'Stand by to lower!' exclaimed the captain; 'all hands; cook, steward, cooper—every d——d one of ye, stand by to lower!'

"An instantaneous rush from all quarters of the vessel answered this appeal, and every man was at his station, almost before the last word had passed the lips of the skipper.

"'Lower away!'—and in a moment the keels splashed in the water. 'Follow down the crews; jump in my boys; ship the crotch; line your oars; now pull, as if the d——l was in your wake!' were the successive orders, as the men slipped down the ship's side, took their places in the boats, and began to give way.

"The second mate had a little the advantage of me in starting. The stern of his boat grated against the bows of mine, at the instant I grasped my steering-oar, and gave the word to shove off. One sweep of my arm, and we sprang foaming in his track. Now came the tug of war. To become a first-rate oarsman, you must understand, requires a natural gift. My crew were not wanting in the proper qualification; every mother's son of them pulled as if he had been born with an oar in his hand; and as they stretched every sinew for the glory of darting the first iron it did my heart good to see the boys spring. At every stroke, the tough blades bent like willow wands, and quivered like tempered steel in the warm sunlight, as they sprang forward from the tension of the retreating wave. At the distance of half a mile and directly before us, lay the object of our emulation and ambition, heaving his huge bulk in unwieldy gambols, as though totally unconscious of our approach.

"'There he blows! An old bull, by Jupiter! Eighty barrels, boys, waiting to be towed alongside! Long and quick—shoot ahead! Now she feels it; waist boat never could beat us, now she feels the touch!—now she walks through it! Again—now!' Such were the broken exclamations and adjurations with which I cheered my rowers to their toil, as, with renewed vigor, I plied my long steering-oar. In another moment, we were alongside our competitor. The shivering blades flashed forward and backward, like sparks of light. The waters boiled under our prow, and the trenched waves closed, hissing and whirling, in our wake, as we swept, I might almost say were lifted, onward in our arrowy course.

"We were coming down upon our fish, and could hear the roar of his spouting above the rush of the sea, when my boat began to take the lead.

"'Now, my fine fellows,' I exclaimed, in triumph, 'now we'll show them our stern—only spring! Stand ready, harpooner, but don't dart, till I give the word.'

"'Carry me on, and his name's Dennis!' cried the boat-steerer, in a confident tone [A whale's name is "Dennis" when he spouts blood.]. We were perhaps a hundred feet in advance of the waist-boat, and within fifty of the whale, about an inch of whose hump only was to be seen above the water, when, heaving slowly into view a pair of flukes some eighteen feet in width, he went down. The men lay on their oars. 'There he blows, again!' cried the tub-oarsman, as a lofty, perpendicular spout sprang into the air, a few furlongs away on the starboard side. Presuming from his previous movement, that the old fellow had been 'gallied' by other boats, and might probably be jealous of our purpose, I was about ordering the men to pull away as softly and silently as possible, when we received fearful intimation that he had no intention of balking our inclination, or even yielding us the honor of the first attack. Lashing the sea with his enormous tail, until he threw about him a cloud of surf and spray, he came down, at full speed, 'jaws on,' with the determination, apparently, of doing battle in earnest. As he drew near, with his long curved back looming occasionally above the surface of the billows, we perceived that it was white as the surf around him; and the men stared aghast at each other, as they uttered, in a suppressed tone, the terrible name of MOCHA DICK!

"'Mocha Dick or the d——l,' said I, 'this boat never sheers off from any thing that wears the shape of a whale. Pull easy; just give her way enough to steer.' As the creature approached, he somewhat abated his frenzied speed, and, at the distance of a cable's length, changed his course to a sharp angle with our own.

"'Here he comes!' I exclaimed. 'Stand up, harpooner! Don't be hasty—don't be flurried. Hold your iron higher—firmer. Now!' I shouted, as I brought our bows within a boat's length of the immense mass which was wallowing heavily by. 'Now!—give it to him solid!'

"But the leviathan plunged on, unharmed. The young harpooner, though ordinarily as fearless as a lion, had imbibed a sort of superstitious dread of Mocha Dick, from the exaggerated stories of that prodigy, which he had heard from his comrades. He regarded him, as he had heard him described in many a tough yarn during the middle watch, rather as some ferocious fiend of the deep, than a regular-built, legitimate whale! Judge then of his trepidation, on beholding a creature, answering the wildest dreams of his fancy, and sufficiently formidable, without any superadded terrors, bearing down upon him with thrashing flukes and distended jaws! He stood erect, it cannot be denied. He planted his foot—he grasped the coil—he poised his weapon. But his knee shook, and his sinewy arm wavered. The shaft was hurled, but with unsteady aim. It just grazed the back of the monster, glanced off, and darted into the sea beyond. A second, still more abortive, fell short of the mark. The giant animal swept on for a few rods, and then, as if in contempt of our fruitless and childish attempts to injure him, flapped a storm of spray in our faces with his broad tail, and dashed far down into the depths of the ocean, leaving our little skiff among the waters where he sank, to spin and duck in the whirlpool.

"Never shall I forget the choking sensation of disappointment which came over me at that moment. My glance fell on the harpooner. 'Clumsy lubber!' I vociferated, in a voice hoarse with passion; 'you a whaleman! You are only fit to spear eels! Cowardly spawn! Curse me, if you are not afraid of a whale!'

"The poor fellow, mortified at his failure, was slowly and thoughtfully hauling in his irons. No sooner had he heard me stigmatize him as 'afraid of a whale', than he bounded upon his thwart, as if bitten by a serpent. He stood before me for a moment, with a glowing cheek and flashing eye; then, dropping the iron he had just drawn in, without uttering a word, he turned half round, and sprang head-foremost into the sea. The tub-oarsman, who was recoiling the line in the after part of the boat, saw his design just in season to grasp him by the heel, as he made his spring. But he was not to be dragged on board again without a struggle. Having now become more calm, I endeavored to soothe his wounded pride with kind and flattering words; for I knew him to be a noble-hearted fellow, and was truly sorry that my hasty reproaches should have touched so fine a spirit so deeply.

"Night being now at hand, the captain's signal was set for our return to the vessel; and we were soon assembled on her deck, discussing the mischances of the day, and speculating on the prospect of better luck on the morrow.

"We were at breakfast next morning, when the watch at the fore-top-gallant head sung out merrily, 'There she breaches!' In an instant every one was on his feet. 'Where away?' cried the skipper, rushing from the cabin, and upsetting in his course the steward, who was returning from the caboose with a replenished biggin of hot coffee. 'Not loud but deep' were the grumblings and groans of that functionary, as he rubbed his scalded shins, and danced about in agony; but had they been far louder, they would have been drowned in the tumult of vociferation which answered the announcement from the mast-head.

"'Where away?' repeated the captain, as he gained the deck.

"'Three points off the leeward bow.'

"'How far?' 'About a league, Sir; heads same as we do. There she blows!' added the man, as he came slowly down the shrouds, with his eyes fixed intently upon the spouting herd.

"'Keep her off two points! Steady!—steady, as she goes!'

"'Steady it is, Sir,' answered the helmsman.

"'Weather braces, a small pull. Loose to'-gallant-s'ls! Bear a hand, my boys! Who knows but we may tickle their ribs at this rising?'

"The captain had gone aloft, and was giving these orders from the main-to'-gallant-cross-trees. 'There she top-tails! there she blows!' added he, as, after taking a long look at the sporting shoal, he glided down the back stay. 'Sperm whale, and a thundering big school of 'em!' was his reply to the rapid and eager inquiries of the men. 'See the lines in the boats,' he continued; 'get in the craft; swing the cranes!'"

"By this time the fish had gone down, and every eye was strained to catch the first intimation of their reappearance. 'There she spouts!' screamed a young greenhorn in the main chains, 'close by; a mighty big whale, Sir!'

"'We'll know that better at the trying out, my son,' said the third mate, drily.

"'Back the main-top-s'l!' was now the command. The ship had little head-way at the time, and in a few minutes we were as motionless as if lying at anchor.

"'Lower away, all hands!' And in a twinkling, and together, the starboard, larboard, and waist-boats struck the water. Each officer leaped into his own; the crews arranged themselves at their respective stations; the boat-steerers began to adjust their 'craft'; and we left the ship's side in company; the captain, in laconic phrase, bidding us to 'get up and get fast', as quickly as possible.

"Away we dashed, in the direction of our prey, who were frolicking, if such a term can be applied to their unwieldy motions, on the surface of the waves. Occasionally, a huge, shapeless body would flounce out of its proper element, and fall back with a heavy splash; the effort forming about as ludicrous a cari-cature of agility, as would the attempt of some over-fed alderman to execute the Highland fling.

"We were within a hundred rods of the herd, when, as if from a common impulse, or upon some preconcerted signal, they all suddenly disappeared. Follow me!' I shouted, waving my hand to the men in the other boats; 'I see their track under water; they swim fast, but we'll be among them when they rise. Lay back,' I continued, addressing myself to my own crew, 'back to the thwarts! Spring hard! We'll be in the thick of 'em when they come up; only pull!'

"And they did pull, manfully. After towing for about a mile, I ordered them to 'lie.' The oars were peaked, and we rose to look out for the first 'noddle-head' that should break water. It was at this time a dead calm. Not a single cloud was passing over the deep blue of the heavens, to vary their boundless transparency, or shadow for a moment the gleaming ocean which they spanned. Within a short distance lay our noble ship, with her idle canvass hang-ing in drooping festoons from her yards; while she seemed resting on her inverted image, which, distinct and beautiful as its original, was glassed in the smooth expanse beneath. No sound disturbed the general silence, save our own heavy breathings, the low gurgle of the water against the side of the boat, or the noise of flapping wings, as the albatross wheeled sleepily along through the stagnant atmosphere. We had remained quiet for about five minutes, when some dark object was descried ahead, moving on the surface of the sea. It proved to be a small 'calf', playing in the sunshine.

"'Pull up and strike it,' said I to the third mate; 'it may bring up the old one—perhaps the whole school.'

"And so it did, with a vengeance! The sucker was transpierced, after a short pursuit; but hardly had it made its first agonized plunge, when an enormous cow-whale rose close beside her wounded offspring. Her first endeavor was to take it under her fin, in order to bear it away; and nothing could be more striking than the maternal tenderness she manifested in her exertions to accomplish this object. But the poor thing was dying, and while she vainly tried to induce it to accompany her, it rolled over, and floated dead at her side. Perceiving it to be beyond the reach of her caresses, she turned to wreak her vengeance on its slayers, and made directly for the boat, crashing her vast jaws the while, in a paroxysm of rage. Ordering his boat-steerer aft, the mate sprang forward, cut the line loose from the calf, and then snatched from the crotch the remaining iron, which he plunged with his gathered strength into the body of the mother, as the boat sheered off to avoid her onset. I saw that the work was well done, but had no time to mark the issue; for at that instant, a whale 'breached' at the distance of about a mile from us, on the starboard quarter. The glimpse I caught of the animal in his descent, convinced me that I once more beheld my old acquaintance, Mocha Dick. That falling mass was white as a snow-drift!

"One might have supposed the recognition mutual, for no sooner was his vast square head lifted from the sea, than he charged down upon us, scattering the billows into spray as he advanced, and leaving a wake of foam a rod in width, from the violent lashing of his flukes.

"'He's making for the bloody water!' cried the men, as he cleft his way toward the very spot where the calf had been killed. 'Here, harpooner, steer the boat, and let me dart!' I exclaimed, as I leaped into the bows. 'May the 'Goneys' eat me, if he dodge us this time, though he were Beelzebub himself! Pull for the red water!'

"As I spoke, the fury of the animal seemed suddenly to die away. He paused in his career, and lay passive on the waves; with his arching back thrown up like the ridge of a mountain. 'The old sog's lying to!' I cried, exultingly. 'Spring, boys! spring now, and we have him! All my clothes, tobacco, every thing I've got, shall be yours, only lay me 'longside that whale before another boat comes up! My grimky! what a hump! Only look at the irons in his back! No, don't look—

PULL! Now, boys, if you care about seeing your sweethearts and wives in old Nantuck!—if you love Yankee-land—if you love me—pull ahead, won't ye? Now then, to the thwarts! Lay back, my boys! I feel ye, my hearties! Give her the touch. Only five seas off! Not five seas off! One minute—half a minute more! Softly—no noise. Softly with your oars! That will do—'

"And as the words were uttered, I raised the harpoon above my head, took a rapid but no less certain aim, and sent it, hissing, deep into his thick white side!

"'Stern all! for your lives!' I shouted; for at that instant the steel quivered in his body, the wounded leviathan plunged his head beneath the surface, and whirling around with great velocity, smote the sea violently, with fin and fluke, in a convulsion of rage and pain.

"Our little boat flew dancing back from the seething vortex around him, just in season to escape being overwhelmed or crushed. He now started to run. For a short time, the line rasped, smoking, through the chocks. A few turns round the loggerhead then secured it; and with oars a-peak, and bows tilted to the sea, we went leaping onward in the wake of the tethered monster. Vain were all his struggles to break from our hold. The strands were too strong, the barbed iron too deeply fleshed, to give way. So that whether he essayed to dive or breach, or dash madly forward, the frantic creature still felt that he was held in check. At one moment, in impotent rage, he reared his immense blunt head, covered with barnacles, high above the surge, while his jaws fell together with a crash that almost made me shiver; then the upper outline of his vast form was dimly seen, gliding amidst showers of sparkling spray; while streaks of crimson on the white surf that boiled in his track, told that the shaft had been driven home.

"By this time, the whole 'school' was about us; and spouts from a hundred spiracles, with a roar that almost deafened us, were raining on every side; while in the midst of a vast surface of chafing sea, might be seen the black shapes of the rampant herd, tossing and plunging, like a legion of maddened demons. The second and third mates were in the very centre of this appalling commotion.

"At length, Dick began to lessen his impetuous speed. 'Now, my boys,' cried I, 'haul me on; wet the line, you second oars-man, as it comes in. Haul away, ship-mates!—why the devil don't you haul? Leeward side—leeward! I tell you! Don't you know how to approach a whale?'

"The boat brought fairly up upon his broadside as I spoke, and I gave him the lance just under the shoulder blade. At this moment, just as the boat's head was laid off; and I was straitening for a second lunge, my lance, which I had 'boned' in the first, a piercing cry from the boat-steerer drew my attention quickly aft, and I saw the waist-boat, or more properly a fragment of it, falling through the air, and underneath, the dusky forms of the struggling crew, grasping at the oars, or clinging to portions of the wreck; while a pair of flukes, descending in the midst of the confusion, fully accounted for the catastrophe. The boat had been struck and shattered by a whale!

"'Good heaven!' I exclaimed, with impatience, and in a tone which I fear showed me rather mortified at the interruption, than touched with proper feeling for the sufferers; 'good heavens—hadn't they sense enough to keep out of the red water! And I must lose this glorious prize, through their infernal stupidity!' This was the first outbreak of my selfishness.

"'But we must not see them drown, boys,' I added, upon the instant; 'cut the line!' The order had barely passed my lips, when I caught sight of the captain, who had seen the accident from the quarter deck, bearing down with oar and sail to the rescue.

"'Hold on!' I thundered, just as the knife's edge touched the line; "for the glory of old Nantuck, hold on! The captain will pick them up, and Mocha Dick will be ours, after all!'

"This affair occurred in half the interval I have occupied in the relation. In the mean time, with the exception of a slight shudder, which once or twice shook his ponderous frame, Dick lay perfectly quiet upon the water. But suddenly, as though goaded into exertion by some fiercer pang, he started from his lethargy with apparently augmented power. Making a leap toward the boat, he darted perpendicularly downward, hurling the after oarsman, who was helmsman at the time, ten feet over the quarter, as he struck the long steering-oar in his descent. The unfortunate seaman fell, with his head forward, just upon the flukes of the whale, as he vanished, and was drawn down by suction of the closing waters, as if he had been a feather. After being carried to a great depth, as we inferred from the time he remained below the surface, he came up, panting and exhausted, and was dragged on board, amidst the hearty congratulations of his comrades.

"By this time two hundred fathoms of line had been carried spinning through the chocks, with an impetus that gave back in steam the water cast upon it. Still the gigantic creature bored his way downward, with undiminished speed. Coil after coil went over, and was swallowed up. There remained but three flakes in the tub!

"'Cut!' I shouted; 'cut quick, or he'll take us down!' But as I spoke, the hissing line flew with trebled velocity through the smoking wood, jerking the knife he was in the act of applying to the heated strands out of the hand of the boat-steerer. The boat rose on end, and her bows were buried in an instant; a hurried ejaculation, at once shriek and prayer, rose to the lips of the bravest when, unexpected mercy! the whizzing cord lost its tension, and our light bark, half filled with water, fell heavily back on her keel. A tear was in every eye, and I believe every heart bounded with gratitude, at this unlooked-for deliverance.

"Overpowered by his wounds, and exhausted by his exertions and the enormous pressure of the water above him, the immense creature was compelled to turn once more upward, for a fresh supply of air. And upward he came, indeed; shooting twenty feet of his gigantic length above the waves, by the impulse of his ascent. He was not disposed to be idle. Hardly had we succeeded in bailing out our swamping boat, when he again darted away, as it seemed to me with renewed energy. For a quarter of a mile, we parted the opposing waters as though they had offered no more resistance than air. Our game then abruptly brought to, and lay as if paralyzed, his massy frame quivering and twitching, as if under the influence of galvanism. I gave the word to haul on; and seizing a boat-spade, as we came near him, drove it twice into his small; no doubt partially disabling him by the vigor and certainty of the blows. Wheeling furiously around, he answered this salutation, by making a desperate dash at the boat's quarter. We were so near him, that to escape the shock of his onset, by any practicable manoeuvre, was out of the question. But at the critical moment, when we expected to be crushed by the collision, his powers seemed to give way. The fatal lance had reached the seat of life. His strength failed him in mid career, and sinking quietly beneath our keel, grazing it as he wallowed along, he rose again a few rods from us, on the side opposite that where he went down.

"'Lay around, my boys, and let us set on him!' I cried, for I saw his spirit was broken at last. But the lance and spade were needless now. The work was done. The dying animal was struggling in a whirlpool of bloody foam, and the ocean far around was tinted with crimson. 'Stern all!' I shouted, as he commenced running impetuously in a circle, beating the water alternately with his head and flukes, and smiting his teeth ferociously into their sockets, with a crashing sound, in the strong spasms of dissolution. 'Stern all! or we shall be stove!'

"As I gave the command, a stream of black, clotted gore rose in a thick spout above the expiring brute, and fell in a shower around, bedewing, or rather drenching us, with a spray of blood.

"'There's the flag!' I exclaimed; 'there! thick as tar! Stern! every soul of ye! He's going in his flurry!' And the monster, under the convulsive influence of his final paroxysm, flung his huge tail into the air, and then, for the space of a minute, thrashed the waters on either side of him with quick and powerful blows; the sound of the concussions resembling that of the rapid discharge of artillery. He then turned slowly and heavily on his side, and lay a dead mass upon the sea through which he had so long ranged a conqueror.

"'He's fin-up at last!' I screamed, at the very top of my voice. 'Hurrah! hurrah! hurrah!' And snatching off my cap, I sent it spinning aloft, jumping at the same time from thwart to thwart, like a madman.

"We now drew alongside our floating spoil; and I seriously question if the brave commodore who first, and so nobly, broke the charm of British invincibility, by the capture of the Guerriere, felt a warmer rush of delight, as he beheld our national flag waving over the British ensign, in assurance of his victory, than I did, as I leaped upon the quarter deck of Dick's back, planted my waif-pole in the midst, and saw the little canvass flag, that tells so important and satisfactory a tale to the whaleman, fluttering above my hard-earned prize.

"The captain and second mate, each of whom had been fortunate enough to kill his fish, soon after pulled up, and congratulated me on my capture. From them I learned the particulars of the third mate's disaster. He had fastened, and his fish was sounding, when another whale suddenly rose, almost directly beneath the boat, and with a single blow of his small, absolutely cut it in twain, flinging the bows, and those who occupied that portion of the frail fabric, far into the air. Rendered insensible, or immediately killed by the shock, two of the crew sank without a struggle, while a third, unable in his confusion to disengage himself from the flakes of the tow-line, with which he had become entangled, was, together with the fragment to which the warp was attached, borne down by the harpooned whale, and was seen no more! The rest, some of them severely bruised, were saved from drowning by the timely assistance of the captain.

"To get the harness on Dick, was the work of an instant; and as the ship, taking every advantage of a light breeze which had sprung up within the last hour, had stood after us, and was now but a few rods distant, we were soon under her stern. The other fish, both of which were heavy fellows, lay floating near; and the tackle being affixed to one of them without delay, all hands were soon busily engaged in cutting in. Mocha Dick was the longest whale I ever looked upon. He measured more than seventy feet from his noddle to the tips of his flukes, and yielded one hundred barrels of clear oil, with a proportionate quantity of 'head-matter.' It may emphatically be said that 'the scars of his old wounds were near his new,' for not less than twenty harpoons did we draw from his back; the rusted mementos of many a desperate rencounter."

The mate was silent. His yarn was reeled off. His story was told; and with far better tact than is exhibited by many a modern orator, he had the modesty and discretion to stop with its termination. In response, a glass of "o-be-joyful" went merrily round [. . . .]

Herman Melville

Herman Melville (1819–91), along with many another famous writer of the American Renaissance, hoped to end the young American nation's "literary flunkyism towards England." He especially abominated his countrymen's "absolute and unconditional" adoration of Shakespeare. "Believe me, my friends," Melville wrote in "Hawthorne and His Mosses," "men not very much inferior to Shakespeare are this day being born on the banks of the Ohio." Melville himself—born just a few blocks from the bustling wharves of Manhattan's South Street Seaport—cherished a secret ambition to be that American Shakespeare. With Nantucket Island and the riches of its whaling history to draw from, he succeeded in Moby-Dick (1851).

Ahab, the novel's tragic protagonist, is a Nantucket whaling captain, not a Shakespearean king, but the stately "thees" and "thous" of the island's Quaker idiom allow him to speak with the cadence and power of a Macbeth or Lear. "Through the mouths of the dark characters of Hamlet, Timon, Lear and Iago," Melville wrote, "[Shakespeare] craftily says, or sometimes insinuates the things which we feel to be so terrifically true that it were all but madness for any good man, in his own proper character, to utter any hint of them." The reputation of the Quakers as freethinkers, coming to truth through their own observations, gives Ahab the license to utter dark truths on Melville's behalf; just as the Calvinist tradition of demonizing Quakers (and even persecuting some as witches) lends a Shakespearean aura of evil, madness, and danger to Ahab's unsanctioned beliefs about God and nature. Ahab's fatal flaw is at once very Shakespearean—"his vaulting ambition doth o'er-leap itself"—and very American, as the Pequod presses back oceanic frontiers in the Pacific and hurls itself into an armed assault on wild nature. Ahab is that dangerous Nantucket species of American that unnerved Edmund Burke and filled Thomas Jefferson with pride.

"My mind was made up to sail in no other than a Nantucket craft," Ishmael tells us. The hierarchy on board a Nantucket whaleship is as rigid as that of the Elizabethan court—something else that contributes to Moby-Dick's Shakespearean organization. But that hierarchy is also uniquely American. The Pequod's crew is not composed of sovereign and nobles, knights and peasants, but captain, mates, harpooneers, and foremast hands. *The crew holds a mirror up to Melville's America—an immigrant and slave-holding society, an amalgam of working men from many races and nationalities. And the harpooneers of Nantucket—Melville insists with a most un-Shakespearean sense of democracy—are worthy to be ranked with the knights of the Order of St. George, despite their "woolen frocks and tarred trousers." Their tragedy will be their mindless obedience to the absolute dominance and unswerving will of authority gone mad, a subject of as much importance in an America trending ever closer to Civil War as it was to an Elizabethan England haunted by the War of the Roses and dreading the death of a Virgin Queen with no heir.*

"O, O, O, O that Shakespeherian Rag," wrote T. S. Eliot in The Waste Land. *"It's so elegant. So intelligent." Here is* Moby-Dick's *most Shakespearean chapter, demonstrating that if Nantucket was, for Ishmael, the most promising port for an adventurous whaleman to embark from, it was, for Herman Melville, the most promising port for an ambitious writer.—SB*

From "The Quarter-Deck," Chapter 36 of *Moby-Dick; or, The Whale*

[....] [O]NE MORNING shortly after breakfast, Ahab, as was his wont, ascended the cabin-gangway to the deck. There most sea-captains usually walk at that hour, as country gentlemen, after the same meal, take a few turns in the garden.

Soon his steady, ivory stride was heard, as to and fro he paced his old rounds, upon planks so familiar to his tread, that they were all over dented, like geological stones, with the peculiar mark of his walk. Did you fixedly gaze, too, upon that ribbed and dented brow; there also, you would see still stranger foot-prints—the foot-prints of his one unsleeping, ever-pacing thought.

But on the occasion in question, those dents looked deeper, even as his nervous step that morning left a deeper mark. And, so full of his thought was Ahab, that at every uniform turn that he made, now at the mainmast and now at the binnacle, you could almost see that thought turn in him as he turned, and pace in him as he paced; so completely possessing him, indeed, that it all but seemed the inward mould of every outer movement.

"D'ye mark him, Flask?" whispered Stubb; "the chick that's in him pecks the shell. 'Twill soon be out."

The hours wore on;—Ahab now shut up within his cabin; anon, pacing the deck, with the same intense bigotry of purpose in his aspect.

It drew near the close of day. Suddenly he came to a halt by the bulwarks, and inserting his bone leg into the auger-hole there, and with one hand grasping a shroud, he ordered Starbuck to send everybody aft.

"Sir!" said the mate, astonished at an order seldom or never given on ship-board except in some extraordinary case.

"Send everybody aft," repeated Ahab. "Mast-heads, there! come down!"

When the entire ship's company were assembled, and with curious and not wholly unappreciative faces, were eyeing him, for he looked not unlike the weather horizon when a storm is coming up, Ahab, after rapidly glancing over the bulwarks, and then darting his eyes among the crew, started from his stand-point; and as though not a soul were nigh him resumed his heavy turns upon the deck. With bent head and half-slouched hat he continued to pace, unmindful of the wondering whispering among the men; till Stubb cautiously whispered to Flask, that Ahab must have summoned them there for the purpose of witnessing a pedestrian feat. But this did not last long. Vehemently pausing, he cried:—

"What do ye do when ye see a whale, men?"

"Sing out for him!" was the impulsive rejoinder from a score of clubbed voices.

"Good!" cried Ahab, with a wild approval in his tones; observing the hearty animation into which his unexpected question had so magnetically thrown them.

"And what do ye do next, men?"

"Lower away, and after him!"

"And what tune is it ye pull to, men?"

"A dead whale or a stove boat!"

More and more strangely and fiercely glad and approving, grew the countenance of the old man at every shout; while the mariners began to gaze curiously at each other, as if marvelling how it was that they themselves became so excited at such seemingly purposeless questions.

But, they were all eagerness again, as Ahab, now half-revolving in his pivot-hole, with one hand reaching up a shroud, and tightly, almost convulsively grasping it, addressed them thus:—

"All ye mast-headers have before now heard me give orders about a white whale. Look ye! d'ye see this Spanish ounce of gold?"—holding up a broad bright coin to the sun—"it is a sixteen dollar piece, men,—a doubloon. D'ye see it? Mr. Starbuck, hand me yon top-maul."

While the mate was getting the hammer, Ahab, without speaking, was slowly rubbing the gold piece against the skirts of his jacket, as if to heighten its lustre, and without using any words was meanwhile lowly humming to himself, producing a sound so strangely muffled and inarticulate that it seemed the mechanical humming of the wheels of the vitality in him.

Receiving the top-maul from Starbuck, he advanced towards the main-mast with the hammer uplifted in one hand, exhibiting the gold with the other, and with a high raised voice exclaiming: "Whosoever of ye raises me a white-headed whale with a wrinkled brow and a crooked jaw; whosoever of ye raises me that white-headed whale, with three holes punctured in his starboard fluke—look ye, whosoever of ye raises me that same white whale, he shall have this gold ounce, my boys!"

"Huzza! Huzza!" cried the seamen, as with swinging tarpaulins they hailed the act of nailing the gold to the mast.

"It's a white whale, I say," resumed Ahab, as he threw down the top-maul; "a white whale. Skin your eyes for him, men, look sharp for white water; if ye see but a bubble, sing out."

All this while Tashtego, Daggoo, and Queequeg had looked on with even more intense interest and surprise than the rest, and at the mention of the wrinkled brow and crooked jaw they had started as if each was separately touched by some specific recollection.

"Captain Ahab," said Tashtego, "that white whale must be the same that some call Moby Dick."

"Moby Dick?" shouted Ahab. "Do ye know the white whale then, Tash?"

"Does he fan-tail a little curious, sir, before he goes down?" said the Gay-Header deliberately.

"And has he a curious spout, too," said Daggoo, "very bushy, even for a parmacetty, and mighty quick, Captain Ahab?"

"And he have one, two, tree—oh! good many iron in him hide, too, Captain," cried Queequeg disjointedly, "all twiske-tee be-twisk, like him—him—" faltering hard for a word, and screwing his hand round and round as though uncorking a bottle—"like him—him—"

"Corkscrew!" cried Ahab, "aye, Queequeg, the harpoons lie all twisted and wrenched in him; aye, Daggoo, his spout is a big one, like a whole shock of wheat, and white as a pile of our Nantucket wool after the great annual sheep-shearing; aye, Tashtego, and he fan-tails like a split jib in a squall. Death and devils! men, it is Moby Dick ye have seen—Moby Dick—Moby Dick!"

"Captain Ahab," said Starbuck, who with Stubb and Flask, had thus far been eyeing his superior with increasing surprise, but at last seemed struck with a thought which somewhat explained all the wonder. "Captain Ahab, I have heard of Moby Dick—but it was not Moby Dick that took off thy leg?"

"Who told thee that"?" cried Ahab; then pausing, "Aye, Starbuck, aye, my hearties all round; it was Moby Dick that dismasted me; Moby Dick that brought me to this dead stump I stand on now. Aye, aye" he shouted with a terrific, loud, animal sob, like that of a heart-stricken moose; "Aye, aye! It was that accursed white whale that razed me; made a poor pegging lubber of me for ever and a day!" Then tossing both arms, with measureless imprecations he shouted out: "Aye, aye! and I'll chase him round Good Hope, and round the Horn, and round the Norway Maelstrom, and round perdition's flames before I give him up. And this is what ye have shipped for, men! to chase that white whale on both sides of land, and over all sides of earth, till he spouts black blood and rolls fin out. What say ye, men, will ye splice hands on it? I think ye do look brave."

"Aye, aye!" shouted the harpooneers and seamen, running closer to the excited old man: "A sharp eye for the White Whale; a sharp lance for Moby Dick!"

"God bless ye," he seemed to half sob and half shout. "God bless ye, men. Steward! go draw the great measure of grog. But what's this long face about,

Mr. Starbuck; wilt thou not chase the white whale? art not game for Moby Dick?"

"I am game for his crooked jaw, and for the jaws of Death too, Captain Ahab, if it fairly comes in the way of the business we follow; but I came here to hunt whales, not my commander's vengeance. How many barrels will thy vengeance yield thee even if thou gettest it, Captain Ahab? It will not fetch thee much in our Nantucket market."

"Nantucket market! Hoot! But come closer, Starbuck; thou requirest a little lower layer. If money's to be the measurer, man, and the accountants have computed their greatest counting-house the globe, by girdling it with guineas, one to every three parts of an inch; then, let me tell thee, that my vengeance will fetch a great premium *here*!"

"He smites his chest," whispered Stubb, "what's that for? methinks it rings most vast, but hollow."

"Vengeance on a dumb brute!" cried Starbuck, "that simply smote thee from blindest instinct! Madness! To be enraged with a dumb thing, Captain Ahab, seems blasphemous."

"Hark ye yet again,—the little lower layer. All visible objects, man, are but as pasteboard masks. But in each event—in the living act, the undoubted deed—there, some unknown but still reasoning thing puts forth the mouldings of its features from behind the unreasoning mask. If man will strike, strike through the mask! How can the prisoner reach outside except by thrusting through the wall? To me, the white whale is that wall, shoved near to me. Sometimes I think that there's naught beyond. But 'tis enough. He tasks me; he heaps me; I see in him outrageous strength, with an inscrutable malice sinewing it. That inscrutable thing is chiefly what I hate; and be the white whale agent, or be the white whale principal, I will wreak that hate upon him. Talk not to me of blasphemy, man; I'd strike the sun if it insulted me. For could the sun do that, then could I do the other; since there is ever a sort of fair play herein, jealousy presiding over all creations. But not my master, man, is even that fair play. Who's over me? Truth hath no confines. Take off thine eye! more intolerable than fiends' glarings is a doltish stare! So, so; thou reddenest and palest; my heat has melted thee to anger-glow. But look ye, Starbuck, what is said in heat, that thing unsays itself. There are men from whom warm words are small indignity. I mean not to incense thee. Let it go! Look! see yonder Turkish cheeks of spotted tawn—living, breathing pictures painted by the sun. The Pagan leopards—the unrecking and unworshipping things, that live; and seek, and give no reasons for the torrid life they feel! The crew, man, the crew! Are they not one and all with Ahab, in this matter of the whale? See Stubb! he laughs! See yonder Chilean! he snorts to think of it. Stand up amid the general hurricane, thy one tossed sapling cannot, Starbuck! And what is it? Reckon it.

'Tis but to help strike a fin; no wondrous feat for Starbuck. What is it more? From this one poor hunt, then, the best lance out of all Nantucket, surely he will not hang back when every foremast-hand has clutched a whetstone? Ah! constrainings seize thee; I see! the billow lifts thee! Speak, but speak!—Aye, aye! thy silence, then, *that* voices thee. [*Aside*] Something shot from my dilated nostrils, he has inhaled it in his lungs. Starbuck now is mine; cannot oppose me now, without rebellion."

"God keep me!—keep us all!" murmured Starbuck, lowly.

But in his joy at the enchanted, tacit acquiescence of the mate, Ahab did not hear his foreboding invocation; nor yet the low laugh from the hold; nor yet the presaging vibrations of the winds in the cordage; nor yet the hollow flap of the sails against the masts, as for a moment their hearts sank in. For again Starbuck's downcast eyes lighted up with the stubborness of life; the subterranean laugh died away; the winds blew on; the sails filled out; the ship heaved and rolled as before. Ah, ye admonitions and warnings! why stay ye not when ye come? But rather are ye predictions than warnings, ye shadows! Yet not so much predictions from without, as verifications of the foregoing things within. For with little external to constrain us, the innermost necessities in our being, these still drive us on.

"The measure! the measure!" cried Ahab.

Receiving the brimming pewter, and turning to the harpooneers, he ordered them to produce their weapons. Then ranging them before him near the capstan, with their harpoons in their hands, while his three mates stood at his side with their lances, and the rest of the ship's company formed a circle around the group; he stood for an instant searchingly eyeing every man of his crew. But those wild eyes met his, as the bloodshot eyes of the prairie wolves meet the eye of their leader, ere he rushes on at their head in the trail of the bison; but, alas! only to fall into the hidden snare of the Indian.

"Drink and pass!" he cried, handing the heavy charged flagon to the nearest seaman. "The crew alone now drink. Round with it, round! Short draughts—long swallows, men; 'tis hot as Satan's hoof. So, so, it goes round excellently. It spiralizes in ye; forks out at the serpent-snapping eye. Well done; almost drained. That way it went, this way it comes. Hand it to me—here's a hollow! Men, ye seem the years; so brimming life is gulped and gone. Steward, refill!

"Attend now, my braves. I have mustered ye all round this capstan; and ye mates, flank me with your lances; and ye harpooneers, stand there with your irons; and ye, stout mariners, ring me in, that I may in some sort revive a noble custom of my fisherman fathers before me. O men, you will yet see that—Ha! boy, come back? bad pennies come not sooner. Hand it me. Why, now, this pewter had run brimming again, wert thou not St. Vitus' imp—away, thou ague!

"Advance, ye mates! Cross your lances full before me. Well done! Let me touch the axis." So saying, with extended arm, he grasped the three level, radiating lances at their crossed centre; while so doing, suddenly and nervously twitched them; meanwhile, gazing intently from Starbuck to Stubb; from Stubb to Flask. It seemed as though, by some nameless, interior volition, he would fain have shocked into them the same fiery emotion accumulated within the Leyden jar of his own magnetic life. The three mates quailed before his strong, sustained, and mystic aspect. Stubb and Flask looked sideways from him. The honest eye of Starbuck fell downright.

"In vain!" cried Ahab; "but, maybe, 'tis well. For did ye three but once take the full-forced shock, then mine own electric thing, *that* had perhaps expired from out me. Perchance, too, it would have dropped ye dead. Perchance ye need it not. Down lances! And now, ye mates, I do appoint ye three cup-bearers to my three pagan kinsmen there—you three most honorable gentlemen and noblemen, my valiant harpooneers. Disdain the task? What, when the great Pope washes the feet of beggars, using his tiara for ewer? Oh, my sweet cardinals! your own condescension, *that* shall bend ye to it. I do not order ye; ye will it. Cut your seizings and draw the poles, ye harpooneers!"

Silently obeying the order, the three harpooneers now stood with the detached iron part of their harpoons, some three feet long, held, barbs up, before him.

"Stab me not with that keen steel! Cant them; cant them over! know ye not the goblet end? Turn up the socket! So, so; now, ye cupbearers, advance. The irons! take them; hold them while I fill!" Forthwith, slowly going from one officer to the other, he brimmed the harpoon sockets with the fiery waters from the pewter.

"Now, three to three, ye stand. Commend the murderous chalices! Bestow them, ye who are now made parties to this indissoluble league. Ha! Starbuck! but the deed is done! Yon ratifying sun now waits to sit upon it. Drink, ye harpooneers! drink and swear, ye men that man the deathful whaleboat's bow—Death to Moby Dick! God hunt us all if we do not hunt Moby Dick to his death!" The long, barbed steel goblets were lifted; and to cries and maledictions against the white whale, the spirits were simultaneously quaffed down with a hiss. Starbuck paled, and turned, and shivered. Once more, and finally, the replenished pewter went the rounds among the frantic crew; when, waving his hand to them, they all dispersed; and Ahab retired within his cabin.

Robert Lowell

Robert Lowell (1917–77) was born into a Boston Brahmin family with a gift for poetry—his grandfather was the prominent nineteenth-century poet and editor James Russell Lowell (1819–91); one of his elder cousins was Amy Lowell (1874–1925), a pivotal figure in the Imagist movement. His own career as a poet was so distinguished that the mid-twentieth century in American poetry is sometimes called "The Age of Lowell"; he would win every major prize, including two Pulitzers, a National Book Award, a Guggenheim Fellowship, and the Bollingen, as well as awards from the American Academy of Poets and the National Institute of Arts and Letters. In a sense, that career began on Nantucket, where Lowell—following his senior year at St. Mark's School and his freshman year at Harvard—spent the summers of 1935 and 1936 in a cottage near the Coast Guard Station in Madaket. "I spent a couple of summers on Nantucket," Lowell wrote to George Santayana on 12 January 1948, ". . .[and] did most of my first writing there." It would be another eight years—years including a remarkable education at Harvard, Kenyon College, and Louisiana State University as well as mentorship by men of letters such as Robert Frost, Ford Madox Ford, Allan Tate, John Crowe Ransom, and Cleanth Brooks—before those two Nantucket summers bore fruit for Lowell in the form of a poetic masterpiece.

Composed in 1944, "The Quaker Graveyard in Nantucket" can seem "unintelligible," as Lowell himself admitted in his letter to Santayana. But islanders who know the actual Quaker graveyard, with its bare rolling ground and lack of headstones, will quickly understand that the graveyard is a metaphor for the sea. Nantucket readers will also recognize that "'The Quaker Graveyard' is built on Moby-Dick," as Lowell acknowledged, and perhaps will notice that "Five lines from section one are lifted from Thoreau's Cape Cod." Less obvious today than when the poem was composed in 1944 is its commentary on World War II. Although Lowell came from a military family—his father was a career naval officer—and early in the war volunteered several times for service, only to be turned down because of poor eyesight, the poet became a conscientious objector after the Allied firebombing of Hamburg in July 1943. Called "Operation Gomorrah," the Hamburg raids left 50,000 German civilians dead—most of them burned alive—and

500,000 homeless. Drafted later that same year, Lowell refused induction and was sentenced to a year and a day. In January 1944, still in prison, Lowell received word that his first cousin Warren Winslow, a naval officer, had been killed when his ship, the ammunition-laden destroyer U.S.S. Turner, *blew up and sank in New York's Gravesend Bay. Dozens of men, in the words of survivor Robert Freear, were "blown to bits, slowly burned to death, [or] drowned" in that tragic accident. When Lowell wrote "The Quaker Graveyard in Nantucket" in Winslow's memory, he was out on parole, compelled to spend his days mopping floors in a dormitory for army nurses in Bridgeport, Connecticut.*

The Nantucket poem, then, is an extended meditation on the savagery of war. But Lowell gives other clues on how to read the poem. Writing to Babette Deutsch in February 1955, the poet remembered that as he wrote he "grew drunker and drunker with the sea. I put all of my chips on rhythm, more than I have ever done since." Readers should appreciate "The Quaker Graveyard in Nantucket" as poetry—a miracle of wild music. Anthologized in Lord Weary's Castle *(1946), the poem helped bring Lowell his first Pulitzer Prize.*

The Quaker Graveyard in Nantucket

[For Warren Winslow, Dead at Sea]

*Let men have dominion over the fishes of the sea and the fowls of
the air and the beasts of the whole earth, and every creeping creature
that moveth upon the earth.*

I

A brackish reach of shoal off Madaket—
The sea was still breaking violently and night
Had steamed into our North Atlantic Fleet,
When the drowned sailor clutched the drag-net. Light
Flashed from his matted head and marble feet,
He grappled at the net
With the coiled, hurdling muscles of his thighs:
The corpse was bloodless, a botch of reds and whites,
Its open staring eyes
Were lustreless dead-lights
Or cabin-windows on a stranded hulk
Heavy with sand. We weight the body, close
Its eyes and heave it seaward whence it came,
Where the heel-headed dogfish barks its nose
On Ahab's void and forehead; and the name
Is blocked in yellow chalk.
Sailors, who pitch this portent at the sea
Where dreadnaughts shall confess
Its hell-bent deity,
When you are powerless
To sand-bag this Atlantic bulwark, faced
By the earth-shaker, green, unwearied, chaste
In his steel scales: ask for no Orphean lute
To pluck life back. The guns of the steeled fleet
Recoil and then repeat
The hoarse salute.

II

Whenever winds are moving and their breath
Heaves at the roped-in bulwarks of this pier,
The terns and sea-gulls tremble at your death
In these home waters. Sailor, can you hear
The Pequod's sea wings, beating landward, fall
Headlong and break on our Atlantic wall
Off 'Sconset, where the yawing S-boats splash
The bell-buoy, with ballooning spinnakers,
As the entangled, screeching mainsheet clears
The blocks: off Madaket, where lubbers lash
The heavy surf and throw their long lead squids
For blue-fish? Sea-gulls blink their heavy lids
Seaward. The winds' wings beat upon the stones,
Cousin, and scream for you and the claws rush
At the sea's throat and wring it in the slush
Of this old Quaker graveyard where the bones
Cry out in the long night for the hurt beast
Bobbing by Ahab's whaleboats in the East.

III

All you recovered from Poseidon died
With you, my cousin, and the harrowed brine
Is fruitless on the blue beard of the god,
Stretching beyond us to the castles in Spain,
Nantucket's westward haven. To Cape Cod
Guns, cradled on the tide,
Blast the eelgrass about a waterclock
Of bilge and backwash, roil the salt and sand
Lashing earth's scaffold, rock
Our warships in the hand
Of the great God, where time's contrition blues
Whatever it was these Quaker sailors lost
In the mad scramble of their lives. They died
Where time was open-eyed,
Wooden and childish; only bones abide
There, in the nowhere, where their boats were tossed
Sky-high, where mariners had fabled news

Of IS the whited monster. What it cost
Them is their secret. In the sperm-whale's slick
I see the Quakers drown and hear their cry:
"If God himself had not been on our side,
If God himself had not been on our side,
When the Atlantic rose against us, why,
Then it had swallowed us up quick."

IV

This is the end of the whaleroad and the whale
Who spewed Nantucket bones on the thrashed swell
And stirred the troubled waters to whirlpools
To send the Pequod packing off to hell:
This is the end of them, three-quarters fools,
Snatching at straws to sail
Seaward and seaward on the turntail whale,
Spouting out blood and water as it rolls,
Sick as a dog to these Atlantic shoals:
Clamavimus, O depths. Let the sea gulls wail

For water, for the deep where the high-tide
Mutters to its hurt self, mutters and ebbs.
Waves wallow in their wash, go out and out,
Leave only the death-rattle of the crabs,
The beach increasing, its enormous snout
Sucking the ocean's side.
This is the end of running on the waves;
We are poured out like water. Who will dance
The mast-lashed master of Leviathans
Up from this field of Quakers in their unstoned graves?

V

When the whale's viscera go and the roll
Of its corruption overruns this world
Beyond tree-swept Nantucket and Woods Hole
And Martha's Vineyard, Sailor, will your sword
Whistle and fall and sink into the fat?
In the great ash-pit of Jehoshaphat
The bones cry for the blood of the white whale,

The fat flukes arch and whack about its ears,
The death-lance churns into the sanctuary, tears
The gun-blue swingle, heaving like a flail,
And hacks the coiling life out: it works and drags
And rips the sperm-whale's midriff into rags,
Gobbets of blubber spill to wind and weather,
Sailor, and gulls go round the stoven timbers
Where the morning stars sing out together
And thunder shakes the white surf and dismembers
The red flag hammered in the mast-head. Hide,
Our steel, Jonas Messias, in Thy side.

V

Nantucket Women

J. Hector St. John de Crèvecoeur

Crèvecoeur's 1773 visit to Nantucket provides us with one of the most detailed early views of Nantucket women. He connects their unique independence, industry, and ability to manage business to their husbands' long absences at sea in the developing whale fishery. In the process, Crèvecoeur gives us a portrait of the island's most successful female entrepreneur, Kesiah Coffin, later immortalized in Joseph C. Hart's Miriam Coffin, or The Whale-Fishermen. *Here, Kesiah is seen before her fall from grace for profiteering during the American Revolution. Crèvecoeur also records that a large number of island women were addicted to opium, a fact contradicting his cheerful insistence that they were "always happy and healthy" and hinting at the loneliness and stress experienced by wives in maritime communities.*

In a sense, Crèvecoeur's Nantucket women illustrate the overall theme of Letters from an American Farmer—*the success of the American experiment. Nantucket women are to their faraway seafaring husbands as the American colonies are to the Old World; they exemplify the unsuspected vigor of a people freed from oppressive governance. Crèvecoeur practiced what he preached, placing great confidence in the prudence and good management of his American-born wife, Mehitabel Tippet. During the American Revolution, when Crèvecoeur was suspected of being a spy by both sides, he went back to Europe with his eldest son, leaving Mehitabel behind to tend their New York farm and two youngest children. Their separation—like many Nantucket separations—would end tragically. When Crèvecoeur returned in 1783, he would find his wife dead, the farm burned by marauding Indians, and the children missing. In 1790, Crèvecoeur returned to France to live out the remainder of his life amid the chaos of the French Revolution, the Reign of Terror, and the Napoleonic Wars. The story of his remarkable life is well-told in a biography by American literary scholar Thomas Philbrick, father of Nantucket author Nathaniel Philbrick.—SB*

"Peculiar Customs at Nantucket"
From Letter VIII of
Letters from an American Farmer

[. . . .] As THE SEA excursions are often very long, their wives in their absence are necessarily obliged to transact business, to settle accounts, and in short, to rule and provide for their families. These circumstances being often repeated, give women the abilities as well as a taste for that kind of superintendency, to which, by their prudence and good management, they seem to be in general very equal. This employment ripens their judgment, and justly entitles them to a rank superior to that of other wives; and this is the principal reason why those of Nantucket as well as those of Montreal are so fond of society, so affable, and so conversant with the affairs of the world. The men at their return, weary with the fatigues of the sea, full of confidence and love, cheerfully give their consent to every transaction that has happened during their absence, and all is joy and peace. "Wife, thee hast done well," is the general approbation they receive for their application and industry. What would the men do without the agency of these faithful mates? The absence of so many of them at particular seasons, leaves the town quite desolate; and this mournful situation disposes the women to go to each other's house much oftener than when their husbands are at home: hence the custom of incessant visiting has infected every one, and even those whose husbands do not go abroad. The house is always cleaned before they set out, and with peculiar alacrity they pursue their intended visit, which consists of a social chat, a dish of tea, and a hearty supper. When the good man of the house returns from his labour, he peaceably goes after his wife and brings her home; meanwhile the young fellows, equally vigilant, easily find out which is the most convenient house, and there they assemble with the girls of the neighborhood. Instead of cards, musical instruments, or songs, they relate stories of their whaling voyages, their various sea adventures, and talk of the different coasts they have visited. "The island of Catherine in the Brazil," says one, "is a very droll island, it is inhabited by none but men; women are not permitted to come in sight of it; not a woman is there on the whole island. Who among us is not glad it is not so here? The Nantucket girls and boys beat the world." At this innocent sally the titter goes round, they whisper to one another their spontaneous reflections: puddings, pies, and custards never fail to be pro-

duced on such occasions; for I believe there never were any people in their circumstances, who live so well, even to superabundance. As inebriation is
unknown, and music, singing, and dancing, are held in equal detestation, they
never could fill all the vacant hours of their lives without the repast of the table.
Thus these young people sit and talk, and divert themselves as well as they can;
if any one has lately returned from a cruise, he is generally the speaker of the
night; they often all laugh and talk together, but they are happy, and would not
exchange their pleasures for those of the most brilliant assemblies in Europe.
This lasts until the father and mother return; when all retire to their respective
homes, the men re-conducting the partners of their affections.

Thus they spend many of the youthful evenings of their lives; no wonder
therefore, that they marry so early. But no sooner have they undergone this ceremony than they cease to appear so cheerful and gay; the new rank they hold in
the society impresses them with more serious ideas than were entertained before.
The title of master of a family necessarily requires more solid behaviour and
deportment; the new wife follows in the trammels of Custom, which are as powerful as the tyranny of fashion; she gradually advises and directs; the new husband
soon goes to sea, he leaves her to learn and exercise the new government, in
which she is entered. Those who stay at home are full as passive in general, at least
with regard to the inferior departments of the family. But you must not imagine
from this account that the Nantucket wives are turbulent, of high temper, and
difficult to be ruled; on the contrary, the wives of Sherburn in so doing, comply
only with the prevailing custom of the island: the husbands, equally submissive to
the ancient and respectable manners of their country, submit, without ever sus-
pecting that there can be any impropriety. Were they to behave otherwise, they
would be afraid of subverting the principles of their society by altering its ancient
rules; thus both parties are perfectly satisfied, and all is peace and concord. The
richest person now in the island owes all his present prosperity and success to the
ingenuity of his wife: this is a known fact which is well recorded; for while he
was performing his first cruises, she traded with pins and needles, and kept a
school. Afterward she purchased more considerable articles, which she sold with
so much judgment, that she laid the foundation of a system of business, that she
has ever since prosecuted with equal dexterity and success. She wrote to London,
formed connections, and, in short, became the only ostensible instrument of that
house, both at home and abroad. Who is he in this country, and who is a citizen of
Nantucket or Boston, who does not know *Aunt Kesiah?* I must tell you that she is
the wife of Mr. C—n, a very respectable man, who, well pleased with all her
schemes, trusts to her judgment, and relies on her sagacity, with so entire a confidence, as to be altogether passive to the concerns of his family. They have the best
country seat on the island, at Quayes, where they live with hospitality, and in perfect union. He seems to be altogether the contemplative man.

To this dexterity in managing the husband's business whilst he is absent, the Nantucket wives unite a great deal of industry. They spin, or cause to be spun in their houses, abundance of wool and flax; and would be forever disgraced and looked upon as idlers if all the family were not clad in good, neat, and sufficient homespun cloth. First Days are the only seasons when it is lawful for both sexes to exhibit some garments of English manufacture; even these are of the most moderate price, and of the gravest colours: there is no kind of difference in their dress, they are all clad alike, and resemble in that respect members of one family.

A singular custom prevails here among the women, at which I was greatly surprised; and am really at a loss how to account for the original cause that has introduced in this primitive society so remarkable a fashion, or rather so extraordinary a want. They have adopted these many years the Asiatic custom of taking a dose of opium every morning; and so deeply rooted is it, that they would be at a loss how to live without this indulgence; they would rather be deprived of any necessary than forego their favourite luxury. This is much more prevailing among the women than the men, few of the latter having caught the contagion; though the sheriff, whom I may call the first person in the island, who is an eminent physician beside, and whom I had the pleasure of being well acquainted with, has for many years submitted to this custom. He takes three grains of it every day after breakfast, without the effects of which, he often told me, he was not able to transact any business.

It is hard to conceive how a people always happy and healthy, in consequence of the exercise and labour they undergo, never oppressed with the vapours of idleness, yet should want the fictitious effects of opium to preserve that cheerfulness to which their temperance, their climate, their happy situation so justly entitle them. But where is the society perfectly free from error or folly; the least imperfect is undoubtedly that where the greatest good preponderates; and agreeable to this rule, I can truly say, that I never was acquainted with a less vicious, or a more harmless one.

Lucretia Coffin Mott

Nineteenth-century women's rights activist, abolitionist, Quaker minister, religious reformer, and co-founder of Swarthmore College, Lucretia Coffin Mott (1793–1880) was born in a big house (since torn down) on Nantucket's Fair Street. Her father, Thomas Coffin Jr., was a sea captain away for years at a time on Pacific whaling voyages. Her mother, Anna Folger Coffin, ran a shop to support the family while Thomas was at sea and held a mariner's power of attorney allowing her to transact business in his stead—a common arrangement on Nantucket, but otherwise a rare form of economic empowerment in an era when married women could not legally own property. Anna herself was often away on business, and when her mother was gone, Lucretia cared for an older, handicapped sister and five younger siblings. Speaking at a women's rights convention in 1853, she would recall how the Nantucket way of life molded smart and independent women:

> On the island of Nantucket—for I was born on that island—I remember how our mothers were employed, while our fathers were at sea. The mothers with the small children around them—'twas not customary to have nurses then—kept small groceries and sold provisions, that they might make something in the absence of their husbands. At that time it required some money and more courage to go to Boston— they were obliged to go to that city—make their trades, exchange their oils and candles for dry goods, and all the varieties of a country store, set their own price, keep their own accounts, and with all of this have very little help in the family, to which they must discharge their duties. Look at the heads of these women; they can mingle with men; they are not triflers; they have intelligent subjects of conversation.

Quakerism was the dominant religion on the island, and Lucretia also benefited from the Quaker belief that all souls are equal in the eyes of the Lord. Writing to fellow suffragist Elizabeth Cady Stanton in 1855, she would boast that on the island "education & intellectual culture have been for years equal for girls & boys—so that their women are prepared to be companions of men in every sense—and their social circles are never divided." In Quaker meetings, where there was no ordained minister but members of the congregation instead rose to speak as the Spirit moved, she found vocal women actively engaged in moral and religious leadership. In the Monthly Meeting of Friends on Nantucket, she would write, "the women have long been regarded as the stronger part—

This is owing to so many of the men being away at sea." Together with her famous ancestor Mary Coffin Starbuck, such women provided role models for Lucretia and gave her a sense of vocation: "In the early settlement of that Island Mary Starbuck bore a prominent place as a wise counselor & a remarkably strong mind—Divers Quaker women since that time have been eminent as preachers."

When Lucretia was almost twelve years old, her father's ship, the Trial, was captured by a Spanish man o' war. In reduced circumstances, Thomas Coffin elected to give up the sea and move his family to the mainland. Lucretia was devastated to leave Nantucket, but excelled as a student and then as a teacher at a Quaker boarding school in New York, eventually marrying the superintendent's son, social activist James Mott. A devoted wife and a loving mother to an eventual six children, Lucretia nevertheless continued to hone her public-speaking skills and her sense of ministry at Quaker meetings. By the age of twenty-eight, she had entered on her life's work as a "Public Friend," a Quaker minister traveling far and wide to give countless speeches and sermons that would change the course of the nation. Her tireless campaigning helped to end slavery and to begin the women's movement in the United States. Throughout it all, Mott's sense of women's potential was deeply rooted in what she called "the Nantucket way."

Here is a selection from one of Mott's best-known speeches on women's rights, delivered at the Assembly buildings in Philadelphia on 17 December 1849.—SB

From "Discourse on Woman"

[. . . .] THE QUESTION is often asked, "What does woman want, more than she enjoys? What is she seeking to obtain? Of what rights is she deprived? What privileges are withheld from her? I answer, she asks nothing as favor, but as right, she wants to be acknowledged a moral, responsible being. She is seeking not to be governed by laws, in the making of which she has no voice. She is deprived of almost every right in civil society, and is a cypher in the nation, except in the right of presenting a petition. In religious society her disabilities, as already pointed out, have greatly retarded her progress. Her exclusion from the pulpit or ministry—her duties marked out for her by her equal brother man, subject to creeds, rules, and disciplines made for her by him—this is unworthy her true dignity. In marriage, there is assumed superiority, on the part of the husband, and admitted inferiority, with a promise of obedience, on the part of the wife. This subject calls loudly for examination, in order that the wrong may be redressed. Customs suited to darker ages in Eastern countries, are not binding upon enlightened society. The solemn covenant of marriage may be entered into without these lordly assumptions, and humiliating concessions and promises. [. . . .]

It is with reluctance that I make the demand for the political rights of woman, because this claim is so distasteful to the age. Woman shrinks, in the present state of society, from taking any interest in politics. The events of the French Revolution and the claim for woman's rights are held up to her as a warning. But let us not look at the excesses of women alone, at that period; but remember that the age was marked with extravagances and wickedness in men as well as women. Indeed, political life abounds with these excesses, and with shameful outrage. Who knows, but that if woman acted her part in governmental affairs, there might be an entire change in the turmoil of political life. It becomes man to speak modestly of his ability to act without her. If woman's judgment were exercised, why might she not aid in making the laws by which she is governed? Lord Brougham remarked that the works of Harriet Martineau upon Political Economy were not excelled by those of any political writer of the present time. The first few chapters of her "Society in America," her views of a Republic, and of Government generally, furnish evidence of woman's capacity to embrace subjects of universal interest.

Far be it from me to encourage woman to vote, or to take an active part in politics, in the present state of our government. Her right to the elective franchise, however, is the same, and should be yielded to her, whether she exercise that right or not. Would that man too, would have no participation in a government based upon the life-taking principle—upon retaliation and the sword. It is unworthy a Christian nation. But when, in the diffusion of light and intelligence, a convention shall be called to make regulations for self-government on Christian, non-resistant principles, I can see no good reason, why woman should not participate in such an assemblage, taking part equally with man.

Walker, of Cincinnati, in his *Introduction to American Law,* says:

With regard to political rights, females form a positive exception to the general doctrine of equality. They have no part or lot in the formation or administration of government. They cannot vote or hold office. We require them to contribute their share in the way of taxes, to the support of government, but allow them no voice in its direction. We hold them amenable to the laws when made, but allow them no share in making them. This language, applied to males, would be the exact definition of political slavery; applied to females, custom does not teach us so to regard it.

Woman, however, is beginning so to regard it.

The law of husband and wife, as you gather it from the books, is a disgrace to any civilized nation. The theory of the law degrades the wife almost to the level of slaves. When a woman marries, we call her condition coverture, and speak of her as a *femme covert.* The old writers call the husband baron, and sometimes, in plain English, lord. The merging of her name in that of her *husband* is emblematic of the fate of all her legal rights. The torch of Hymen serves but to light the pile, on which these rights are offered up. The legal theory is that marriage makes the husband and wife one person, and that person is the husband. On this subject, reform is loudly called for. There is no foundation in reason or expediency, for the absolute and slavish subjection of the wife to the husband, which forms the foundation of the present legal relations. Were woman, in point of fact, the abject thing which the law, in theory, considers her to be when married, she would not be worthy the companionship of man.

I would ask if such a code of laws does not require change? If such a condition of the wife in society does not claim redress? On no good ground can reform be delayed. Blackstone says, "The very being and legal existence of woman is suspended during marriage,—incorporated or consolidated into that of her husband, under whose protection and cover she performs every thing." Hurlbut, in his *Essays upon Human Rights,* says:

The laws touching the rights of woman are at variance with the laws of the Creator. Rights are human rights, and pertain to human beings, without distinction of sex. Laws should not be made for man or for woman, but for mankind. Man was not born to command, nor woman to obey. The law of France, Spain, and Holland, and one of our own States, Louisiana, recognizes the wife's right to property, more than the common law of England. The law depriving woman of the right of property is handed down to us from dark and feudal times, and not consistent with the wiser, better, purer spirit of the age. The wife is a mere pensioner on the bounty of her husband. Her lost rights are appropriated to himself. But justice and benevolence are abroad in our land, awakening the spirit of inquiry and innovation; and the Gothic fabric of the British law will fall before it, save where it is based upon the foundation of truth and justice.

May these statements lead you to reflect upon this subject, that you may know what woman's condition is in society—what her restrictions are, and seek to remove them. In how many cases in our country, the husband and wife begin life together, and by equal industry and united effort accumulate to themselves a comfortable home. In the event of the death of the wife, the household remains undisturbed, his farm or his workshop is not broken up, or in any way molested. But when the husband dies, he either gives his wife a *portion* of their joint accumulation, or the law apportions to her a *share;* the homestead is broken up, and she is dispossessed of that which she earned equally with him; for what she lacked in physical strength, she made up in constancy of labor and toil, day and evening. The sons then coming into possession of the property, as has been the custom until of latter time, speak of having to *keep* their mother, when she in reality is aiding to keep them. Where is the justice of this state of things? The change in the law of this State and of New York, in relation to the property of the wife, go to a limited extent, toward the redress of these wrongs; but they are far more extensive, and involve much more, than I have time this evening to point out.

On no good ground can the legal existence of the wife be suspended during marriage, and her property surrendered to her husband. In the intelligent ranks of society, the wife may not in point of fact, be so degraded as the law would degrade her; because public sentiment is above the law. Still, while the law stands, she is liable to the disabilities which it imposes. Among the ignorant classes of society, woman is made to bear heavy burdens, and is degraded almost to the level of the slave.

There are many instances now in our city, where the wife suffers much from the power of the husband to claim all that she can earn with her own hands. In my intercourse with the poorer class of people, I have known cases of extreme cruelty, from the hard earnings of the wife being thus robbed by the husband, and no redress at law.

An article in one of the daily papers lately, presented the condition of needle women in England. There might be a presentation of this class in our own country, which would make the heart bleed. Public attention should be turned to this subject, in order that avenues of more profitable employment may be opened to women. There are many kinds of business which women, equally with men, may follow with respectability and success. Their talents and energies should be called forth, and their powers brought into the highest exercise. The efforts of women in France are sometimes pointed to in ridicule and sarcasm, but depend upon it, the opening of profitable employment to women in that country, is doing much for the enfranchisement of the sex. In England also, it is not an uncommon thing for a wife to take up the business of her deceased husband and carry it on with success.

Our respected British Consul stated to me a circumstance which occurred some years ago, of an editor of a political paper having died in England; it was proposed to his wife, an able writer, to take the editorial chair. She accepted. The patronage of the paper was greatly increased, and she a short time since retired from her labors with a handsome fortune. In that country however, the opportunities are by no means general for Woman's elevation.

In visiting the public school in London, a few years since, I noticed that the boys were employed in linear drawing, and instructed upon the black board, in the higher branches of arithmetic and mathematics; while the girls, after a short exercise in the mere elements of arithmetic, were seated, during the bright hours of the morning, *stitching wristbands*. I asked, Why there should be this difference made; why they too should not have the black board? The answer was, that they would not probably fill any station in society requiring such knowledge.

But the demand for a more extended education will not cease, until girls and boys have equal instruction, in all the departments of useful knowledge. We have as yet no high school for girls in this state. The normal school may be a preparation for such an establishment. In the late convention for general education, it was cheering to hear the testimony borne to woman's capabilities for head teachers of the public schools. A resolution there offered for equal salaries to male and female teachers, when equally qualified, as practised in Louisiana, I regret to say was checked in its passage, by Bishop Potter; by him who has done so much for the encouragement of education, and who gave his countenance and influence to that convention. Still the fact of such a resolution being offered, augurs a time coming for woman, which she may well hail. At the last examination of the public schools in this city, one of the alumni delivered an address on Woman, not as is too common, in eulogistic strains, but directing the attention to the injustice done to woman in her position in society, in a variety of ways. The unequal wages she receives for her constant toil, &c., presenting facts calculated to arouse attention to the subject.

Women's property has been taxed, equally with that of men's, to sustain colleges endowed by the states; but they have not been permitted to enter those high seminaries of learning. Within a few years, however, some colleges have been instituted, where young women are admitted, nearly upon equal terms with young men; and numbers are availing themselves of their long denied rights. This is among the signs of the times, indicative of an advance for women. The book of knowledge is not opened to her in vain. Already is she aiming to occupy important posts of honor and profit in our country. We have three female editors in our state—some in other states of the Union. Numbers are entering the medical profession—one received a diploma last year; others are preparing for a like result.

Let woman then go on—not asking as favor, but claiming as right, the removal of all the hindrances to her elevation in the scale of being—let her receive encouragement for the proper cultivation of all her powers, so that she may enter profitably into the active business of life; employing her own hands in ministering to her necessities, strengthening her physical being by proper exercise and observance of the laws of health. Let her not be ambitious to display a fair hand, and to promenade the fashionable streets of our city, but rather, coveting earnestly the best gifts, let her strive to occupy such walks in society, as will befit her true dignity in all the relations of life. No fear that she will then transcend the proper limits of female delicacy. True modesty will be as fully preserved, in acting out those important vocations to which she may be called, as in the nursery or at the fireside, ministering to man's self-indulgence.

Then in the marriage union, the independence of the husband and wife will be equal, their dependence mutual, and their obligations reciprocal.

In conclusion, let me say, "Credit not the old fashioned absurdity, that woman's is a secondary lot, ministering to the necessities of her lord and master! It is a higher destiny I would award you. If your immortality is as complete, and your gift of mind as capable as ours, of increase and elevation, I would put no wisdom of mine against God's evident allotment. I would charge you to water the undying bud, and give it healthy culture, and open its beauty to the sun—and then you may hope, that when your life is bound up with another, you will go on equally, and in a fellowship that shall pervade every earthly interest."

Lucretia Coffin Mott, Elizabeth Cady Stanton, Mary Ann McClintock, Martha Coffin Wright, Jane Hunt

The abolition of slavery was the first cause of Nantucket-born reformer Lucretia Coffin Mott (1793-1880). As a Quaker schoolgirl on Nantucket, she received her introduction to the anti-slavery movement in a primer titled Mental Improvement, by English Friend Priscilla Wakefield, a text dwelling in graphic detail on infants torn from their mothers' arms and on the horrors of the Middle Passage. Fired with a sense of injustice, Lucretia memorized a long section for recitation to her classmates. As an adult, she would aid William Garrison in the foundation of the American Anti-Slavery Society and, on her own, create the Philadelphia Female Anti-Slavery Society. A brilliant public speaker, Mott won thousands to the cause and would risk her life to address hostile mobs. About her efforts, black orator and abolitionist Frederick Douglass would recall:

> When the true history of the anti-slavery cause shall be written, woman shall occupy a large space in its pages; for the cause of the slave has been peculiarly woman's cause.
> . . . Foremost among these notable women who in point of clearness of vision, breadth of understanding, fullness of knowledge, catholicity of spirit, weight of character, and widespread influence, was Lucretia Mott. . . . In a few moments after she began to speak, I saw before me no more a woman, but a glorified presence, bearing a message of light and love from the Infinite to a benighted and strangely wandering world. . . .

In 1840, Mott and her husband, James, were elected delegates to the World's Anti-Slavery Convention held in London. When Mott arrived, however, this consummate orator learned that female delegates would not be permitted to speak or even allowed on the convention floor. Women were not to be seen or heard; instead they were forced to listen to the proceedings from behind a screen at the back of the hall. There Mott found herself standing next to a young woman named Elizabeth Cady Stanton (1815–1902), and *the historic friendship kindled in that moment would bring forth out of the anti-slavery cause the woman suffrage movement.*

Perhaps their finest moment came in 1848, when a Quaker woman named Jane Hunt (1812–89) invited Mott and Stanton to a tea party with another friend, Mary Ann McClintock (1800–84), and with Mott's younger sister, Martha Coffin Wright (1806–75). Sitting around a mahogany tea table, the five women found themselves pouring out their grievances at the position of women in society. Stanton was especially fired up, and later remembered: "I stirred myself, as well as the rest of the party, to do and dare anything." Over the next few days, the women would plan the nation's first Women's Rights Convention, to be held in Seneca Falls, New York. Together, they would write the convention's resolutions and plan its speeches. And, together, they would draft the foundation document of the American women's movement, the "Declaration of Sentiments." Lucretia Coffin Mott, the eldest and most experienced reformer and speaker, and the mentor of the young women, would not only do the lion's share of the speaking at the convention, but would be the first of sixty-eight women and thirty-two men to sign the document. Thus did a woman steeped in "the Nantucket way" help set the nation on the long and arduous road to the passage of the Nineteenth Amendment in 1920.—SB

The Declaration of Sentiments

WHEN, IN THE course of human events, it becomes necessary for one portion of the family of man to assume among the people of the earth a position different from that which they have hitherto occupied, but one to which the laws of nature and of nature's God entitle them, a decent respect to the opinions of mankind requires that they should declare the causes that impel them to such a course.

We hold these truths to be self-evident: that all men and women are created equal; that they are endowed by their Creator with certain inalienable rights; that among these are life, liberty, and the pursuit of happiness; that to secure these rights governments are instituted, deriving their just powers from the consent of the governed. Whenever any form of government becomes destructive of these ends, it is the right of those who suffer from it to refuse allegiance to it, and to insist upon the institution of a new government, laying its foundation on such principles, and organizing its powers in such form, as to them shall seem most likely to effect their safety and happiness. Prudence, indeed, will dictate that governments long established should not be changed for light and transient causes; and accordingly all experience hath shown that mankind are more disposed to suffer, while evils are sufferable, than to right themselves by abolishing the forms to which they were accustomed. But when a long train of abuses and usurpations, pursuing invariably the same object, evinces a design to reduce them under absolute despotism, it is their duty to throw off such government, and to provide new guards for their future security. Such has been the patient sufferance of the women under this government, and such is now the necessity which constrains them to demand the equal station to which they are entitled.

The history of mankind is a history of repeated injuries and usurpations on the part of man toward woman, having in direct object the establishment of an absolute tyranny over her. To prove this, let facts be submitted to a candid world.

He has never permitted her to exercise her inalienable right to the elective franchise.

He has compelled her to submit to laws, in the formation of which she had no voice.

He has withheld from her rights which are given to the most ignorant and degraded men—both natives and foreigners.

Having deprived her of this first right of a citizen, the elective franchise, thereby leaving her without representation in the halls of legislation, he has oppressed her on all sides.

He has made her, if married, in the eye of the law, civilly dead.

He has taken from her all right in property, even to the wages she earns.

He has made her, morally, an irresponsible being, as she can commit many crimes with impunity, provided they be done in the presence of her husband. In the covenant of marriage, she is compelled to promise obedience to her husband, he becoming to all intents and purposes, her master—the law giving him power to deprive her of her liberty, and to administer chastisement.

He has so framed the laws of divorce, as to what shall be the proper causes, and in case of separation, to whom the guardianship of the children shall be given, as to be wholly regardless of the happiness of women—the law, in all cases, going upon a false supposition of the supremacy of man, and giving all power into his hands.

After depriving her of all rights as a married woman, if single, and the owner of property, he has taxed her to support a government which recognizes her only when her property can be made profitable to it.

He has monopolized nearly all the profitable employments, and from those she is permitted to follow, she receives but a scanty remuneration. He closes against her all the avenues to wealth and distinction which he considers most honorable to himself. As a teacher of theology, medicine, or law, she is not known.

He has denied her the facilities for obtaining a thorough education, all colleges being closed against her.

He allows her in Church, as well as State, but a subordinate position, claiming Apostolic authority for her exclusion from the ministry, and, with some exceptions, from any public participation in the affairs of the Church.

He has created a false public sentiment by giving to the world a different code of morals for men and women, by which moral delinquencies which exclude women from society, are not only tolerated, but deemed of little account in man.

He has usurped the prerogative of Jehovah himself, claiming it as his right to assign for her a sphere of action, when that belongs to her conscience and to her God.

He has endeavored, in every way that he could, to destroy her confidence in her own powers, to lessen her self-respect, and to make her willing to lead a dependent and abject life.

Now, in view of this entire disfranchisement of one-half the people of this country, their social and religious degradation—in view of the unjust laws above mentioned, and because women do feel themselves aggrieved, oppressed, and fraudulently deprived of their most sacred rights, we insist that they have immediate admission to all the rights and privileges which belong to them as citizens of the United States.

In entering upon the great work before us, we anticipate no small amount of misconception, misrepresentation, and ridicule; but we shall use every instrumentality within our power to effect our object. We shall employ agents, circulate tracts, petition the State and National legislatures, and endeavor to enlist the pulpit and the press in our behalf. We hope this Convention will be followed by a series of Conventions embracing every part of the country.

Eliza Spencer Brock

Contemporary women readers, spurred on, perhaps, by contemporary novels such as *Sena Jeter Naslund's* Ahab's Wife, *love to imagine the fictive adventures of Nantucket's whaling women, sailing with their captain husbands into exotic seas on the far side of the world. But the fact is, as whaling scholar Joan Druett reminds us, that "over the first four and a half decades of the [nineteenth] century, when thousands of whaleships departed American ports, only about two dozen New England wives accompanied their men to sea." Whaling was a brutal, greasy, and dangerous business pursued by brutal, greasy, and dangerous men who often "hung up their morals on Cape Horn" to be picked up on the return voyage. A whaleship was no place for a respectable woman; her role was to keep the home fires burning. Not until the middle of the nineteenth century, when whaling had already begun its long decline, did new ideas about the capacities of women and increasingly civilized ports of call in the Pacific make it acceptable for some wives to accompany their captain husbands. Even then, the practice often owed more to the captains' desires for female companionship and domestic comfort than to the women's interest in spending months and even years away from family, friends, and the company of their own sex, confined in an all-male shipboard society where they had no important role to play.*

Nantucketer Eliza Spencer Brock (1810–99), who accompanied her husband Captain Peter C. Brock on a whaling voyage from 21 May 1853 to 25 June 1856, has left us one of the most important written records of what this experience was really like. Her "Journal Kept On Board the Ship Lexington," which made a whaling voyage around the Cape of Good Hope, into the South Pacific, and far up into dangerous Arctic seas pursuing increasingly scarce whales, is one of the great treasures of the Nantucket Historical Association's manuscript collections. The journal records her intense loneliness "shut up" in her "Ocean dwelling." Eliza's five-year-old son, Joseph Chase, accompanied her on the Lexington's voyage, but she left behind three other children—William, a boy just seven years old; Lydia, her second born; and Oliver, a son who had gone to sea two years before his mother's departure. For Eliza, life at sea is tedium and monotony punctuated by moments of fear, when men are carried out of boats by whales, icebergs growl along the hull, news comes of ships wrecked and husbands lost, and death seems

omnipresent. Even ashore on those exotic Pacific islands, homesickness rules her sensibil-
ities. The Sandwich Islands are memorable because there is mail from home waiting there.
In New Zealand, surrounded by tattooed Maori natives with baskets of fruit, she thinks
of how her children would enjoy it. Delighted to spend a couple of weeks with other
Nantucket captains' wives when the Lexington refits at Bay of Islands, she finds herself
devastated to leave them when the time comes to depart.

For Eliza, the three-year voyage of the Lexington seemed endless. Even her unusual
punctuation attests to this—phrases, sentence fragments, and sentences alike are often
spliced together with commas and semicolons. She almost never uses a period—even daily
entries in her journal sometimes end with semicolons, as one day flows into the next, and
the ship sails on and on. Eliza Brock's life aboard the Lexington may seem romantic to
us today, but her journal is living proof of why Nantucket women famously located freedom and empowerment at home—on shore—and not at sea. —SB

From "Journal Aboard the Whaleship *Lexington*"

Ship *Lexington,* on the coast of New Zealand

Saturday, November the 12th [1853]
Light wind at east and pleasant, steered SSE saw nothing, dreary dull pastime here no whales. I am anxious to see whaling begun but will try to have Patience we are almost six months out and no Oil. . . .

Sunday, November the 13 [1853]
Light wind at NE; ship headed ESE saw nothing at night shortened sail; this is a lonesome quiet day upon the Ocean, no unnecessary work done on the Sabbath; plenty of time to read and write. . . .

Tuesday, November the 15, [1853]
Light wind at SE by E, Ship headed SSW four men at mast head on the look out all day long no Whales to be seen, dull times with us, but Hope for better days if it was not for Hope the heart would break, F. Thayer the carpenter quite sick Middle part pleasant bright moonlight, Last fresh breeze, Ship headed South

Sunday, November the 20, [1853]
Light wind at ESE, pleasant weather for this Coast, no Whales to be seen; dull times with us, six months out Tomorrow, time flies swiftly away after awhile the voyage will be over whales or none; it is quite discouraging cruising about here day after day looking for Sperm Whales and not seeing any; we are now bound South, again to try our luck there, perhaps we may be more successful Middle and Last pleasant, weather warm, Ship headed SSW.

Monday, November the 21, [1853]
Light wind at ENE, Steered SSW fine pleasant weather; caught an Albacore fish that weighed 70 [lbs?], a monster, at night took in sail, Middle moderate cloudy weather, Last wind North and Rainy, Ship headed SW, six months yesterday since I left my Native Isle, my home, Children and Friends, I long to see them all but now the Time seems far distant for us to return home again; but it flies swiftly away and the years will come round, there will be an end to this voyage, the same as there is to all things beneath the Sun;

Ship *Lexington,* Cruising About the Curtiss Islands

Monday, December the 12th [1853]
Light wind at west, at 2 pm saw a school of Whales; at 2:30 lowered and struck him had two Boats stove; and the Third Mate Mr. Luces Leg Broke short off just above the ankle; a sad accident; Capt and Mate set the bone; here he lays in the Cabin helpless; how little we know in the morning what will be before night; at 3 pm got the Stoven Boats on board, a Loose Iron cut off the line and I am sorry to say that they lost the Whale; a sad disappointment to all; Two Ships in sight Sunday and Macauleys Islands in sight; Last Part, calm; some employed in mending the Stoven Boats . . . .

Tuesday, December the 13th, 1853
Light aires and calm; at 2 pm finished one Boat; hard rain; Mr. Luces leg in great Pain this is a gloomy day to me; but an alwise God is ever watching over us and ordereth all things aright; this is a troublesome world; but it is not our home, we are passing along through this vale of tears; our life is a dream; there is a better world than this and a rest that remaineth for the People of God; where there shall be no more sighing neither any more Dying; . . . .Middle part moderate and rainy, two ships in sight; Last part Strong Wind; at 11 am spoke Ship Caroline of New Bedford, 250 bbls 16 mos. out; Capt. Gifford very unwell; he reported the loss of Ship Susan in the Arctic Ocean crushed by the ice; very bad weather there, most of the Fleet had done nothing, he also reported Ship Norman of Nantucket in November lost at Mowee with 600 bbls sperm Oil. . . .

Monday, January the 9, 1854;
Strong wind at SE thick and Rainy very Rugged; Ship under the Foresail, and Close Reefed Main Topsails; at 3 pm; began to moderate, Clear; set the Mizzen Topsail, nothing to be seen but the dark heaving Sea and dark heavy Clouds hanging all around, and nothing to be heard but the screaming of the Sea Bird and the howling of the wind; how true the saying they that go down to the Sea in Ships that traverse the deep, these are they that see the works of God and his Wonders in the Mighty Deep; Middle & Last light wind saw a sail and Macauleys Rocks. Saw grampuses mistook them to be a school of Whales; lowered the boats & chased but could not get up with them; Boats still off chasing;

Ship *Lexington* Under Way bound out of Maui

Sunday, November the 19, 1854
Light wind at S, ship ready for sea, at 2 pm got under way, Ship lying off and on; at 4 pm Boat came on Board, from on Shore, made Sail and passed out, between the two islands, Morotoi and Rania, bound down to Atooi for

recruits. Last part wind SW, Ten Ships in sight weather fine very cool and comfortable, on board the Ship I am quite glad to get back again, after spending
Twelve Days on Shore; have had a pleasant visit and met with many old
acquaintances all of whom I was glad to see. I received a lot of letters from my
family and Friends at home, feel that I have great cause to be thankful, that they
all were enjoying good health and so many other blessings, hope in time to
meet them all again;

Ship *Lexington* Bound Into the Bay of Islands

Tuesday morning the 13, [February 1855]
Fine weather, but Cool two Boats alongside loaded, with Peaches, the Decks
Thronged with Natives, Men Women and Children their Faces all Tatooed and
for an Ornament a Whale's Tooth tied around the neck, Their Dresses, made
Loose and very Short; all Barefooted and Headed. It is quite amusing to see
them and hear them jabber and see them go up and down the side of the Ship
just like cats. . . .

Ship *Lexington* at Anchor in the Bay of Islands

Tuesday noon the 13, [February 1855]
Ship *Enterprise* of New Bedford here five months from home. Deck still thronged
with natives; loaded down with Peaches; if I could only pass a few baskets of
them to my Children at home, I should like it. One large canoe paddled by eight
Ladies. They seem to manage them as easily as our Sailors do their Boats. It is a
matter of wonder to me how they do it. Capt Nickerson of the *Ganges* called on
board, Mrs Nickerson on shore has an infant six weeks old. Staying at Dr. Fords.
This is a beautiful Bay, much pleasanter to me than Maui. . . .

Wednesday the 14 [February 1855]
All ready for a Start, Boat waiting, Carpenter on Board repairing the Mast. Deck
thronged with Native visitors with loads of Peaches, and Pears, Honey, Fish, etc.
One head of Tobacco will buy a basketful. 10 o'clock am on Shore. Stopping at
the Russell Hotel, kept by Mr Evens and Lady, English residents have been here
Twelve years, been Burned out once in the time, keep a Bar Room in one
Room of the house. Capt gone off on Board the Cutter, to buy Potatoes and
Onions. Joseph Chase quite delighted running about seeing the Goats, and Dogs,
which are very plenty, Wednesday noon Dr Ford's Wife and Mrs Nickerson called
on me, went with them up to the house and took Tea, found Mrs Grant, well, and
in good Spirits. Stayed until 3 o'clock, heard some sweet music a German teacher
Played and Sung on the Piano Forte, he is the most delightful singer I ever heard

Sunday the 25 [February 1855]

Received a note this morning from Mrs Ford saying Mrs Grant was confined this morning at 5 o'clock requesting me to come directly on Shore; Sunday eve just came on board the Ship; spent the day with Mrs Grant and found and left her very comfortable, has a beautiful Babe named Elinor [?] Baker, hard rain storm; Capt Pease spent the day on board, Mr Fisher gone up river after Peaches, Mr Fisher just got back dripping wet without any Peaches, the Natives would not trade on the Sabbath. Boat going up again Tomorrow.

Ship *Lexington* at the Bay of Islands, Ready for Sea

Monday eve, February the 26, [1855]

Just returned on Board been at Doctor Fords and took tea, found Mrs Grant and Babe doing well, felt very bad in parting with her, knowing that it will be a long time before we meet again, if ever, she is a very fine woman, one that I dearly love, Tomorrow morning if it is a fair wind we leave this beautiful Bay of Islands, and wend our way to the Cold Stormy Regions of the North, there to spend one more Summer amongst the Ice and Snow. . . .

Ship *Lexington* Under Way Bound out of the Bay of Islands

Tuesday, the 27 of February [1855] Tuesday evening

Ship out all clear of the land, Pilot gone on Shore, the Planter going along in Company with us. Strong wind and rugged, the shades of evening fast approaching and the dim distant land receding from my view, causing me to feel sad and lonely; my home is on the deep waters.

> Shades of evening close not o'er us,
> Leave our lonely bark awhile,
> Morn, alas, will not restore us,
> Yonder, dim, and distant Isle. . . .

Ship *Lexington* Cruising Round about Jonas Island

Thursday the 7, [June 1855]

Light wind at S at 1 pm Fog lighted a little seven Ships all near us and Ice all round, a dismal looking sight one Ship closed up in it with all sail clued down, at 5 pm spoke Ship *Eliza Adams* Hawse of New Bedford, seven months out, two whales. They reported the loss of Ship *Edgar* of Fall River on Jonas Island, went on Shore, Sunday night last, in the fog all hands saved Ship high up on the Beach; why they did not hear the Howl of the Seal in time to keep off Shore is quite a matter of wonder to all; they are distinctly heard one mile, or more.

They howl and bark just like a Dog. Middle and Last a Calm and thick Fog, as usual. Seven Ships round us, so ends

> And they feared exceedingly, and said to one another; what manner of man is this that even the winds and the Sea obey him, the disciples stand aghast, and hear the winds, rebuked, and the Sea, becalmed;

Ship *Lexington* Cruising in the Ochotsk Sea; 1855

Friday the 15, [June]
Light wind at NNW steering W, heavy Ice, on the larboard side; three ships in sight running down to us, at 7 pm, spoke Ship *Montreal* of New Bedford; we went on board at 9 o'clock in the evening and stopped until Eleven had a first rate gam and social visit, with Mrs. Gray; they have two children with them, the little Boy eighteen months old, was born off Cape Horn, the little girl Kate was quite delighted seeing Joseph Chase Middle fine weather, nine ships in sight Last the same Boats down in the Ice looking for Whales; Ship running along the edge of the Ice; the *Montreal*'s boats in the Ice, this is a hard way of Whaling to have to lower to look the Whales up, it reminds me of going a Blackberrying;

Ship *Lexington* Cruising on the Line for Whales

Tuesday, January the 1, 1856. I wish a happy New Year to All.

> Tis the New Year's Morn; but ah, alone.
> Shut up in the Ocean dwelling,
> There comes to my ear no cheering tone,
> From the heart of Friendship swelling,
> And I think of the friends I left on land,
> And how they today are meeting
> And pledging anew the friendly hand,
> With a hearty New Year's greeting.

Middle and Last part of this day Strong Trades, Ship headed NW at Night took in Sail and Lought too.
Bound to the Westward, Towards Starbucks Island

Sunday, January the 13, 1856,
My dear Sailor Boy's Birth Day twenty two years old; if living, and a wanderer like his Mother upon the wide Ocean; five long years have passed away since I last saw him leave his home a Boy, seventeen years old, oh, the many changes since that sad day when last I saw him; and yet many more weary long months will elapse before we meet again; and perhaps never, life is uncertain; may heaven's Blessings rest upon him.

This holy Day begins with a light breeze at N. Ship headed west, light Showers of Rain and very warm have employed most of this sacred day of rest in reading and writing a quiet Sabbath spent on the Ocean; Middle and Last light winds at N.

Ship *Lexington* at Anchor in Holmes Hole

[Wednesday, June 25th, 1856]
At 2 o clock this morning Ship came to anchorage here, at 5 am the Pilot came on board to take the Ship down to Nantucket Bar

Ship *Lexington* under way from Holmes Hole, Bound to Nantucket

[Wednesday, June 25th, 1856]
A Boat alongside with fish and milk to sell, about Twenty Sail in sight fine weather but very Cold, at 7 am abreast Cape Poge, at 7 ? o clock Steamboat *Island Home* passed us, a fine looking Boat, saw the Nantucket Light Boat at 9 am Nantucket in sight, its Barren Hills I see; five Boats in sight coming off Strong; wind at SW at 10 am Sail Boat *Thorn* came Along side with several Persons, among the crowd I see Charles Cathcart and Joseph Cook. Ship almost down to the Bar, the Ship *Massachusetts* Lying at Anchor there, at Eleven am our Ship came too at Anchor at Nantucket Bar, after a long weary voyage of 37 Months and four Days.

Eighty three days from Pernambuco, all well and in good Spirits. So ends my Journal, and my voyage in the Good & Faithful Ship *Lexington*

> Home again; home again; from a foreign Shore
> And oh; it fills my soul with joy
> To meet my friends once more.
>
> Here I dropped the parting tear and crossed the Ocean's foam
> But now I am once again with those
> Who kindly greet me home.
>
> Eliza.

Martha Ford

On 12 February 1855, the Nantucket whaleship Lexington dropped anchor in New Zealand's Bay of Islands, just off the small but bustling port of Russell, a popular place for whalers to exchange mail; clean and refit their ships; and take on water, firewood, and fresh produce. While her husband oversaw such matters, Eliza Brock, wife of the Lexington's captain, went ashore to stay at the Russell Hotel and soon was on her way to call at the home of a resident American couple—Dr. Samuel Hayward Ford and his lively wife, Martha. There, visiting captains and their wives found warm hospitality. In the afternoons, the women enjoyed tea with Martha and gathered around her fine piano forte to play and sing. In the evenings, Dr. Ford made a hot brandy punch with sliced lemons and lumps of sugar, and moved sliding panels to enlarge the drawing room, where couples danced the quadrille to live music by Russell's talented local musicians. One sea-faring guest remembered the Fords' old-fashioned furniture, thick carpets, lovely lamps with dangling glass drops, and lavish use of candles.

More important, the Fords offered a safe haven to whaling wives who had become pregnant at sea—a place for giving birth and for recovery while husbands either waited in port or continued on their cruises. Dr. Ford, who had arrived in New Zealand in 1837 with the Christian Missionary Society, was the country's first resident physician, and offered the security of medical attention. While not much is known about Martha's background, we do know she was an experienced mother (she may have had as many as ten children; in 1848 she lost four children to scarlet fever and in 1852 a fifth to unspecified causes) who offered friendship, support, and practical advice. And so when Eliza Brock came to call, she found two other Nantucket captains' wives at the Fords—pregnant Nancy Grant, of the Mohawk, who would deliver a healthy baby girl during Eliza's two-week stay in Russell, and Mrs. Nickerson, of the Ganges, with a six-week-old infant—shortly to set sail. The three "Nantucket girls," half a world away from home, were especially glad to see one another and exchange news of the island; at the Fords, they spent time clustered around Martha's piano or gossiping with one another. When Nancy gave birth, the socializing shifted to her bedside.

When Eliza Brock left Russell, she carried away one of the most charming relics of Nantucket women's history—the witty lyrics to "Nantucket Girls' Song." Martha Ford was apparently the author; Eliza copied the ditty in the back of her journal of the Lexington's whaling voyage, noting at the song's conclusion: "February 1855. Martha Ford. Bay of Islands, Reefside. New Zealand, Russell." While we can't know the exact circumstances of composition, it's not hard to imagine musical Martha at the piano keyboard, mocking the complaints of the three seafaring Nantucket women gathered in her New Zealand parlor—women who apparently wished that they had never gone to sea. Perhaps they joined in to help in craft the lyrics. Maritime historian Lisa Norling has called the "Nantucket Girls' Song" "a high-spirited and funny (if conflicted) vision of women's autonomy on shore in the absence of their seafaring men." Therein lies the song's unexpected irony—that Nantucket's whaling wives, sailing the globe with their captain husbands, should have located true freedom in remaining at home without them. —SB

"Nantucket Girls' Song"

I have made up my mind now to be a Sailor's wife,
To have a purse full of money and a very easy life.
For a clever sailor Husband is so seldom at his home,
That his wife can spend the dollars with a will that's all her own.
Then I'll haste to wed a Sailor, and send him off to sea,
For a life of independence is the pleasant life for me.
But every now and then I shall like to see his face,
For it always seems to me to beam with manly grace,
With his brow so nobly open and his dark and kindly eye,
Oh my heart beats fondly towards him whenever he is nigh,
But when he says "Goodbye my love, I'm off across the sea,"
First I cry for his departure, then laugh because I'm free.
But I'll welcome him most gladly, whenever he returns,
And share with him most cheerfully all the money that he earns,
For he's a loving husband though he leads a roving life
And well I know how good it is to be a Sailor's wife.

María Mitchell

For most Nantucketers, Maria Mitchell (1818–89) needs no introduction as the female astronomer who, in 1847, discovered a telescopic comet that catapulted her to international fame. The King of Denmark awarded Mitchell a gold medal for her discovery—an award somewhat equivalent to winning a Nobel Prize today—and a young America was especially enchanted that a young Quaker woman from Nantucket, working from a makeshift observatory atop the Pacific National Bank, had edged out the top male astronomers of Europe for the honor. More honors and a lifetime of achievement as a scientist and educator flowed to Mitchell from this point. She would become the first woman elected to the American Academy of Sciences and the first female member of the American Association for the Advancement of Science. She would be the first woman employed to make computations for the Nautical Almanac—*arguably America's first professional woman scientist. In 1865, she would become the first Professor of Astronomy at newly founded Vassar College for Women—a demanding, nurturing teacher of the nation's first generation of college-educated women scientists. The indefatigable Mitchell would also help found the Association for the Advancement of Women and serve as its president, becoming a powerful advocate of women's right to higher education.*

Mitchell's Nantucket background was integral to her success. Like so many of the island's illustrious women, she benefited from the Quaker belief in equal education for girls. Maria was the third of ten children born to Lydia Coleman and William Mitchell. Her mother was extraordinarily well-read, having volunteered as a librarian to two circulating libraries, and the Mitchell household was full of books. Her father was a gifted teacher, surveyor, and amateur astronomer, a widely respected man who became both the cashier of the Pacific National Bank (a position equivalent to president) and an Overseer of Harvard College. Maria grew up surrounded by telescopes, celestial globes, sextants, and chronometers—astronomy was the lifeblood of a seafaring community that used celestial navigation to send whaleships halfway around the world and bring them safely home again. When she showed an aptitude for the necessary mathematics, William made his daughter his pupil and assistant in astronomy.

Maria's formal education ended when she was sixteen, but after a brief stint as a schoolteacher, she was appointed the first librarian of the Nantucket Atheneum, a position that placed her among the nation's first female library professionals. There, when not involved in day-to-day operations such as purchasing and cataloguing books, she attended lectures by the likes of Ralph Waldo Emerson, Louis Agassiz, Lucy Stone, and Dorothea Dix, and studied diligently, reading George Biddell Airy on gravitation, for instance, and Karl Friedrich Gauss on the motion of celestial bodies. In an era when colleges were closed to women, Mitchell used the resources of the Nantucket Atheneum to design her own curriculum. She was well-prepared for fame when it arrived. Unitarian minister Theodore Parker, who spoke at the Atheneum in 1856, might have been thinking in part of Mitchell when he observed of Quaker Nantucket: "[T]here is no town in New England where the whole body of women is so well-educated. There are no balls, no theatres, no public amusements—even courting is the rarest of luxuries. . . . So they fall upon their heads, the poor women. . . . and make for the Tree of Knowledge when debarred from the Tree of Life."

Here we offer some selections from Mitchell's diaries and notebooks. They reveal a woman of humor, warmth, and intelligence—a woman with a matchless work ethic and sense of woman's potential. —SB

Selections from her Diaries and Notebooks

[On Astronomy]

Dec. 5, 1854. The love of one's own sex is precious, for it is neither provoked by vanity nor retained by flattery; it is genuine and sincere. I am grateful that I have had much of this in my life.

The comet looked in upon us on the 29th. It made a twilight call, looking sunny and bright, as if it had just warmed itself in the equinoctial rays. A boy on the street called my attention to it, but I found on hurrying home that father had already seen it, and had ranged it behind buildings so as to get a rough position.

It was piping cold, but we went to work in good earnest that night, and the next night on which we could see it, which was not until April.

I was dreadfully busy, and a host of little annoyances crowded upon me. I had a good star near it in the field of my comet-seeker, but *what* star?

On that rested everything, and I could not be sure even from the catalogue, for the comet and the star were so much in the twilight that I could get no good neighboring stars. We called it Arietes, or 707.

Then came a waxing moon, and we waxed weary in trying to trace the fainter and fainter comet in the mists of twilight and the glare of moonlight.

Next I broke a screw of my instrument, and found that no screw of that description could be bought in the town.

I started off to find a man who could make one, and engaged him to do so the next day. The next day was Fast Day; all the world fasted, at least from labor.

However, the screw was made, and it fitted nicely. The clouds cleared, and we were likely to have a good night. I put up my instrument, but scarcely had the screw-driver touched the new screw than out it flew from its socket, rolled along the floor of the "walk," dropped quietly through a crack into the gutter of the house-roof. I heard it click, and felt very much like using language unbecoming to a woman's mouth.

I put my eye down to the crack, but could not see it. There was but one thing to be done—the floor-boards must come up. I got a hatchet, but could do nothing. I called father; he brought a crowbar and pried up the board, then crawled under it and found the screw. I took good care not to lose it a second time.

The instrument was fairly mounted when the clouds mounted to keep it company, and the comet and I again parted.

In all observations, the blowing out of a light by a gust of wind is a very common and very annoying accident; but I once met with a much worse one, for I dropped a chronometer, and it rolled out of its box on to the ground. We picked it up in a great panic, but it had not even altered its rate, as we found by later observations.

The glaring eyes of the cat, who nightly visited me, were at one time very annoying, and a man who climbed up a fence and spoke to me, in the stillness of the small hours, fairly shook not only my equanimity, but the pencil which I held in my hand. He was quite innocent of any intention to do me harm, but he gave me a great fright.

The spiders and bugs which swarm in my observing-houses I have rather an attachment for, but they must not crawl over my recording-paper. Rats are my abhorrence, and I learned with pleasure that some poison had been placed under the transit-house.

One gets attached (if the term may be used) to certain midnight apparitions. The Aurora Borealis is always a pleasant companion; a meteor seems to come like a messenger from departed spirits; and the blossoming of trees in the moonlight becomes a sight looked for with pleasure.

Aside from the study of astronomy, there is the same enjoyment in a night upon the housetop, with the stars, as in the midst of other grand scenery; there is the same subdued quiet and grateful seriousness; a calm to the troubled spirit, and a hope to the desponding.

Even astronomers who are as well cared for as are those of Cambridge have their annoyances, and even men as skilled as they are make blunders.

I have known one of the Bonds [of the Harvard College Observatory], with great effort, turn that huge telescope down to the horizon to make an observation upon a blazing comet seen there, and when he had found it in his glass, find also that it was not a comet, but the nebula of Andromeda, a cluster of stars on which he had spent much time, and which he had made a special object of study.

Dec. 26, 1854. They were wonderful men, the early astronomers. That was a great conception, which now seems to us so simple, that the earth turns upon its axis, and a still greater one that it revolves about the sun (to show this last was worth a man's lifetime, and it really almost cost the life of Galileo). Somehow we are ready to think that they had a wider field than we for speculation, that truth being all unknown it was easier to take the first step in its paths. But is the region of truth limited? Is it not infinite? ... We know a few things which were once hidden, and being known they seem easy; but there are the flashings of the Northern Lights—"Across the lift they start and shift;" there is the conical zodiacal beam seen so beautifully in the early evenings of spring and the early mornings of autumn; there are the startling comets, whose use is all unknown; there are the brightening and flickering variable stars, whose cause is all unknown; and the meteoric showers—and for all of these the reasons are as clear as for the succession of day and night; they lie just beyond the daily mist of our minds, but our eyes have not yet pierced through it.

Jan. 1, 1855. I put some wires into my little transit this morning. I dreaded it so much, when I found yesterday that it must be done, that it disturbed my sleep. It was much easier than I expected. I took out the little collimating screws first, then I drew out the tube, and in that I found a brass plate screwed on the diaphragm which contained the lines. I was at first a little puzzled to know which screws held this diaphragm in its place, and, as I was very anxious not to unscrew the wrong ones, I took time to consider and found I need turn only two. Then out slipped the little plate with its three wires where five should have been, two having been broken. As I did not know how to manage a spider's web, I took the hairs from my own head, taking care to pick out white ones because I have no black ones to spare. I put in the two, after first stretching them over pasteboard, by sticking them with sealing-wax dissolved in alcohol into the little grooved lines which I found. When I had, with great labor, adjusted these, as I thought, firmly, I perceived that some of the wax was on the hairs and would make them yet coarser, and they were already too coarse; so I washed my little camel's-hair brush which I had been using, and began to wash them with clear alcohol. Almost at once I washed out another wire and soon another and another. I went to work patiently and put in the five perpendicular ones besides the horizontal one, which, like the others, had frizzled up and appeared to melt away. With another hour's labor I got in the five, when a rude motion raised them all again and I began over. Just at one o'clock I had got them all in again. I attempted then to put the diaphragm back into its place. The sealing-wax was not dry, and with a little jar I sent the wires all agog. This time they did not come out of the little grooved lines into which they were put, and I hastened to take out the brass plate and set them in parallel lines. I gave up then for the day, but, as they looked well and were certainly in firmly, I did not consider that I had made an entire failure. I thought it nice ladylike work to manage such slight threads and turn such delicate screws; but fine as are the hairs of one's head, I shall seek something finer, for I can see how clumsy they will appear when I get on the eyepiece and magnify their imperfections. They look parallel now to the eye, but with a magnifying power a very little crook will seem a billowy wave, and a faint star will hide itself in one of the yawning abysses.

January 15. Finding the hairs which I had put into my instrument not only too coarse, but variable and disposed to curl themselves up at a change of weather, I wrote to George Bond to ask him how I should procure spider lines. He replied that the web from cocoons should be used, and that I should find it difficult at this time of year to get at them. I remembered at once that I had seen two in the library room of the Atheneum, which I had carefully refrained from disturbing. I found them perfect, and unrolled them. . . . Fearing that I might not succeed in managing them, I procured some hairs from C.'s head. C. being not quite a year old, his hair is remarkably fine and sufficiently long. . . . I made the perpendicular wires of the spider's webs, breaking them and doing the work over again a great many times. . . . I at length got all in, crossing the five perpendicular ones with a horizontal one from C.'s spinning-wheel. . . . After twenty-four hours' exposure to the weather, I looked at them. The spider-webs had not changed, they were plainly used to a chill and made to endure changes of temperature; but C.'s hair, which had never felt a cold greater than that of the nursery, nor a change more decided than from his mother's arms to his father's, had knotted up into a decided curl!—N.B. C. may expect ringlets.

[On Nantucket Life]

Oct. 21, 1854. This morning I arose at six, having been half asleep only for some hours, fearing that I might not be up in time to get breakfast, a task which I had volunteered to do the preceding evening. It was but half light, and I made a hasty toilet. I made a fire very quickly, prepared the coffee, baked the graham bread, toasted white bread, trimmed the solar lamp, and made another fire in the dining-room before seven o'clock.

I always thought that servant-girls had an easy time of it, and I still think so. I really found an hour too long for all this, and when I rang the bell at seven for breakfast I had been waiting fifteen minutes for the clock to strike.

I went to the Atheneum at 9.30, and having decided that I would take the Newark and Cambridge places of the comet, and work them up, I did so, getting to the three equations before I went home to dinner at 12.30. I omitted the corrections of parallax and aberrations, not intending to get more than a rough approximation. I find to my sorrow that they do not agree with those from my own observations. I shall look over them again next week.

At noon I ran around and did up several errands, dined, and was back again at my post by 1.30. Then I looked over my morning's work—I can find no mistake. I have worn myself thin trying to find out about this comet, and I know very little now in the matter.

I saw, in looking over Cooper, elements of a comet of 1825 which resemble what I get out for this, from my own observations, but I cannot rely upon my own.

I saw also, to-day, in the "Monthly Notices," a plan for measuring the light of stars by degrees of illumination,—an idea which had occurred to me long ago, but which I have not practised.

October 23. Yesterday I was again reminded of the remark which Mrs. Stowe makes about the variety of occupations which an American woman pursues.

She says it is this, added to the cares and anxieties, which keeps them so much behind the daughters of England in personal beauty.

And to-day I was amused at reading that one of her party objected to the introduction of waxed floors into American housekeeping, because she could seem to see herself down on her knees doing the waxing.

But of yesterday. I was up before six, made the fire in the kitchen, and made coffee. Then I set the table in the dining-room, and made the fire there. Toasted bread and trimmed lamps. Rang the breakfast bell at seven. After breakfast, made my bed, and "put up" the room. Then I came down to the Atheneum and looked over my comet computations till noon.

Before dinner I did some tatting, and made seven button-holes for K. I dressed and then dined. Came back again to the Atheneum at 1.30, and looked over another set of computations, which took me until four o'clock. I was pretty tired by that time, and rested by reading *Cosmos*. Lizzie E. came in, and I gossiped for half an hour. I went home to tea, and that over, I made a loaf of bread. Then I went up to my room and read through (partly writing) two exercises in German, which took me thirty-five minutes. It was stormy, and I had no observing to do, so I sat down to my tatting. Lizzie E. came in and I took a new lesson in tatting, so as to make the pearl-edged. I made about half a yard during the evening. At a little after nine I went home with Lizzie, and carried a letter to the post-office. I had kept steadily at work for sixteen hours when I went to bed.

Jan. 22, 1857. Hard winters are becoming the order of things. Winter before last was hard, last winter was harder, and this surpasses all winters known before.

We have been frozen into our island now since the 6th. No one cared much about it for the first two or three days; the sleighing was good, and all the world was out trying their horses on Main Street—the racecourse of the world. Day after day passed, and the thermometer sank to a lower point, and the winds rose to a higher, and sleighing became uncomfortable; and even the dullest man longs for the cheer of a newspaper. The "Nantucket Inquirer" came out for awhile, but at length it had nothing to tell and nothing to inquire about, and so kept its peace.

After about a week a vessel was seen off Siasconset, and boarded by a pilot. Her captain said he would go anywhere and take anybody, as all he wanted was a harbor. Two men whose business would suffer if they remained at home took passage in her, and with the pilot, Patterson, she left in good weather and was seen off Chatham at night. It was hoped that Patterson would return and bring at least a few newspapers, but no more is known of them. Our postmaster thought he was not allowed to send the mails by such a conveyance.

Yesterday we got up quite an excitement because a large steamship was seen near the Haul-over. She set a flag for a pilot, and was boarded. It was found that she was out of course, twenty days from Glasgow, bound to New York. What the European news is we do not yet know, but it is plain that we are nearer to Europe than to Hyannis. Christians as we are, I am afraid we were all sorry that she did not come ashore. We women revelled in the idea of the rich silks she would probably throw upon the beach, and the men thought a good job would be made by steamboat companies and wreck agents.

Last night the weather was so mild that a plan was made for cutting out the steamboat; all the Irishmen in town were ordered to be on the harbor with axes, shovels, and saws at seven this morning. The poor fellows were exulting in the prospect of a job, but they are sadly balked, for this morning at seven a hard storm was raging—snow and a good north-west wind. What has become of the English steamer no one knows, but the wind blows off shore, so she will not come any nearer to us.

Inside of the house we amuse ourselves in various ways. F.'s family and ours form a club meeting three times a week, and writing "machine poetry" in great quantities. Occasionally something very droll puts us in a roar of laughter. F., E., and K. are, I think, rather the smartest, though Mr. M. has written rather the best of all. At the next meeting, each of us is to produce a sonnet on a subject which we draw by lot. I have written mine and tried to be droll. K. has written hers and is serious.

I am sadly tried by this state of things. I cannot hear from Cambridge [the *Nautical Almanac* office], and am out of work; it is cloudy most of the time, and I cannot observe; and I had fixed upon just this time for taking a journey. My trunk has been half packed for a month.

January 23. Foreseeing that the thermometer would show a very low point last night, we sat up until near midnight, when it stood one and one-half below zero. The stars shone brightly, and the wind blew freshly from west north-west.

This morning the wind is the same, and the mercury stood at six and one-half below zero at seven o'clock, and now at ten A.M. is not above zero. The Coffin School dismissed its scholars. Miss F. suffered much from the exposure on her way to school.

The "Inquirer" came out this morning, giving the news from Europe brought by the steamer which lies off 'Sconset. No coal has yet been carried to the steamer, the carts which started for 'Sconset being obliged to return.

There are about seven hundred barrels of flour in town; it is admitted that fresh meat is getting scarce; the streets are almost impassable from the snow-drifts.

K. and I have hit upon a plan for killing time. We are learning poetry—she takes twenty lines of Goldsmith's "Traveller," and I twenty lines of the "Deserted Village." It will take us twenty days to learn the whole, and we hope to be stopped in our course by the opening of the harbor. Considering that K. has a fiancé from whom she cannot hear a word, she carries herself very amicably towards mankind. She is making herself a pair of shoes, which look very well; I have made myself a morning-dress since we were closed in.

Last night I took my first lesson in whist-playing. Learned in one evening to know the king, queen, and jack apart, and to understand what my partner meant when she winked at me.

The worst of this condition of things is that we shall bear the marks of it all our lives. We are now sixteen daily papers behind the rest of the world, and in those sixteen papers are items known to all the people in all the cities, which will never be known to us. How prices have fluctuated in that time we shall not know—what houses have burned down, what robberies have been committed. When the papers do come, each of us will rush for the latest dates; the news of two weeks ago is now history, and no one reads history, especially the history of one's own country.

I bought a copy of "Aurora Leigh" just before the freezing up, and I have been careful, as it is the only copy on the island, to circulate it freely. It must have been a pleasant visitor in the four or five households which it has entered. We have had Dr. Kane's book and now have the "Japan Expedition."

The intellectual suffering will, I think, be all. I have no fear of scarcity of provisions or fuel. There are old houses enough to burn. Fresh meat is rather scarce because the English steamer required so much victualling. We have a barrel of pork and a barrel of flour in the house, and father has chickens enough to keep us a good while.

There are said to be some families who are in a good deal of suffering, for whom the Howard Society is on the lookout. Mother gives very freely to Bridget, who has four children to support with only the labor of her hands.

The Coffin School has been suspended one day on account of the heaviest storm, and the Unitarian church has had but one service. No great damage has been done by the gales. My observing-seat came thundering down the roof one evening, about ten o'clock, but all the world understood its cry of "Stand from under," and no one was hurt. Several windows were blown in at midnight, and houses shook so that vases fell from the mantelpieces.

The last snow drifted so that the sleighing was difficult, and at present the storm is so smothering that few are out. A. has been out to school every day, and I have not failed to go out into the air once a day to take a short walk.

January 24. We left the mercury one below zero when we went to bed last night, and it was at zero when we rose this morning. But it rises rapidly, and now, at eleven A.M., it is as high as fifteen. The weather is still and beautiful; the English steamer is still safe at her moorings.

Our little club met last night, each with a sonnet. I did the best I could with a very bad subject. K. and E. rather carried the honors away, but Mr. J. M.'s was very taking. Our "crambo" playing was rather dull, all of us having exhausted ourselves on the sonnets. We seem to have settled ourselves quietly into a tone of resignation in regard to the weather; we know that we cannot "get out," any more than Sterne's Starling, and we know that it is best not to fret.

The subject which I have drawn for the next poem is "Sunrise," about which I know very little. K. and I continue to learn twenty lines of poetry a day, and I do not find it unpleasant, though the "Deserted Village" is rather monotonous.

We hear of no suffering in town for fuel or provisions, and I think we could stand a three months' siege without much inconvenience as far as the physicals are concerned.

January 26. The ice continues, and the cold. The weather is beautiful, and with the thermometer at fourteen I swept with the telescope an hour and a half last night, comfortably. The English steamer will get off to-morrow. It is said that they burned their cabin doors last night to keep their water hot. Many people go out to see her; she lies off 'Sconset, about half a mile from shore. We have sent letters by her which, I hope, may relieve anxiety.

K. bought a backgammon board to-day. Clifford [the little nephew] came in and spent the morning.

January 29. We have had now two days of warm weather, but there is yet no hope of getting our steamboat off. Day before yesterday we went to 'Sconset to see the English steamer. She lay so near the shore that we could hear the orders given, and see the people on board. When we went down the bank the boats were just pushing from the shore, with bags of coal. They could not go directly to the ship, but rowed some distance along shore to the north, and then falling into the ice drifted with it back to the ship. When they reached her a rope was thrown to them, and they made fast and the coal was raised. We watched them through a glass, and saw a woman leaning over the side of the ship. The steamer left at five o'clock that day.

It was worth the trouble of a ride to 'Sconset to see the masses of snow on the road. The road had been cleared for the coal-carts, and we drove through a narrow path, cut in deep snow-banks far above our heads, sometimes for the length of three or four sleighs. We could not, of course, turn out for other sleighs, and there was much waiting on this account. Then, too, the road was much gullied, and we rocked in the sleigh as we would on shipboard, with the bounding over hillocks of snow and ice.

Now, all is changed: the roads are slushy, and the water stands in deep pools all over the streets. There is a dense fog, very little wind, and that from the east. The thermometer above thirty-six.

[On Women's Rights, ca. 1865–73]

[. . . .] I am far from thinking that every woman should be an astronomer or a mathematician or an artist, but I do think that every woman should strive for perfection in everything she undertakes.

If it be art, literature or science, let her work be incessant, continuous, life-long. If she be gifted and talented above the average, by just so much is the demand on her for higher labor, by just that amount is the pressure of duty increased. Any special capability, and sense of peculiar fitness for a certain line is of itself an inspiration from God, the line is marked out for her by His finger. Who dare turn from that path? And if she be of only moderate capacity, the duty of using to the utmost her power for good is still upon her. The Germans have a proverb "Life is not a pleasure journey, but partly a battlefield and partly a pilgrimage."

Think of the steady effort, the continuous labor of those whom the world calls "geniuses." Believe me, the poet who is "born and not made" works hard for what you consider his birthright. Newton said his whole power lay in "patient thought" and patient thought, patient labor and firmness of purpose are almost omnipotent.

Let me give you an instance, from my own observations. The telescope maker Mr. Clark, who has just improved the glass of our telescope, stands over such a glass eight hours a day, for six months, patiently rubbing the surface with a fine powder. It is mere manual labor, you will say. But at the end of that six months he has made a glass which reveals to the world heavenly bodies which no mortal eye ever saw before. [. . . .]

Are we women using all the rights we have? We have the right to steady and continuous effort after knowledge, after truth. Who denies our right to life-long study? Yet you will find most women leave their studies when they leave the schoolroom. You have heard many a woman say "I was very fond of Latin when I went to school but I've forgotten all I knew" or "I used to love mathematical studies but I don't know the first thing now." Now if Latin was worth studying in youth, it is worthy of study in middle life. If needed for dis-cipline in youth, it is needed as culture later [. . . .]

We have another right, which I am afraid we do not use, the right to do our work well, *as well as men do theirs*. I have thought of this part of the subject a good deal and I am almost ready to say that women do their work less thoroughly than men. Perhaps from the need of right training, perhaps because they enter upon occupations only temporarily, they keep school a year, they write one magazine story, they keep accounts for a few months for some uncle, they take hold of some benevolent enterprise for one winter, when it's "all the rage."

The woman who does her work better than ever woman did before helps all woman kind, not only now, but in all the future, she moves the whole race no matter if it is only a differential movement, it is growth. And this seems to me woman's greatest wrong, the wrong which she does to herself by work loosely done, ill finished, or not finished at all. The world has not yet outgrown the idea that women are playthings, because women have not outgrown it themselves.

No man dares say that Mrs. Browning was not a poet, that Rosa Bonheur is no painter, that Harriet Hosmer is no sculptor, and, although you may be neither poet, painter, nor sculptor, your work should be the best of its kind, nothing short of the highest mark should be your aim.

I would urge upon you earnestly, the consideration of this one of your wrongs, a wrong if it come to *you* of your own doing. Whatever apology other women may have for loose, ill finished work, or work not finished at all, you will have none. When you leave Vassar College, you leave it the best educated women in the world.

Living a little outside of the college beyond the reach of the little currents that go up and down the corridors, I think I am a fairer judge of your advantages than you can be yourselves, and when I say that you will be the best-educated women in the world, I do not mean the education of textbooks and classrooms and apparatus only, but the broader education which you attain unconsciously, that higher teaching which comes to you all unknown to the givers, from daily association with the noble-souled women who are around you.

The ideas, the thoughts which have grown into this College are your inheritance from all the ages. Guard it and treasure it and develop it as you would any other inheritance. [. . . .]

You and I think a great deal about our rights! I have thought more on that subject since I have been in Vassar College than in my whole life before. For myself it is of little consequence; for you, who have long lives before you and to whom new responsibilities are sure to come, it is of great moment.

VI

Refuge of the Free

Anonymous

Believing that all souls were equal in the eyes of the Lord, Nantucket Quakers were among the first opponents of slavery in the American colonies. As early as 1716, the monthly meeting of Nantucket Friends recorded that "It is not agreeable to Truth to purchase Slaves." In 1733, Elihu Coleman produced one of the first abolitionist tracts published in America: A Testimony Against That Anti-Christian Practice of Making Slaves of Men. A form of pure venture capitalism requiring a skilled and motivated work force, the whaling industry too, was inimical to slavery. *The whaling industry, too, was inimical to slavery. A pure form of venture capitalism requiring a skilled and motivated work force. Whalemen were paid with a share, or "lay," of the voyage's profits, a system that rewarded merit. In 1773, a Nantucket jury granted black slave Prince Boston both his freedom and his wages on his return from a highly successful whaling cruise. His lay—£28 for a three-and-a-half-month voyage—was the equivalent, on a monthly basis, of what the captain of a slave ship might be paid. Quaker whaling baron William Rotch, who sponsored the court case, was perhaps less interested in the injustice of slavery than in wresting Boston, a highly skilled harpooneer, away from his owner, John Swain. But the end result was the same. The decision effectively ended slavery on Nantucket. By 1782, J. Hector St. John de Crèvecoeur could write "there is not a slave I believe on the whole island, while slavery prevails all around them."*

During the nineteenth century, Jeffrey Bolster tells us, "whaling ships offered the best chances for promotion and responsibility" to free black men. In 1848, when whaling was in its heyday, Bolster estimates that "some 700 men of color then sailed as officers and harpooners on American whalers." Nantucket's most famous black sea officer was Captain Absalom Boston (1785–1855). The free-born son of a manumitted black slave and an Indian mother, Boston as a boy did outdoor work for the Macy family, who probably taught him to read and write. At age fifteen, he went to sea, and over the course of several voyages learned to navigate and earned the right to be called "master mariner." Back on the island, he invested his carefully husbanded pay in real estate, opened a pub, and began to build a fortune. By 1822, Boston was able to outfit his own whaling vessel, the Industry, and captain her all-black crew on a voyage to the Atlantic whaling grounds. On his return, he continued his investments, opened an inn, and became a benefactor to *his community, helping to build the island's African school and meeting house (1825) and hiring a lawyer to press for integration of Nantucket's public schools. By the time of his death in 1855, Absalom Boston was the wealthiest African-American on Nantucket, and a greatly admired and respected citizen.*

The Nantucket Historical Association preserves in its collections a holograph copy of the words to a song composed on board the Industry, *giving all the details of that historic whaling voyage by Captain Boston and his black crew. Composed by an anonymous sailor—or perhaps the collective endeavor of several crew members—the ballad's poetic form is a classic one for describing momentous voyages, and its tune, while not given, probably dates back at least to the Elizabethan era. Sometimes erroneously referred to as a ship, the* Industry *was actually a schooner, a fore-and-aft rigged vessel ideal for hugging the coast in a circumnavigation of the Atlantic basin, but lacking the stability and cargo capacity for a voyage around Cape Horn into the Pacific. Confined to the overhunted Atlantic grounds, the* Industry *was not especially successful, taking just seventy barrels of oil, and Boston would auction off the vessel on his return. But the ballad is remarkable, recording every detail of the voyage from the mundane (days without sighting a whale, taking on onions and potatoes) to the extraordinary (black and white crews hunting cooperatively, the sighting of a possible pirate—a matter of high anxiety to black men at risk of being kidnapped into slavery). But most of all, the ballad rings with the pride the* Industry's *men took in their captain, their vessel, and their work. It is a song about freedom and the dignity of labor.* —SB

From "Schooner Industry a [expedi]tion on a Whaling Cruse A Song Composed On Board of Her"

Come all you noble colored tars
That plough the raging main
Come listen to my story boys
A thing that is quite strange

It was on the 12th of May my boys
Eighteen hundred and twenty two
A schooner from Nantucket boys
With all a colored crew

A. F. Boston was commander
And him we will obey
We took our anchor on our bow
Intend to go to sea

In company with schooner Franklin
Being pleasant all around
We steered out for the Western [illegible]
But unfortunately got a ground

There we lay all the first day
Our wives and girls on board
At a PM flood tide again
We sent our friends on shore

We steered out for the Great Point Light
Until we got our bearings on
Then we hauled out about ESE
Until daylight did dawn

Then we hauled up to the Westward
Where we intend to cruise awhile
From thence to the Westward Islands
In hopes to get some oil

For a Whaling voyage intended
And it we mean to pursue
On board of the schooner Industry boys
Fourteen was all our crew

We cruised a fortnight and over
Nothing could we discern
Except fin backs and grampuses
They would not answer our turn

We fell in with the brig Urchin
She was something like two years out
She had been cruising a long time here
Never seen a sperm whale spout

Then says our captain to the mate
I think it is high time
We put away for the Western Islands
For that is my design

[. . . .] Then we clapt her up to the eastward boys
Under a crowd of sail
We touched along on Georges Bank
In hopes to get some whale

There we were disappointed
No whale could we find there
We continued our course to the eastward boys
While the wind it being fair

In cruising of the current boys
We had two smocking gales of wind
We kept her on before the sea
As long as our sails would stand

At [length] were obliged to heave to
We could not longer run
For fear of losing caboose and boats
And then our voyage is done

The gale continued not a [illegible]
Before it did abate
All hands were called immediately
And we made sail again

We still sailed on to eastward
For the space of 12 more days
Then we made the Island of Flores
Right ahead distance about 10 leagues

Early the next morning
We ran down of the port
And there we sent the mate on shore
For to get some recruit

Got a few potatoes and onions
With what he had to trade
Some pigs some hens and other things
And returned on board again

[. . . .] On the 4th day of July my boys
As you shall understand
It was off between the Island[s] boys
We had one noble game

There were brigs ships and schooners
The masters all dandy men
They all dined on board of the brig Traveller
Joseph Warren in command

There we agreed to cruise together
Until something new prevailed
On the 14th day of July my boys
We raised a noble Whale

We lowered away our boats my boys
To leeward we did row
Our second mate having the chase
Up to her we did go

Our consort[']s boats the next came up
Thinking to get a lance
But she did run and fought at such a [illegible]
They could not get a chance

At last the whale being pretty [illegible]
Beat out and began to lag
The other boats just got up
And raised the body flag

We took her alongside of our comrade
And there we cut her in
She made but 65 barrels
And she ought to have made 110

We cruised a short time together
Then we divided spoil
For we were bound to St. Michaels bay
In hopes to get more oil

[. . . .] We got up with Terceira
The wind did very light prevail
The next we heard was Town O
My boys theres a school of noble whales

We wore ship directly
The whales all round in sight
We dropped our boats got fast to one
Some time before it was night

The other boat she came up
To the second whale got fast
She stove the boat wounded one man
We lost both whales at last

[. . . .] We had not searched long my boys
Before a noble school we espied
We lowered away our boats my boys
And took one alongside

We got all things in order
Ready to cut them in
First coiled our lines filled our boats
And was ready for them again

And now we had her all cut in
My boys to trying we will go
A gale of wind came on my boys
Most tremendously did blow

We still continued trying
In spite of all the blow
And what we saved of that large whale
The number of barrels was forty two

[. . . .] On the first day of October
The wind fair at NE
We [clapt] her [off] before the wind
And steered our course SW

Towards America we are bound
My boys before comes hail and frost
Still in hopes to get another whale
Before we reach the American coast

[. . . .] Then we kept off to the Northern
Bermudas for to make
To see if our reckoning was right
Or [whether] we had made a mistake

But we found there was no mistake my boys
As you shall understand
On the 31st day of October boys
We made Bermuda land

[. . . .] With a light wind at S-E my boys
Two days from the land
We saw a sloop off the lee bow
And towards us she did stand

He stood along right at us
Until within a mile or two
Then wore ship hauled on the wind
And from us he seemed to go

Yet he seemed to be manoeuvering
Until late in the afternoon
Then he again [clapt] her off before the wind
As if going athwart our stern

We supposed the fellow to be a rogue
With the manoeuvres that he made
Therefore every man being prepared
With iron and lance in hand

We thought she was waiting for the night
As pirates often do
And if he had made the attempt
He would have lost the whole boats crew

We were agre[e]ably disappointed
For he never came any nigher
All hands upon the deck until PM
A waiting for the fire

We did not intend to make any attempt
Until they were safe on deck
Then pointed straight and darts [in hand]
Fasten to the back of their necks

Early the next morning
Soon as it was day light
A man aloft to look all around
But no fellow was in sight

In five days after we left that rogue
Acrost the current we came
With a gentle S W wind my boys
We made a noble run

In the latitude of 39°
To the Northward we did stand
We spoke a schooner from New York
In to Charleston she was bound

The next day after we left him
We had the wind NE
To the back of Long Island
Was the land that we made first

We wore ship directly
And began to take in sail
For the sea it ran full mountains high
It blew a tremendous gale

The gale continued 22 hours
And then it died away
We tacked ship directly boys
And stood in shore again

Early the next morning
The wind fair at S W
We steered in right for Gay Head
With the wind a blowing fresh

There we lay five hours a waiting
For the tide to make its flood
Then we took our anchor on our [bow]
And got into the Road

Then we warpt into the wharf my boys
And there made her well fast
First furled our sails sleaved up our [illegible]
And discharged every cask

Now to conclude my ditty
Put an end unto my Song
A set of better fellows
To a whaleman never belonged

Here is health to Capt. Boston
His officers and crew
And if he gets another craft
To sea with him I'll go.

End

William Lloyd Garrison

Born in Newburyport, Massachusetts, the son of a merchant sailing master, William Lloyd Garrison (1805–79) would become America's best-known radical abolitionist. A writer and editor who began his newspaper career with the Newburyport Herald, *Garrison was ready on 1 January 1831 to begin publishing a newspaper of his own— the anti-slavery* Liberator. *Through thirty-five years and 1,820 issues, never ceasing in his efforts until the Civil War was over and slavery formally ended by the Thirteenth Amendment, Garrison supplied anti-slavery news and rhetoric to the nation's activists. Networking regional anti-slavery societies into a larger whole, the* Liberator *used the printed word to develop, unite, and arm a powerful faction for the abolition of slavery. Garrison's editorial stance was passionate and unyielding:*

> *On this subject, I do not wish to think, or to speak, or write, with moderation. No! no! Tell a man whose house is on fire to give a moderate alarm; tell him to moderately rescue his wife from the hands of the ravisher; tell the mother to gradually extricate her babe from the fire into which it has fallen;—but urge me not to use moderation in a cause like the present. I am in earnest—I will not equivocate—I will not excuse—I will not retreat a single inch—AND I WILL BE HEARD.*

On Nantucket, black Captain Absalom Boston was the first citizen to subscribe to the Liberator, *and eighteen-year-old Anna Gardner—a white abolitionist teacher in the island's African school—the second. Black businessman Edward Pompey would become Nantucket's subscription agent for the* Liberator, *drawing more islanders to the cause.*

In 1833, with help from Nantucket native Lucretia Coffin Mott, Garrison would found the American Anti-Slavery Society, an organization whose radical ideas included admitting blacks and women on terms of equality with white men. Nantucket's Anti-Slavery Society, formed in 1838, would follow suit, with Anna Gardner and Edward Pompey serving as officers. The American Anti-Slavery Society, with Garrison at the helm, served communities like Nantucket by helping to organize anti-slavery conventions and by supplying abolitionist speakers for the lecture circuit. Garrison himself was a fiery and sought-after orator, known for his belief that the United States Constitution was a

proslavery document—"a Covenant with Death and an Agreement with Hell"—and
for burning copies on-stage.

Garrison would speak on Nantucket many times, but his best-known visit came in
1841, when he attended an anti-slavery convention held at the old Atheneum. On that
historic occasion, a fugitive slave named Frederick Douglass stood up for the first time to
address a predominantly white audience about the evils of slavery. Both Douglass's testi-
mony and his delivery electrified the crowd, and Garrison immediately drafted him as a
lecturing agent for the Massachusetts Anti-Slavery Society. In that moment a star was
born, as the escaped slave launched a career that would make him the most celebrated
African-American intellectual of the nineteenth century—orator, author, editor, and
diplomat. Here, in his preface to Narrative of the Life of Frederick Douglass, An
American Slave *(1845), Garrison recalls the scene in the Nantucket Atheneum as*
Douglass made his debut. —SB

From Preface to *Narrative of the Life of Frederick Douglass, An American Slave*

IN THE MONTH of August, 1841, I attended an anti-slavery convention in Nantucket, at which it was my happiness to become acquainted with Frederick Douglass, the writer of the following Narrative. He was a stranger to nearly every member of that body; but, having recently made his escape from the southern prison-house of bondage, and feeling his curiosity excited to ascertain the principles and measures of the abolitionists,—of whom he had heard a somewhat vague description when he was a slave,—he was induced to give his attendance, on the occasion alluded to, though at that time a resident in New Bedford.

Fortunate, most fortunate occurrence!—fortunate for the millions of manacled brethren, yet panting for deliverance from their awful thraldom!—fortunate for the land of his birth, which he has already done so much to save and bless!—fortunate for a large circle of friends and acquaintances, whose sympathy and affection he has strongly secured by the many sufferings he has endured, by his virtuous traits of character, by his ever-abiding remembrance of those who are in bonds, as being bound with them!—fortunate for the multitudes, in various parts of our republic, whose minds he has enlightened on the subject of slavery, and who have been melted to tears by his pathos, or roused to virtuous indignation by his stirring eloquence against the enslavers of men!—fortunate for himself, as it at once brought him into the field of public usefulness, "gave the world assurance of a MAN," quickened the slumbering energies of his soul, and consecrated him to the great work of breaking the rod of the oppressor, and letting the oppressed go free!

I shall never forget his first speech at the convention—the extraordinary emotion it excited in my own mind—the powerful impression it created upon a crowded auditory, completely taken by surprise—the applause which followed from the beginning to the end of his felicitous remarks. I think I have never hated slavery so intensely as at that moment; certainly, my perception of the enormous outrage which is inflicted by it, on the godlike nature of its victims, was rendered far more clear than ever. There stood one, in physical proportion commanding and exact—in intellect richly endowed—in natural eloquence a prodigy—in soul manifestly "created but a little lower than the angels"—yet a slave, ay, a fugitive slave—trembling for his safety, hardly daring to believe that on the American soil, a single white person could be found who would befriend him at all hazards, for the love of God and humanity! Capable of high attainments as an intellectual and moral being—needing nothing but a comparatively small amount of cultivation to make him an ornament to society and a blessing to his race—by the law of the land, by the voice of the people, by the terms of the slave code, he was only a piece of property, a beast of burden, a chattel personal, nevertheless!

A beloved friend from New Bedford prevailed on Mr. DOUGLASS to address the convention. He came forward to the platform with a hesitancy and embarrassment, necessarily the attendants of a sensitive mind in such a novel position. After apologizing for his ignorance, and reminding the audience that slavery was a poor school for the human intellect and heart, he proceeded to narrate some of the facts in his own history as a slave, and in the course of his speech gave utterance to many noble thoughts and thrilling reflections. As soon as he had taken his seat, filled with hope and admiration, I rose, and declared that PATRICK HENRY, of revolutionary fame, never made a speech more eloquent in the cause of liberty, than the one we had just listened to from the lips of that hunted fugitive. So I believed at the time—such is my belief now. I reminded the audience of the peril which surrounded this self-emancipated young man at the North,—even in Massachusetts, on the soil of the Pilgrim Fathers, among the descendants of revolutionary sires; and I appealed to them, whether they would ever allow him to be carried back into slavery,—law or no law, constitution or no constitution. The response was unanimous and in thunder-tones—"NO!" "Will you succor and protect him as a brother-man—a resident of the old Bay-State?" "YES!" shouted the whole mass, with an energy so startling that the ruthless tyrants south of Mason and Dixon's line might almost have heard the mighty burst of feeling, and recognized it as the pledge of an invincible determination, on the part of those who gave it, never to betray him that wanders, but to hide the outcast, and firmly to abide the consequences.

It was at once deeply impressed upon my mind, that, if Mr. DOUGLASS could be persuaded to consecrate his time and talents to the promotion of the anti-slavery enterprise, a powerful impetus would be given to it, and a stunning blow at the same time inflicted on northern prejudice against a colored complexion. I therefore endeavored to instill hope and courage into his mind, in order that he might dare to engage in a vocation so anomalous and responsible for a person in his situation; and I was seconded in this effort by warm-hearted friends, especially by the late General Agent of the Massachusetts Anti-Slavery Society, Mr. JOHN A. COLLINS, whose judgment in this instance entirely coincided with my own. At first, he could give no encouragement; with unfeigned diffidence, he expressed his conviction that he was not adequate to the performance of so great a task; the path marked out was wholly an untrodden one; he was sincerely apprehensive that he should do more harm than good. After much deliberation, however, he consented to make a trial; and ever since that period, he has acted as a lecturing agent, under the auspices either of the American or the Massachusetts Anti-Slavery Society. In labors he has been most abundant; and his success in combating prejudice, in gaining proselytes, in agitating the public mind, has far surpassed the most sanguine expectations that were raised at the commencement of his brilliant career. He has borne himself with gentleness and meekness, yet with true manliness of character. As a public speaker, he excels in pathos, wit, comparison, imitation, strength of reasoning, and fluency of language. There is in him that union of head and heart, which is indispensable to an enlightenment of the heads and a winning of the hearts of others. May his strength continue to be equal to his day! May he continue to "grow in grace, and in the knowledge of God," that he may be increasingly serviceable in the cause of bleeding humanity, whether at home or abroad! [. . . .]

Reader! are you with the man-stealers in sympathy and purpose, or on the side of the down-trodden victims? If with the former, then you are the foe of God and man. If with the latter, what are you prepared to do and dare in their behalf? Be faithful, be vigilant, be untiring in your efforts to break every yoke and let the oppressed go free. Come what may—cost what it may—inscribe on the banner which you unfurl to the breeze, as your religious and political motto—"NO COMPROMISE WITH SLAVERY! NO UNION WITH SLAVEHOLDERS!"

Frederick Douglass

Few Americans born in freedom can boast a political and literary life as distinguished as that of African-American Frederick Douglass (1818?–95), born a slave. Douglass spent the first twenty years of his life as a field hand and houseboy before escaping north to freedom and a job as a stevedore on the New Bedford docks. Yet within just three years of his escape, the fugitive slave had embarked on a career as a professional platform speaker in the anti-slavery cause, a powerful and sought-after orator. Success followed success, as Douglass published the international bestseller and now classic Narrative of the Life of Frederick Douglass, An American Slave *(1845), made a triumphant speaking tour of Britain, and found influential friends to purchase his freedom. He would establish his own weekly abolitionist newspaper,* The North Star, *and publish other important books—*The Heroic Slave *(1853), a novella about a historic slave revolt on the vessel* Creole, *and two autobiographical works,* My Bondage and My Freedom *(1855) and* Life and Times of Frederick Douglass *(1881, revised edition 1892). Over the course of a long career, Douglass would continue to speak in the anti-slavery cause. When the Civil War broke out, he recruited black troops for the Union Army. When the war and slavery ended, he worked on behalf of black suffrage and civil rights. Always an advocate of women's rights, Douglass would join Nantucketer Lucretia Coffin Mott on stage at the historic 1848 Women's Rights Convention in Seneca Falls, New York. Toward the end of his life he was honored with a variety of presidential appointments, and in 1891, Douglass became U.S. consul-general to Haiti, the only independent black nation in the Western Hemisphere.*

This illustrious career began on Nantucket on 11 August 1841. The twenty-three year-old fugitive slave had traveled to the island to attend an anti-slavery convention organized by Nantucket abolitionist Anna Gardner, who had led a campaign among fellow proprietors of the Atheneum to force that institution to open its doors to blacks for the occasion. Some of the most prominent abolitionists of the day were there, including Wendell Phillips and William Lloyd Garrison. As the convention progressed, William C. Coffin, who had heard Douglass speak at a black church in New Bedford, encouraged him to address the audience. Douglass hesitantly agreed: "It was a severe cross," he later recalled, "and I took it up reluctantly. The truth was, I felt myself a slave and the idea of speaking to white people weighed me down." "It was with the utmost difficulty I could stand erect," he remembered, "or that I could command and articulate two words without hesitation and stammering. I trembled in every limb." But after speaking for a few moments, Douglass recovered from his nerves—"I felt a degree of freedom, and said what I desired with considerable ease." He left his Nantucket audience in the throes of "extraordinary emotion," and he left the island with a contract to lecture for the Massachusetts Anti-Slavery Society.

Douglass surely stunned the island convention. Because it was illegal in the South to teach slaves to read and write, many former slaves were illiterate. Not so Douglass, who had not only clawed his way to literacy by various clandestine means, but had steeped himself in great speeches of English parliamentarians such as Pitt and Sheridan, as well as in the abolitionist rhetoric of The Liberator. Nor was Douglass a stranger to public speaking—he had been teaching and preaching in black assemblies since age fourteen—and had sat through many an anti-slavery convention thinking about what he would say if given the chance. And he was blessed with a magnificent baritone voice—a crucial gift in an era before microphones. When Douglass stood up in the old Nantucket Atheneum, he was more than ready to take the audience by storm. His oratorical powers aside, the very idea of this intelligent, articulate, self-educated man as chattel was an outrage.

Douglass's first visit to Nantucket was not his last. He attended island anti-slavery conventions in 1842 and 1843, lectured at the Atheneum in 1850, and in 1885 toured as a much-fêted celebrity, the guest of honor at an ice-cream-and-cake social hosted by Mrs. Matthew Starbuck. We don't know precisely what he said in that fateful first speech in 1841, but we do know that he spoke about "the fresh recollections of the scenes through which I had passed as a slave." Those recollections are the subject of his 1845 Narrative, and here, to represent the advent of Douglass on Nantucket, is the opening chapter of that remarkable book, which, as Henry Louis Gates reminds us, "opens itself to all classes of readers, from those who love an adventure story to those who wish to have rendered for them in fine emotional detail the facts of human bondage." —SB

Chapter 1 of *Narrative of the Life of Frederick Douglass, An American Slave*

I WAS BORN in Tuckahoe, near Hillsborough, and about twelve miles from Easton, in Talbot county, Maryland. I have no accurate knowledge of my age, never having seen any authentic record containing it. By far the larger part of the slaves know as little of their ages as horses know of theirs, and it is the wish of most masters within my knowledge to keep their slaves thus ignorant. I do not remember to have ever met a slave who could tell of his birthday. They seldom come nearer to it than planting-time, harvest-time, cherry-time, spring-time, or fall-time. A want of information concerning my own was a source of unhappiness to me even during childhood. The white children could tell their ages. I could not tell why I ought to be deprived of the same privilege. I was not allowed to make any inquiries of my master concerning it. He deemed all such inquiries on the part of a slave improper and impertinent, and evidence of a restless spirit. The nearest estimate I can give makes me now between twenty-seven and twenty-eight years of age. I come to this, from hearing my master say, some time during 1835, I was about seventeen years old.

My mother was named Harriet Bailey. She was the daughter of Isaac and Betsey Bailey, both colored, and quite dark. My mother was of a darker complexion than either my grandmother or grandfather.

My father was a white man. He was admitted to be such by all I ever heard speak of my parentage. The opinion was also whispered that my master was my father; but of the correctness of this opinion, I know nothing; the means of knowing was withheld from me. My mother and I were separated when I was but an infant—before I knew her as my mother. It is a common custom, in the part of Maryland from which I ran away, to part children from their mothers at a very early age. Frequently, before the child has reached its twelfth month, its mother is taken from it, and hired out on some farm a considerable distance off, and the child is placed under the care of an old woman, too old for field labor. For what this separation is done, I do not know, unless it be to hinder the development of the child's affection toward its mother, and to blunt and destroy the natural affection of the mother for the child. This is the inevitable result.

I never saw my mother, to know her as such, more than four or five times in my life; and each of these times was very short in duration, and at night. She was hired by a Mr. Stewart, who lived about twelve miles from my home. She made her journeys to see me in the night, travelling the whole distance on foot, after the performance of her day's work. She was a field hand, and a whipping is the penalty of not being in the field at sunrise, unless a slave has special permission from his or her master to the contrary—a permission which they seldom get, and one that gives to him that gives it the proud name of being a kind master. I do not recollect of ever seeing my mother by the light of day. She was with me in the night. She would lie down with me, and get me to sleep, but long before I waked she was gone. Very little communication ever took place between us. Death soon ended what little we could have while she lived, and with it her hardships and suffering. She died when I was about seven years old, on one of my master's farms, near Lee's Mill. I was not allowed to be present during her illness, at her death, or burial. She was gone long before I knew any thing about it. Never having enjoyed, to any considerable extent, her soothing presence, her tender and watchful care, I received the tidings of her death with much the same emotions I should have probably felt at the death of a stranger.

Called thus suddenly away, she left me without the slightest intimation of who my father was. The whisper that my master was my father, may or may not be true; and, true or false, it is of but little consequence to my purpose whilst the fact remains, in all its glaring odiousness, that slaveholders have ordained, and by law established, that the children of slave women shall in all cases follow the condition of their mothers; and this is done too obviously to administer to their own lusts, and make a gratification of their wicked desires profitable as well as pleasurable; for by this cunning arrangement, the slaveholder, in cases not a few, sustains to his slaves the double relation of master and father.

I know of such cases; and it is worthy of remark that such slaves invariably suffer greater hardships, and have more to contend with, than others. They are, in the first place, a constant offence to their mistress. She is ever disposed to find fault with them; they can seldom do any thing to please her; she is never better pleased than when she sees them under the lash, especially when she suspects her husband of showing to his mulatto children favors which he withholds from his black slaves. The master is frequently compelled to sell this class of his slaves, out of deference to the feelings of his white wife; and, cruel as the deed may strike any one to be, for a man to sell his own children to human flesh-mongers, it is often the dictate of humanity for him to do so; for, unless he does this, he must not only whip them himself, but must stand by and see one white son tie up his brother, of but few shades darker complexion than himself, and ply the gory lash to his naked back; and if he lisp one word of disapproval, it is set down to his parental partiality, and only makes a bad matter worse, both for himself and the slave whom he would protect and defend.

Every year brings with it multitudes of this class of slaves. It was doubtless in consequence of a knowledge of this fact, that one great statesman of the south predicted the downfall of slavery by the inevitable laws of population. Whether this prophecy is ever fulfilled or not, it is nevertheless plain that a very different-looking class of people are springing up at the south, and are now held in slavery, from those originally brought to this country from Africa; and if their increase do no other good, it will do away the force of the argument, that God cursed Ham, and therefore American slavery is right. If the lineal descendants of Ham are alone to be scripturally enslaved, it is certain that slavery at the south must soon become unscriptural; for thousands are ushered into the world, annually, who, like myself, owe their existence to white fathers, and those fathers most frequently their own masters.

I have had two masters. My first master's name was Anthony. I do not remember his first name. He was generally called Captain Anthony—a title which, I presume, he acquired by sailing a craft on the Chesapeake Bay. He was not considered a rich slaveholder. He owned two or three farms, and about thirty slaves. His farms and slaves were under the care of an overseer. The overseer's name was Plummer. Mr. Plummer was a miserable drunkard, a profane swearer, and a savage monster. He always went armed with a cowskin and a heavy cudgel. I have known him to cut and slash the women's heads so horribly, that even master would be enraged at his cruelty, and would threaten to whip him if he did not mind himself. Master, however, was not a humane slaveholder. It required extraordinary barbarity on the part of an overseer to affect him. He was a cruel man, hardened by a long life of slave-holding. He would at times seem to take great pleasure in whipping a slave. I have often been awakened at the dawn of day by the most heart-rending shrieks of an own aunt of mine, whom he used to tie up to a joist, and whip upon her naked back till she was literally covered with blood. No words, no tears, no prayers, from his gory victim, seemed to move his iron heart from its bloody purpose. The louder she screamed, the harder he whipped; and where the blood ran fastest, there he whipped longest. He would whip her to make her scream, and whip her to make her hush; and not until overcome by fatigue, would he cease to swing the blood-clotted cowskin. I remember the first time I ever witnessed this horrible exhibition. I was quite a child, but I well remember it. I never shall forget it whilst I remember any thing. It was the first of a long series of such outrages, of which I was doomed to be a witness and a participant. It struck me with awful force. It was the blood-stained gate, the entrance to the hell of slavery, through which I was about to pass. It was a most terrible spectacle. I wish I could commit to paper the feelings with which I beheld it.

This occurrence took place very soon after I went to live with my old master, and under the following circumstances. Aunt Hester went out one night,—where or for what I do not know,—and happened to be absent when my master desired her presence. He had ordered her not to go out evenings, and warned her that she must never let him catch her in company with a young man who was paying attention to her belonging to Colonel Lloyd. The young man's name was Ned Roberts, generally called Lloyd's Ned. Why master was so careful of her, may be safely left to conjecture. She was a woman of noble form, and of graceful proportions, having very few equals, and fewer superiors, in personal appearance, among the colored or white women of our neighborhood.

Aunt Hester had not only disobeyed his orders in going out, but had been found in company with Lloyd's Ned; which circumstance, I found, from what he said while whipping her, was the chief offence. Had he been a man of pure morals himself, he might have been thought interested in protecting the innocence of my aunt; but those who knew him will not suspect him of any such virtue. Before he commenced whipping Aunt Hester, he took her into the kitchen, and stripped her from neck to waist, leaving her neck, shoulders, and back, entirely naked. He then told her to cross her hands, calling her at the same time a d—d b—h. After crossing her hands, he tied them with a strong rope, and led her to a stool under a large hook in the joist, put in for the purpose. He made her get upon the stool, and tied her hands to the hook. She now stood fair for his infernal purpose. Her arms were stretched up at their full length, so that she stood upon the ends of her toes. He then said to her, "Now, you d—d b—h, I'll learn you how to disobey my orders!" and after rolling up his sleeves, he commenced to lay on the heavy cowskin, and soon the warm, red blood (amid heart-rending shrieks from her, and horrid oaths from him) came dripping to the floor. I was so terrified and horror-stricken at the sight, that I hid myself in a closet, and dared not venture out till long after the bloody transaction was over. I expected it would be my turn next. It was all new to me. I had never seen any thing like it before. I had always lived with my grandmother on the outskirts of the plantation, where she was put to raise the children of the younger women. I had therefore been, until now, out of the way of the bloody scenes that often occurred on the plantation.

Stephen S. Foster

If the Nantucket anti-slavery convention of 1841 saw the advent of Frederick Douglass as an abolitionist orator, a second convention, held in 1842, would also make history, culminating in a violent riot and in publication of one of the most remarkable efforts of the abolitionist era, Stephen Symonds Foster's (1809–81) The Brotherhood of Thieves; or, A True Picture of the American Church and Clergy: A Letter to Nathaniel Barney of Nantucket *(1843). The six-day convention, which began in the old Atheneum, involved adopting a slate of resolutions that would become the subject of set-piece orations by the invited speakers (in addition to Foster, both William Lloyd Garrison and Frederick Douglass were on stage in 1842) and lively debate by members of the island audience. One resolution in particular would be responsible for the events of 1842: "Resolved, That it is a dreadful libel on the Christian church to affirm that slave-holders, or the apologists of slavery, were ever members of it; and therefore, the real disciples of Christ, who is the Prince of Emancipators, will never give the right hand of fellowship to any such persons, nor recognize them as among those who are born of God." Trouble began when Foster, no relation whatsoever to the Stephen Foster who wrote the syrupy Southern song, "My Old Kentucky Home," stood up to address this resolution. An articulate man educated at Dartmouth College and Union Theological Seminary, one of the most extreme and vitriolic of anti-slavery orators, Foster was described by poet James Russell Lowell as—*

> *A kind of maddened John the Baptist,*
> *To whom the harshest word comes aptest,*
> *Who, struck by stone or brick ill-starred,*
> *Hurls back an epithet as hard,*
> *Which deadlier than stone or brick*
> *Has a propensity to stick.*
> *His oratory is like the scream,*
> *Of the iron horse's phrenzied steam*
> *Which warns the world to leave wide space*
> *For the black engine's swerveless race.*

Foster's now-infamous oration argued that the institution of slavery involved men in the commission of five particular crimes—theft, adultery, kidnapping, piracy, and murder. What's more, Foster continued, because members of the Southern clergy in the Methodist, Episcopalian, Baptist, and Presbyterian churches held slaves, and Northern members of those denominations kept fellowship with these slaveholders, they were all, by extension, guilty. The church, Foster proclaimed, was "The Bulwark of Slavery," its clergy "a designing priesthood," and its membership a "Brotherhood of Thieves." As if that wasn't enough, Foster got personal, singling out Nantucket ministers. The editor of the Inquirer *expressed his indignation: "We have been told that our people were a set of thieves, pirates, and man-stealers—that our clergymen were 'pimps to Satan'—that there was not a drunkard or a rum-seller in town that was not nearer the Kingdom of Heaven than our clergymen. We have been told that one of our ministers of religion, eminent for his talents and piety, and warmly endeared to the hearts of his people, was an INFA-MOUS WRETCH."*

As news of Foster's speech flashed around the island, a hostile mob formed, drowning out convention proceedings with hooting and whistling, and throwing rotten eggs, stones, and chunks of paving. Windows were broken, at least one home was damaged, and women and children were struck by flying missiles. Over the course of three days, the mob pursued the convention from one site to another before finally breaking it up altogether. The Nantucket community was left deeply shaken and divided by the violence. Nathaniel Barney, an island abolitionist who had served as vice-president of the convention, was concerned that the riot had damaged the anti-slavery cause. Barney wrote to Foster and urged him to publish his speech, that the world might "hear both sides." Here we offer some selected passages from the best-selling result, Foster's The Brotherhood of Thieves, *which went through twenty printings. His words still ring from the page in a scathing denunciation of the support given to slavery by religious hypocrisy. —SB*

From *The Brotherhood of Thieves; or, A True Picture of the American Church and Clergy: A Letter to Nathaniel Barney, of Nantucket.*

Esteemed friend:

In the early part of last autumn, I received a letter from you, requesting me to prepare an article for the press, in vindication of the strong language of denunciation of the American church and clergy, which I employed at the late Anti-Slavery Convention on your island, and which was the occasion of the disgraceful mob, which disturbed and broke up that meeting [. . . .]

I have no pacificatory explanations to offer, no coward disclaimers to make.

But I shall aim to present to the comprehension of the humblest individual, into whose hands this letter may chance to fall, a clear and comprehensive view of the intrinsic moral character of that class of our countrymen who claim our respect and veneration, as ministers and followers of the Prince of Peace.

I am charged with having done them great injustice in my public lectures, on that and various other occasions.

Many of those, who make this charge, doubtless, honestly think so. To correct their error—to reflect on their minds the light which God has kindly shed on mine—to break the spell in which they are now held by the sorcery of a designing priesthood, and prove that priesthood to be a "Brotherhood of Thieves" and the "Bulwark of American Slavery"—is all that I shall aim to do.

But I ought, perhaps, in justice to those who know nothing of my religious sentiments, except from the misrepresentations of my enemies, to say, that I have no feelings of personal hostility towards any portion of the church or clergy of our country. As children of the same Father, they are endeared to me by the holiest of all ties: and I am as ready to suffer, if need be, in defence of their rights, as in defence of the rights of the Southern slave.

My objections to them are purely conscientious. I am a firm believer in the Christian religion, and in Jesus, as a divine being, who is to be our final Judge. I was born and nurtured in the bosom of the church, and for twelve years was among its most active members.

At the age of twenty-two, I left the allurements of an active business life, on which I had just entered with fair prospects, and for seven successive years, cloistered myself within the walls of our literary institutions, in "a course of study preparatory to the ministry."

The only object I had in view in changing my pursuits, at this advanced period of life, was to render myself more useful to the world, by extending the principles of Christianity, as taught and lived out by their great Author.

In renouncing the priesthood and an organized church, and laboring for their overthrow, my object is still the same.

I entered them on the supposition that they were, what from a child I had been taught to regard them, the enclosures of Christ's ministers and flock, and his chosen instrumentalities for extending his kingdom on the earth.

I have left them from an unresistible conviction, in spite of my early prejudices, that they are a "hold of every foul spirit," and the devices of men to gain influence and power.

And, in rebuking their adherents as I do, my only object is to awaken them, if possible, to a sense of their guilt and moral degradation, and bring them to repentance, and a knowledge of the true God, of whom most of them are now lamentably ignorant, as their lives clearly prove.

The remarks which I made at your Convention were of a most grave and startling character. They strike at the very foundation of all our popular ecclesiastical institutions, and exhibit them to the world as the apologists and supporters of the most atrocious system of oppression and wrong, beneath which humanity has ever groaned.

They reflect on the church the deepest possible odium, by disclosing to public view

- the chains and hand-cuffs,
- the whips and branding-irons
- the rifles and bloodhounds

with which her ministers and deacons bind the limbs and lacerate the flesh of innocent men and defenceless women.

They cast upon the clergy the same dark shade which Jesus threw over the ministers of his day, when he tore away the veil beneath which they had successfully concealed their diabolical schemes of personal aggrandizement and power, and denounced them before all the people,

- as a "den of thieves,"
- as "fools and blind,"
- "whited sepulchres,"
- "blind guides, which strain at a gnat, and swallow a camel,"
- "hypocrites, who devour widows' houses, and for a pretence make long prayers,"
- "liars,"
- "adulterers,"
- "serpents,"

· "a generation of vipers,"
· who could not "escape the damnation of hell."

But, appalling and ominous as they were, I am not aware that I gave the parties accused, or their mobocratic friends, any just cause of complaint. [. . . .]

In exposing the deep and fathomless abominations of those *pious* thieves, who gain their livelihood by preaching sermons and stealing babies, I am not at liberty to yield to any intimidations, however imposing the source from whence they come.

The right of speech—the liberty to utter our own convictions *freely*, at all times and in all places, at discretion, unawed by fear, unembarrassed by force— is the gift of God to every member of the family of man, and should be pre- served inviolate; and for one, I can consent to surrender it to no power on earth, but with the loss of life itself.

Let not the petty tyrants of our land, in church or state, think to escape the censures which their crimes deserve, by hedging themselves about with the frightful penalties of human law, or the more frightful violence of a drunken and murderous mob. [. . . .]

I said at your meeting, among other things,

· that the American church and clergy, as a body, were thieves, adulterers, man-stealers, pirates, and murderers;
· that the Methodist Episcopal church was more corrupt and profligate than any house of ill-fame in the city of New York;
· that the Southern ministers of that body were desirous of perpetuating slavery for the purpose of supplying themselves with concubines from among its hapless victims;
· and that many of our clergymen were guilty of enormities that would disgrace an Algerine pirate!!

These sentiments called forth a burst of holy indignation from the *pious* and *dutiful* advocates of the church and clergy, which overwhelmed the meeting with repeated showers of stones and rotten eggs, and eventually compelled me to leave your island, to prevent the shedding of human blood.

But whence this violence and personal abuse, not only of the author of these obnoxious sentiments, but also of your own unoffending wives and daughters, whose faces and dresses, you will recollect, were covered with the most loathsome filth?

It is reported of the ancient Pharisees and their adherents, that they stoned Stephen to death for preaching doctrines at war with the popular religion of their times, and charging them with murder of the Son of God; but their suc-

cessors of the modern church, it would seem, have discovered some new principle in theology, by which it is made their duty not only to stone the heretic
himself, but all those also who may at any time be found listening to his discourse without a permit from their priest.

Truly, the church is becoming "terrible as an army with banners."

This violence and outrage on the part of the church were, no doubt, committed to the glory of God and the honor of religion, although the connection
between rotten eggs and holiness of heart is not very obvious.

It is, I suppose, one of the mysteries of religion which laymen cannot
understand without the aid of the clergy; and I therefore suggest that the pulpit make it a subject of Sunday discourse.

But are not the charges here alleged against the clergy strictly and literally
true?

I maintain that they are true to the very letter; that the clergy and their
adherents are literally, and beyond all controversy, a "brotherhood of thieves";
and, in support of this opinion, I submit the following considerations:—

You will agree with me, I think, that slaveholding involves the commission
of all the crimes specified in my first charge, viz., theft, adultery, man-stealing,
piracy, and murder. But should you have any doubts on this subject, they will
be easily removed by analyzing this atrocious outrage on the laws of God, and
the rights and happiness of man, and examining separately the elements of
which it is composed. Wesley, the celebrated founder of the Methodists, once
denounced it as the "sum of all villanies."

Whether it be the sum of *all* villanies, or not, I will not here express an
opinion; but that it is the sum of at least *five,* and those by no means the least
atrocious in the catalogue of human aberrations, will require but a small tax on
your patience to prove.

1. Theft. To steal, is to take that which belongs to another, without his consent. Theft and robbery are, *morally,* the same act, different only in form. Both
are included under the command, "Thou shalt not steal"; that is, thou shalt not
take thy neighbor's property.

Whoever, therefore, either secretly or by force, possesses himself of the
property of another, is a thief.

Now, no proposition is plainer than that every man owns his own industry.
He who tills the soil has a right to its products, and cannot be deprived of them
but by an act of felony. This principle furnishes the only solid basis for the right
of private or individual property; and he who denies it, either in theory or
practice, denies that right, also.

But every slave-holder takes the entire industry of his slaves, from infancy
to gray hairs; they dig the soil, but he receives its products.

No matter how kind or humane the master may be, —he lives by plunder. He is emphatically a freebooter; and, as such, he is as much more despicable a character than the common horse-thief, as his depredations are more extensive.

2. Adultery. This crime is disregard for the requisitions of marriage. The conjugal relation has its foundation deeply laid in man's nature, and its strict observance is essential to his happiness. Hence Jesus Christ

- has thrown around it the sacred sanction of his written law
- and expressly declared that the man who violates it, even by a lustful eye, is an adulterer.

But does the slave-holder respect this sacred relation? Is he cautious never to tread upon forbidden ground? No! His very position makes him the minister of unbridled lust.

By converting woman into a commodity to be bought and sold, and used by her claimant as his avarice or lust may dictate, he totally annihilates the marriage institution, and transforms the wife into what he very significantly terms a "BREEDER," and her children into "STOCK."

This change in woman's condition, from a free moral agent to a chattel, places her domestic relations entirely beyond her own control, and makes her a mere instrument for the gratification of another's desires. The master claims her body as his property, and, of course, employs it for such purposes as best suit his inclinations,—demanding free access to her bed; nor can she resist his demands but at the peril of her life.

Thus is her chastity left entirely unprotected, and she is made the lawful prey of every pale-faced libertine who may choose to prostitute her.

To place woman in this situation, or to retain her in it when placed there by another, is the highest insult that any one could possibly offer to the dignity and purity of her nature; and the wretch who is guilty of it deserves an epithet compared with which adultery is spotless innocence. Rape is his crime! death his desert,—if death be ever due to criminals!

Am I too severe?

Let the offence be done to a sister or daughter of yours; nay, let the Rev. Dr. Witherspoon, or some other *ordained* miscreant from the South, lay his vile hands on your own bosom companion, and do to her what he has done to the companion of another,—and what Prof. Stuart and Dr. Fisk say he may do, "without violating the Christian faith,"—and I fear not your reply.

None but a moral monster ever consented to the enslavement of his own daughter, and none but fiends incarnate ever enslave the daughter of another.

Indeed, I think the demons in hell would be ashamed to do to their fellow-demons what many of our clergy do to their own church members.

3. Man-stealing. What is it to steal a man? Is it not to claim him as your property?—to call him yours?

God has given to every man an inalienable right to himself,—a right of which no conceivable circumstance of birth, or forms of law, can divest him; and he who interferes with the free and unrestricted exercise of that right, who, not content with the proprietorship of his own body, claims the body of his neighbor, is a man-stealer.

This truth is self-evident. Every man, idiots and the insane only excepted, knows that he has no possible right to another's body; and he who persists, for a moment, in claiming it, incurs the guilt of man-stealing.

The plea of the slave-claimant, that he has bought, or inherited, his slaves, is of no avail. What right had he, I ask, to purchase, or to inherit, his neighbors?

The purchase, or inheritance of them as a legacy, was itself a crime of no less enormity than the original act of kidnapping. But every slave-holder, whatever his profession or standing in society may be, lays his felonious hands on the body and soul of his equal brother, robs him of himself, converts him into an article of merchandise, and leaves him a mere chattel personal in the hands of his claimants. Hence he is a kidnapper, or man-thief.

4. Piracy. The American people, by an act of solemn legislation, have declared the enslaving of human beings on the coast of Africa to be piracy, and have affixed to the crime the penalty of death.

And can the same act be piracy in Africa, and not be piracy in America? Does crime change its character by changing longitude? Is killing, with malice aforethought, no murder, where there is no human enactment against it? Or can it be less piratical and Heaven-daring to enslave our own native country-men, than to enslave the heathen sons of a foreign and barbarous realm?

If there be any difference in the two crimes, the odds [are] in favor of the foreign enslaver. Slaveholding loses none of its enormity by a voyage across the Atlantic, nor by baptism into the Christian name.

It is piracy in Africa; it is piracy in America; it is piracy the wide world over; and the American slave-holder, though he possess all the sanctity of the ancient Pharisees, and make prayers as numerous and long, is a *pirate* still; a base, profligate adulterer, and wicked contemner of the holy institution of marriage; identical in moral character with the African slave-trader, and guilty of a crime which, if committed on a foreign coast, he must expiate on the gallows.

5. Murder. Murder is an act of the mind, and not of the hand. "Whosoever hateth his brother is a murderer."

A man may kill,—that is his hand may inflict a mortal blow,—without committing murder. On the other hand, he may commit murder without actu-ally taking life. The intention constitutes the crime.

He who, with a pistol at my breast, demands my pocket-book or my life, is a murderer, whichever I may choose to part with.

And is not he a murderer, who, with the same deadly weapon, demands the surrender of what to me is of infinitely more value than my pocket-book, nay, than life itself—my liberty—myself—my wife and children—all that I possess on earth, or can hope for in heaven?

But this is the crime of which every slaveholder is guilty.

He maintains his ascendancy over his victims, extorting their unrequited labor, and sundering the dearest ties of kindred, only by the threat of extermination.

With the slave, as every intelligent person knows, there is no alternative. It is submission or death, or, more frequently, protracted torture more horrible than death.

Indeed, the South never sleeps, but on dirks, and pistols, and bowie knives, with a troop of blood-hounds standing sentry at every door!

What, I ask, means this splendid enginery of death, which gilds the palace of the tyrant master?

It tells the story of his guilt. The burnished steel which waits beneath his slumbering pillow, to drink the life-blood of outraged innocence, brands him as a murderer. It proves, beyond dispute, that the submission of his victims is the only reason why he has not already shed their blood. [. . . .]

My task is done. My pledge is redeemed. I have here drawn a true but painful picture of the American church and clergy. I have proved them to be a BROTHERHOOD OF THIEVES!

I have shown that multitudes of them subsist by ROBBERY and make THEFT their trade!—that they plunder the cradle of its precious contents, and rob the youthful lover of his bride!—that they steal "from principle," and teach their people that slavery "is not opposed to the will of God," but "IS A MERCIFUL VISITATION!"—that they excite the mob to deeds of violence, and advocate LYNCH LAW for the suppression of the sacred right of speech!—

I have shown that they sell their own sisters in the church for the SERAGLIO, and invest the proceeds of their sales in BIBLES for the heathen!—that they rob the forlorn and despairing mother of her babe, and barter away that babe to the vintner for wine for the Lord's supper!

I have shown that nearly all of them *legalise* slavery, with all its barbarous, bitter, burning wrongs, and make PIRACY lawful and honorable commerce; and that they dignify slave-holding, and render it popular, by placing MANSTEALERS in the Presidential chair!

I have shown that those who themselves abstain from these enormities, are in church fellowship with those who perpetrate them; and that, by this connection, they countenance the wrong, and strengthen the hands of the oppressor!

I have shown that while with their lips they profess to believe that LIB-ERTY is God's free and impartial gift to all, and that it is "*inalienable,*" they hold 2,500,000 of their own countrymen in the most abject bondage; thus proving to the world, that they are not *Infidels* merely, but blank ATHEISTS—disbeliev-ers in the existence of a God who will hold them accountable for their actions!

These allegations are all supported by evidence which none can contro-vert, and which no impartial mind can doubt. The truth of them is seen on every page of our country's history; and it is deeply *felt* by more than two mil-lions of our enchained countrymen, who now demand their plundered rights at their hands.

In making this heart-rending and appalling disclosure of their hypocrisy and crimes, I have spoken with great plainness, and at times with great severity; but it is the severity of truth and love.

I have said that *only* which I could not in kindness withhold! and in dis-charging the painful duty which devolved upon me in this regard, I have had but a single object in view—the redemption of the oppressor from his guilt, and the oppressed from his chains.

To this darling object of my heart, this letter is now dedicated.

As it goes out through you, to the public, a voice of terrible warning and admonition to the guilty oppressor, but of consolation, as I trust, to the despair-ing slave, I only ask for it, that it may be received with the same kindness, and read with the same candor, in which it has been written.

With great respect and affection,

Your sincere friend,

S. S. FOSTER.

Canterbury, N. H, July, 1843.

Edward J. Pompey and 104 Other Black Citizens of Nantucket

About the African school founded on Nantucket by, among others, black mariner Absalom Boston in 1825, the Inquirer *of the day would write: "a development of the human faculties in the pursuit of arts and sciences is the surest passport to honour and happiness, and the best guarantee of our civil and religious liberties." Sure enough, just fifteen years after the school opened its doors to provide an elementary education to the island's black children, a young graduate named Eunice Ross was ready to challenge the segregation of Nantucket's public high school. Examined by the School Committee in 1840, she was found amply qualified for admission, but was refused entrance by a vote of the Town, on account of her color. Five years of struggle over school integration ensued, with hotly contested School Committee elections, public school boycotts, and acrimonious town meetings pitting the island's black citizens and their white sympathizers—a minority—against a bigoted majority of white segregationists. The tide began to turn in 1845, however, when the black community realized that the only way to force desegregation of the schools was to change state law to allow those excluded from public education to sue for damages.*

Edward J. Pompey (?–1848) stepped forward to draft a petition to the state legislature. Like Captain Absalom Boston, Pompey was the free-born scion of an old island slave family, and had begun his career as a mariner. He parlayed his earnings at sea into ownership of a store and bought shares in the schooner Highlander. *Edward Pompey was not only an officer of the Nantucket Anti-Slavery Society and the island subscription agent for William Lloyd Garrison's* Liberator, *he was an avid reader whose personal library included books on religion, law, slavery, American history and geography, English grammar and literature, biography, accounting, and health—as well as three copies of* Narrative of the Life of Frederick Douglass. *He perfectly understood the importance of education, and was the ideal author for the petition of Nantucket's black citizens. Pompey's petition was successful in changing Massachusetts law in 1845, enabling Captain Absalom Boston to hire a lawyer and sue the Town of Nantucket on behalf of his daughter Phebe Ann, "for depriving her of the advantages of Public School instruction." By 1847, Captain Boston was able to drop his suit. Fifteen years before the Emancipation Proclamation ended slavery in this country, Nantucket's public schools—primary and secondary—were integrated. Here are two of the documents that made this achievement possible. —SB*

Petition to the Massachusetts State House

To the Senate and House of Representatives of Massachusetts in General Court assembled.

The undersigned inhabitants of Nantucket respectfully present that they have between thirty and forty children who are deprived of their right to equal instruction with other children in our Common Schools; and that they can have no instruction from the town, unless, they submit to insults, and outrages upon their rights, quite equal to being imprisoned in a *South Carolina* jail; and for no other reason but . . . color.

They have applied to some of the first lawyers in the Commonwealth, and are informed that they can get no redress, through the law as it is, they therefore pray that there may be some enactment, which will protect all children in their equal right to the schools, against the majorities of School Committees, or of those who assemble in town meetings.

[Signed by Edward J. Pompey and 104 other Black Citizens of Nantucket, including Absalom Boston, Arthur Cooper, and several members of the Ross family]

Massachusetts House Bill No. 45, 1845

An Act concerning Public Schools

Any child unlawfully excluded from any public school, which such child has a legal right to attend, or from public school instruction, in this Commonwealth, shall recover damages therefore, in an action on the case, to be brought in the name of said child by his guardian, or next friend, or any court of competent jurisdiction to try the same, against the city or town, by which said school is supported.

VII

Distressing Calamities

William Lay and Cyrus M. Hussey

In 1824, a psychotic harpooneer named Samuel Comstock made literary history—and mayhem—when he and a handful of accomplices ran amok with axes, boarding knives, and bayonets during the midnight watch on board the whaleship Globe *of Nantucket. After murdering the captain and all but one of the officers, Comstock sailed the ship to a tiny island in the remote Pacific, intending to establish himself as king. There chaos ensued, as Comstock was murdered in a counter-mutiny; a portion of the crew escaped with the* Globe, *marooning the rest; and island natives rose up and massacred all of the remaining survivors except two terrified teenagers—William Lay of Saybrook, Connecticut (ca. 1805–?) and Cyrus Hussey of Nantucket (ca. 1805–29). Enslaved by the natives, the boys would remain on the island for almost two full years before their rescue by the U.S. Navy. Fortunately for us, Lay and Hussey (perhaps with help from a ghost writer named William Coffin, Jr.) would give their remarkable story to the world in* A Narrative of the Mutiny on Board the Ship Globe of Nantucket *(1828).*

So great was the nineteenth-century public's thirst for the grim details of the Globe *mutiny that Samuel Comstock's skull and cutlass were disinterred and brought to New York for display in a museum. The story galvanized contemporary readers when Lay and Hussey published their narrative, and other principals too attempted to capitalize. The mutineer's younger brother, Nantucket-born William Comstock, published* The Life of Samuel Comstock, The Terrible Whaleman *(1824), while Lieutenant Hiram Paulding published* Journal of the Cruise of the United States Schooner Dolphin . . . . In Pursuit of the Mutineers of the Whaleship Globe *(1831). Great writers also found imaginative inspiration in the story. Edgar Allan Poe was understandably enchanted, and made "mutiny and atrocious butchery" pivotal to the plot of his* Narrative of Arthur Gordon Pym of Nantucket *(1838). Herman Melville, taken by the idea of a ship in the grip of a madman, acknowledged both the Lay and Hussey narrative and the Comstock narrative in the extracts of* Moby-Dick *(1851). Twentieth* *and twenty-first century writers have also known how to exploit reader relish for this Nantucket disaster classic. We have Edouard Stackpole's novel,* Mutiny at Midnight *(1939), Edwin Hoyt's nonfiction account* The Mutiny on the Globe *(1975), and, in 2002, with the public's thirst for maritime disaster narratives driven to an all-time high by Sebastian Junger's bestselling* The Perfect Storm *(1997) and Nathaniel Philbrick's* In the Heart of the Sea *(2000), we have two dueling books about the mutiny— Gregory Gibson's* Demon of the Waters *and Thomas Farel Heffernan's* Mutiny on the Globe: The Fatal Voyage of Samuel Comstock.*

Here, we offer a selection from the Nantucket narrative that started it all, by the two young shipmates who experienced it all. —SB

Chapter 1 of *A Narrative of the Mutiny on Board the Ship Globe of Nantucket*

THE SHIP *Globe,* on board of which occurred the horrid transactions we are about to relate, belonged to the Island of Nantucket; she was owned by Messrs. C. Mitchell & Co. and other merchants of that place; and commanded on this voyage by Thomas Worth of Edgartown, Martha's Vineyard. William Beetle, mate, John Lumbert, 2nd mate, Nathaniel Fisher, 3rd mate, Gilbert Smith, boat-steerer, Samuel B. Comstock, do., Stephen Kidder, seaman, Peter C. Kidder, do., Columbus Worth, do., Rowland Jones, do., John Cleveland, do., Constant Lewis, do., Holden Henman, do., Jeremiah Ingham, do., Joseph Ignasius Prass, do., Cyrus M. Hussey, cooper, Rowland Coffin, do., George Comstock, sea-man, and William Lay, do.

On the 15th day of December, we sailed from Edgartown, on a whaling voyage, to the Pacific Ocean, but in working out, having carried away the cross–jack–yard, we returned to port, and after having refitted and sent aloft another, we sailed again on the 19th and on the same day anchored in Holmes Hole. On the following day a favourable opportunity offering to proceed to sea, we got under way, and having cleared the land, made sail, and performed the necessary duties of stowing the anchors, unbending and coiling away the cables, etc. On the 1st of January 1823, we experienced a heavy gale from the N.W. which was but the first in the catalogue of difficulties we were fated to encounter. As this was our first trial of a seaman's life, the scene presented to our view, "mid the howling storm," was one of terrific grandeur, as well as of real danger. But as the ship scudded well, and the wind was fair, she was kept before it, under a close-reefed main-top-sail and fore-sail, although during the gale, which lasted forty-eight hours, the sea frequently threatened to board us, which was prevented by a skillful management of the helm. On the 9th of January we made the Cape Verde Islands, bearing S.W. twenty-five miles dis-tant, and on the 17th, crossed the Equator. On the 29th of the same month we saw sperm whales, lowered our boats, and succeeded in taking one; the blubber of which, when boiled out, yielded us seventy-five barrels of oil. Pursuing our voyage, on the twenty-third of February we passed the Falkland Islands, and about the 5th of March, doubled the great promontory of South America, Cape Horn, and stood to the northward.

We saw whales only once before we reached the Sandwich Islands, which we made on the first of May early in the morning. When drawing in with the Island of Hawaii about four in the afternoon, the man at the mast head gave notice that he saw a shoal of black fish on the lee bow; which we soon found to be canoes on their way to meet us. It falling calm at this time prevented their getting along side until night fall, which they did, at a distance of more than three leagues from the land. We received from them a very welcome supply of potatoes, sugar cane, yams, coconuts, bananas, fruit, fish, etc. for which we gave them in return pieces of iron hoop, nails, and similar articles. We stood off and on during the next day, and after obtaining a sufficient supply of vegetables and fruit, we shaped our course for Oahu, at which place we arrived the following day, and, after lying there twenty hours, sailed for the coast of Japan, in company with the whaling ship *Palladium* of Boston, and *Pocahontas* of Falmouth; from which ships we parted company when two days out. After cruising in the Japan seas several months, and obtaining five hundred and fifty barrels of oil, we again shaped out course for the Sandwich Islands, to obtain a supply of vegetables, etc.

While lying at Oahu, six of the men deserted in the night; two of them having been re-taken were put in irons, but one of them having found means to divest himself of his irons set the other at liberty and both escaped.

To supply their places, we shipped the following persons, viz: Silas Payne, John Oliver, Anthony Hanson, a native of Oahu, W. M. Humphries, a black man, and steward, and Thomas Lilliston. Having accommodated ourselves with as many vegetables and as much fruit as could be preserved, we again put to sea, fondly anticipating a successful cruise, and a speedy and happy meeting with our friends. After leaving Oahu we ran to the south of the equator, and after cruising a short time for whales without much success, we steered for Fanning Island, which lies in lat. 3°49' N. and long. 158°29' W. While cruising off this island, an event occurred which, whether we consider the want of motives, or the cold blooded and obstinate cruelty with which it was perpetrated, has not often been equalled. We speak of the want of motives because, although some occurrences which we shall mention had given the crew some ground for dissatisfaction, there had been no abuse which could in the least degree excuse so barbarous a mode of redress and revenge. During our cruise to Japan the season before, many complaints were uttered by the crew among themselves with respect to the manner and quantity in which they received their *meat*, the quantity sometimes being more than sufficient for the number of men, and at others not enough to supply the ship's company; and it is fair to presume that the most dissatisfied deserted the ship at Oahu.

But the reader will no doubt consider it superfluous for us to attempt an unrequired vindication of the conduct of the officers of the *Globe* whose aim was to maintain a correct discipline, which should result in the furtherance of the voyage and be a benefit to all concerned, more especially when he is informed that part of the men shipped at Oahu, in the room of the deserters, were abandoned wretches, who frequently were the cause of severe reprimands from the officers, and in one instance one of them received a severe flogging. The reader will also please to bear in mind that Samuel B. Comstock, the ringleader of the mutiny, was an officer (being a boat-steerer) and as is customary, ate in the cabin. The conduct and deportment of the Captain towards this individual was always decorous and gentlemanly, a proof of intentions long premeditated to destroy the ship. Some of the crew were determined to leave the ship provided she touched at Fanning Island, and we believe had concerted a plan of escape, but of which the perpetration of a deed chilling to humanity precluded the necessity. We were at this time in company with the ship *Lyra,* of New Bedford, the Captain of which had been on board the *Globe* during most of the day, but had returned in the evening to his own ship. An agreement had been made by him with the Captain of the *Globe* to set a light at midnight as a signal for tacking. It may not be amiss to acquaint the reader of the manner in which whalemen keep watch during the night. They generally carry three boats, though some carry four, five, and sometimes six; the *Globe,* however, being of the class carrying three. The Captain, mate, and second mate stand no watch except there is *blubber* to be boiled; the boat-steerers taking charge of the watch and managing the ship with their respective boat's crews, and in this instance dividing the night into three parts, each taking a third. It so happened that Smith, after keeping the first watch, was relieved by Comstock (whom we shall call by his sir name [*sic*] in contradistinction to his brother George) and the *waist boat's crew,* and the former watch retired below to their berths and hammocks. George Comstock took the helm during his *trick,* received orders from his brother to "keep the ship a good full," swearing that the ship was too nigh the wind. When his time at the helm had expired he took the *rattle* (an instrument used by whalemen to announce the expiration of the hour, the watch, etc.) and began to shake it, when Comstock came to him, and, in the most peremptory manner, ordered him to desist, saying "If you make the least damn bit of noise, I'll send you to hell!" He then lighted a lamp and went into the steerage. George, becoming alarmed at this conduct of his unnatural brother, again took the *rattle* for the purpose of alarming some one; Comstock arrived in time to prevent him, and, with threatenings dark and diabolical, so congealed the blood of his trembling brother, that even had he possessed the power of alarming the unconscious and fated victims below, his life would have been the forfeit of his temerity!

Comstock now laid something heavy upon a small work bench near the cabin gangway, which was afterwards found to be a boarding knife. It is an instrument used by whalers to cut the *blubber* when hoisting it in, is about four feet in length, two or three inches wide, and necessarily kept very sharp, and, for greater convenience when in use, is two edged.

In giving a detail of this transaction, we shall be guided by the description given of it by the younger Comstock, who, as has been observed, was upon deck at the time, and afterwards learned several particulars from his brother, to whom alone they could have been known. Comstock went down into the cabin accompanied by Silas Payne or Paine, of Sag Harbour, John Oliver, of Shields, Eng., William Humphries, the steward of Philadelphia, and Thomas Lilliston; the latter, however, went no farther than the cabin gangway, and then ran forward and *turned in*. According to his own story he did not think they would attempt to put their designs into execution, until he saw them descending into the cabin, having gone so far, to use his own expression, to show himself as brave as any of them. But we believe he had not the smallest idea of assisting the villains. Comstock entered the cabin so silently as not to be perceived by the man at the helm, who was first apprised of his having begun the work of death by the sound of a heavy blow with an axe, which he distinctly heard.

The Captain was asleep in a hammock, suspended in the cabin, his state room being uncomfortably warm; Comstock approaching him with the axe, struck him a blow upon the head, which was nearly severed in two by the first stroke! After repeating the blow, he ran to Payne, who it seems was stationed with the before mentioned boarding knife, to attack the mate, as soon as the Captain was killed. At this instant, Payne making a thrust at the mate, he awoke, and terrified, exclaimed, "What! what! what!" "Is this—Oh! Payne! Oh! Comstock!" "Don't kill me, don't." "Have I not always—." Here Comstock interrupted him saying, "Yes! you have always been a d—d rascal; you tell lies of me out of the ship, will you? It's a d—d good time to beg now, but you're too late." Here the mate sprang, and grasped him by the throat. In the scuffle, the light which Comstock held in his hand was knocked out and the axe fell from his hand; but the grasp of Mr. Beetle upon his throat did not prevent him from making Payne understand that his weapon was lost, who felt about until he found it, and, having given it to Comstock, he managed to strike him a blow upon the head which fractured his skull; when he fell into the pantry where he lay groaning until dispatched by Comstock! The steward held a light at this time, while Oliver put in a blow as often as possible!

The second and third mates, fastened in their state rooms, lay in their berths listening, fearing to speak, and being ignorant of the numerical strength of the mutineers, and unarmed, thought it best to wait the dreadful issue, hoping that their lives might be spared.

Comstock, leaving a watch at the second mate's door, went upon deck to light another lamp at the binnacle, it having again been accidentally extinguished. He was there asked by his terrified brother, whose agony of mind we will not attempt to portray, if he intended to hurt Smith, the other boat-steerer. He replied that he did; and inquired where he was. George, fearing that Smith would be *immediately* pursued, said he had not seen him. Comstock then perceiving his brother to be shedding tears asked sternly, "What are you crying about?" "I am afraid," replied George, "that they will hurt me!" "I *will* hurt you" said he, "if you talk in that manner!"

But the work of death was not yet finished. Comstock took his light into the cabin and made preparations for attacking the second and third mates, Mr. Fisher, and Mr. Lumbert. After loading two more muskets, he fired one through the door, in the directions as near as he could judge of the officers, and then inquired if either was shot! Fisher replied, "Yes, I am shot in the mouth!" Previous to his shooting Fisher, Lumbert asked if he was going to kill him? To which he answered with apparent unconcern, "Oh no, I guess not."

They now opened the door, and Comstock, making a pass at Mr. Lumbert, missed him, and fell into the state room. Mr. Lumbert collared him, but he escaped from his hands. Mr. Fisher had got the gun, and actually presented the bayonet to the monster's heart! But Comstock assuring him that his life should be spared if he gave it up, he did so; when Comstock immediately ran Mr. Lumbert through the body several times!

He then turned to Mr. Fisher, and told him there was no hope for *him*!! "You have got to die," said he, "remember the scrape you got me into, when in company with the *Enterprise* of Nantucket." The "scrape" alluded to was as follows. Comstock came up to Mr. Fisher to wrestle with him. Fisher being the most athletic of the two, handled him with so much ease, that Comstock in a fit of passion *struck* him. At this Fisher seized him, and laid him upon the deck several times in a pretty rough manner.

Comstock then made some violent threats, which Fisher paid no attention to, but which now fell upon his soul with all the horrors of reality. Finding his cruel enemy deaf to his remonstrances and entreaties, he said, "If there is no hope, I will at least die like a man!" and having, by order of Comstock, turned back too, said in a firm voice, "*I am ready!!*"

Comstock then put the muzzle of the gun to his head, and fired, which instantly put an end to his existence! Mr. Lumbert, during this time, was begging for life, although no doubt mortally wounded. Comstock, turned to him and said, "I am a bloody man! I have a bloody hand and *will* be avenged!" and *again* ran him through the body with a bayonet! He then begged for a little water; "I'll give you water," said he, and once more plunging the weapon in his body, left him for dead!

Thus it appears that this more than demon, murdered with his own hand, the whole! Gladly would we wash from "memory's waste" all remembrance of that bloody night. The compassionate reader, however, whose heart sickens within him at the perusal, as does ours at the recital, of this tale of woe, will not, we hope, disapprove of our publishing these melancholy facts to the world. As, through the boundless mercy of Providence we have been restored to the bosom of our families and homes, we deemed it a duty we owe to the world to record our "unvarnished tale."

Nathaniel Philbrick

Boston-born Nathaniel Philbrick (b. 1956) grew up with a penchant for American litera-
ture and history nurtured by a scholarly father, Professor Thomas Philbrick of the University
of Pittsburgh, and a passion for sailing that brought him the North American Sunfish
Championship at age 22. After graduating from Brown University and earning an M.A.
in American literature from Duke, Philbrick worked for four years as a staff writer for
Sailing World, *and then as a freelance sailing journalist, writing or editing a number of*
books about sailing, including Yaahting: A Parody *(1984).*

Together with his wife Melissa, an attorney, and their two children, Philbrick moved
to Nantucket year-round in 1986, and while directing sailing programs for the Nantucket
Yacht Club was inspired to begin writing about the island and its history. Three
Nantucket books followed: Away Off Shore: Nantucket Island and Its People,
1602–1890 *(1994) and* Abram's Eyes: The Native American Legacy of Nantucket
Island *(1998), both histories, as well as* Second Wind: A Sunfish Sailor's Odyssey
(1999) a personal narrative that includes Philbrick's adventures sailing on Nantucket's
ponds. During this period, Philbrick became the founding director of the island's Egan
Institute for Maritime Studies.

His big break came in June 1998 when he sold a proposal for what would become
In the Heart of the Sea *(2000) to Viking Penguin. Combining Philbrick's scholarly*
gift for original research with his journalist's talent for fast-paced story-telling strong in
human interest, In the Heart of the Sea *recounts the 1820 tragedy of the Nantucket*
whaleship Essex, *rammed and sunk by a whale in the middle of the Pacific Ocean, and*
the subsequent sufferings of her crew in open boats. Perhaps the most literary event in
island history, the Essex *disaster riveted the nineteenth-century reading public in the*
form of survivor Owen Chase's personal narrative, and inspired both Herman Melville
and Edgar Allan Poe. Philbrick's twenty-first-century retelling would top The New
York Times *best seller lists for weeks and bring him a National Book Award.*

Today, Philbrick is a nationally renowned, critically acclaimed author of best-selling histories. Sea of Glory *(2003), the story of the 1838 U.S. Exploring Expedition to Antarctica and the Pacific Ocean, won the Theodore and Franklin D. Roosevelt Naval History Prize, while* Mayflower: A Story of Courage, Community, and War *(2006) was nominated for the Pulitzer Prize in History. Here we offer a selection from* In the Heart of the Sea, *the Nantucket story that launched his career.—SB*

From "Games of Chance," Chapter 11
of *In the Heart of the Sea*

On January 26, the sixty-sixth day since leaving the wreck, their noon observation indicated that they had sunk to latitude 36° south, more than 600 nautical miles south of Henderson Island and 1,800 miles due west of Valparaiso, Chile. That day the searing sun gave way to a bitterly cold rain. Starvation had lowered their body temperatures by several degrees, and with few clothes to warm their thin bodies, they were now in danger of dying of hypothermia. They had no choice but to try to head north, back toward the equator.

With the breeze out of the east, they were forced to tack, turning with the steering oar until the wind came from the starboard side of the boat. Prior to reaching Henderson, it had been a maneuver they accomplished with ease. Now, even though the wind was quite light, they no longer had the strength to handle the steering oar or trim the sails. "[A]fter much labor, we got our boat about," Chase remembered, "and so great was the fatigue attending this small exertion of our bodies, that we all gave up for a moment and abandoned her to her own course."

With no one steering or adjusting the sails, the boat drifted aimlessly. The men lay helpless and shivering in the bilge as, Chase wrote, "the horrors of our situation came upon us with a despairing force and effect." After two hours, they finally marshaled enough strength to adjust the sails so that the boat was once again moving forward. But now they were sailing north, parallel to, but not toward, the coast of South America. Like Job before him, Chase could not help but ask, "[What] narrow hopes [still] bound us to life?"

As Chase's men lay immobilized by hunger in the bottom of their boat, yet another member of Hendricks's crew died. This time it was Isaiah Sheppard, who became the third African American to die and be eaten in only seven days. The next day, January 28—the sixty-eighth day since leaving the wreck—Samuel Reed, the sole black member of Pollard's crew, died and was eaten. That left William Bond in Hendricks's boat as the last surviving black in the *Essex*'s crew. There was little doubt who had become the tropic birds and who had become the hawks.

Sailors commonly accepted that eating human flesh brought a person's moral character down to the level of those "brutish savages" who voluntarily indulged in cannibalism. On Boon Island in 1710, Captain Dean had noticed a shocking transformation among his crew once they began to eat the carpenter's body. "I found (in a few days) their natural disposition changed," Dean wrote, "and that affectionate, peaceable temper they had all along hitherto, discovered totally lost; their eyes staring and looking wild, their countenances fierce and barbarous."

But it wasn't the act of cannibalism that lowered a survivor's sense of civility; rather, it was his implacable hunger. During the first leg of their voyage, Chase had noticed that their sufferings had made it difficult for them to maintain "so magnanimous and devoted a character to our feelings."

Even under the controlled circumstances of the 1945 Minnesota starvation experiment, the participants were aware of a distressing change in their behavior. A majority of the volunteers were members of the Church of the Brethren, and many had hoped that the period of deprivation would enhance their spiritual lives. But they found just the opposite to be true. "Most of them felt that the semi-starvation had coarsened rather than refined them," it was reported, "and they marveled at how thin their moral and social veneers seemed to be."

In another notorious case of survival cannibalism, sailors aboard the badly damaged *Peggy* were reaching the final stages of starvation on the stormy Atlantic in 1765. Although they still had more than enough left of the vessel's cargo of wine and brandy, it had been eighteen days since they'd eaten the last of their food. Emboldened by alcohol, the first mate informed the captain that he was going to kill and eat a black slave. The captain refused to take part and, too weak to oppose them, overheard the terrifying sounds of the execution and subsequent feast from the cabin. A few days later, the crew appeared at the captain's door, looking for another man to kill. "I . . . [told them] that the poor Negro's death had done them no service," Captain Harrison wrote, "as they were as greedy and as emaciated as ever. . . . The answer which they gave to this, was, that they were now hungry and must have something to eat."

Like the crew of the *Peggy*, the *Essex* survivors were no longer operating under the rules of conduct that had governed their lives prior to the ordeal; they were members of what psychologists studying the Nazi concentration camps have called a "modern feral community"—a group of people reduced to "an animal state very closely approaching 'raw' motivation." Just as concentration camp inmates underwent, in the words of one psychologist, "starvation . . . in a state of extreme stress," so did the men of the *Essex* live from day to day not knowing which of them would be the next to die.

Under these circumstances, survivors typically undergo a process of psychic deadening that one Auschwitz survivor described as a tendency to "kill my feelings." Another woman expressed it as an amoral, even immoral, will to live: "Nothing else counted but that I wanted to live. I would have stolen from husband, child, parent or friend, in order to accomplish this. Therefore, every day I disciplined myself with a sort of low, savage cunning, to bend every effort, to devote every fiber of my being, to do those things which would make that possible."

Within a feral community, it is not uncommon for subgroups to develop as a collective form of defense against the remorseless march of horror, and it was here that the Nantucketers—their ties of kinship and religion stitching them together—had an overwhelming advantage. Since there would be no black survivors to contradict the testimonies of the whites, the possibility exists that the Nantucketers took a far more active role in insuring their own survival than has been otherwise suggested. Certainly the statistics raise suspicion—of the first four sailors to be eaten all were black. Short of murdering the black crew members, the Nantucketers could have refused to share meat with them.

However, except for the fact that the majority of blacks were assigned to a whaleboat commanded by a sickly mate, there is no evidence of overt favoritism in the boats. Indeed, what appears to have distinguished the men of the *Essex* was the great discipline and human compunction they maintained throughout. If necessity forced them to act like animals, they did so with the deepest regrets. There was a reason why William Bond in Hendricks's boat was the last African American left alive. Thanks to his position as a steward in the officers' quarters, Bond had enjoyed a far more balanced and plentiful diet than his shipmates in the forecastle. But now that he was the only black among six whites, Bond had to wonder what the future held.

Given the cruel mathematics of survival cannibalism, each death not only provided the remaining men with food but reduced by one the number of people they had to share it with. By the time Samuel Reed died on January 28, the seven survivors each received three thousand calories' worth of meat (up by almost a third since the death of Lawson Thomas). Unfortunately, even though this portion may have been roughly equivalent to each man's share of a Galapagos tortoise, it lacked the fat that the human body requires to digest meat. No matter how much meat they now had available to them, it was of limited nutritional value without a source of fat.

The following night, January 29, was darker than most. The two boat-crews were finding it difficult to keep track of each other; they also lacked the strength to manage the steering oar and sails. That night, Pollard and his men looked up to find that the whaleboat containing Obed Hendricks, William Bond, and Joseph West had disappeared. Pollard's men were too weak to attempt to find the missing boat—either by raising a lantern or firing a pistol. That left George Pollard, Owen Coffin, Charles Ramsdell, and Barzillai Ray—all Nantucketers—alone for the first time since the sinking of the *Essex*.

They were at latitude 35° south, longitude 100° west, 1,500 miles from the coast of South America, with only the half-eaten corpse of Samuel Reed to keep them alive.

But no matter how grim their prospects might seem, they were better than those of Hendricks's boat-crew. Without a compass or a quadrant, Hendricks and his men were now lost in an empty and limitless sea.

On February 6, the four men in Pollard's boat, having consumed "the last morsel" of Samuel Reed, "began to "[look] at each other with horrid thoughts in our minds," according to one survivor, "but we held our tongues." Then the youngest of them, sixteen-year-old Charles Ramsdell, uttered the unspeakable. They should cast lots, he said, to see who would be killed so that the rest could live.

The drawing of lots in a survival situation had long been an accepted custom of the sea. The earliest recorded instance dates back to the first half of the seventeenth century, when seven Englishmen sailing from the Caribbean island of St. Kitts were driven out to sea in a storm. After seventeen days, one of the crew suggested that they cast lots. As it turned out, the lot fell to the man who had originally made the proposal, and after lots were cast again to see who should execute him, he was killed and eaten.

In 1765, several days after the crew of the *Peggy* had eaten the remains of the black slave, lots were drawn to see who would be the next to serve as food. The lot fell to David Flatt, a foremastman and one of the most popular sailors in the crew. "The shock of the decision was great," wrote Captain Harrison, "and the preparations for execution dreadful." Flatt requested that he be given some time to prepare himself for death, and the crew agreed to postpone the execution until eleven the next morning. The dread of his death sentence proved too much for Flatt. By midnight he had become deaf; by morning he was delirious. Incredibly, a rescue ship was sighted at eight o' clock. But for David Flatt it was too late. Even after the *Peggy*'s crew had been delivered to England, Harrison reported that "the unhappy Flatt still continued out of his senses."

Drawing lots was not a practice to which a Quaker whaleman could, in good conscience, agree. Friends not only have a testimony against killing people but also do not allow games of chance. Charles Ramsdell, the son of a cabinetmaker, was a Congregationalist. However, both Owen Coffin and Barzillai Ray were members of Nantucket's Friends Meeting. Although Pollard was not a Quaker, his grandparents had been, and his great-grandmother, Mehitable Pollard, had been a minister.

Faced with similarly dire circumstances, other sailors made different decisions. In 1811, the 139-ton brig *Polly,* on her way from Boston to the

Caribbean, was dismasted in a storm, and the crew drifted on the waterlogged hull for 191 days. Although some of the men died from hunger and exposure, their bodies were never used for food; instead, they were used for bait. Attaching pieces of their dead shipmate's body to a trolling line, the survivors managed to catch enough sharks to sustain themselves until their rescue. If the *Essex* crew had adopted this strategy with the death of Matthew Joy, they might never have reached the extreme that confronted them now.

When first presented with young Ramsdell's proposal, Captain Pollard "would not listen to it," according to an account related by Nickerson, "saying to the others, 'No, but if I die first you are welcome to subsist on my remains.'" Then Owen Coffin, Pollard's first cousin, the eighteen-year-old son of his aunt, joined Ramsdell in requesting that they cast lots.

Pollard studied his three young companions. Starvation had ringed their sunken eyes with dark, smudge-like pigmentation. There was little doubt that they were all close to death. It was also clear that all of them, including Barzillai Ray, the orphaned son of a noted island cooper, were in favor of Ramsdell's proposal. As he had two times before—after the knockdown in the Gulf Stream and the sinking of the *Essex*—Pollard acquiesced to the majority. He agreed to cast lots. If suffering had turned Chase into a compassionate yet forceful leader, Pollard's confidence had been eroded further by events that reduced him to the most desperate extreme a man can ever know.

They cut up a scrap of paper and placed the pieces in a hat. [. . . .]

Edgar Allan Poe

The morbid and brilliant Edgar Allan Poe (1809–49) may never have visited Nantucket, but the exploits of the island's world-wandering whalemen as they pressed back maritime frontiers in the Pacific and South Atlantic captured his imagination nonetheless. Criticism, short fiction, and poetry were his usual genres, but Nantucket inspired Poe's only novel, The Narrative of Arthur Gordon Pym of Nantucket *(1838), a fictional yarn masquerading as a firsthand nonfiction account of a voyage towards the South Pole by the redoubtable Pym. The novel's breathless subtitle says it all:*

> *Comprising the details of a mutiny and atrocious butchery on board the American brig Grampus, on her way to the South Seas, in the month of June, 1827. With an account of the recapture of the vessel by the survivers [sic]; their shipwreck and subsequent horrible sufferings from famine; their deliverance by means of the British schooner Jane Guy; the brief cruise of this latter vessel in the Antarctic Ocean; her capture, and the massacre of her crew among a group of islands in the EIGHTY-FOURTH PARALLEL OF SOUTHERN LATITUDE; together with the incredible adventures and discoveries STILL FARTHER SOUTH to which that distressing calamity gave rise.*

As the subtitle suggests, Poe was thoroughly familiar with the maritime disaster narratives so popular during this period. He almost certainly had read about Nantucket's two most famous disasters—the "mutiny and atrocious butchery" on board the whaleship Globe, *as well as the wreck of the whaleship* Essex *and her crew's "subsequent horrible sufferings from famine." In some ways, the adventures of Poe's improbably unlucky Mr. Pym constitute a spoof of the disaster genre.*

When Poe began writing Pym in 1836, he was also actively engaged in the national debate over launching a U.S. Exploring Expedition to investigate the newly recognized continent of Antarctica and probe towards the South Pole. Writing for the Southern Literary Messenger, *Poe backed the efforts of Jeremiah Reynolds—an author and explorer with strong Nantucket ties—to form such an expedition, and may even have hoped to go along. During this period, the South Pole was still so mysterious that even serious men could believe in John Cleve Symmes's "Theory of Concentric Spheres," the idea that there might be holes at the earth's poles and vast oceanic vortices where the world's seas poured into a hollow planet. For Poe, who pioneered the science fiction and fantasy genres in American literature, the subject was irresistible. Ultimately, both Reynolds and Poe would be disappointed when command of the Expedition went to Lieutenant Charles Wilkes, who set sail in 1838, the year* Pym *was published.*

Nantucket readers should also note Pym's *influence on French literature. During the nineteenth century, Poe's fiction was far more admired in France than in America. The symbolist poet Charles Baudelaire (1821–67) translated* Pym *into French (the Nantucket Historical Association has a first edition of the 1858 translation), while Arthur Rimbaud (1854–1891) paid homage to* Pym *in his 1871 poem, "Le bateau ivre" ("The Drunken Boat"). And French science fiction writer Jules Verne (1828–1905) wrote a sequel to* The Narrative of Arthur Gordon Pym of Nantucket—Le Sphinx des Glaces *(1897), available in English translation as* An Antarctic Mystery; Or, The Sphinx of the Ice Fields. *Readers who tackle Poe's novel in its entirety and find the ending to be a real cliffhanger may enjoy Verne's solution.*

Here we offer a selection covering just one of Pym's *many remarkable adventures.—SB*

From Chapters 20 through 22 of *The Narrative of Arthur Gordon Pym of Nantucket*

It was on the first of February that we went on shore for the purpose of visiting the village. Although, as said before, we entertained not the slightest suspicion, still no proper precaution was neglected. Six men were left in the schooner, with instructions to permit none of the savages to approach the vessel during our absence, under any pretence whatever, and to remain constantly on deck. The boarding-nettings were up, the guns double-shotted with grape and canister, and the swivels loaded with canisters of musket-balls. She lay, with her anchor apeak, about a mile from the shore, and no canoe could approach her in any direction without being distinctly seen and exposed to the full fire of our swivels immediately.

The six men being left on board, our shore-party consisted of thirty-two persons in all. We were armed to the teeth, having with us muskets, pistols, and cutlasses; besides, each had a long kind of seaman's knife, somewhat resembling the bowie knife now so much used throughout our western and southern country. A hundred of the black skin warriors met us at the landing for the purpose of accompanying us on our way. We noticed, however, with some surprise, that they were now entirely without arms; and, upon questioning Too-wit in relation to this circumstance, he merely answered that Mattee non we pa pa si—meaning that there was no need of arms where all were brothers. We took this in good part, and proceeded.

We had passed the spring and rivulet of which I before spoke, and were now entering upon a narrow gorge leading through the chain of soapstone hills among which the village was situated. This gorge was very rocky and uneven, so much so that it was with no little difficulty we scrambled through it on our first visit to Klock-klock. The whole length of the ravine might have been a mile and a half, or probably two miles. It wound in every possible direction through the hills (having apparently formed, at some remote period, the bed of a torrent), in no instance proceeding more than twenty yards without an abrupt turn. The sides of this dell would have averaged, I am sure, seventy or eighty feet in perpendicular altitude throughout the whole of their extent, and in some portions they arose to an astonishing height, overshadowing the pass so completely that but little of the light of day could penetrate. The general width was about forty feet, and occasionally it diminished so as not to allow the passage of more than five or six persons abreast. In short, there could be no place in the world better adapted for the consummation of an ambuscade, and it was no more than natural that we should look carefully to our arms as we entered upon it. When I now think of our egregious folly, the chief subject of astonishment seems to be, that we should have ever ventured, under any circumstances, so completely into the power of unknown savages as to permit them to march both before and behind us in our progress through this ravine. Yet such was the order we blindly took up, trusting foolishly to the force of our party, the unarmed condition of Too-wit and his men, the certain efficacy of our firearms (whose effect was yet a secret to the natives), and, more than all, to the long-sustained pretension of friendship kept up by these infamous wretches. Five or six of them went on before, as if to lead the way, ostentatiously busying themselves in removing the larger stones and rubbish from the path. Next came our own party. We walked closely together, taking care only to prevent separation. Behind followed the main body of the savages, observing unusual order and decorum.

Dirk Peters, a man named Wilson Allen, and myself were on the right of our companions, examining, as we went along, the singular stratification of the precipice which overhung us. A fissure in the soft rock attracted our attention. It was about wide enough for one person to enter without squeezing, and extended back into the hill some eighteen or twenty feet in a straight course, sloping afterward to the left. The height of the opening, as far as we could see into it from the main gorge, was perhaps sixty or seventy feet. There were one or two stunted shrubs growing from the crevices, bearing a species of filbert which I felt some curiosity to examine, and pushed in briskly for that purpose, gathering five or six of the nuts at a grasp, and then hastily retreating. As I turned, I found that Peters and Allen had followed me. I desired them to go back, as there was not room for two persons to pass, saying they should have some of my nuts. They accordingly turned, and were scrambling back, Allen being close to the mouth of the fissure, when I was suddenly aware of a concussion resembling nothing I had ever before experienced, and which impressed me with a vague conception, if indeed I then thought of anything, that the whole foundations of the solid globe were suddenly rent asunder, and that the day of universal dissolution was at hand.

As soon as I could collect my scattered senses, I found myself nearly suffocated, and grovelling in utter darkness among a quantity of loose earth, which was also falling upon me heavily in every direction, threatening to bury me entirely. Horribly alarmed at this idea, I struggled to gain my feet, and at last succeeded. I then remained motionless for some moments, endeavouring to conceive what had happened to me, and where I was. Presently I heard a deep groan just at my ear, and afterward the smothered voice of Peters calling to me for aid in the name of God. I scrambled one or two paces forward, when I fell directly over the head and shoulders of my companion, who, I soon discovered, was buried in a loose mass of earth as far as his middle, and struggling desperately to free himself from the pressure. I tore the dirt from around him with all the energy I could command, and at length succeeded in getting him out.

As soon as we sufficiently recovered from our fright and surprise to be capable of conversing rationally, we both came to the conclusion that the walls of the fissure in which we had ventured had, by some convulsion of nature, or probably from their own weight, caved in overhead, and that we were consequently lost for ever, being thus entombed alive. For a long time we gave up supinely to the most intense agony and despair, such as cannot be adequately imagined by those who have never been in a similar position. I firmly believed that no incident ever occurring in the course of human events is more adapted to inspire the supremeness of mental and bodily distress than a case like our own, of living inhumation. The blackness of darkness which envelops the victim, the terrific oppression of lungs, the stifling fumes from the damp earth, unite with the ghastly considerations that we are beyond the remotest confines of hope, and that such is the allotted portion of the dead, to carry into the human heart a degree of appalling awe and horror not to be tolerated—never to be conceived.

At length Peters proposed that we should endeavour to ascertain precisely the extent of our calamity, and grope about our prison; it being barely possible, he observed, that some opening might yet be left us for escape. I caught eagerly at this hope, and, arousing myself to exertion, attempted to force my way through the loose earth. Hardly had I advanced a single step before a glimmer of light became perceptible, enough to convince me that, at all events, we should not immediately perish for want of air. We now took some degree of heart, and encouraged each other to hope for the best. Having scrambled over a bank of rubbish which impeded our farther progress in the direction of the light, we found less difficulty in advancing and also experienced some relief from the excessive oppression of lungs which had tormented us. Presently we were enabled to obtain a glimpse of the objects around, and discovered that we were near the extremity of the straight portion of the fissure, where it made a turn to the left. A few struggles more, and we reached the bend, when to our inexpressible joy, there appeared a long seam or crack extending upward a vast distance, generally at an angle of about forty-five degrees, although sometimes much more precipitous. We could not see through the whole extent of this opening; but, as a good deal of light came down it, we had little doubt of finding at the top of it (if we could by any means reach the top) a clear passage into the open air.

I now called to mind that three of us had entered the fissure from the main gorge, and that our companion, Allan, was still missing; we determined at once to retrace our steps and look for him. After a long search, and much danger from the farther caving in of the earth above us, Peters at length cried out to me that he had hold of our companion's foot, and that his whole body was deeply buried beneath the rubbish beyond the possibility of extricating him. I soon found that what he said was too true, and that, of course, life had been long extinct. With sorrowful hearts, therefore, we left the corpse to its fate, and again made our way to the bend.

[. . . .] At length we reached what might be called the surface of the ground; for our path hitherto, since leaving the platform, had lain beneath an archway of high rock and foliage, at a vast distance overhead. With great caution we stole to a narrow opening, through which we had a clear sight of the surrounding country, when the whole dreadful secret of the concussion broke upon us in one moment and at one view.

The spot from which we looked was not far from the summit of the highest peak in the range of the soapstone hills. The gorge in which our party of thirty-two had entered ran within fifty feet to the left of us. But, for at least one hundred yards, the channel or bed of this gorge was entirely filled up with the chaotic ruins of more than a million tons of earth and stone that had been artificially tumbled within it. The means by which the vast mass had been precipitated were not more simple than evident, for sure traces of the murderous work were yet remaining. In several spots along the top of the eastern side of the gorge (we were now on the western) might be seen stakes of wood driven into the earth. In these spots the earth had not given way, but throughout the whole extent of the face of the precipice from which the mass had fallen, it was clear, from marks left in the soil resembling those made by the drill of the rock blaster, that stakes similar to those we saw standing had been inserted, at not more than a yard apart, for the length of perhaps three hundred feet, and ranging at about ten feet back from the edge of the gulf. Strong cords of grape vine were attached to the stakes still remaining on the hill, and it was evident that such cords had also been attached to each of the other stakes. I have already spoken of the singular stratification of these soapstone hills; and the description just given of the narrow and deep fissure through which we effected our escape from inhumation will afford a further conception of its nature. This was such that almost every natural convulsion would be sure to split the soil into perpendicular layers or ridges running parallel with one another, and a very moderate exertion of art would be sufficient for effecting the same purpose. Of this stratification the savages had availed themselves to accomplish their treacherous ends. There can be no doubt that, by the continuous line of stakes, a partial rupture of the soil had been brought about probably to the depth of one or two feet, when by means of a savage pulling at the end of each of the cords (these cords being attached to the tops of the stakes, and extending back from the edge of the cliff), a vast lever-age power was obtained, capable of hurling the whole face of the hill, upon a given signal, into the bosom of the abyss below. The fate of our poor compan-ions was no longer a matter of uncertainty. We alone had escaped from the tem-pest of that overwhelming destruction. We were the only living white men upon the island.

Our situation, as it now appeared, was scarcely less dreadful than when we had conceived ourselves entombed forever. We saw before us no prospect but that of being put to death by the savages, or of dragging out a miserable exis-tence in captivity among them. We might, to be sure, conceal ourselves for a time from their observation among the fastnesses of the hills, and, as a final resort, in the chasm from which we had just issued; but we must either perish in the long Polar winter through cold and famine, or be ultimately discovered in our efforts to obtain relief.

The whole country around us seemed to be swarming with savages, crowds of whom, we now perceived, had come over from the islands to the southward on flat rafts, doubtless with a view of lending their aid in the capture and plunder of the *Jane*. The vessel still lay calmly at anchor in the bay, those on board being apparently quite unconscious of any danger awaiting them. How we longed at that moment to be with them! either to aid in effecting their escape, or to perish with them in attempting a defence. We saw no chance even of warning them of their danger without bringing immediate destruction upon our own heads, with but a remote hope of benefit to them. A pistol fired might suffice to apprise them that something wrong had occurred; but the report could not possibly inform them that their only prospect of safety lay in getting out of the harbour forthwith—nor tell them no principles of honour now bound them to remain, that their companions were no longer among the living. Upon hearing the discharge they could not be more thoroughly pre-pared to meet the foe, who were now getting ready to attack, than they already were, and always had been. No good, therefore, and infinite harm, would result from our firing, and after mature deliberation, we forbore.

Our next thought was to attempt to rush toward the vessel, to seize one of the four canoes which lay at the head of the bay, and endeavour to force a pas-sage on board. But the utter impossibility of succeeding in this desperate task soon became evident. The country, as I said before, was literally swarming with the natives, skulking among the bushes and recesses of the hills, so as not to be observed from the schooner. In our immediate vicinity especially, and blockad-ing the sole path by which we could hope to attain the shore at the proper point were stationed the whole party of the black skin warriors, with Too-wit at their head, and apparently only waiting for some re-enforcement to commence his onset upon the *Jane*. The canoes, too, which lay at the head of the bay, were manned with savages, unarmed, it is true, but who undoubtedly had arms within reach. We were forced, therefore, however unwillingly, to remain in our place of concealment, mere spectators of the conflict which presently ensued.

In about half an hour we saw some sixty or seventy rafts, or flatboats, with outriggers, filled with savages, and coming round the southern bight of the harbor. They appeared to have no arms except short clubs, and stones which lay in the bottom of the rafts. Immediately afterward another detachment, still larger, appeared in an opposite direction, and with similar weapons. The four canoes, too, were now quickly filled with natives, starting up from the bushes at the head of the bay, and put off swiftly to join the other parties. Thus, in less time than I have taken to tell it, and as if by magic, the *Jane* saw herself surrounded by an immense multitude of desperadoes evidently bent upon capturing her at all hazards.

That they would succeed in so doing could not be doubted for an instant. The six men left in the vessel, however resolutely they might engage in her defence, were altogether unequal to the proper management of the guns, or in any manner to sustain a contest at such odds. I could hardly imagine that they would make resistance at all, but in this was deceived; for presently I saw them get springs upon the cable, and bring the vessel's starboard broadside to bear upon the canoes, which by this time were within pistol range, the rafts being nearly a quarter of a mile to windward. Owing to some cause unknown, but most probably to the agitation of our poor friends at seeing themselves in so hopeless a situation, the discharge was an entire failure. Not a canoe was hit or a single savage injured, the shots striking short and ricocheting over their heads. The only effect produced upon them was astonishment at the unexpected report and smoke, which was so excessive that for some moments I almost thought they would abandon their design entirely, and return to the shore. And this they would most likely have done had our men followed up their broadside by a discharge of small arms, in which, as the canoes were now so near at hand, they could not have failed in doing some execution, sufficient, at least, to deter this party from a farther advance, until they could have given the rafts also a broadside. But, in place of this, they left the canoe party to recover from their panic, and, by looking about them, to see that no injury had been sustained, while they flew to the larboard to get ready for the rafts.

The discharge to larboard produced the most terrible effect. The star and double-headed shot of the large guns cut seven or eight of the rafts completely asunder, and killed, perhaps, thirty or forty of the savages outright, while a hundred of them, at least, were thrown into the water, the most of them dreadfully wounded. The remainder, frightened out of their senses, commenced at once a precipitate retreat, not even waiting to pick up their maimed companions, who were swimming about in every direction, screaming and yelling for aid. This great success, however, came too late for the salvation of our devoted people. The canoe party were already on board the schooner to the number of more than a hundred and fifty, the most of them having succeeded in scrambling up the chains and over the boarding-netting even before the matches had been applied to the larboard guns. Nothing now could withstand their brute rage. Our men were borne down at once, overwhelmed, trodden under foot, and absolutely torn to pieces in an instant.

Seeing this, the savages on the rafts got the better of their fears, and came up in shoals to the plunder. In five minutes the *Jane* was a pitiable scene indeed of havoc and tumultuous outrage. The decks were split open and ripped up; the cordage, sails, and everything movable on deck demolished as if by magic, while, by dint of pushing at the stern, towing with the canoes, and hauling at the sides, as they swam in thousands around the vessel, the wretches finally forced her on shore (the cable having been slipped), and delivered her over to the good offices of Too-wit, who, during the whole of the engagement, had maintained, like a skilful general, his post of security and reconnaissance among the hills, but, now that the victory was completed to his satisfaction, condescended to scamper down with his warriors of the black skin, and become a partaker in the spoils.

[. . .] [The savages] had already made a complete wreck of the vessel, and were now preparing to set her on fire. In a little while we saw the smoke ascending in huge volumes from her main hatchway, and, shortly afterward, a dense mass of flame burst up from the forecastle. The rigging, masts and what remained of the sails caught immediately, and the fire spread rapidly along the decks. Still a great many of the savages retained their stations about her, hammering with large stones, axes, and cannon balls at the bolts and other iron and copper work. On the beach, and in canoes and rafts, there were not less, altogether, in the immediate vicinity of the schooner, than ten thousand natives, besides the shoals of them who, laden with booty, were making their way inland and over to the neighbouring islands. We now anticipated a catastrophe, and were not disappointed. First of all there came a smart shock (which we felt as distinctly where we were as if we had been slightly galvanized), but unattended with any visible signs of an explosion. The savages were evidently startled, and paused for an instant from their labours and yellings. They were upon the point of recommencing, when suddenly a mass of smoke puffed up from the decks, resembling a black and heavy thundercloud—then, as if from its bowels, arose a tall stream of vivid fire to the height, apparently, of a quarter of a mile—then there came a sudden circular expansion of the flame—then the whole atmosphere was magically crowded, in a single instant, with a wild chaos of wood, and metal, and human limbs—and, lastly, came the concussion in its fullest fury, which hurled us impetuously from our feet, while the hills echoed and re-echoed the tumult, and a dense shower of the minutest fragments of the ruins tumbled headlong in every direction around us.

The havoc among the savages far exceeded our utmost expectation, and they had now, indeed, reaped the full and perfect fruits of their treachery. Perhaps a thousand perished by the explosion, while at least an equal number were desperately mangled. The whole surface of the bay was literally strewn with the struggling and drowning wretches, and on shore matters were even worse. They seemed utterly appalled by the suddenness and completeness of their discomfiture, and made no efforts at assisting one another. At length we observed a total change in their demeanour. From absolute stupor, they appeared to be, all at once, aroused to the highest pitch of excitement, and rushed wildly about, going to and from a certain point on the beach, with the strangest expressions of mingled horror, rage, and intense curiosity depicted on their countenances, and shouting, at the top of their voices, "Tekeli-li! Tekeli-li!"

Presently we saw a large body go off into the hills, whence they returned in a short time, carrying stakes of wood. These they brought to the station where the crowd was the thickest, which now separated so as to afford us a view of the object of all this excitement. We perceived something white lying upon the ground, but could not immediately make out what it was. At length we saw that it was the carcass of the strange animal with the scarlet teeth and claws which the schooner had picked up at sea on the eighteenth of January. Captain Guy had had the body preserved for the purpose of stuffing the skin and taking it to England. I remember he had given some directions about it just before our making the island, and it had been brought into the cabin and stowed away in one of the lockers. It had now been thrown on shore by the explosion; but why it had occasioned so much concern among the savages was more than we could comprehend. Although they crowded around the carcass at a little distance, none of them seemed willing to approach it closely. By-and-by the men with the stakes drove them in a circle around it, and no sooner was this arrangement completed, than the whole of the vast assemblage rushed into the interior of the island, with loud screams of "Tekeli-li! Tekeli-li!"

Peter Benchley

Born in New York City, Peter Benchley (1940–2006) arrived with both authorship and Nantucket in his genes. His grandfather, celebrated humorist and New Yorker *theater critic Robert Benchley, began the family tradition of summering on the island. His father, the prolific Nathaniel Benchley, author of many books for both adults and children, purchased "Flagstaff," the family's 'Sconset cottage. There Peter and his brother Nat would spend virtually every summer of their boyhoods swimming, fishing, and listening to their father's tall tales about the sea and its creatures, including a white whale named Moby-Dick. In the family boat, they hunted sharks off Great Point, and young Peter developed a fascination with sharks akin to that which some children reserve for dinosaurs. And just to be sure that authorship gene "took," during the summer that Peter turned 15, his father paid him for writing every day.*

Take it did, and the payoff was huge. After graduating from Harvard, Benchley wrote for the Washington Post *and* Newsweek, *served as a speechwriter for the Johnson administration, and even published a travelogue,* Time and a Ticket *(1964). Then, with help from the literary agency that represented his father and from Tom Congdon, a young editor at Doubleday, Benchley sold his first novel. About a great white shark that terrorizes a small summer resort and exposes the dubious morals of the citizenry,* Jaws *(1974) became the best-selling first novel in literary history, topping* The New York Times *fiction list for forty weeks. Made into an Academy Award-winning movie directed by a young Steven Spielberg and with an unforgettable score by an as-yet-unknown composer named John Williams,* Jaws *shattered records for box office gross, bringing in over $470 million, spawning a number of sequels, and sealing its creators' fame.*

*Benchley would go on to write a number of thrillers about the ocean and marine menaces from pirates to giant squid—*The Deep *(1976),* The Island *(1979), and* Beast *(1991) are among the best-known. Repentant about the impact of "Jawsmania" on the world's endangered population of sharks, he would also become a highly visible and* *compelling spokesman for ocean conservation. His fourth novel,* The Girl from the Sea of Cortez *(1982), has been called "a poetic fable with an environmental theme." His last book,* Shark Trouble: True Stories of Sharks and the Sea *(2002), reminds readers that "for every human being killed by a shark, roughly ten million sharks are killed by human beings." Still, none of this lessens the delicious frisson of primal dread still evoked by* Jaws . . . . —SB

From Chapter 1 of *Jaws*

THE GREAT FISH moved silently through the night water, propelled by short sweeps of its crescent tail. The mouth was open just enough to permit a rush of water over the gills. There was little other motion: an occasional correction of the apparently aimless course by the slight raising or lowering of a pectoral fin—as a bird changes direction by dipping one wing and lifting the other. The eyes were sightless in the black, and the other senses transmitted nothing extraordinary to the small, primitive brain. The fish might have been asleep, save for the movement dictated by countless millions of years of instinctive continuity: lacking the flotation bladder common to other fish and the fluttering flaps to push oxygen-bearing water through its gills, it survived only by moving. Once stopped, it would sink to the bottom and die of anoxia.

The land seemed almost as dark as the water, for there was no moon. All that separated sea from shore was a long, straight stretch of beach—so white that it shone. From a house behind the grass-splotched dunes, lights cast yellow glimmers on the sand.

The front door to the house opened, and a man and a woman stepped out onto the wooden porch. They stood for a moment staring at the sea, embraced quickly, and scampered down the few steps onto the sand. The man was drunk, and he stumbled on the bottom step. The woman laughed and took his hand, and together they ran to the beach.

"First a swim," said the woman, "to clear your head."

"Forget my head," said the man. Giggling, he fell backward onto the sand, pulling the woman down with him. They fumbled with each other's clothing, twined limbs around limbs, and thrashed with urgent ardor on the cold sand.

Afterward, the man lay back and closed his eyes. The woman looked at him and smiled. "Now, how about that swim?" she said.

"You go ahead. I'll wait for you here."

The woman rose and walked to where the gentle surf washed over her ankles. The water was colder than the night air, for it was only mid-June. The woman called back, "You're sure you don't want to come?" But there was no answer from the sleeping man.

She backed up a few steps, then ran at the water. At first her strides were long and graceful, but then a small wave crashed into her knees. She faltered, regained her footing, and flung herself over the next waist-high wave. The water was only up to her hips, so she stood, pushed the hair out of her eyes, and continued walking until the water covered her shoulders. There she began to swim—with the jerky, head-above-water stroke of the untutored.

A hundred yards offshore, the fish sensed a change in the sea's rhythm. It did not see the woman, nor yet did it smell her. Running within the length of its body were a series of thin canals, filled with mucus and dotted with nerve endings, and these nerves detected vibrations and signaled the brain. The fish turned toward shore.

The woman continued to swim away from the beach, stopping now and then to check her position by the lights shining from the house. The tide was slack, so she had not moved up or down the beach. But she was tiring, so she rested for a moment, treading water, and then started for the shore.

The vibrations were stronger now, and the fish recognized prey. The sweeps of its tail quickened, thrusting the giant body forward with a speed that agitated the tiny phosphorescent animals in the water and caused them to glow, casting a mantle of sparks over the fish.

The fish closed on the woman and hurtled past, a dozen feet to the side and six feet below the surface. The woman felt only a wave of pressure that seemed to lift her up in the water and ease her down again. She stopped swimming and held her breath. Feeling nothing further, she resumed her lurching stroke.

The fish smelled her now, and the vibrations—erratic and sharp—signaled distress. The fish began to circle close to the surface. Its dorsal fin broke water, and its tail, thrashing back and forth, cut the glassy surface with a hiss. A series of tremors shook its body.

For the first time, the woman felt fear, though she did not know why. Adrenaline shot through her trunk and limbs, generating a tingling heat and urging her to swim faster. She guessed that she was fifty yards from shore. She could see the line of white where the waves broke on the beach. She saw the lights in the house, and for a comforting moment she thought she saw someone pass by one of the windows.

The fish was about forty feet from the woman, off to the side, when it turned suddenly to the left, dropped entirely below the surface, and, with two quick thrusts of its tail, was upon her.

At first, the woman thought she had snagged her leg on a rock or a piece of floating wood. There was no initial pain, only one violent tug on her right leg. She reached down to touch her foot, treading water with her left leg to keep her head up, feeling in the blackness with her left hand. She could not find her foot. She reached higher on her leg, and then she was overcome by a rush of nausea and dizziness. Her groping fingers had found a nub of bone and tattered flesh. She knew that the warm, pulsing flow over her fingers was her own blood.

Pain and panic struck together. The woman threw her head back and screamed a guttural cry of terror.

The fish had moved away. It swallowed the woman's limb without chewing. Bones and meat passed down its gullet in a single spasm. Now the fish turned again, homing on the stream of blood flushing from the woman's femoral artery, a beacon as true and clear as a lighthouse on a cloudless night. This time the fish attacked from below. It hurtled up under the woman, jaws agape. The great conical head struck her like a locomotive, knocking her up out of the water. The jaws snapped shut around her torso, crushing bones and flesh and organs into a jelly. The fish, with the woman's body in its mouth, smashed down on the water with a thunderous splash, spewing foam and blood and phosphorescence in a gaudy shower.

Below the surface, the fish shook its head from side to side, its serrated triangular teeth sawing through what little sinew still resisted. The corpse fell apart. The fish swallowed, then turned to continue feeding. Its brain still registered the signals of nearby prey. The water was laced with blood and shreds of flesh, and the fish could not sort signal from substance. It cut back and forth through the dissipating cloud of blood, opening and closing its mouth, seining for a random morsel. But by now, most of the pieces of the corpse had dispersed. A few sank slowly, coming to rest on the sandy bottom, where they moved lazily in the current. A few drifted away just below the surface, floating in the surge that ended in the surf.

The man awoke, shivering in the early morning cold. His mouth was sticky and dry, and his wakening belch tasted of bourbon and corn. The sun had not yet risen, but a line of pink on the eastern horizon told him that daybreak was near. The stars still hung faintly in the lightening sky. The man stood and began to dress. He was annoyed that the woman had not woken him when she went back to the house, and he found it curious that she had left her clothes on the beach. He picked them up and walked to the house.

He tiptoed across the porch and gently opened the screen door, remembering that it screeched when yanked. The living room was dark and empty, littered with half-empty glasses, ashtrays, and dirty plates. He walked across the living room, turned right down a hall, past two closed doors. The room he shared with the woman was open, and a bedside light was on. Both beds were made. He tossed the woman's clothes on one of the beds, then returned to the living room and switched on a light. Both couches were empty.

There were two more bedrooms in the house. The owners slept in one. Two other house guests occupied the other. As quietly as possible, the man opened the door to the first bedroom. There were two beds, each obviously containing only one person. He closed the door and moved to the next room.

The host and hostess were asleep on each side of a king-size bed. The man closed the door and went back to his room to find his watch. It was nearly five.

He sat on one bed and stared at the bundle of clothes on the other. He was certain the woman wasn't in the house. There had been no other guests for dinner, so unless she had met someone on the beach while he slept, she couldn't have gone off with anyone. And even if she had, he thought, she would probably have taken at least some of her clothes.

Only then did he permit his mind to consider the possibility of an accident. Very quickly the possibility became a certainty. He returned to the host's bedroom, hesitated for a moment beside the bed, then softly placed his hand on a shoulder.

"Jack," he said, patting the shoulder. "Hey, Jack."

The man sighed and opened his eyes. "What?"

"It's me, Tom. I hate like hell to wake you up, but I think we may have a problem."

Jane Langton

Boston-born Jane Langton (b. 1922) is the Edgar Award-winning author of eighteen adult mystery novels featuring detective Homer Kelly. Langton lives in Lincoln, Massachusetts, the town next to historic Concord, and many of her mysteries are either set in Concord or in other Massachusetts locations equally rich in history. The Minuteman Murder *(1974),* The Memorial Hall Murder *(1978),* Emily Dickinson Is Dead *(1984),* Murder at the Gardner *(1988), and* God in Concord *(1992) are fine examples. Langton is equally well-known and equally prolific in the field of children's fiction. Her work for children includes picture books, several stand-alone novels, and a series—*The Hall Family Chronicles—*which begins with* The Diamond in the Window *(1962) and most recently has included* The Mysterious Circus *(2005). In 1980, her juvenile novel* The Fledgling, *about a little girl whose dreams of flying come true when she rides on the back of a Canada goose, was a Newbery Honor Book.*

Langton once observed that "My books start with an interest in place." Fortunately for island aficionados of the murder mystery, her interest in place has included Nantucket. Langton's Dark Nantucket Noon *(1975) is on the Independent Mystery Booksellers' List of "100 Favorite Mysteries of the Twentieth Century." The author researched the novel through several visits to the island and a course of study at the University of Massachusetts Nantucket Field Station. The multifaceted Langton is an artist as well as a writer;* Dark Nantucket Noon *is charmingly illustrated with her line drawings of island scenes. The novel opens with an event some Nantucketers may remember—the total eclipse of the sun that took place on 7 March 1970. —SB*

From Chapter 1 of *Dark Nantucket Noon*

Below the little plane the water of Nantucket Sound slipped over itself, the gusty wind from the east rippling the surface in an endless rapid sparkling hastening succession of white-capped waves, while the larger waves below them seemed motionless from the air, a geologic mold of ocean water. But of course the larger waves were moving too, more slowly. And, obeying a deeper compulsion, the vast watery volume of the Atlantic Ocean was rising in response to an urgent tide that yearned across the earth, sending a bulge of water dragging after the moon from the old world to the new, carrying it heaving and pulsing along the New England coast, smashing up after last night's storm upon the granite boulders of Penobscot Bay, running up into the tidal flats of the Ipswich River and the clam beds of the town of Essex, stirring the lobster pots of Gloucester and Marblehead, agitating the scum and garbage floating around T Wharf in Boston Harbor, pounding on the fisted forearm of Cape Cod, carrying away granules of colored clay from the cliffs of Gay Head on Martha's Vineyard, washing in the white breakers against the shoal that curved northeastward from the body of the island rising below the plane.

Everywhere at once the Atlantic was in motion, rocking in its bed, lifting at the summons of the massive moon, shifting the uneasy hulks of sunken vessels lying on the bottom: the *Andrea Doria*, many fathoms down, the *City of Columbus*. The tide was running in the sea; it was an ocean walking.

Kitty was coming to the island only to see the total eclipse of the sun, that was all. She had taken the plane at Boston, and when it came down at the Nantucket airport she would jump into the rented car that would be waiting for her, drive to the remotest corner of the island, look up at the eclipse, and then take the next plane home.

She was coming only to see the eclipse. There was no chance at all that she would run into Joe Green. The fact that he was living on the island with his wife had nothing whatever to do with her coming. Nothing at all. She had wanted to see a total solar eclipse all her life, and here it was, only a few miles offshore. Nantucket happened to be the only place on the North Atlantic seaboard where totality would be visible, so she had no choice. And just because she had once made a fool of herself over Joe Green, just because he had settled down on the island and married his second or third cousin or whatever it was, that was of no consequence. She would see what she had come to see, and go home.

Therefore it was odd the way the sight of the gray sickle-shaped island in the glittering sunshaft on the Atlantic Ocean alarmed her. It was positively crawling with invisible antlike Joseph Greens. They were everywhere. Kitty imagined herself aiming a powerful telescope at the island at random—at that long neck of sand ending in a little stick that must be a lighthouse, or perhaps at that stretch of red carpet in the middle of the island. She would squint one eye through the telescope and adjust the focus until the fuzzy field of view sharpened, and there before her would be Joe's face with its amiable mouth and big kindly nose and light eyes. And those eyes would be staring up at her, seeing her, identifying her through the plane window and the wrong end of the telescope, turning cold with anger at this invasion of his privacy.

At the Nantucket airport Kitty climbed out of the plane, letting the wind blow her hair like a veil over her scowling face, avoiding the eyes of the people clustered at the gate. Joe Greens, every one of them. He had multiplied, he was just on the edge of her averted gaze, he was looking through the baggage on the pavement, he was shouting greetings into the wind, he was selling her a local paper and a map of the island, he was handing her the key to her rented car, he was crowding the waiting room, he was loaded down with sleeping bags and heavy parkas and eclipse-viewing apparatus, he was talking excitedly in a loud voice. All the Joe Greens were exchanging congratulations about the brilliant day after the storm during the night, and they were swapping information about what to watch for—the solar corona, and Baily's beads, and the shadow bands, and the flash of red at the very end. But of course when any of these multitudinous Joe Greens opened his mouth Kitty knew it wasn't really Joe, because his voice had been different. She couldn't remember it exactly, but it wasn't this one or that one.

So it was a relief to find the little green car in the parking lot just where the man had said it would be, and her key worked in the lock, and she got in and slammed the door, grateful to be out of the wind, and dumped her bag on the seat beside her, and heaved a great sigh. Joe Green couldn't see her now, unless of course he was the man off vaguely to the left climbing into a station wagon—there, now he was gone.

Kitty started the engine to warm the car, and unfolded her new map. Where was that long neck of sand she had seen from the air? There had been a lighthouse at the end, but the rest of the long sandy beach looked roadless and deserted. There it was. Great Point. She would go to Great Point. How much time did she have? She looked at her watch. Almost two hours before the partial phase of the eclipse began, three before totality. And it was the two-and-a-half minutes of totality that she had come to see, when the light of the sun would be completely blocked out by the moon, and the sky would darken, and the solar corona would appear. It was supposed to be awe-inspiring, breath-taking, wonderful. Three hours. Plenty of time. Kitty picked up the Nantucket *Inquirer and Mirror* and turned the pages idly.

On page three there was a picture of Nantucket's Maria Mitchell Observatory, and an article about the expeditions from Johns Hopkins and the Oceanographic Institute at Woods Hole. They were going to photograph the eclipse at the observatory and make spectrographic studies of the solar prominences. They would all be there now, thought Kitty, the scientists, milling around, checking their instruments, getting ready, jubilant because of the crystal sky after last night's storm.

There was an article with the headline WHAT TO LOOK FOR, and Kitty made a mental note to read it carefully later on. Then a name caught her eye—"Homer Kelly." Homer Kelly? It had a familiar ring somehow. She ran her eye down the paragraph. "Ex-Lieutenant-Detective Homer Kelly, noted scholar in the field of nineteenth-century American literature, is spending a few weeks on the island to complete his study of the men who sailed with Melville." Oh yes, that was who Homer Kelly was. Kitty had read the biography of Thoreau he had written with his wife. What did this article mean by calling him an Ex-Lieutenant-Detective? Had he been some kind of policeman?

Well, enough of that. Kitty folded the newspaper and stuck it into her bag, which was a roomy canvas carryall with a pair of leather handles. Then she looked at the map again. To get to Great Point she would have to go west first, then turn a sharp corner and head northeast on a road marked "Polpis." Good. Kitty put the map into her carryall next to the newspaper and shifted gears.

On the road she kept her eyes straight ahead, looking neither left nor right, while Joe Greens whizzed past her every now and then, going the other way. There were torn leaves and twigs on the pavement, and Kitty guessed they had been blown off in last night's storm.

SOFT TIRES ONLY BEYOND THIS POINT

The road had petered out into sand beyond the big gray shuttered hotel, and now it had come to an end altogether. Kitty pulled up, locked the car, and set off with her bag over her arm. There was nothing in her ears but the noise she made cleaving the air, the slightest of slight sounds, diminishing as she picked up each foot in turn, increasing as she swung it forward. There were muddy puddles in the wheel ruts, and she skirted them. To her right, a row of houses looked uninhabited, boarded up. To her left lay the wind-streaked water of the harbor. Where was the open ocean? Kitty stopped and opened out her fluttering map, then struggled to fold it up again. The sea should be just over there to the right. She plowed up a steep slope, clutching at beach grass, and came out on the open Atlantic. The water was a cold dark blue, foaming up at the bottom of the steep short beach. And there was something in the water, far out, sleek black heads and finny tails. Seals! sporting and playing, diving for fish.

Exhilarated, Kitty ran down to the sand at the water's edge and whirled around, her bag a driving force at the end of one arm, her hair swatting her neck, slapping her face. Then she walked straight ahead in big strides, the sunshine striking down upon her shoulders.

The simple facts of the seashore made her happy. Air, water, earth, and fire, everything reduced to its ancient elements. She had been wanting for a long time to do something with those four things, a long funny exercise in rhymed couplets. Why didn't she just stay, abandon her students, her apartment in Cambridge, and just stay? With only those four gigantic things to think about—the salt air, the blue water, the clean sand and the fiery sun. Only three in a little while, because the sun was about to have its eye put out by the murdering moon.

The northwest wind knocked and shouldered against her. Kitty leaned into it, adapted herself to it, let it whip her hair and at the two ends of her wrapped skirt. Suddenly she felt hungry, terribly hungry. She sank down on the sand and reached for her sandwiches. Then she had to get up and plump herself down higher up the beach, because she hadn't counted on the reach of the waves. The tide must be rising. She unwrapped a sandwich and took a lusty bite. It tasted marvelous. Then she unscrewed the top of her Thermos and poured out a little coffee. That tasted marvelous too. She felt around in her bag for the photographic plate she had wrapped carefully in a cotton handkerchief and held it to the sun. There! A tiny nibble had been taken from the lower right-hand side. Kitty glanced around at the bluff and the sand and the sea, wondering if there would be any diminishing yet of the daylight. Not yet. Everything seemed just as before.

She stood up, let the wind carry the crumbs away from her skirt, gathered up the debris from her lunch, chased a flying sandwich wrapper, pounced on it, stuffed it into her bag and walked on. The going was hard, because the sand was mushy even at the wet edge of the water. Every now and then she rested by stopping to look up at the sun through her photographic plate. The bite that was being taken by the hungry moon was growing bigger, but still the light shining on the sea seemed as bright as ever. The shore continued to curve out of sight ahead of her as if she were walking always in the same place. Once Kitty climbed the bluff to examine a pile of shells and fragments of sponge and bits of beach glass that had been dumped there by some child. They had not come from this place, because here the shore was bare except for flotsam tossed up by the storm, pieces of broken lumber, a plastic jug. There was no other debris on the coarse golden sand, only the overlapping lines traced by the farthest-flung waves, delicate scalloped edgings the thickness of a single grain of sand, beaded with miniature pebbles and fragile tassels of seaweed and pearly fragments of sponge like crumbs of bread. Kitty scooped up some of the shells and dropped them into her bag.

The lighthouse was in sight at last, a white object far away. She looked at her watch. Only an hour before totality. Impulsively Kitty made up her mind to watch the eclipse from the lighthouse. There was no time to waste. She ran back down again to the edge of the water and began striding along, dragging her heels out of the clinging sand, feeling the pull in the small of her back. By the time the moon had effaced half of the sun's disk she was tired, but she kept her eyes fixed on the curving shore ahead of her, willing the lighthouse now to come in sight. The sky was noticeably darker now, the blue deeper and more intense, the sea more forbidding, the air chillier and sharp. The crescent sun was slanting down through the beach grass on the bluff, making miraculous images of itself between the interfering blades, and the dancing sparkles on the rushing waves were crescents too. The light filtering through Kitty's hair made small crescents amid the shadow that floated beside her. But Kitty had eyes now only for the lighthouse, a faraway gleaming tower above the bluff. She hurried her heavy feet, feeling giddy, high-spirited. *I am running a race with the moon. So is the sun, which comes forth like a bridegroom leaving his chamber, and like a strong man runs its course with joy.*

Where were the birds? There had been small ones skittering along the edge of the waves, and herring gulls dipping and soaring. They were gone. *I must be moonstruck,* thought Kitty, giggling. *I'm suffering from moon madness.* She pounded on, her feet doggedly taking turns, her chest rising and falling in gasping breaths. The land had narrowed. She could see the ocean on either side. The sandy neck was all one beach. Suddenly her shoes were in water. A shock of cold went through her, and she looked down. A wave had run up the shore and spilled over on the other side. Kitty tried to dodge the next, but it caught her and dashed against her legs, soaking her shoes and woolly stockings and drenching the hem of her skirt with the freezing water of the North Atlantic. Ankle-deep, Kitty stood still and cried out with the bitterness of the cold. The wave slipped sideways back, and the next impulse was not as high. Swiftly she pulled off her sopping shoes and stockings and stuffed them in her carryall. The sand seemed almost warm to her bare feet. The sky was darker now, the wind freshening, lifting her hair, blowing up the loose heavy edge of her skirt. Light footed, Kitty began to run again, glancing up at the streaking rays glaring over the edge of the moon. *Not yet, moon, don't put the sun out yet. I want to touch base first.* Gasping, she ran, shivering with the cold, the wind tossing her hair in a long streamer, blowing the flap of her skirt up about her waist, exposing one pale cold leg. At first Kitty tried to push her skirt down, but it was too much trouble. And why bother? There was no one to see. Even the all-seeing eye of the sun was about to be put out. It was really dark now, quite dark. She stopped running and plodded along for another half mile. Then with a breathless laugh Kitty suddenly reached up and wrenched off her sunglasses. Sunglasses! At a time like this.

Touch base! She was nearly there. She ran across the wet sand, her hands stretched out, the stone side of the lighthouse looming up before her, and at last her fingers touched the peeling white paint of the wall. Then she turned and tottered a few steps, her heart in her mouth as a pall of darkness suddenly dropped upon her shoulders. The sand was fluttering with strange shadows. She threw her head back and looked up. The sun was going. A single piercing ray glistened at one side, and then—

Kitty screamed. The sea screamed, the sand, the sky. The sun was gone. There was a black stone in its place. A small black stone. Pearly brightness flared up around it. Two planets welled up in the midnight sky near it.

God have mercy. Kitty shuddered, struggling not to burst into hysterical tears. She should never have come out here alone. No one should have to behold the end of the world like this alone. Oh, God, the black stone. She should fall on her knees and pray, she should offer herself up as a sacrifice, she should wail and hammer some brazen gong. But all she could do was cry, and stare up, mesmerized, shaking, weeping—until the moon at last drifted to the left and released a blaze of sunlight to the right. Choked with relief, Kitty laughed, and wiped her face with the backs of her hands, and then stumbled around the base of the lighthouse, holding her palms out to catch a handful of sunlight, circumambulating the round tower like a pilgrim praying his way around a holy place, babbling to herself. She felt cracked, unhinged, deranged, delirious. Everything was suddenly at high pitch. And so when she saw the empty cars parked down near the beach on the other side of the dune, a pickup truck and a jeep, she whirled around and looked up at the top of the lighthouse, because she knew immediately exactly where people were. They were up there! But she was too near, it was too dark, she couldn't see, she laughed with understanding, she was only looking up into blackness. And then her attention was caught by something at the foot of the lighthouse wall. There was a woman there. A woman was lying at the base of the wall, her head bent sideways to look at Kitty. She had been hurt. There was a red stain on her skirt. It was not surprising. Kitty did not feel shocked. The moon had thrown down a bolt like a thunderstone. She ran up to the woman. Perhaps she could help her. Perhaps the woman wasn't dead.

There was a great deal of blood. Kitty knelt down on the cold sand and pulled her kerchief out of her bag and dabbed at the brimming wound. But there was too much blood, and the kerchief was soon soaked. Puzzled, Kitty looked at it in disbelief, then wadded it into a sopping ball, dropped it back in her bag, and scrabbled around for a sweater that was rolled up in there somewhere. Had she lost it?

Impatiently, Kitty upended the bag and dumped everything out on the sand. Ah, there was the sweater. She pressed it against the woman's breast. But it was no use. The woman was dead. The cage of her chest was not rising and falling. Kitty shook her head and abandoned the effort, and began picking up her possessions from the sand and dropping them back into her bag. What a mess. They were all bloody from the bloody kerchief. And there was too much stuff. She put a big shell in her skirt pocket.

There. Kitty stood up, the bag in her hand, and saw the people in the lighthouse coming out. They were looking at her, looking down at the dead woman.

There were four of them. Three men and a woman. They were staring, exclaiming. One of the men dropped to his knees beside the dead woman. It was Joe Green. Kitty was not surprised. One of the other men was looking at her, choking, saying something ridiculous. "You killed her," he said. He meant Kitty. He thought she, Kitty, had killed the woman.

"No," said Kitty. "It was the moon, you see. The moon did it."

The third man had his camera out. He was taking her picture. The woman was crying, her hand over her mouth, her horrified eyes looking at Kitty. Now the man with the camera was bending down, pointing at something in the sand. He wasn't a man, after all, not a grown man. He was a young student of Kitty's, Arthur Bird. "Hello, Arthur," said Kitty.

Arthur's face was pale. Usually it was pink, Kitty remembered, with boyish red patches on his plump fair jowls. "There's the knife," he said.

"Oh, thank you," said Kitty. "That's mine. It fell out of my bag." She picked it up. It had fallen point down and nearly buried itself in the sand.

The three men and the woman all recoiled, staring at her. Then Arthur lifted his camera and took another picture.

"No, no," Kitty said. "You don't understand. I didn't kill her." She dropped the knife back in her bag. "It was the moon, don't you see? The moon did it."

VIII

Humor

Robert Benchley

Humorist, theater critic, screenwriter, actor, and raconteur Robert Benchley (1889–1945) produced more than six hundred comic essays in his lifetime, many of them written for The New Yorker. *Together with fellow theater critics Dorothy Parker and Robert Sherwood, he was a founder of the Algonquin Round Table, a luncheon meeting of New York's funniest people—a group that included Edna Ferber, Noel Coward, Harold Ross, Harpo Marx, and Tallulah Bankhead, among others—who met weekly at the Algonquin Hotel for verbal jousting and word play. Also known as "The Vicious Circle," the Algonquins were known for their epigrammatic wit (one thinks of Bankhead's apocryphal "You can take Nantucket and shove it up Woods Hole"). Benchley had no trouble keeping pace; his many quotable bon mots include "A freelance writer is one who is paid per word, per page, or perhaps"; "Tell us your phobias and we will tell you what you are afraid of"; and "A boy can learn a lot from a dog: loyalty, obedience, and the importance of turning around three times before lying down."*

Benchley's second career was launched when actors annoyed by the Algonquins' scathing reviews challenged the drama critics to perform. The result, a 1922 revue called No Sirree! *included Benchley performing a skit of his own composition called "The Treasurer's Report." When it brought down the house, Irving Berlin put Benchley on the Broadway stage, and before long he was on his way to Hollywood to write and film some forty-eight comic shorts for the new "talkies." With his plastic face, toothbrush mustache, and endearing persona as a bumbling and pedantic expert, Benchley was a hit, and in 1935 his* How to Sleep *won the Academy Award for Best Short Film.*

On Nantucket, Robert Benchley is best known as the founding sire of a talented dynasty whose members include son Nathaniel (author of The Off-Islanders*) and grandsons Peter (author of* Jaws*), Nat (actor and playwright), and Robert III (author and photographer). His earliest visit to the island was probably in 1908, when a family friend treated Robert to a recuperative week at the Sea Cliff Inn for swimming, sailing, and dancing prior to the start of his freshman year at Harvard, where he would hone his comic talents as a member of the Hasty Pudding Club and a contributor to the* Harvard Lampoon. *In 1922, friends from New York's theater circles coaxed Benchley to return* *to the island and join their summer colony in 'Sconset. Benchley was a natural asset to summer theatricals at the 'Sconset Casino, but disliked the beach, where he made only occasional appearances, clad in moccasins, a long robe, sunglasses, and a yachting cap to protect himself from dive-bombing terns. Nevertheless, Benchley, his wife, Gertrude, and two young sons, Nathaniel and Robert Jr., fell in love with the island, and would return again and again over many summers, usually staying at the Underhill Cottages. Shortly before his death, Benchley purchased the first family property on Nantucket—a burial plot in Prospect Hill Cemetery.*

Here, we offer two selections: "Why I Am Pale," Benchley's comic reflection on the difficulties of reading at the beach, and "Abandon Ship!" inspired in part by his many voyages from New Bedford to Nantucket on the steamer Nobska. *Unlike today's motor vessels, the* Nobska *had small staterooms for napping. That may sound like cause for nostalgia, but island readers will discover that the ferry experience hasn't changed much since Benchley's day. —SB*

Why I Am Pale

O NE OF THE reasons (in case you give a darn) for that unreasonable pallor of mine in midsummer, is that I can seem to find no comfortable position in which to lie in the sun. A couple of minutes on my elbows, a couple of minutes on my back, and then the cramping sets in and I have to scramble to my feet. And you can't get very tanned in four minutes.

I see other people, especially women (who must be made of rubber), taking books to the beach or up on the roof for a whole day of lolling about in the sun in various attitudes of relaxation, hardly moving from one position over a period of hours. I have even tried it myself.

But after arranging myself in what I take, for the moment, to be a comfortable posture, with vast areas of my skin exposed to the actinic rays and the book in a shadow so that I do not blind myself, I find that my elbows are beginning to dig their way into the sand, or that they are acquiring "sheet-burns" from the mattress; that the small of my back is sinking in as far as my abdomen will allow, and that both knees are bending backward, with considerable tugging at the ligaments.

This is obviously not the way for me to lie. So I roll over on my back, holding the book up in the air between my eyes and the sun. I am not even deluding myself by this maneuver. I know that it won't work for long. So, as soon as paralysis of the arms sets in, I drop the book on my chest (without having read more than three consecutive words), thinking that perhaps I may catch a little doze.

But the sun shining on closed eyelids (on *my* closed eyelids) soon induces large purple azaleas whirling against a yellow background, and the sand at the back of my neck starts crawling. (I can be stark naked and still have something at the back of my neck for sand to get in under.) So it is a matter of perhaps a minute and a half before I am over again on my stomach with a grunt, this time with the sand on my lips.

There are several positions in which I may arrange my arms, all of them wrong. Under my head, to keep the sand or mattress out of my mouth; down straight at my sides, or stretched out like a cross; no matter which, they soon develop unmistakable symptoms of arthritis and have to be shifted, also with grunting.

Lying on one hip, with one elbow supporting the head, is no better, as both joints soon start swelling and aching, with every indication of becoming infected, and often I have to be assisted to my feet from this position.

Once on my feet, I try to bask standing up in various postures, but this results only in a sunburn on the top of my forehead and the entire surface of my nose, with occasional painful blisters on the tops of my shoulders. So, gradually, trying to look as if I were just ambling aimlessly about, I edge my way toward the clubhouse, where a good comfortable chair and a long, cooling drink soon put an end to all this monkey business.

I am afraid that I am more the pale type, and should definitely give up trying to look rugged.

Abandon Ship!

THERE HAS BEEN a great deal of printed matter issued, both in humorous and instructive vein, about ocean travel on those mammoth ships which someone, who had never ridden on one, once designated as "ocean greyhounds." "Ocean camels" would be an epithet I would work up for them, if anyone should care enough to ask me. Or I might even think of a funnier one. There is room for a funnier one.

But, whether one calls them "ocean greyhounds" or "ocean camels" or something to be thought up at a later date, no one can deny that the ships which ply between this country and foreign lands get all the publicity. Every day, through this "broad" land of ours, on lakes, rivers, gulfs, and up and down the coast line, there are plying little steamers carrying more American passengers than Europe, in its most avid moments, ever dreamed of. And yet, does anyone ever write any travel hints for them, other than to put up signs reading: "Please leave your stateroom keys in the door upon departure"? Are colorful sea stories ever concocted, or gay pamphlets issued, to lend an air of adventure to this most popular form of travel by water? I hope not, for I had rather hoped to blaze a literary trail in this tantalizing bit of marine lore.

There are three different types of boat in use on our inland waterways and coastwise service: (1) Ferries, which are so silly that even *we* won't take them up for discussion. (2) Day, or excursion, boats, which take you where you are going, and, if you get fascinated by the thing, back in the same day. (3) Night boats, mostly in the Great Lakes or coastwise service, which have, as yet, never fascinated anyone to the point of making a return trip on the same run. And then, of course, you can always row yourself.

There is one peculiar feature of travel on these smaller craft of our merchant marine. Passengers are always in a great hurry to embark and in an equally great hurry to disembark. The sailing of an ocean liner, on which people are really going somewhere and at considerable expense, is marked by leisurely and sometimes haphazard arrivals right up to the last minute. But let an excursion boat called the *Alfred F. Parmenter* announce that it will leave one end of a lake at 9 A.M. bound for one end of the lake and return, and at 6 A.M. there will be a crowd of waiting passengers on the dock so great as to give passersby the impression that a man-eating shark has just been hauled up. On the other hand, fully half an hour before one of these "pleasure" boats is due to dock on its return trip, the quarterdeck will be jammed with passengers who evidently can hardly wait to get off and who have to be restrained by the officers from jumping overboard and beating the boat in to shore. At least a quarter of the time on one of these recreation trips is spent standing patiently in a crowd waiting for a chance to be the first ones on and the first ones off.

Just why anyone should want to be the first one aboard an excursion boat is one of the great mysteries of the sea. Of course, there is the desire to get good positions on deck, but even if you happen to be the first one on board, the good positions are always taken by people who seem to have swum around and come up from the other side. And then there is the question: "What *is* a good position?" No matter where you settle yourself, whether up in the bow or way aft under the awning, by the time the boat has started it turns out to be too sunny or too windy or too much under the pattering soot from the stack. The first fifteen minutes of a trip are given over to a general changing of positions among the passengers. People who have torn on board and fought for preferred spots with their lives are heard calling out: "Hey, Alice, it's better over here!" and "You hold these and I'll go see if we can't get something out of the wind." The wise tripper gets on board at the last minute and waits until the boat has swung around into her course. Then he can see how the sun, wind, and soot are falling and choose accordingly.

Of course, getting on a day boat at the last minute is a difficult thing to figure out. No matter how late you embark, there is always a wait of twenty minutes before the thing starts, a wait with no breeze in a broiling sun to the accompanying rumble of outbound freight. I have not the statistics at hand, but I venture to say that no boat of less than 4,000 tons ever sailed on time. The captain always has to have an extra cup of coffee up at the Greek's, or a piece of freight gets caught against a stanchion or the engineer can't get the fire to catch. The initial rush to get on board and the scuffle to get seats is followed by a great deal of tooting and ringing of bells—and then a long wait. People who have called out frantic good-bys find themselves involved in what seems to be an endless and footless conversation over the rail which drags on through remarks such as "Don't get seasick" and "Tell mother not to worry" into a forced interchange of flat comments which would hardly have served for any basis of conversation on shore. It finally ends by the relatives and friends on the pier being the first to leave. The *voyageurs* then return dispiritedly to their seats and bake until the thing sails. Thus, before the trip has even begun, the letdown has set in.

It has always been my theory that the collapsible chairs on the day boat are put out by one firm, the founders of which were the Borgias of medieval Italy. In the old sadistic days, the victim was probably put into one of these and tied so that he could not get out. Within two hours' time the wooden crosspiece on the back would have forced its way into his body just below the shoulder blades, while the two upright knobs at the corners of the seat would have destroyed his thigh bones, thereby making any further torture, such as the Iron Maiden or the thumbscrews, unnecessary. Today, the steamboat company does not go so far as to tie its victims in, but it gives them no other place to sit on deck, and the only way in which a comfortable reading posture can be struck is for the passenger to lie sideways across the seat with his left arm abaft the cross-bar and his left hip resting on the cloth. The legs are then either stretched out straight or entwined around another chair. Sometimes one can be comfortable for as long as four minutes in this position. The best way is to lie down flat on the deck and let people walk over you.

This deliberate construction of chairs to make sitting impossible would be understandable if there were any particular portion of the boat, such as a good lunch counter, to which the company wanted to drive its patrons. But the lunch counters on day boats seem to be run on the theory that Americans, as a nation, eat too much. Ham, Swiss cheese, and, on the dressier boats, tongue sandwiches constitute the *carte du jour* for those who, driven from their seats by impending curvature of the spine, rush to the lunch counter. If the boat happens to be plying between points in New England, that "vacation-land of America" where the business slogan is "the customer is always in the way," the customer is lucky if the chef in attendance furnishes grudgingly a loaf of bread and a piece of ham for him to make his own sandwiches. And a warm bottle of "tonic" is considered all that any epicure could demand as liquid refreshment.

All of this would not be so bad if, shortly after the boat starts, a delicious aroma of cooking onions and bacon were not wafted up through the ventilators, which turns out to be coming from the galley where the crew's midday meal is being prepared.

If the boat happens to be a "night boat," there is a whole new set of experiences in store for the traveler. Boarding at about five or six in the afternoon, he discovers that, owing to the *Eastern Star* or the *Wagumsett* having been lying alongside the dock all day in the broiling sun, the staterooms are uninhabitable until the boat has been out a good two hours. Even then he has the choice of putting his bags in or getting in himself. A good way to solve this problem is to take the bags with him into one of the lifeboats and spend the night there. Of course, if there are small children in the party (and there always are) two lifeboats will be needed.

Children on a night boat seem to be built of hardier stock than children on any other mode of conveyance. They stay awake later, get up earlier, and are heavier on their feet. If, by the use of sedatives, the traveler finally succeeds in getting to sleep himself along about 3 A.M., he is awakened sharp at four by footraces along the deck outside which seem to be participated in by the combined backfields of Notre Dame and the University of Southern California. Two children can give this effect. Two children and one admonitory parent calling out, "Don't run so hard, Ethel; you'll tire yourself all out!" can successfully bring the half-slumbering traveler to an upright position, crashing his head against the upper bunk with sufficient force to make at least one more hour's unconsciousness possible.

It is not only the children who get up early on these night boats. There is a certain type of citizen who, when he goes on a trip, "doesn't want to miss anything." And so he puts on his clothes at 4:30 A.M. and goes out on the deck in the fog. If he would be careful only not to miss anything on the coastline, it might not be so bad, but he is also determined not to miss anything in the staterooms, with the result that sleepers who get through the early-morning childish prattle are bound to be awakened by the uncomfortable feeling that they are being watched. Sometimes, if the sleeper is picturesque enough, there will be a whole family looking in at him, with the youngest child asking, "Is that daddy?" There is nothing left to do but get up and shut the window. And, with the window shut, there is nothing left to do but get out into the air. Thus begins a new day.

Sometime a writer of sea stories will arise who will immortalize this type of travel by water. For it has its heroes and its hardships, to say nothing of its mysteries, and many a good ringing tale could be built around the seamen's yarns now current among the crews of our day- and night-excursion boats. I would do it myself, but it would necessitate at least a year's apprenticeship and right now I do not feel up to that.

Frank B. Gilbreth Jr. and Ernestine Gilbreth Carey

The Gilbreth family's connection to Nantucket, which continues to this day, began in 1921 when Frank Gilbreth Sr. and his wife, Lillian Moller Gilbreth, purchased a small lot near Cliff Beach that included one of two "bug-lights" (small lighthouses built in 1838 to serve as rangefinders for the main channel into the harbor) and the keeper's small workshop-cottage. The Gilbreths then had the second bug-light moved to the property, a job accomplished by a group of Nantucket men with a horse and a ship's capstan. Highly regarded professional partners in the fields of motion study and industrial efficiency, Frank Sr. and Lillian (who received a Ph.D. from Brown University in 1915) produced a brood of twelve children—six girls and six boys—born over a period of seventeen years, and often the subjects of parental experiments. The bug-lights and the cottage (fondly nicknamed "The Shoe") would become the Gilbreth clan's much-loved summer home (in 1952 the old Shoe was replaced by a new and larger Shoe).

Two of the twelve children, Frank B. Gilbreth Jr. (1911–2001) and Ernestine Gilbreth Carey (1908–2006), would immortalize the adventures of this wonderfully wacky family in two coauthored bestsellers, Cheaper by the Dozen (1948) and its sequel Belles on Their Toes (1950). Book-of-the-Month-Club selections translated into fifty-two languages, both books also became successful films. Ernestine, third-born and the older member of the brother-and-sister team, graduated from Smith College in 1929 with a degree in English. She enjoyed a successful career as a department-store buyer and manager in New York City for many years, and published a number of books on her own, including Jumping Jupiter (1952) and Rings Around Us (1956), comedies based on her department-store experiences and married life. Frank Jr. was the fifth-born child and first boy. A University of Michigan graduate, he became a journalist, served in the U.S. Navy during World War II (becoming a lieutenant commander and winning the Bronze Star and Air Medal), and went on to a career as vice-president, assistant publisher, and columnist for the Charleston, South Carolina, Post and

Courier. *He too was an author in his own right. Among his many books,* Innside Nantucket *(1954; about the family's experiences running an island bed-and-breakfast) and* Of Whales and Women: One Man's View of Nantucket History *(1956) ought to interest Nantucket readers. Here, we offer a look at the Gilbreths' island adventures from* Cheaper By the Dozen. *—SB*

From Chapters 11 and 12
of *Cheaper by the Dozen*

WE SPENT OUR summers at Nantucket, Massachusetts, where Dad bought two lighthouses, which had been abandoned by the government, and a ramshackle cottage, which looked as if it had been abandoned by Coxey's Army. Dad had the lighthouses moved so that they flanked the cottage. He and mother used one of them as an office and den. The other served as a bedroom for three of the children.

He named the cottage "The Shoe," in honor of Mother, who, he said, reminded him of the old woman who lived in one.

The cottage and lighthouses were situated on a flat stretch of land between the fashionable Cliff and the Bathing Beach. Besides our place, there was only one other house in the vicinity. This belonged to an artist couple named Whitney. But after our first summer at Nantucket, the Whitneys had their house jacked up, placed on rollers, and moved a mile away to a vacant lot near the tip of Brant Point. After that, we had the strip of land all to ourselves. . . .

When we first started going to Nantucket, which is off the tip of Cape Cod, automobiles weren't allowed on the island, and we'd leave the Pierce-Arrow in a garage at New Bedford, Massachusetts. Later, when the automobile ban was lifted, we'd take the car with us on the *Gay Head* or the *Sankaty,* the steamers that plied between the mainland and the island. Dad had a frightening time backing the automobile up the gangplank. Mother insisted that we get out of the car and stand clear. Then she'd beg Dad to put on a life preserver.

"I know you and it are going to go into the water one of these days," she warned.

"Doesn't anybody, even my wife, have confidence in my driving?" he would moan. Then, on a more practical note: "Besides, I can swim."

The biggest problem, on the boat and in the car, was Martha's two canaries, which she had won for making the best recitation in Sunday school. All of us, except Dad, were fond of them. Dad called one of them Shut Up and the other You Heard Me. He said they smelled so much they ruined his whole trip, and were the only creatures on earth with voices louder than his children. Tom Grieves, the handyman, who had to clean up the cage, named the birds Peter Soil and Maggie Mess. Mother wouldn't let us use those full names, she said they were "Eskimo." (Eskimo was Mother's description of anything that was off-color, revolting, or evil-minded.) We called the birds simply Peter and Maggie.

On one trip, Fred was holding the cage on the stern of the ship, while Dad backed the car aboard. Somehow, the wire door popped open and the birds escaped. They flew to a piling on the dock, then to the roof of a warehouse. When Dad, with the car finally stowed away, appeared on deck, three of the younger children were sobbing. They made so much noise that the captain heard them and came off the bridge.

"What's the trouble now, Mr. Gilbreth?" he asked.

"Nothing," said Dad, who saw a chance to put thirty miles between himself and the canaries. "You can shove off at any time, Captain."

"No one tells me to shove off until I'm ready to shove off," the captain announced stubbornly. He leaned over Fred. "What's the matter, son?"

"Peter and Maggie," bawled Fred. "They've gone over the rail."

"My God," the captain blanched. "I've been afraid this would happen ever since you Gilbreths started coming to Nantucket."

"Peter and Maggie aren't Gilbreths," Dad said irritatedly. "Why don't you just forget about the whole thing and shove off?"

The captain leaned over Fred again. "Peter and Maggie who? Speak up, boy!"

Fred stopped crying. "I'm not allowed to tell you their last names. Mother says they're Eskimo."

The captain was bewildered. "I wish someone would make sense. You say Peter and Maggie, the Eskimos, have disappeared over the rail?"

Fred nodded. Dad pointed to the empty cage. "Two canaries," Dad shouted, "known as Peter and Maggie and by other aliases, have flown the coop. No matter. We wouldn't think of delaying you further."

"Where did they fly to, sonny?"

Fred pointed to the roof of the warehouse. The captain sighed.

"I can't stand to see children cry," he said. He walked back to the bridge and started giving orders.

Four crew members, armed with crab nets, climbed to the roof of the warehouse. While passengers shouted encouragement from the rail, the men chased the birds across the roof, back to the dock, onto the rigging of the ship, and back to the warehouse again. Finally Peter and Maggie disappeared altogether, and the captain had to give up.

"I'm sorry, Mr. Gilbreth," he said. "I guess we'll have to shove off without your canaries."

"You've been too kind already," Dad beamed.

Dad felt good for the rest of the trip, and even managed to convince Martha of the wisdom of throwing the empty, but still smelly, bird cage over the side of the ship.

The next day, after we settled in our cottage, a cardboard box arrived from the captain. It was addressed to Fred, and it had holes punched in the top.

"You don't have to tell *me* what's in it," Dad said glumly. "I've got a nose." He reached in his wallet and handed Martha a bill. "Take this and go down to the village and buy another cage. And after this, I hope you'll be more careful of your belongings."

Our cottage had one small lavatory, but no hot water, shower, or bathtub. Dad thought that living a primitive life in the summer was healthful. He also believed that cleanliness was next to godliness, and as a result all of us had to go swimming at least once a day. The rule was never waived, even when the temperature dropped to the fifties, and a cold, gray rain was falling. Dad would lead the way from the house to the beach, dog-trotting, holding a bar of soap in one hand, and beating his chest with the other.

"Look out, ocean, here comes a tidal wave. Brrr. Last one in is Kaiser Bill."

Then he'd take a running dive and disappear in a geyser of spray. He'd swim under water a ways, allow his feet to emerge, wiggle his toes, swim under water some more, and then come up head first, grinning and spitting a thin stream of water through his teeth.

"Come on," he'd call. "It's wonderful once you get in." And he'd start lathering himself with soap.

Mother was the only non-swimmer, except the babies. She hated cold water, she hated salt water, and she hated bathing suits. Bathing suits itched her, and although she wore the most conservative models, with long sleeves and black stockings, she never felt modest in them. Dad used to say Mother put on more clothes than she took off when she went swimming.

Mother's swims consisted of testing the water with the tip of a black bathing shoe, wading cautiously out to her knees, making some tentative dabs in the water with her hands, splashing a few drops on her shoulders, and, finally, in a moment of supreme courage, pinching her nose and squatting down until the water reached her chest. The nose pinch was an unnecessary precaution, because her nose never came within a foot of the water.

Then, with teeth chattering, she'd hurry back to the house, where she'd take a cold-water sponge bath, to get rid of the salt.

"My, the water was delightful this morning, wasn't it?" she'd say brightly at the lunch table.

"I've seen fish who found the air more delightful than you do the water," Dad would remark.

As in every other phase of teaching, Dad knew his business as a swimming instructor. Some of us learned to swim when we were as young as three years old, and all of us had learned by the time we were five. It was a sore point with Dad that Mother was the only pupil he ever had encountered with whom he had no success.

"This summer," he'd tell Mother at the start of every vacation, "I'm really going to teach you, if it's the last thing I do. It's dangerous not to know how to swim. What would you do if you were on a boat that sank? Leave me with a dozen children on my hands, I suppose! After all, you should have some consideration for me."

"I'll try again," Mother said patiently. But you could tell she knew it was hopeless.

Once they had gone down to the beach, Dad would take her hand and lead her. Mother would start out bravely enough, but would begin holding back about the time the water got to her knees. We'd form a ring around her and offer her what encouragement we could.

"That's the girl, Mother," we'd say. "It's not going to hurt you. Look at me. Look at me."

"Please don't splash," Mother would say. "You know how I hate to be splashed."

"For Lord's sakes, Lillie," said Dad. "Come out deeper."

"Isn't this deep enough?"

"You can't learn to swim if you're hard aground."

"No matter how deep we go, I always end up aground anyway."

"Don't be scared now. This time will be different. You'll see."

Dad towed her out until the water was just above her waist. "Now, the first thing you have to do," he said, "is learn the dead man's float. If a dead man can do it, so can you."

"I don't even like its name. It sounds ominous."

"Like this, Mother. Look at me."

"You kids clear out," said Dad. "But, Lillie, if the children can do it, you, a grown woman, should be able to. Come on now. You can't help but float, because the human body, when inflated with air, is lighted than the water."

"You know I always sink."

"That was last year. Try it now. Be a sport. I won't let anything happen to you."

"I don't want to."

"You don't want to show the white feather in front of all the kids."

"I don't care if I show the whole albatross," Mother said. "But I don't suppose I'll have another minute's peace until I try it. So here goes. And remember, I'm counting on you not to let anything happen to me."

"You'll float. Don't worry."

Mother took a deep breath, stretched herself out on the surface, and sank like a stone. Dad waited awhile, still convinced that under the laws of physics she must ultimately rise. When she didn't, he finally reached down in disgust and fished her up. Mother was gagging, choking up water, and furious.

"See what I mean?" she finally managed.

Dad was furious too. "Are you sure you didn't do that on purpose?" he asked her.

"Mercy, Maud," Mother sputtered. "Mercy, mercy, Maud. Do you think that I like it down there in Davey Jones' locker?"

"Davey Jones' locker," scoffed Dad. "Why, you weren't even four feet underwater. You weren't even in his attic."

"Well, it seemed like his locker to me. And I'm never going down there again. You ought to be convinced that Archimedes' principle simply doesn't apply, so far as I am concerned."

Coughing and blowing her nose, Mother started for the beach.

"I still don't understand it, Dad muttered. "She's right. It completely refutes Archimedes." [. . . .]

Dad acquired the *Rena* to reward us for learning to swim. She was a catboat, twenty feet long and almost as wide. She was docile, dignified, and ancient.

Before we were allowed on board the *Rena*, Dad delivered a series of lectures about navigation, tides, the magnetic compass, seamanship, rope-splicing, right-of-way, and nautical terminology. It is doubtful if, outside the Naval Academy at Annapolis, any group of Americans ever received a more thorough indoctrination before setting foot on a catboat.

Next followed a series of dry runs, on the front porch of the Shoe. Dad, sitting in a chair and holding a walking stick as if it were a tiller, would bark out orders while maneuvering his imaginary craft around a tricky harbor.

We'd sit in line on the floor alongside of him, pretending we were holding down the windward rail. Dad would rub imaginary spray out of his eyes, and scan the horizon for possible sperm whale, Flying Dutchmen, or floating ambergris.

"Great Point Light off the larboard bow," he'd bark. "Haul in the sheet and we'll try to clear her on this tack."

He'd ease the handle of the cane over toward the imaginary leeward rail, and two of us would haul in an imaginary rope.

"Steady as she goes," Dad would command. "Make her fast."

We'd make believe to twist the rope around a cleat.

"Coming about," he'd shout. "Low bridge. Ready about, hard a'lee."

This time he'd push the cane handle all the way over to the leeward side. We'd duck our heads and then scramble across the porch to man the opposite rail.

"Now we'll come up and pick up our mooring. You do that at the end of every sail. Good sailors always make the mooring on the first try. Landlubbers sometimes have to go around three or four times before they can catch it."

He'd stand up in the stern, the better to squint at the imaginary mooring.

"Now. Let go your sheet, Bill. Stand by the center-board, Mart. Up on the bow with the boat-hook, Anne and Ernestine, and mind you grab that mooring. Stand by the throat, Frank. Stand by the peak, Fred. . . ."

We'd scurry around the porch going through our duties, until at last Dad was satisfied his new crew was ready for the high seas.

Dad was never happier than when aboard the *Rena*. From the moment he climbed into our dory to row out to *Rena*'s mooring, his personality changed. On the *Rena*, we were no longer his flesh and blood, but a crew of landlubberly scum shanghaied from the taverns and fleshpots of many exotic ports. *Rena* was no scow-like catboat, but a sleek four-master, bound around the Horn with a bone in her teeth in search of rare spices and the priceless treasures of the Indies. He insisted that we address him as Captain, instead of Daddy, and every remark must needs be civil and end with a "Sir."

"It's just like when he was in the Army," Ernestine whispered. "Remember those military haircuts for Frank and Bill, and all that business of snapping to attention, and learning to salute, and the kitchen police?"

"Avast there, you swabs," Dad hollered. "No mutinous whispering on the poop deck!"

Anne, being the oldest, was proclaimed first mate of the *Rena*. Ernestine was second mate, Martha third, and Frank fourth. All the younger children were able-bodied seamen who, presumably, ate hardtack and bunked before the mast.

"Seems to be blowing up, Mister," Dad said to Anne. "I'll have a reef in that mains'l."

"Aye, aye, Sir."

"The *Rena*'s got just one sail, Daddy," Lill said. Is that the mains'l?"

"Quiet, you landlubber, or you'll get the merrie rope's end. Of course it's the mains'l."

The merrie rope's end was no idle threat. Able-bodied seamen or mates who failed to leap when Dad barked an order did in fact receive a flogging with a piece of rope. It hurt, too.

Dad's mood was contagious, and soon the mates were as dogmatic and full of invective as he, when dealing with the sneaking pickpockets and rum-palsied derelicts who were their subordinates. And somehow, Dad passed along to us the illusion that placid old *Rena* was a taut ship.

"I'll have those halliards coiled," he told Anne.

"Aye, aye, Sir. Come on, you swabs. Look alive now, or shiver my timbers if I don't keel haul the lot of you."

Sometimes, without warning, Dad would start to bellow out tuneless chanties about the fifteen men on a dead man's chest and, especially, one that went, "He said heave her to, she replied make it three."

If there had been any irons aboard, they would have been occupied by the fumbling landlubber or scurvy swab who forgot his duties and made Dad miss the mooring. Dad felt that to have to make a second try for the mooring was the supreme humiliation, and that fellow yachtsmen and professional sea captains all along the waterfront were splitting their sides laughing at him. He'd drop the tiller, grow red in the face, and advance rope in hand on the offender. More than once, the scurvy swab made a panic-stricken dive over the side, preferring to swim ashore, where he would cope ultimately with Dad, instead of meeting the captain on the latter's own quarterdeck.

On one occasion, when Dad blamed missing a mooring on general inefficiency and picked up a merrie rope's end to inflict merrie mass punishment, the entire crew leaped over the side in an unrehearsed abandon-ship maneuver. Only the captain remained at the helm, from which vantage point he hurled threatening reminders about the danger of sharks and the penalties of mutiny. On that occasion, he brought *Rena* up to the mooring by himself, without any trouble, thus proving something we had long suspected—that he didn't really need our help at all, but enjoyed teaching us and having a crew to order around.

Through the years, the old *Rena* remained phlegmatic, paying no apparent attention to the bedlam which had intruded into her twilight years. She was too old a seadog to learn new tricks.

Only once, just for a second, did she display any sign of temperament. It was after a long sail. A fog had come up, and *Rena* was as clammy as a shower curtain. We had missed the mooring on the first go-round, and the captain was in an ugly mood. We made the mooring all right on the second try. The captain, as was his custom, was standing in the stern, merrie rope in hand, shouting orders about lowering the sail. Just before the sail came down, a squall hit *Rena*, and she retaliated by whipping her boom savagely across the hull. The captain saw it coming, but didn't have time to duck. The boom caught him on the side of the head with a terrific clout, a blow hard enough to lift him off his feet and tumble him, stomach first, into the water.

The captain didn't come up for almost a minute. The crew, while losing little love for their captain, became frightened for their Daddy. We were just about to dive in after him when a pair of feet emerged from the water and the toes wiggled. We knew everything was all right then. The feet disappeared, and a few moments later Dad came up head first. His nose was bleeding, but he was grinning and didn't forget to spit the fine stream of water through his front teeth.

"The bird they call the elephant," he whispered weakly, and he was Dad then. But not for long. As soon as his head cleared and his strength came back, he was the captain again.

"All right, you red lobsters, avast there," he bellowed. "Throw your captain a line and help haul me aboard. Or, shiver my timbers, I'll take a belaying pin to the swab who lowered the boom on me."

Reprinted by permission of HarperCollins Publishers.

Nathaniel Benchley

Nathaniel Benchley (1915–81) marks the middle generation of Nantucket's literary dynasty. He was the son of a famous father, Robert Benchley of the Algonquin Round Table, and the father of a famous son, Peter Benchley, author of Jaws. Nathaniel distinguished himself as the most prolific author of the Benchley clan. After beginning his career as a reporter for the New York Herald Tribune, serving in the U.S. Naval Reserve during World War II, and working briefly for Newsweek as an editor, Benchley had gained enough experience and recognition to be able to support his family as a freelance writer and artist. Over the course of a forty-year career, he would write twenty books for adults, including fifteen novels, twenty-four books for children and young adults, and a number of theatrical and film adaptations—not to mention articles and short stories for magazines including The New Yorker, Esquire, McCall's, Ladies Home Journal, and Vogue. His connection to Nantucket was lifelong, beginning with boyhood summers in 'Sconset, a tradition he continued for his own sons. Ten years before his death, Benchley and his wife Marjorie moved to Nantucket year-round.

A sampler of Nathaniel Benchley's notable writing might include the 1968 thriller Welcome to Xanadu, about a mental patient who kidnaps a sixteen-year-old farm girl, or the 1960 comic novel Sail a Crooked Ship, about a group of bank robbers who highjack a ship they don't know how to sail. It might include his 1975 biography of Humphrey Bogart, a close personal friend, or his 1954 anthology of his father's essays, The Benchley Roundup. His award-winning young-adult novels, Only Earth and Sky Last Forever (1972, about a young Indian survivor of the battle of the Little Big Horn) and Bright Candles (1974, about a Danish boy's experiences during the Nazi occupation of his country), would certainly be on the list. So would many of his children's books, including Sam the Minuteman (1969), Small Wolf (1972), and George the Drummer Boy (1977), all still available today as part of Harper Trophy's successful "I Can Read" series. Island children might vote to include an out-of-print favorite, The Deep Dives of Stanley Whale (1973), about a young whale whose desire to explore the deepest, blackest water gets him into trouble with a giant squid but helps him to save his Uncle Moby from whalers.

But on Nantucket, and to the world at large, Nathaniel Benchley is best known for his 1961 novel The Off-Islanders, *a comedy lampooning Cold War paranoia. The plot involves a Soviet submarine that runs aground on Nantucket shoals and the adventures that ensue when a Russian landing party sneaks ashore to steal a boat and winds up confronting a hysterical citizenry determined to defend the island from invasion.* The Off-Islanders *was made into the popular 1966 film* The Russians Are Coming, The Russians Are Coming, *directed by Norman Jewison and starring Eva Marie Saint and Alan Arkin, among others. However, we've chosen to represent Nathaniel Benchley with a selection from a lesser-known novel set on the island,* Sweet Anarchy *(1979), a comedy loosely based on Nantucket's historic 1977 attempt to secede from the Commonwealth of Massachusetts. Here, Benchley serves up a familiar island scenario that's always good for laughs—the clash of pompous personalities at town meeting.* —SB

From *Sweet Anarchy*

Town meeting was usually held in the American Legion hall, on the theory that the assorted battle flags and trophies would be a fitting reminder to the citizens of their patriotic duty, but on this occasion it was decided to move to larger quarters, the better to handle the anticipated crowd. The high school gymnasium was selected as the largest indoor space available, and row upon row of folding chairs were set up on the basketball court. These were for the qualified voters; observers either stood at the rear or found what seats they could in the bleachers that lined both sides. Chief Maddox stood at the door, and under his watchful eye the incoming townspeople gave their names to be checked against the voting sheet. When Sam arrived, the chief hesitated for a fraction of an instant, then waved him toward the back of the room.

The moderator was Dennis Fenwick, who had conducted every town meeting in recent memory. Although technically an attorney, he had spent most of his time in real-estate and land-court matters, and there were few areas on the island that he had not, at one point or another, either surveyed or examined in the books, with an eye toward possible purchase. He was large, with a florid complexion, and when he walked he wheezed as though he had air brakes. Town meetings were mercifully short, because he could stand on his feet for only so long before his arches began to give way. There had been a time, before his tenure, when the meetings ran on into the night, and those with the strongest bladders were those who cast the deciding votes, but now it was an unusual one that lasted past ten o'clock, and if there was still work on the agenda it was put over until the following evening. Since this was a special meeting there was only one item, but nobody could guess how long it would take.

Sam watched the people as they filed in and took their seats, and although he tried to classify them by type they resisted any overall description. There were the obvious workmen and fishermen, with large, heavy hands and leathery necks; there were youths of his own age group, some with beards and some with long hair and some with neither; there were white-collar types, with pale faces and soft, pudgy hands; and among the women there were some lean and leathery and some young and attractive, but on the average they were of medium height and tended toward heaviness in the hips. The clothes ranged from padded vests, like Sam's, to business suits to sweaters to horse-blanket sports jackets, and among the women there was a preponderance of tweeds and housedresses. Experienced meeting-goers wore clothing that could with decency be removed as the place grew hotter, because by ten o' clock it had usually taken on the characteristics of a Senegalese locker room.

Lennie was among the last to arrive. She looked around the crowded room, saw Sam, and had started toward him when Chief Maddox steered her toward one of the bleacher seats along the side. She turned obediently and picked her way through the other spectators until she found a seat on the top row, where she sat down and again looked over toward Sam. He saw her, and tried to pantomime that he would see her afterward, but he was sure she didn't get the message because she just looked puzzled. Then he reminded himself of his oath of celibacy, and decided it was probably just as well.

On the podium, Dennis Fenwick rapped his gavel for order, then blew into the microphone. No sound came from the speakers, and he blew again with the same result. He turned to a man behind him and said something, and all other conversation ceased. From across the room someone called an unintelligible remark, and someone else laughed, and then there was silence.

"It'll be just a minute," Fenwick said, his voice sounding strangely small. "Soon as Buster finds out WHAT THE TROUBLE IS." The speakers blared the last words, and everyone laughed. "All right," Fenwick continued, in a lower voice. "The meeting will come to order." He cleared his throat. "You all know why we're here, but in order for everything to be legal, I'll read the notice anyway." He read the call for a special meeting, for the purpose of drawing up a list of grievances against the state and making the case for secession, such document as finally agreed upon to be submitted to the voters not later than the second Tuesday after the first Monday in the month following the adoption of the declaration. "Is that all clear?" he asked when he had finished reading. There were murmured sounds of assent, and Fenwick went on, "Now, following the usual procedure, I'm going to ask each speaker to wait until a microphone is brought to him, and identify himself loud and clear so everyone'll know who's talking. Just raise your hand if you want to speak, and Buster or Albert will bring you a mike."

A man raised his hand; Fenwick nodded at him, and the man rose and began to talk. Sam recognized the owner of the pickup truck who'd given him a lift the night before, but he couldn't hear a word the man was saying.

"Just a minute, Edgar," Fenwick cut in. "Wait till you get a mike, then give your name, and *then* talk. What have I just been saying?"

A microphone on a long cord was passed in to where the man was standing, and he took it and said, "Edgar Morris. I just want to make sure that at the top of the list you make a note to abolish the excise tax. I just bought a new pickup truck, with steel-belted heavy-duty radials, overhead camshaft—"

"Edgar—" Fenwick tried to break in, but Morris wouldn't be stopped.

"—torsion-bar suspension, synchronized maxi-flex gear-box—"

"Edgar—"

"—and you know what it cost me? Sixty-eight hundred and fifty bucks, and that was *before* the excise tax. The excise tax added—now get this—the excise tax added three hundred and fifty bucks, so in all I'm looking at a tab for seventy-two hundred bucks, and that's a goddam outrage. That's all I've got to say."

"We should be so lucky," a man near Sam observed as Morris handed back the microphone and sat down.

"We'll make a note of your observation," Fenwick said. "For the moment, I think we should confine ourselves to—ah—broader matters."

A heavyset man in a madras sports jacket stood up. His complexion suggested that he had spent the winter in Florida, and the contrast between that and his shock of bushy white hair made him look almost like a photo negative. He produced a paper from his inside pocket, and cleared his throat. "I've made a few notes here," he began.

"The mike, George, wait for the mike," Fenwick said.

The microphone was passed to him, and he said, "I've made a few—"

"Your name first," Fenwick prompted.

In obvious irritation, the man said, "George Markey. M-a-r-k-e-y. I've made a few notes for what I think should be the preamble to our declaration, and with the chair's permission I'd like to read them."

"Go right ahead," Fenwick said.

Holding the paper at arm's length, Markey read: "When in the course of human events it becomes necessary for the people of an island to separate themselves from the mainland, and to assume the responsibility for governing themselves that God granted to them or should have, a decent respect for the opinions of others requires that they say why. We hold—"

"Why what?" Fenwick interrupted.

Markey looked up, and glared at the moderator. "What do you mean?"

"Does it mean why are we separating, or why did God grant us the responsibility? Or should have?"

"Look, Mr. Moderator, this is patterned on—"

"I know what it's patterned on, but if you ask me you should either have stuck to the original or made up a whole new preamble. Preferably in English."

Markey's face turned from light tan to dark mahogany. "Am I going to be allowed to read this, or not?"

"Read it, but let's confine ourselves to the grievances." Fenwick paused, and puffed for air. We've got enough business ahead of us here, without wasting time on preambles."

"The hell with it." Markey crammed the paper in his pocket, and sat down. He handed the microphone back as though he were making a sword thrust.

Sam leaned toward the man next to him. "Who's he?" he asked.

"Who ain't he?" the man replied. "Chairman of the selectmen, president of the bank—Christ, you name it, he's probably it."

"Has quite a temper, hasn't he?"

"That's his Sicilian blood."

"Markey? Sicilian?"

"Try spelling it M-a-r-c-h-i."

Fenwick rapped once with his gavel and looked around. "Does anyone care to list any specific grievances?" he asked. Several hands went up, and he nodded to a woman in a print dress wearing a hat trimmed with cherries. "Madam Selectwoman," he said. "Or should I say Selectperson?"

"Selectwoman will do." She stood up, and when the microphone reached her she said, "Agnes Tuttle. If you ask me, our most valid complaint is our lack of representation in the statehouse. They're passing laws that concern us—that have a direct effect on us—but they're not letting us have a say in the making of those laws. That's taxation without representation, which, you will remember, our forefathers classed a tyranny."

"Amen to that," someone said, and there was scattered applause.

"So be it," Fenwick said, making a note. "Grievance Number One is so recorded. Any others?" He pointed to one of the upraised hands, and said, "All right, Norris."

A small man, wearing a gray cardigan and plaid shirt buttoned at the neck, stood up. "Norris Webster. What bugs me is the amount of money we pay in taxes as against what the state does for us. Every bottle of liquor I sell I've not only had to pay a federal tax on, but also a walloping big state tax, *and* the cost of getting it here, so I'm having to sell liquor at two, three times what it cost on the mainland. Now—"

"The mainland people pay those taxes, too," Fenwick reminded him.

"I know, but the cost of getting it here makes it that much worse. My point is, here we're pouring all this money into the state, and what do they do for us? They patch up a stretch of road every now and then, and they pick up some of the tab for the school, but what else? Nothing! I figured out that for every five dollars we give them we get one in return, and that just don't make sense. I don't mind paying taxes, just so's I get something out of it, but this way it's utter damn foolishness. We're being suckered, is what we are."

Again there was applause, and Fenwick wrote on his pad. "Next?" he said.

This time the man was a speaker who looked superficially like Primo Carnera, with a bulbous jaw and prominent gums. He gave his name as Emil Corning, and went on, "What gripes my ass—"

Fenwick interrupted him with a rap of the gavel. "Let's mind our language, Emil. This isn't the Waterfront Club."

"What gives me a pain," Corning said, amidst scattered laughter, "is the damn-fool government regulations and the inspectors they send down here to enforce them. Out at the boatyard we got inspectors crawling around like termites, and every time I sell an outboard I almost got to strip it down to the piston rings to prove it don't violate some ordinance dreamed up by a guy sitting on his—uh—butt up in State Street. The government got their noses into everything, to the point where a decent American don't have a chance to make a living. I say live and let live, and screw all government inspectors."

He sat down to loud applause, and a number of hands went up. Fenwick recognized a tall, lanky man wearing a tweed suit and holding an unlighted pipe in his teeth. "Dr. Amberson," he said.

Dr. Amberson removed his pipe, took the microphone, and for a moment seemed undecided as to which he should talk into. Then he said, "One thing we haven't mentioned yet is the matter of land. We all know there's only so much land on an island, and that land can support just so many people. Once the developers take over we're lost, because they care only for the fast dollar and disregard the future. And the state has the power to mandate a development any place they see fit, no matter what the feelings of the affected community may be. There has already been talk of a state-mandated housing program here, and if it goes through we might as well kiss the island goodbye. As I see it, our only hope is to declare ourselves outside the jurisdiction of the state—in other words, to secede, and secede now, while there's still time."

When the applause had died down, Corning was on his feet, speaking without the microphone. "I don't think we should go on record against builders," he said loudly. "Building's a big part of our economy, and—"

"You've already had your say, Emil," Fenwick broke in. "Lots of people want to talk, and we don't have all night." He nodded to a short man with large ears, whose features seemed to be compressed into the middle of his face, clustered around his nose like the petals of a flower. "Mr. Turpin," he said.

"Lester Turpin," the man said into the microphone. "I don't think we ought to be too hasty with this secession business. I mean, look where it got the Confederate states. Secession means trouble, and trouble won't attract people to the island. Whenever I sit down to write an editorial, I try to think what the island is all about, so's the paper will reflect what we really are. And nine times out of ten I'll write my lead editorial on the autumn colors on the moors, or the beauty of the surf, or the sight of a deer in the morning fog, and I think that's what people like to read. If we get all hot and bothered and secede, then we're going to be like one of those cockamamie countries over in Africa, and we all know nobody wants to go *there*. If you put a gun at my head you couldn't get me to write an editorial attacking the United States, and as I see it, that's what you'll be wanting me to do. I want everything to be peaceful because that's what most people want, and I think they want to read about the good things rather than the bad."

"Nobody's asking you to attack the United States," Fenwick said. "Seceding from one state don't mean we're attacking the country as a whole."

"As far as I'm concerned we are," Corning put in. "If any more of them goddam government inspectors—"

Fenwick rapped his gavel smartly. "Save it for the general discussion, Emil," he said, and Corning subsided, muttering.

The next speaker was a lady in her mid-forties who still showed the traces of earlier good looks. Her eyes were clear and her figure was trim, but her facial muscles showed the effect of years of strain, and her hair was in slight disarray. She identified herself as Muriel Baxter, and said, "Before we cut ourselves off from the mainland completely I think we should look ahead, and see what we'll be losing. Without state aid of some sort, the school is going to be in really desperate straits. For just one thing, the matter of textbooks—we're able to get our books through various government programs, and the wear and tear on them is such that they're in need of replacement every year. If we don't have the books we'll be reduced to teaching from the blackboard, and we might as well go back to the one-room-schoolhouse system."

"And not a bad idea, either," Corning remarked loudly. "My pa was taught in a one-room schoolhouse, and it didn't do *him* no harm." He said it fast, to get it all in before Fenwick cracked his gavel, and the result was an approximate dead heat.

"I say good riddance if we get rid of government textbooks," Morris added, from his seat. "Just because they give us books they think they can tax us for everything else, and I wind up paying seventy-two hundred bucks for a pickup—"

"Let's have some order here!" Fenwick shouted, pounding his gavel. "Miss Baxter still has the floor."

"That's all I have to say," Miss Baxter concluded quietly. "There are some things we can't do without and some things we can't supply ourselves, and I believe we should think twice before we throw them away." She sat down as three people stood up, all shouting to be heard. Fenwick motioned to one of them, and the others sat down.

The speaker was a short man wearing a windbreaker and clutching a Day-Glo orange hunter's cap in both hands. "I say that's a goddam insult to us Americans—"he began, but Fenwick cut him off.

"Please identify yourself," Fenwick said, "and mind your language."

The man gave a name that sounded like "Glamis Tillik," and went on, "I still say it's a goddamn insult to us as Americans. If we—"

"I said mind your language!" Fenwick cut in sharply.

"I am minding my language! I mean every goddam word of it, and no legal-minded son of a bitch is going to stop me! If we can't use a little good old American know-how, and—"

"Sergeant at Arms, eject this man!" Fenwick ordered, to Maddox, and Maddox came down the aisle eyeing the man warily, as though he were a sparking catherine wheel.

"You can eject me but you can't shut me up!" the man shouted. "I know my rights! What the hell ever became of free speech in this country? Whatever became of a man's liberty? What ever became of free enterprise? The govern-ment's taken the whole goddam thing away from us, and is trying to brainwash our children with Communist books they deal out in the schools! Well, I ain't about to—" He stopped, and grappled with Maddox, who had slipped up behind him and pinned his arms. Two other men came up to help Maddox, and as they carried him out of the room he shouted, "They're after us right now! The Communists got boats lying off shore, waiting to take over! Look off Gander Rip, and you'll see! You'll see!" There was a brief silence, and then the sound of a slamming door.

"Sorry about that," Fenwick said. "Freedom of speech is one thing, but freedom to disrupt is quite another. This is a legal meeting, and I intend to keep it that way." He paused, breathing hard, and the overhead lights picked up a glis-ten of perspiration on his forehead. "Now," he said when his breathing returned to normal, "does anyone have any further grievances? Specific grievances against the state, that is." He looked around but saw no hands, so went on, "All right, then, let's consider those we have already noted. Are there any comments?" A forest of hands appeared, and he hesitated before selected a speaker. "Mrs. Tuttle," he said at last, and the selectwoman arose, brushed imaginary crumbs from her lap, and folded her hands in front of her. It was clear she was trying to establish an attitude of dignity and calm.

"We have heard several suggestions tonight," she said in measured tones, "some concerning the general good, and some stemming from more—ah— personal motives. I think we should separate these two, because personal griev-ances have no place in a decision that will affect the entire community. I mentioned taxation without representation, and this is, I believe, in the field of the general good. However, we have heard other complaints, from people who simply don't like the idea of taxes, and this I think is simply unrealistic." Both Webster and Morris started to their feet, but were stopped by two taps from Fenwick's gavel, and Mrs. Tuttle continued, "If we are to have a government at all we must have taxes, and those who want them abolished are putting their own selfish interests above those of the community. A community without taxes is a community without government, which is anarchy, and I don't believe that anyone here would knowingly vote for anarchy." She sat down, and Webster and Morris shot up as though impelled by springs. Fenwick recog-nized Webster.

"I resent the implication I'm against taxes," he said, looking at Mrs. Tuttle. "What I said was—"

"Nobody mentioned you by name," she replied. "If the shoe fits—"

"You might as well have. What I said was I was against paying all these taxes and getting nothing in return, but since you bring *up* the matter of taxes, how come the assessor raised the rates on every property in town but yours? You got something going with—"

"Order!" Fenwick shouted, with a resounding crack of his gavel. "The speaker will limit himself to the subject at hand."

"She was talking about taxes," Webster replied. "So was I."

"You will avoid personalities, or you will be denied the floor."

Webster shrugged. "I was only wondering," he said, and sat down.

Mrs. Tuttle rose, and looked at Fenwick. "May I be allowed to reply to this accusation?" she said.

"Nobody accused you of nothing," Webster replied from his seat. If the shoe—"

"To this implication, then?"

Wearily, Fenwick said, "Madam Selectwoman, I am trying to confine this discussion to the question of secession, and if—"

"I feel that I have been publicly insulted, and should be allowed a public rebuttal."

"Then someone else will have something personal to add, and we'll be here all night. I understand your feeling, but your request is denied. Mr. Morris has the floor."

Red-faced, her eyes glazed with rage, Mrs. Tuttle sat down, and Morris said, "I'm not so sure that anarchy would be a bad idea. Anarchy is freedom, and the American Revolution was fought for just that. Anarchy allows a man to do as he damn well pleases, without the government looking over his shoulder and stealing his money and butting in on everything he does, and if you want my opinion I say that's a good thing. We got no more freedom now than they got in Russia, and to me that's a hell of a way to live. Now, I figure that without taxes, my pickup truck would have cost about—if you figure no taxes anywhere along the line, and no government regulations—about two thousand—"

Fenwick tapped his gavel. "Can we leave the pickup truck out of it?" he asked. "I'd like to deal in broader terms."

"I was making a point," Morris replied tartly. "Some people don't seem to understand what you're talking about unless you spell it out for them."

"Why don't we take that chance?" said Fenwick. "I think most of us get your drift."

"It sure as hell don't sound that way."

"If you have nothing further to add, I'll recognize Mr. Corning." A tap of the gavel, and Webster sat down slowly, as though trying to think of something more to say, but Corning was already talking.

"I think we should settle this matter of land development," he said. "Conservation is one thing, but restricting all building is another, and I don't think we should make laws that are going to keep people from building. If you stop building you stop business, and that's going to be worse than what we got now."

Dr. Amberson was on his feet in an instant. "I didn't say I was against *all* building," he said. "I said I was against state-mandated housing programs which order building without regard to local conditions."

Fenwick rapped his gavel, but Corning ignored him. "It comes to the same thing," he said. "You're against one kind of building, you're against 'em all, just like if you're pregnant, you're pregnant, and no halfway in between."

"That's the most idiotic statement I ever heard!" Dr. Amberson began to gesticulate with his pipe, disregarding the now steady rapping of Fenwick's gavel. "You can no more lump all building together than you can lump all diseases—you can't say if a patient has gout he also has pneumonia, just—"

"How would *you* know the difference?" Corning replied loudly. "Think back a little, and you may—"

"Gentlemen!" Fenwick bellowed, but by now others had joined the fray, and the tattered remains of order had vanished into chaos. Markey stood up and added his bullhorn voice to the din.

"Mr. Chairman!" he shouted. "If I may have the floor!"

Fenwick rolled his eyes toward Markey like a heifer going to slaughter, and made a futile waving gesture with the broken shaft of his gavel. Markey took it as a signal to proceed and, invoking his office as Chairman of the Board of Selectmen, he gestured to Chief Maddox to blow his whistle. The piercing trill cut through the pandemonium and people stopped, frozen in mid-action. Corning and Dr. Amberson had been removing their jackets, Lester Turpin was halfway under his chair, Mrs. Tuttle had her umbrella raised over Webster's head, and Morris had made his way behind Miss Baxter and was crouched like a panther, ready to spring. With the blowing of the whistle they stopped, paused, and then resumed their seats.

Markey glared about the room, imperious as Napoleon. "This meeting will come to order," he said. "And the first person to be out of order will be ejected. Is that clear?" Nobody spoke, and he went on, "At the beginning, I read the proposed preamble to our declaration, and I think that, in spite of some minor quibbles, it sets a tone that—"

"Hey, George," Morris said, raising his hand. "Look at—"

"If you don't mind, I have the floor!" Markey snarled. "Save what you have to say until I'm finished. This preamble is the spirit of our—"

Other people were now murmuring, and Morris said, "I'm not kidding. Just look—"

"Are you trying to be ejected?" Markey replied.

"No, but look at Dennis. I think he's dead."

Markey looked behind him, and there, slumped across the podium, was Fenwick. His face was purple, and before anyone could reach him he slid quietly to the floor, as limp as wet seaweed.

"Jesus Christ, why didn't you say so?" Markey exclaimed, and then Dr. Amberson made his way up to the dais, kneeled down, and reached for Fenwick's wrist. Next he put his ear against Fenwick's chest, and after a moment he straightened up.

"He's alive," he said. "But only just. Get the ambulance."

The business of the meeting was forgotten; people stood quietly and waited. Sam went across to where Lennie was standing, and she took his hand and clutched it in silence. Then they heard the wheep-wheep-wheep of the ambulance siren, and saw the windows blink with its flashing light, and finally two orderlies appeared, wheeling a stretcher between them. With some difficulty they managed to clamp an oxygen mask to Fenwick's face, which was rapidly losing color, and bundle him onto the stretcher. Then, with Dr. Amberson acting as outrider, they hurried down the aisle. In a few moments there came the thump of the ambulance doors; the siren started up, then faded in the distance.

Markey mounted the dais, and took the speaker's microphone. "Ladies and gentlemen," he announced, "this meeting is adjourned."

"What about secession?" someone asked.

"The main points have already been made," Markey replied. "I—the selectmen will draw them up in legal form, and they will be presented to the voters for final consideration. I think we should all go home now, and pray for the speedy recovery of our beloved town moderator. Good night."

As the somber crowd shuffled toward the exits, Sam remembered an incident earlier in the evening, and said to Lennie, "That man who was thrown out—what did he mean there are Communist boats off the shore?"

"Search me," she said. "I think he's just out of his tree."

A man next to them overheard, and said, "There's been a boat off Gander Rip the last week or so, but it ain't no Communist boat. Looks more like a yacht to me."

"What's it doing?" Sam asked.

The man shook his head. "I ain't about to explain people in yachts," he said.

Reprinted by permission of Doubleday, a division of Random House, Inc.

Russell Baker

Nantucket is fortunate to have enjoyed a long relationship with Russell Baker (b. 1925), one of twentieth-century America's foremost humorists. Something of a scholar of humor, Baker edited the Norton Book of Light Verse *(1986) and* Russell Baker's Book of American Humor *(1993) in addition to exercising his own comic gift in regular "Observer" columns for* The New York Times. *Here, in two columns published in 1983 and 1984, respectively, Baker lampoons Nantucket's carefully regulated and self-conscious historicity. —SB*

The Taint of Quaint

I WAS NOT SURPRISED to discover that Nantucket had suffered a severe outbreak of cobblestones in my absence. The symptoms of an onset were obvious
before I left in January when a telltale rash of electrified fake gas street lamps
was beginning to spread along the sidewalks.

I cautioned my friend Crowley. "If you're not careful, you may be caught
here in a raging epidemic of quaintness," I said. I had seen these plagues before.
The onset of fake gas lamps was always a bad sign.

"What's the worst that can happen?" Crowley asked.

I hesitated to tell him, but felt obliged by the duty of friendship. "In the
worst cases, inhabitants find themselves dressed in wigs, hoop skirts, knee
britches and such, while standing in public places stirring boiling vats of candle
wax for tourist snapshots."

Did I think there was danger of that?

"Not for two or three years yet," I said. "Usually the onset of fake gas lamps
is followed by an intermediate stage characterized by a severe outbreak of cobblestones. In this stage, the disease's tendency is to expand the summer tourist
season into the winter. Saloonkeepers start referring to their merchandise as
'wassail cups' while hotel keepers refer to their fireplace wood as 'yule logs.'"

"But that's already happened here," Crowley cried.

"Then the disease may be progressing backward," I said. "I wouldn't be
surprised to see a severe outbreak of cobblestones by summer."

I should note that Nantucket is an island located south of Cape Cod,
eighty minutes by air from Columbus Avenue. Heavily dependent on tourism,
it is highly vulnerable to the epidemics rampant among the middle class of the
great northeastern megalopolis, a group in which the fever for chic smolders
constantly alongside the damp smoke of nostalgia.

Thus, cobblestones were always easily predictable, just as the gourmet del-
icatessen was easily predictable. The cobblestones were Nantucket's reaction to
the city dweller's hunger for nostalgia, just as the gourmet food shops were an
attempt to assuage the city dweller's uneasiness about being denied Columbus
Avenue cuisine.

If my diagnosis is correct, Nantucket's ailment results from a misreading of
the chic urban crowd it yearns to attract. Consider the cobblestones. Nantucket
has always had one cobblestoned street, overarched with giant elms and lined
with architecturally handsome houses.

It is a magnificent street to photograph but, because of the cobblestones, a terrible street to walk or drive on, and an agonizing street on which to ride a bicycle. For this reason, most Nantucketers try to avoid it as much as possible and leave it to the tourists.

Last year, a great many of the giant elms died of the elm blight, which diminished the street's grandeur. New plantings will improve matters forty years from now, but in the meantime. . . ? The fake gas lamps sprouted, then cobblestones broke out all over heavily trafficked side streets.

It is obvious that Nantucket has overestimated the city dwellers' thirst for quaintness. What well-heeled spenders want when they depart Boston, New York and Philadelphia for the seashore is to take the elegance of Boston, New York and Philadelphia with them.

This is why gourmet food shops blossom wherever they go and why singles' bars replace the carpenters' beer joints in seaside towns. When the $100,000-a-year people take to the seaside, they don't want to eat the fried seafood platter at Cy's Green Coffee Pot while a television set blares the Red Sox game from the bar. They want to dine in a restaurant so exclusive that nobody else on the beach can get a reservation.

While they want the elegant side of city life waiting wherever they go, they do not want its seamy side. This is why most of the people you see standing around the streets of the Hamptons, Martha's Vineyard, and Nantucket in what looks like underwear have it embroidered with alligators to show that it isn't underwear.

They don't want to be reminded that back home people sprawl all over the streets in real underwear. Nor do they want a lot of potholes. And what is a batch of cobblestones but an out-of-date precursor to the modern city pothole?

One cobbled street is amusing. Two cobbled streets remind us that quaintness was something Americans worked hard to put behind them, for good reason.

Whether the fever for quaintness has become terminal for Nantucket, it is too soon to say, but the crisis is now. Once total quaintness occurs, as it has in Williamsburg, all you have left is a two-day town. I pray for Nantucket's recovery, if only so Crowley doesn't end up in a wig and knee britches, stirring hot candle wax in front of the camera shop.

Reprinted by permission of *The New York Times*.

Quaintness

I WENT TO NANTUCKET to see how the quainting was coming along and whether it had done in my old friend Crowley.

Faithful readers may recall that my last visit had left me fearful that Crowley would end up wearing a Pilgrim costume and dipping candles in front of the Moby Dick Antique Post Card Shop. That could happen to a person who, like Crowley, lives in a place that's being quainted.

And Nantucket was being quainted at a prodigious rate. At that time, there had been an intense onset of cobblestones. Cobblestones, cobblestones. Cobblestones everywhere. Cobblestones covering up once smooth streets as relentlessly as the lava burying old Pompeii.

Cobblestones are the favorite assault weapon of quainters. First they fill all the streets with cobblestones, then they put up fake gas street lights, and then they slap people like Crowley into Pilgrim costumes and make them dip candles in public.

The good news from this year's trip is that Crowley has not succumbed to candle dipping, though it was a close thing after he heard about the Texans.

The Texans came in force this year to Nantucket and, according to the islanders, brought all their money with them and dispensed it with a generosity infuriating to the chintzy New England spirit.

In New England, a millionaire driving a car fancier than a 1967 Pontiac is regarded as an ostentatious spendthrift. Texans, who see nothing remarkable about buying the Taj Mahal if Italy is not for sale, scandalized Nantucket with their $500 tips to the mailman and the boy who raked the lawn.

When Crowley heard about the $500 tips, naturally—Crowley is a New Englander, after all—he went shopping for a Pilgrim suit and enrolled in the Moby Dick Academy of Antique Auctioneering and Public Candle Dipping.

He wanted to be in position to hold his palm out if any Texans went looking for an entertaining demonstration of candle dipping.

Crowley abandoned the project after someone told him the Texans never left their rental digs, day or night. "I was told they all traveled with computers plugged into the world and never left them for fear they'd miss a change in the price of soybeans in Hong Kong, Paris or Addis Ababa," Crowley said.

True, he still might have got several $500 tips if he had rapped on the Texans' rental doors in his Pilgrim suit and offered to dip a candle, but the humiliation of posing as a door-to-door candle dipper in order to be tipped by Texans was more than Crowley's New England spirit could countenance.

In short, Crowley had not actually been quainted, but he had been mightily tempted. I fear the time is short for Crowley. In the old days on Nantucket, before the quainting began, people like Crowley usually ended up covered with gray cedar shingles.

That's because in the days before it was quainted, Nantucket was proud to be different from the mainland, whose inhabitants were always described a bit superciliously as "off-islanders."

In those days, merely being a Nantucketer was quaintness enough, and, to distinguish themselves from "off-islanders," Nantucketers had their houses, their cars and themselves shingled in gray cedar.

Though an "off-islander," Crowley has always wanted to pass as a native, and for several years I expected to return to the island one day and find him shingled from head to toe.

Now that the quainting is proceeding at a gallop, I have graver worries. Is it not a bad sign that Crowley has had a fake gas street light installed outside his house?

I remarked on the absurdity of it. The light it emits at night is a pink electric glow. One has the prurient impression of looking at the world through gauzy pink lingerie. And since there is no gas on the island, the fakery of the thing is completed by the surge of electricity needed to make it give fraudulent gaslight.

Crowley ignored my criticisms. He was too eager to show me the mountain of cobblestones recently delivered to his house. Next week he plans to start cobblestoning his parlor floor.

When that is done he intends to strip the shingles from his house and replace them with cobblestones. A house covered with cobblestones? Is this not madness? Nonsense, says Crowley, who gives me the same argument the town made for cobblestoning the streets:

"When my house is covered with cobblestones, I'll never have to worry about it getting potholes again."

Reprinted by permission of *The New York Times.*

Tom Congdon

A summer resident for decades, and a year-round resident of Nantucket for fourteen years, freelance writer and editor Tom Congdon (1931-2008) is perhaps best-known in literary circles as the editor who hooked and landed Peter Benchley's Jaws. *Congdon was working as a senior editor at Doubleday in New York when some of Benchley's writing in* National Geographic *caught his eye. In an interview with Joshua Balling of the* Inquirer and Mirror, *Congdon recalled what happened next: "[S]o I asked him to come to lunch, and usually, all novelists want to do is talk about their books, but he didn't want to do that. Finally, at the end, I asked if he had any ideas for novels. He said 'Yes. I want to write a novel about a great white shark that fastens on an American seaport town and provokes a moral crisis. . . .' [T]he next thing we knew, we were drowning in book orders and cash and movie deals from one little luncheon in a second-rate French restaurant." As a result, Congdon became editor-in-chief at E. P. Dutton, a position he held for many years.*

Congdon found his vocation as an editor at the Saturday Evening Post *before moving on to New York's major publishing houses, and necessarily spent much of his career nurturing the work of other writers. For instance, Congdon edited Russell Baker's* Growing Up, *David Halberstam's* The Reckoning, *and Christopher Buckley's* Steaming to Bamboola. *But Congdon was a fine writer himself, and an especially fine humorist. His occasional pieces about Nantucket life enlivened* Forbes *magazine in the late 1990s. Nothing is sacred and no one is safe from Congdon's trenchant wit and relish for island eccentricities. Here we offer two selections reprinted from* Forbes. *"Mrs. Coffin's Consolation" is a naughty gem which, like its subject matter, has become something of an underground legend on Nantucket. "While You Were Away" beautifully captures a number of island characters, the tenor of life off-season, and the depth of the Nantucketer's patriotic feeling for the bay scallop. —SB.*

Mrs. Coffin's Consolation

At the Wharf Rat Club, where the old guys meet to gab, and at the post office and the Fog Island Café . . . wherever the year-round residents congregate, Nantucketers are congratulating themselves this month on another long summer survived. Once again the summer people, playing their traditional role, have left their money and vanished, freeing islanders to conjecture on important matters, such as the price scallops will bring when the commercial season starts, and what happened to Edouard A. Stackpole's stash of antique dildos.

Nantucket, as you know from your reading of *Moby-Dick* (or maybe you caught the movie), was once a whaling island. In the eighteenth and nineteenth centuries, its ships roamed the oceans of the world in pursuit of the great oil-sodden beasts. With the fortunes they made, the ship owners and captains built the stunning mansions that still line Main Street. The whaling is long gone, and the island now trades in a different kind of blubber: its history. The romance of the past lures the tourists and lubricates the real-estate market. The more romantic the past can be made, the better. But it's more than just money; it's personal. Many islanders still bear the famous old whaling surnames like Coffin and Folger and Macy, and they don't take kindly to rude suggestions about their forebears' morals.

The great expert on Nantucket history was Edouard A. Stackpole. If you had a question about Nantucket in the old days, you went to Eddie; he knew it all. A charming, white-maned old gentleman, built like a bollard, he was revered on the island, especially by those who prefer their history comfortable. He was the keeper of the flame.

The Stackpolians were dismayed when, several years ago, a young scholar named Nathaniel Philbrick wrote, of all things, an honest history of the island. Along with other demolitions, for example, Philbrick debunked the hallowed myth that Nantucket's founding fathers were lovely to the Indians. They enslaved the Indians, Philbrick revealed politely.

Tactfully hidden in the endnotes of Philbrick's forthright history was a paragraph which, though just a few lines long and set in tiny type, nonetheless lifted local eyebrows. In the course of researching his book, Philbrick wrote, he'd encountered a number of Nantucket old-timers who made the same shocking allegation—that many of the whalers, returning from the Pacific, brought their wives Chinese sex appliances ironically called "he's-at-homes." Often made from carved ivory, these implements were designed to help the good women of the island get by while their husbands were off on three- and four-year voyages. But the scholars weren't certain that any he's-at-homes had survived.

The dildo reports, though interesting, were mere hearsay, so Philbrick left the topic out of the main body of his text.

It's one thing to hear that your forefathers were a bit rough on the aborigines; it's another to be told your great-great-great grandma used a dildo. But because his scholarly reputation was unassailable and his smile disarming, Philbrick got away with both affronts, only a few diehard traditionalists electing to cross the cobblestones rather than speak to him.

The island's historians—some published, some just knowledgeable buffs—had already heard the he's-at-home rumors but, as members of a more circumspect generation, hadn't seen fit to circulate them. Among themselves, however, and loosened by sherry, they often debated the existence of these exotic devices. Rarer were they than the great white whale, and some said just as mythical. But one historian, Wes Tiffney, claimed that years before, he'd had a drink with Stackpole, who'd shown him a small sea-chest full of them—ivory, exotic hardwoods, and gutta-percha.

Stackpole is said to have later denied that he had any he's-at-homes, but most local scholars disbelieved him. Doubters speculated that he'd hidden them under his floorboards or buried them in his cellar. When Stackpole died, at the age of 89, his house was put up for sale, which gave interested parties a chance to get in there and poke around. No he's-at-homes. "He must have taken them with him," quipped one buff. In the archives he bequeathed to the Nantucket Historical Association, however, someone did find a photo of a white-bearded seaman displaying a whale's penis eight-and-a-half feet long.

As it happened, my wife and I had something important to contribute to the Nantucket dildo discussion. Seventeen years ago, we'd bought an old house in the island's historic district. All the fireplaces had been closed off, so we hired a mason, Kevin Thurston, to open them up and install dampers. One afternoon, when we came by to check on his progress, Kevin greeted us with a peculiar expression on his face. "I found these on the damper ledge of the middle-room fireplace," he said. Blushing, he handed us an assortment of strange objects.

There was a little green bottle—a laudanum vial, it later turned out. There was a man's shirt collar and a pipe. There was a stack of scorched letters from James Coffin, a captain in the navy, begging his wife's forgiveness for some unnamed scandal he had brought upon the family. And there was an eight-inch homemade plaster dildo. Somewhat sooty, it was very realistic, well-proportioned, with a pink tip and a hole running through the center from fore to aft (an innovation subsequently lost to the dildo maker's art, it seems, probably during mechanization). To see that dildo was to feel a sudden and unexpected kinship with generations long gone, to be overwhelmed by a sense of shared humanity.

"My God," I thought. "They were people, too."

My wife and I tried to imagine how those articles came to be in that chimney, and of course I liked my theory best. "Here's the scenario," I said. "When Captain Coffin died of a broken heart, Mrs. Coffin invited her daughter and her family to share the house. Mrs. Coffin grew very old and was moved into the middle room, along with her belongings, hidden among which were the items we've found. Mrs. Coffin was a bit ashamed of several of them—the scandalous letters, the dope bottle, the dildo—and she didn't know what to do with them. She became obsessed with the fear that she'd die and her daughter would find these mortifying items in her bureau drawer.

"Mrs. Coffin got more and more infirm," I continued, trying to hold my wife's attention, "and there came the day when they had to put her into Our Island Home. The home sent over a carriage to take her away. When it arrived at the house, the daughter went to fetch Mrs. Coffin. She tried to enter her mother's room, but she found the door locked.

"'Mother,' the daughter called. 'Why is this door locked? What on earth are you doing in there?'

"'Just a moment, dear,' Mrs. Coffin called back. 'I'll be right out.'

"In a panic, she went to the bureau drawer and took out the relics of her secret life. She had no idea how to dispose of them. She thought of throwing them into the fireplace, but it was summer, no fire, and plaster doesn't burn. Then she blindly reached up into the chimney, found the ledge that in these old-time houses was often used as a hiding place for keys and coins, and shoved the relics up onto it. She rose, brushed the soot from her fingers, unlocked the door, and tottered out to the carriage."

"Interesting," my wife said patiently.

"No, wait, here's the best part. As soon as Mrs. Coffin left, her daughter said to her husband, 'I'll miss Mother terribly. But now we can close off these nasty old-fashioned fireplaces she liked so much. Now at last we can have nice modern coal-burning stoves.' Don't you see? The fact that the fireplaces were sealed saved the letters and the collar from being burned; they were just singed by heat from the stove-pipe."

"Very plausible, I'm sure," my wife said, "but what are we going to do with these things?"

I said I thought they were important historic artifacts and therefore should be taken to the Nantucket Historical Association. I wrapped the dildo in tissue and put the whole collection in a Bloomingdale's box and, with my wife, now infected by grudging curiosity, went down to the association's headquarters. We waited in a hall full of whale's skeletons, harpoons and other whaling paraphernalia, and finally a tall, distinguished-looking woman with tightly curled white hair received us. She listened to our story of the discovery, took the box, and told us to come back in two weeks. We came back in two weeks.

"The letters are important," she said. "They should be in our archives." Then she handed back the box.

I opened it. Everything but the letters was still there. "What about the rest of this?"

"No, thank you," said the woman, her face set. "We have lots of those." I had a mental picture of hundreds of elegant ivory dildos stacked like cordwood in the association's vault . . . and in the air surrounding them, a ghostly, gratified murmur. I felt a bit foolish, having pushed my workaday plaster model.

Some time after Edouard A. Stackpole's death, I read the Philbrick history of Nantucket—it's called *Away Off Shore: Nantucket Island and Its People, 1602–1890* and was published by Mill Hill Press. I saw the endnote about he's-at-homes and called Philbrick up. We had lunch at the Brotherhood of Thieves, and over coffee I summoned the courage to mention our discovery.

"You've got a he's-at-home?" Philbrick said, clearly amazed.

"Sure," I said, swelling with pride of ownership, though I was a little uneasy about going public as a dildo owner.

"Can I see it?" he asked, surprisingly excited. "Can I bring a few people?"

Promptly at 4:00 that afternoon, Philbrick and three Nantucket history mavens appeared at my door. One of them was Wes Tiffney, the fellow who claimed to have seen Stackpole's trove. He and another man were carrying large, impressive cameras, and the third carried a tripod. I could tell that these men were in no mood for pleasantries, so I took them directly into the dining room. The Bloomingdale's box was on the table. "There it is," I said. No one made a move, so I opened the box and unwrapped the dildo. Jaws dropped. One sensed that if there were doubters among them, they were instantly converted. "May I . . . ?" asked one of them, Charley Walters, and I handed him the he's-at-home. He studied it closely and hefted it. Then Bud Egan and Wes Tiffney in turn did the same.

Walters carried it into the living room, as solemnly as the bearer of the mace at a coronation, and placed it on our settee; the claret-colored velvet, he said, was the ideal background for photos. Calipers were used to gauge its diameter, and a steel ruler was put alongside it on the velvet to indicate length in the photos. For one silly minute I wondered if they hoped that with their measurements they'd be able to identify the whaler endowed with the prototype.

Light meters were held out to the dildo, then photos were taken. There were no coarse jokes. The atmosphere was flawlessly scholarly, the aura of dedication palpable.

"Why all the fuss over just one he's-at-home?" I asked Philbrick when the others had left. "The lady at the Historical Association told me they have lots of them."

Philbrick laughed. "Take my word for it," he said. "There are no he's-at-homes in the Historical Association. This is the only surviving specimen that any of us knows of."

"But the lady. . . ."

"Perhaps the lady was flustered."

I felt vindicated. My humble dildo, spurned so frostily, was a historical treasure after all, the only known artifact of its kind on the island, highly pertinent to the annals of Nantucket women of the whaling period, who were famous for their self-reliance. It explained so much.

Ever since my lunch with Philbrick, I've been sitting around waiting for a revisionist to take over at the Historical Association and summon my he's-at-home to a place of honor in the permanent collection. Of course I'll donate the thing itself, but could I, I've wondered, ask for a small percentage when they sell reproductions in the museum gift shop?

But I can't wait much longer. What if I should get hit by a car and my executor should find this Bloomingdale's box in my bureau drawer?

Reprinted by permission of the author.

While You Were Away

If you own a house on Nantucket and occupy it for just a month or so a year, it may surprise you to learn that even though the island is thirty miles at sea and bleaker than bleak in the winter, a lot goes on in your absence. To bring you up to speed, here's a rundown on this year's off-season highlights.

Halfway through the high school football schedule, Vito Capizzo, coach of Nantucket's beloved Whalers, spotted a pretty coed in a corridor and called out, "Yo, sexy broad! Get your tail over here!"

The remark was reported in the local paper, and school officials were faced with a dilemma. On the one hand, the island's feminists, among whom Capizzo already had a lively reputation for gender-specific exuberance, started talking harassment. On the other hand, the Whalers were depending on Capizzo to get them through the big game against their rival, Martha's Vineyard (whose team is called the Vineyarders at home but on Nantucket, irreverently, the Grapes). Beyond that, no one wanted to say anything that might offend this winning coach and prompt him to look for greener gridirons.

The superintendent said something delicate to the coach, who made a perfunctory apology in the paper's letters column "to those who were offended." A few weeks later the Whalers, led by Capizzo, stomped the Grapes and went on to triumph in the regional superbowl. "Superintendents come and go," he was said to have observed at a meeting of the Boosters Club, "but I'll be here forever."

John Husted sold his handsome Federal-period house in the historic district and moved out into the moors. People wondered why in the world he ever gave up such a beautiful place.

One plausible theory came from a house painter who spent much of last summer working on the house next door. When Jacqueline Onassis died and her obituary revealed that Husted had been her first fiancé, tour buses began stopping at Husted's house, the painter said, their loudspeakers booming out the choice bit of Kennediana.

It was easy to imagine poor Husted, a reserved, retired Wall Streeter, cowering in his house, not daring to come near his front windows, resolving to flee to where the buses couldn't find him.

If he had peeped through the curtains, the sightseers would have had a bewildering bonus: Husted is a dead ringer for Claus von Bulow. (What the *National Enquirer* could have done with that one.)

❄

To year-round Nantucketers, the tiny bay scallops taken from their shallows are soul food—not only a mainstay of their economy but emblems of their maritime island life. They know how bone-chilling it is to dredge scallops from icy water and how tedious to shuck them. You have to know these things, they say, to really appreciate them.

Just before Christmas, Joanne Jones, the French teacher at the high school, set off on her annual trip to relatives in Indianapolis. As always, she was carrying a special, much-anticipated gift: five pounds of Nantucket bay scallops. At $15 a pound in the local markets ($20 a pound in Manhattan), they were a delicacy indeed.

In the waiting room at Nantucket Airport, early for the plane that would take her on the first leg of the trip, she placed her small suitcase and the container of scallops on a chair in the waiting room, then went into the coffee shop for a sandwich. (Nantucketers aren't very security-conscious; it comes from living on an island.) When she heard the plane announced, she went right out to it and got in, entirely forgetting her carry-on. The pilot climbed in through his hatch and started the engines, and the plane, a nine-seater, taxied from the terminal.

As the plane approached the head of the runway, Jones fell into conversation with the man sitting next to her, a tourist who said the high point of his visit to the island had been a scallop dinner. Jones realized what she had done.

The pilot, Ryan Hudson, was only three seats ahead of her, so she got up her courage and went forward. "I left my luggage back in the waiting room!" she shouted over the engine noise.

Hudson shrugged. "Sorry, Ma'am," he shouted back. "There's nothing I can do. We're about to take off."

"But you don't understand," Jones wailed. "I've got five pounds of scallops in my bags!"

Hudson is a Nantucketer. He pushed the microphone button on the control wheel. "Nantucket Ops," he said, hailing the airline's staff in the terminal. "Passenger left five pounds of scallops in the waiting room. We're coming back for them."

As islanders and Yankees, Nantucketers are seldom ruffled by eccentricity, but when Roger Schmidt bought a house in Codfish Park this January, their equanimity was challenged.

Codfish Park is a spit of sand sticking out into the Atlantic from the eastern end of the island. A century ago it was the base for Nantucket's cod fishery, and a quaint little settlement of houses and cottages grew up there. When the cod went away, summer people arrived, and for generations they enjoyed the cottages and their orchestra seats on one of the world's best beaches.

Ten years ago the ocean began chomping off great chunks of Codfish Park. Whenever a major nor'easter blew up, Nantucketers came out from town to watch whole houses riding out to sea, sometimes with curtains flapping and geraniums still bobbing in the window boxes. Codfish Park became to erosion what Malibu is to mudslides. Even the island's most aggressive realtors, the ones who could effortlessly sell acreage around the town's smoldering dump, gave up on Codfish Park.

Beyond the power of salesmanship, it vanished from their brochures.

Enter Roger Schmidt. This winter, as Codfish Park homeowners continued the doleful task of dragging their dwellings to plots elsewhere on the island, Schmidt bought a Codfish Park house, a pretty little place just twenty-six paces from the teeth of *mare horribilis*. He not only bought it but began sinking money into it. Once again Nantucketers drove out from town, this time to gape as Schmidt installed copper plumbing and electrical conduit and banged on rows of fresh cedar shingling.

At the Atlantic Café, especially when the wind comes strongly out of the northeast, drinkers debate whether they're dealing with an idiot here or with a mythic hero about whom an island bard should be writing "The Ballad of Roger Schmidt." King Canute couldn't hold back the sea, but maybe Schmidt can. "I'm an optimist," Schmidt says. "If I get a few good years before the ocean takes it, I'll have gotten my money's worth. In the meantime, I've got an uninterrupted view right over to Portugal."

Or in the words of Tennyson:

"And may there be no moaning [at] the bar / When I put out to sea."

Timothy Lepore is quite possibly the island's favorite general practitioner and definitely its most fanatic outdoorsman. A tall, hearty man, he shaves his head and decorates the walls of his waiting room with pistols and animal skulls.

One dark day in February, Lepore had just finished his examination of Nina Murray, a retired Harvard lecturer, when his nurse called him to the phone in the next room. "Great!" Murray could hear Dr. Lepore saying excitedly. "I'll be right over!"

He hastily hung up the phone and hurried back to his patient. "Sorry to rush off like this, Nina," he said, shedding his white smock and donning a windbreaker. "But I've just heard about some fresh roadkill." And with that he was gone.

Murray looked at the nurse in bewilderment.

"Dr. Lepore is a falconer," the nurse explained. "He needs the roadkill to feed his falcon."

Winter is a tough time on the island, as booze and boredom tatter civility. There's not enough work, and people run out of money. To save rent and fuel, they cram into small spaces and get on each other's nerves. The stores are mostly shut, and there's not much entertainment except in taverns. The police-blotter page in the local newspaper bulges with DWIs and restraining orders, along with occasional laconic little items that scream for amplification. Take for example the report that appeared in February concerning one Robert M. DiCarlo, of Littleton. DiCarlo, it stated, pled guilty to an assault charge: shaving a woman's pubic hair without her consent. That was the extent of the report, nothing else but the admonition from Judge James O'Neill. "The court," the judge rumbled, "is becoming a lot less tolerant of behavior like this."

March is called "hate month" in Nantucket. In a March meeting of the Nantucket Conservation Commission, the typically heated discussion was getting out of hand, and commissioner Andy Lowell rose from his chair to restore order. "We're acting like a bunch of third graders having a tizzy fit," he said. His remark was printed in the Nantucket paper.

A week later the paper ran a response from the third grade at Nantucket Elementary School, which as it happened was fresh from special instruction in "life skills":

"We read what you said, and we don't like it. We don't have tizzy fits when we don't agree with each other. We find ways to solve our problems without throwing fits.

"When your members can work out your differences and still be kind to each other, then you will be acting like third graders."

Reprinted by permission of the author.

IX

Contemporary Voices

John Cheever

John Cheever (1912–82) is considered one of the finest American short-story writers of the twentieth century. His collected short fiction, The Stories of John Cheever *(1978), won both the National Book Award (1979) and the Pulitzer Prize (1981). He is a noteworthy novelist as well; his major works include* The Wapshot Chronicle *(1957) as well as* Bullet Park *(1969) and* The Falconer *(1977). In 1982, Cheever received the National Medal for Literature. He is best known for chronicling the quiet desperation and spiritual malaise of New England's white, Protestant, suburban middle-class. Cheever writes with grim humor of passive protagonists alienated from their families and their jobs, nostalgic for a time when work and home were more meaningful.*

Born in Quincy, Massachusetts, Cheever was the son of unhappily married parents—Frederick Cheever, a hard-drinking shoe salesman and manufacturer who lost the family savings in the Crash of 1929, and Mary Liley Cheever, a gift-shop owner. Although he would receive an honorary doctorate from Harvard University before his death, Cheever's formal education consisted of being expelled from Thayer Academy. Yet, he was a voracious reader and a precocious writer who sold his first short story to the New Republic *by age seventeen and became a regular contributor to* The New Yorker *just five years later. Except for a brief tour in the U. S. Army Signal Corps during World War II, and occasional teaching stints in creative writing, Cheever made his living as a professional writer right from the start. In 1941, he married Mary Winternitz, a poet and teacher, and went on to father three children with her, although their marriage would be darkened by his alcoholism and closeted bisexuality.*

Cheever discovered Nantucket in the 1950s, when he and Mary began a tradition of renting seaside cottages for summer holidays with their children. One early Nantucket visit by the Cheevers was to the Yates-Shepard cottage in Surfside. Martha's Vineyard and Friendship, Maine, were also popular destinations for these family vacations, but Nantucket swiftly became the favorite when Cheever discovered the Wauwinet House, then a comfortable, casual place ideal for writing and indulging his passion for sailing. He would return to Wauwinet over and over again through the years. Nothing could speak to Cheever's love for Nantucket more plainly than his response to an offer made to him by the Franklin Library. When Franklin brought out a deluxe limited edition of The Wapshot Chronicle, *with each volume to be autographed by the author, they offered to send Cheever, all expenses paid, to an island anywhere in the world. Instead of choosing to sign books on Tahiti, say, or Bali, Cheever could think of no island he'd rather visit than the one he'd been to so many times before—Nantucket.*

Biographer Scott Donaldson has observed of Cheever that "the fictionalizing exploration of other people's houses, other people's lives . . . was, for him, part of the charm of rented summer places. . . . Summer cottages revealed their past in the books left behind, or the absence of them, and in the paintings or other displays on the wall. At Wauwinet on Nantucket, pencil markings recorded the growth of children who had lived there for the past sixty years, and Cheever could not resist inventing tales about them. At Nantucket's Surfside, in the Yates-Shepard cottage, Cheever conjured up a divorce. She was a watercolorist and he a slim young man from New York. Why did they quarrel? When did he leave?" Here we offer a Cheever story likely to haunt every Nantucket reader who has ever rented a cottage.—SB

The Seaside Houses

Each year, we rent a house at the edge of the sea and drive there in the first of the summer—with the dog and cat, the children, and the cook—arriving at a strange place a little before dark. The journey to the sea has its ceremonious excitements, it has gone on for so many years now, and there is a sense that we are, as in our dreams we have always known ourselves to be, migrants and wanderers—travelers, at least, with a traveler's acuteness of feeling. I never investigate the houses that we rent, and so the wooden castle with a tower, the pile, the Staffordshire cottage covered with roses, and the Southern mansion all loom up in the last of the sea light with the enormous appeal of the unknown. You get the sea-rusted keys from the house next door. You unfasten the lock and step into a dark or light hallway, about to begin a vacation—a month that promises to have no worries of any kind. But as strong as or stronger than this pleasant sense of beginnings is the sense of having stepped into the midst of someone else's life. All my dealings are with agents, and I have never known the people from whom we have rented, but their ability to leave behind them a sense of physical and emotional presences is amazing. Our affairs are certainly not written in air or water, but they do seem to be chronicled in scuffed baseboards, odors, and tastes in furniture and paintings, and the climates we step into in these rented places are as marked as the changes of weather on the beach. Sometimes there is in the long hallway a benignness, a purity, and a clearness of feeling to which we all respond. Someone was enormously happy here, and we rent their happiness as we rent their beach and their catboat. Sometimes the climate of the place seems mysterious, and remains a mystery until we leave in August. Who, we wonder, is the lady in the portrait in the upstairs hallway? Whose was the Aqualung, the set of Virginia Woolf? Who hid the copy of *Fanny Hill* in the china closet, who played the zither, who slept in the cradle, and who was the woman who painted red enamel on the nails of the claw-footed bathtub? What was this moment in her life?

The dog and the children run down to the beach, and we bring in our things, wandering, it seems, through the dense histories of strangers. Who owned the *Lederhosen*, who spilled ink (or blood) on the carpet, who broke the pantry window? And what do you make of a bedroom bookshelf stocked with *Married Happiness: An Illustrated Guide to Sexual Happiness in Marriage, The Right to Sexual Felicity,* and *A Guide to Sexual Happiness for Married Couples?* But outside the windows we hear the percussive noise of the sea; it shakes the bluff where the house stands, and sends its rhythm up through the plaster and timbers of the place, and in the end, we all go down to the beach—it is what we came for, after all—and the rented house on the bluff, burning now with our lights, is one of those images that have preserved their urgency and their fitness. Fishing in the spring woods, you step on a clump of wild mint and the fragrance released is like the essence of that day. Walking on the Palatine, bored with antiquities and life in general, you see an owl fly out of the ruins of the palace of Septimius Severus and suddenly that day, that raffish and noisy city all make sense. Lying in bed, you draw on your cigarette and the red glow lights an arm, a breast, and a thigh around which the world seems to revolve. These images are like the embers of our best feelings, and standing on the beach, for that first hour, it seems as if we could build them into a fire. After dark we shake up a drink, send the children to bed, and make love in a strange room that smells of someone else's soap—all measures taken to exorcise the owners and secure our possession of the place. But in the middle of the night, the terrace door flies open with a crash, although there seems to be no wind, and my wife says, half asleep, "Oh, why have they come back? Why have they come back? What have they lost?"

Broadmere is the rented house I remember most clearly, and we got there at the usual time of day. It was a large white house, and it stood on a bluff facing south, which was the open sea on that coast. I got the key from a Southern lady in a house across the garden, and opened the door onto a hallway with a curved staircase. The Greenwoods, the owners, seemed to have left that day, seemed in fact to have left a minute earlier. There were flowers in the vases, cigarette butts in the ashtrays, and a dirty glass on the table. We brought in the suitcases and sent the children down to the beach, and I stood in the living room waiting for my wife to join me. The stir, the discord of the Greenwoods' sudden departure still seemed to be in the air. I felt that they had gone hastily and unwillingly, and that they had not wanted to rent their summer house. The room had a bay window looking out to sea, but in the twilight the place seemed drab, and I found it depressing. I turned on a lamp, but the bulb was dim and I thought that Mr. Greenwood had been a parsimonious and mean man. Whatever he had been, I seemed to feel his presence with uncommon force. On the bookshelf there was a small sailing trophy that he had won ten years before. The books were mostly Literary Guild selections. I took a biography of Queen Victoria off the shelf, but the binding was stiff, and I think no one had read it. Hidden behind the book was an empty whiskey bottle. The furniture seemed substantial and in good taste, but I was not happy or at ease in the room. There was an upright piano in the corner, and I played some scales to see if it was in tune (it wasn't) and opened the piano bench to look for music. There was some sheet music, and two more empty whiskey bottles. Why hadn't he taken out his empties like the rest of us? Had he been a secret drinker? Would this account for the drabness of the room? Had he learned to take the top off the bottle without making a sound, and mastered the more difficult trick of canting the glass and the bottle so that the whiskey wouldn't splash? My wife came in, carrying an empty suitcase, which I took up to the attic. This part of the house was neat and clean. All the tools and paints were labeled and in their places, and all this neatness, unlike the living room, conveyed an atmosphere of earnestness and probity. He must have spent a good deal of time in the attic, I thought. It was getting dark, and I joined my wife and children on the beach.

The sea was running high and the long white line of the surf reached, like an artery, down the shore for as far as we could see. We stood, my wife and I, with our arms loosely around one another—for don't we all come down to the sea as lovers, the pretty woman in her pregnancy bathing suit with a fair husband, the old couples who bathe their gnarled legs, and the bucks and the girls, looking out to the ocean and its fumes for some riggish and exalted promise of romance? When it was dark and time to go to bed, I told my youngest son a story. He slept in a pleasant room that faced the east, where there was a lighthouse on a point, and the beam swept in through the window. Then I noticed something on the corner baseboard—a thread or a spider, I thought—and knelt down to see what it was. Someone had written there, in a small hand, "My father is a rat. I repeat. My father is a rat." I kissed my son good night and we all went to sleep.

Sunday was a lovely day, and I woke in very high spirits, but, walking around the place before breakfast, I came on another cache of whiskey bottles hidden behind a yew tree, and I felt a return of that drabness—it was nearly like despair—that I had first experienced in the living room. I was worried and curious about Mr. Greenwood. His troubles seemed inescapable. I thought of going into the village and asking about him, but this kind of curiosity seems to me indecent. Later in the day, I found his photograph in a shirt drawer. The glass covering the picture was broken. He was dressed in the uniform of an Air Force major, and had a long and romantic face. I was pleased with his handsomeness, as I had been pleased with his sailing trophy, but these two possessions were not quite enough to cure the house of its drabness. I did not like the place, and this seemed to affect my temper. Later I tried to teach my oldest son how to surfcast with a drail, but he kept fouling his line and getting sand in the reel, and we had a quarrel. After lunch we drove to the boatyard where the sailboat that went with the house was stored. When I asked about the boat, the proprietor laughed. It had not been in the water for five years and was falling to pieces. This was a grave disappointment, but I did not think angrily of Mr. Greenwood as a liar, which he was; I thought of him sympathetically as a man forced into those embarrassing expedients that go with a rapidly diminishing income. That night in the living room, reading one of his books, I noticed that the sofa cushions seemed unyielding. Reaching under them, I found three copies of a magazine dealing with sunbathing. They were illustrated with many pictures of men and women wearing nothing but their shoes. I put the magazines into the fireplace and lighted them with a match, but the paper was coated and they burned slowly. Why should I be made so angry, I wondered; why should I seem so absorbed in this image of a lonely and drunken man? In the upstairs hallway there was a bad smell, left perhaps by an unhousebroken cat or a stopped drain, but it seemed to me like the distillate, the essence, of a bitter quarrel. I slept poorly.

On Monday it rained. The children baked cookies in the morning. I walked on the beach. In the afternoon we visited the local museum where there was one stuffed peacock, one spiked German helmet, an assortment of shrapnel, a collection of butterflies, and some old photographs. You could hear the rain on the museum roof. On Monday night I had a strange dream. I dreamed I was sailing for Naples on the *Cristoforo Colombo* and sharing a tourist cabin with an old man. The old man never appeared, but his belongings were heaped on the lower berth. There was a greasy fedora, a battered umbrella, a paperback novel, and a bottle of laxative pills. I wanted a drink. I am not an alcoholic, but in my dream I experienced all the physical and emotional torments of a man who is. I went up to the bar. The bar was closed. The bartender was there, locking up the cash register, and all the bottles were draped in cheesecloth. I begged him to open the bar, but he said that he had spent the last ten hours cleaning staterooms and that he was going to bed. I asked if he would sell me a bottle, and he said no. Then—he was an Italian—I explained slyly that the bottle was not for me but for my little daughter. His attitude changed at once. If it was for my little daughter, he would be happy to give me a bottle, but it must be a beautiful bottle, and after searching around the bar he came up with a swan-shaped bottle, full of liqueur. I told him my daughter wouldn't like this at all, that what she wanted was gin, and he finally produced a bottle of gin and charged me ten thousand lire. When I woke, it seemed that I had dreamed one of Mr. Greenwood's dreams.

We had our first caller on Wednesday. This was Mrs. Whiteside, the Southern lady from whom we got the key. She rang our bell at five and presented us with a box of strawberries. Her daughter, Mary-Lee, a girl of about twelve, was with her. Mrs. Whiteside was formidably decorous, but Mary-Lee had gone in heavily for make-up. Her eyebrows were plucked, her eyelids were painted, and the rest of her face was highly colored. I suppose she didn't have anything else to do. I asked Mrs. Whiteside in enthusiastically, because I wanted to cross-question her about the Greenwoods. "Isn't it a beautiful staircase?" She asked when she stepped into the hall. "They had it built for their daughter's wedding. Dolores was only four at the time, but they liked to imagine that she would stand by the window in her white dress and throw her flowers down to her attendants." I bowed Mrs. Whiteside into the living room and gave her a glass of sherry. "We're pleased to have you here, Mr. Ogden," she said. "It's so nice to have children running on the beach again. But it's only fair to say that we all miss the Greenwoods. They were charming people, and they've never rented before. This is their first summer away from the beach. Oh, he loved Broadmere. It was his pride and joy. I can't imagine what he'll do without it." If the Greenwoods were so charming, I wondered who had been the secret drinker. "What does Mr. Greenwood do?" I asked, trying to finesse the direct- ness of my question by crossing the room and filling her glass again. "He's in synthetic yarns," she said. "Although I believe he's on the lookout for some- thing more interesting." This seemed to be a hint, a step perhaps in the right direction. "You mean he's looking for a job?" I asked quickly. "I really can't say," she replied.

She was one of those old women who you might say were as tranquil as the waters under a bridge, but she seemed to me monolithic, to possess some of the community's biting teeth, and perhaps to secrete some of its venom. She seemed by her various and painful disappointments (Mr. Whiteside had passed away, and there was very little money) to have been pushed up out of the stream on life to sit on its banks in unremittent lugubriousness, watching the rest of us speed down to sea. What I mean to say is that I thought I detected beneath her melodious voice a vein of corrosive bitterness. In all, she drank five glasses of sherry.

She was about to go. She sighed and started to get up. "Well, I'm so glad of this chance to welcome you," she said. "It's so nice to have children running on the beach again, and while the Greenwoods were charming, they had their dif- ficulties. I say that I miss them, but I can't say that I miss hearing them quarrel, and they quarreled every single night last summer. Oh, the things he used to say! They were what I suppose you would call incompatible." She rolled her eyes in the direction of Mary-Lee to suggest that she could have told us much more. "I like to work in my garden sometimes after the heat of the day, but when they were quarreling I couldn't step out of the house, and I sometimes had to close the doors and windows. I don't suppose I should tell you all of this, but the truth will out, won't it?" She got to her feet and went into the hall. "As I say, they had the staircase built for the marriage of their daughter, but poor Dolores was married in the Municipal Building eight months pregnant by a garage mechanic. It's nice to have you here. Come along, Mary-Lee."

I had, in a sense, what I wanted. She had authenticated the drabness of the house. But why should I be so moved, as I was, by the poor man's wish to see his daughter happily married? It seemed to me that I could see them standing in the hallway when the staircase was completed. Dolores would be playing on the floor. They would have their arms around each other; they would be smiling up at the arched window and its vision of cheer, propriety, and enduring happiness. But where had they all gone, and why had this simple wish ended in disaster?

In the morning it rained again, and the cook suddenly announced that her sister in New York was dying and that she had to go home. She had not received any letters or telephone calls that I knew of, but I drove her to the airport and let her go. I returned reluctantly to the house. I had got to hate the place. I found a plastic chess set and tried to teach my son to play chess, but this ended in a quarrel. The other children lay in bed, reading comics. I was short-tempered with everyone, and decided that for their own good I should return to New York for a day or two. I lied to my wife about some urgent business, and she took me to the plane the next morning. It felt good to be airborne and away from the drabness of Broadmere. It was hot and sunny in New York—it felt and smelled like midsummer. I stayed at the office until late, and stopped at a bar near Grand Central Station. I had been there a few minutes when Greenwood came in. His romantic looks were ruined, but I recognized him at once from the photograph in the shirt drawer. He ordered a Martini and a glass of water, and drank off the water, as if that was what he had come for.

You could see at a glance that he was one of the legion of wage-earning ghosts who haunt midtown Manhattan, dreaming of a new job in Madrid, Dublin, or Cleveland. His hair was slicked down. His face had the striking ruddiness of a baseball-park or race-track burn, although you could see by the way his hands shook that the flush was alcoholic. The bartender knew him, and they chatted for a while, but then the bartender went over to the cash register to add up his slips and Mr. Greenwood was left alone. He felt this. You could see it in his face. He felt that he had been left alone. It was light, all the express trains would have pulled out, and the rest of them were drifting in—the ghosts, I mean. God knows where they come from or where they go, this host of prosperous and well-dressed hangers-on who, in spite of the atmosphere of a fraternity they generate, would not think of speaking to one another. They all have a bottle hidden behind the Literary Guild selections and another in the piano bench. I thought of introducing myself to Greenwood, and then thought better of it. I had taken his beloved house away from him, and he was bound to be unfriendly. I couldn't guess the incidents in his autobiography, but I could guess its atmosphere and drift. Daddy would have died or absconded when he was young. The absence of a male parent is not so hard to discern among the marks life leaves on our faces. He would have been raised by his mother and his aunt, have gone to the state university and have majored (my guess) in general merchandising. He would have been in charge of PX supplies during the war. He had lost his daughter, his house, the love of his wife, and his interest in business, but none of these losses would account for his pain and bewilderment. The real cause would remain concealed from him, concealed from me, concealed from us all. It is what makes the railroad-station bars at that hour seem so mysterious. "Stupid," he said to the bartender. "Oh, stupid. Do you think you could find the time to sweeten my drink?"

It was the first note of ugliness, but there would be nothing but ugliness afterward. He would get very mean. Thin, fat, choleric or merry, young or old, all of the ghosts do. In the end, they all drift home to accuse the doorman of incivility, to rail at their wives for extravagance, to lecture their bewildered children on ingratitude, and then to fall asleep on the guest-room bed with all their clothes on. But it wasn't this image that troubled me but the image of him standing in the new hallway, imagining that he saw his daughter at the head of the stairs in her wedding dress. We had not spoken, I didn't know him, his losses were not mine, and yet I felt them so strongly that I didn't want to spend the night alone, and so I spent it with a sloppy woman who works in our office. In the morning, I took a plane back to the sea, where it was still raining and where I found my wife washing pots in the kitchen sink. I had a hangover and felt painfully depraved, guilty, and unclean. I thought that I might feel better if I went for a swim, and I asked my wife for my bathing trunks.

"They're around here somewhere," she said crossly. "They're kicking around underfoot somewhere. You left them wet on the bedroom rug and I hung them up in the shower."

"They're not in the shower," I said.

"Well, they're around here somewhere," she said. "Have you looked on the dining room table?"

"Now, listen," I said. "I don't see why you have to speak of my bathing trunks as if they had been wandering around the house, drinking whiskey, breaking wind, and telling dirty stories to mixed company. I'm just asking for an *innocent* pair of bathing trunks." Then I sneezed, and I waited for her to bless me as she always did but she said nothing. "And another thing I can't find," I said, "is my handkerchiefs."

"Blow your nose on Kleenex," she said.

"I don't want to blow my nose on Kleenex," I said. I must have raised my voice, because I could hear Mrs. Whiteside calling Mary-Lee indoors and shutting a window.

"Oh, God, you bore me this morning," my wife said.

"I've been bored for the last six years," I said.

I took a cab to the airport and an afternoon plane back to the city. We had been married twelve years and had been lovers for two years before our marriage, making a total of fourteen years in all that we had been together, and I never saw her again.

This is being written in another seaside house with another wife. I sit in a chair of no discernible period or inspiration. Its cushions have a musty smell. The ashtray was filched from the Excelsior in Rome. My whiskey glass once held jelly. The table I'm writing on has a bum leg. The lamp is dim. Magda, my wife, is dyeing her hair. She dyes it orange, and this has to be done once a week. It is foggy, we are near a channel marked with buoys, and I can hear as many bells as I would hear in any pious village on a Sunday morning. There are high bells, low bells, and bells that seem to ring from under the sea. When Magda asks me to get her glasses, I step quietly onto the porch. The lights from the cottage, shining into the fog, give an illusion of substance, and it seems as if I might stumble on a beam of light. The shore is curved, and I can see the lights of other haunted cottages where people are building up an accrual of happiness or misery that will be left for the August tenants or the people who come next year. Are we truly this close to one another? Must we impose our burdens on strangers? And is our sense of the universality of suffering so inescapable? "My glasses, my glasses!" Magda shouts. "How many times do I have to ask you to bring them for me?" I get her her glasses, and when she is finished with her hair we go to bed. In the middle of the night, the porch door flies open, but my first, my gentle wife is not there to ask, "Why have they come back? What have they lost?"

Nancy Thayer

Novelist Nancy Thayer (b. 1943) is a year-round resident of Nantucket, where she and her husband Charley Walters share a historic house from the island's whaling era. Thayer is the author of sixteen novels as of this writing, including the critically acclaimed Stepping *(1980),* Three Women at the Water's Edge *(1981), and* Custody *(2001); and, most recently, the popular and whimsical* Hot Flash *series—*The Hot Flash Club *(2003),* The Hot Flash Club Strikes Again *(2005),* Hot Flash Holidays *(2005), and* The Hot Flash Club Chills Out *(2006). In her own words, Thayer's books concern "the mysteries and romance of families and relationships: marriage and friendships, divorce and love, custody and step-parenting, family secrets and private self-affirmation, the quest for independence and the normal human hunger for personal connections."*

Our selection is from Spirit Lost *(1988), a Gothic romance with a twist. Set on contemporary Nantucket, the novel follows a happily married couple, John and Willy Constable, as they move into an old house and set about restoring it, only to find their relationship threatened by a lonely and love-starved female ghost in the attic, a spectral "widowed bride" from the island's seafaring past. Willy must fight to save her marriage and ultimately her husband's life from this dangerously seductive presence. Thayer's characters are drawn with her trademark warmth and empathy, and Nantucket readers will especially enjoy her detailed descriptions of the Constables' daily lives and island surroundings. Suspenseful and entertaining,* Spirit Lost *is the perfect book to curl up with on a dark and stormy Nantucket night, with a gale howling around the house and rain rattling the windowpanes.*

Other novels by Thayer set on Nantucket include Morning *(1987),* Belonging *(1995),* Between Husbands and Friends *(1999), and* The Hot Flash Club Chills Out *(2006).* —SB

From Chapter 5 of *Spirit Lost*

Tₕₑ ꜰᴇʀʀʏ ᴀᴘᴘʀᴏᴀᴄʜᴇᴅ over dark water. Fathoms deep lay treasure, jewels and gold, sunken boats, lovers lost forever, their white bones gleaming, caught in the streaming seaweed, washed along with stones and rubies and brass buckles from belts and shoes, froth and plunder of the sea.

John leaned on the railing of the ferry, liking the cold slap of wet wind, the darkness. The lights of Nantucket were in the distance. Below him now lay mysteries, joys and terrors he could not imagine. And he thought how the land was all man knew of civilization and security; the sea was all he could bear to know of the wild, the amoral, the unguessed.

It was just after midnight when Willy and John unlocked their front door and entered their Orange Street house. It was silent inside, and cold, for they had left the heat turned down while they were gone.

They turned up the thermostat; then Willy, who was tired in spite of her nap in the car, headed for the bedroom.

"Coming?" she asked John, and when he shook his head and said he wasn't sleepy just yet, she only paused a moment, then swallowed whatever it was she had been going to say and went on into the bedroom alone.

John poured himself a brandy and soda and, keeping on his parka, because it would be coldest of all in the attic, where there was no heat, pulled on the light chain and went up the stairs into the cold, bright attic.

She was there, as he had thought she might be. She was in the darkest corner of the attic, without her cape now, dressed simply in a long dress of creamy, lacy cotton, and her hair was pulled back and up in thick, dark sloping loops secured with ivory-headed pins. Somehow it amused him that she had a shawl of gray wool wrapped loosely around her shoulders, as if she were guarding against the cold. As if a ghost could feel cold, or warmth.

"You've come back," she said, smiling, advancing just one step toward him. Her face was so beautiful, her expression so sweetly pleased by his presence.

"I've come back," he agreed. He had vowed to himself not to be afraid, not anymore, and it wasn't only fear that he felt now, really, though his heart knocked in his chest.

"It was cruel of you to go away," she said, again smiling that sweet smile, almost flirtatiously.

"It is cruel of you to come here," John responded, but he smiled, too, as he spoke to show this apparition he was friendly.

She drew back, surprised. "But this is my home!" she said.

"*Was* your home, perhaps," John said. "It's mine now—mine and my wife's."

The woman dropped her eyes. She was offended.

"I don't like your wife," she said petulantly, and then she let her shawl drop off one shoulder and trail to the ground. She began to wander around the attic, slowly, trailing her shawl along the ground as she walked. Every now and then she would glance sidelong at John, with a sweet, challenging smile, and as she turned this way and that, as she traced her seemingly aimless path, John realized that she was showing off for him. Showing off her winsome beauty. She was petite and very slender. Thin as a wraith, he thought, and smiled to himself at the expression. He thought he would easily be able to close his hands around her waist. Through the stuff of her dress he could see the push of her breasts, which were like a girl's, still small and high and peaked.

"Who are you?" he asked. "What's your name?"

"Such impertinence!" she said in reply, stopping still in her movement. She had turned toward him, full face, and she was indignant. A flush rose up her neck, a rosiness so vivid against her pale skin that John almost felt the heat of it. They were only a few feet apart. "This is *my* house. My dearest husband built it for *me*. For me to come into as his bride. And you ask who I am!"

She was so angry that John would not have been surprised if she had hit him; he felt her anger that strongly.

But she turned away and walked slowly back to the end of the attic. Her shawl still trailed gracefully over one arm, its feathery tips dancing against the wooden floor.

She stopped, looking over her shoulder at him, and now she was smiling again, a different sort of smile, a suggestive, provocative, openly sexual smile.

"Perhaps you should find out who I am," she said. "Perhaps you might like to make my acquaintance."

Then she was gone.

She had vanished, disappeared, before his eyes. Now John was not surprised. He had told himself he should expect such a thing, and now that it had happened, he really was not surprised. He was, though, admiring. And curious. But not unhappy. And strangely, not frightened anymore. He felt invigorated. But now he turned and went back down the stairs and stood next to the bed, where he stripped off his parka and clothes and let them fall into a pile where he stood. He sank heavily into bed next to Willy and fell asleep at once.

The great white-columned neoclassic library, with the name Atheneum announced in huge gold letters on the façade, looked forbiddingly grand compared to the modest village buildings surrounding it. Inside, it was surprisingly cozy. John was directed by a librarian to the section along the side of one wall that was devoted entirely to books on Nantucket. There were dozens. He selected a few of the oldest histories and carried them to a corner where the afternoon sun fell from high windows across the wooden table, making the yellow oak gleam.

There were entire books or sections of books devoted to the most famous families of the island, the Coffins and Starbucks and Macys and Husseys. There were ships' logs and chronicles and lists and charts and documents by the score, but it wasn't until the library was almost ready to close, two hours after he had started his search, that John found what he wanted. In a dog-eared, cottony-paged, leather-bound book published in the 1920s, in the section entitled "Tragedies, Disasters and Bizarre Misfortunes," among tales of shipwrecks and mutinies, town fires and scandals, was an entry about "The Widowed Bride."

> One of Nantucket's most romantic and saddest histories is that of Captain John Wright and Jesse Orsa Barnes.
>
> Captain Wright met Miss Barnes in 1823 when he was twenty-four, a young Nantucket man who had just finished his first and extremely successful whaling cruise. Captain Wright had gone to Boston on legal matters and had visited at the home of relatives, where he met Miss Barnes, who was then seventeen and already known for her beauty. She is said to have been a slight, slender woman, graceful and delicate, with large dark eyes and long, thick, lustrous dark hair. (This in contrast to the descriptions of the island women, who, according to reports, tended to be large, husky, practical, and strong enough to perform the work of men—which, as their men were always gone, they had to do.)
>
> Captain Wright was smitten at once and vowed to make young Miss Barnes his bride. He stayed on and on in Boston, delaying the next sailing of his ship, in order to meet Miss Barnes and persuade her to be his wife. Miss Barnes was reluctant to leave the society of Boston for the isolation of Nantucket, but Captain Wright persuaded her by saying that if she would be his wife, he would build her a fine, elegant home on Orange Street, which was where the "aristocracy" of Nantucket lived at that time. In addition, it must be stated that Captain Wright was himself a fine figure of a man, though not overly tall, still of noble bearing, and strikingly handsome, with blue eyes and dark hair and a graceful demeanor.

Finally, against the advice of her friends and guardian (for Miss Barnes was an orphan and an only child), she agreed to marry Captain Wright when he returned from his next whaling expedition. Miss Barnes's love for her fiancé must have been strong, for during the three years he was away, she was proposed to so many times by men far wealthier than the captain, with far more to offer her in the way of culture and position and society. But for three years she waited for her affianced, attending only small gatherings and spending most of her time hand sewing her wedding trousseau.

In May 1826, Captain Wright returned home from his second and even more profitable whaling voyage. In the summer of that year the work was completed on the elegant neoclassic house he had had built on Orange Street, complete with servants' quarters, six fireplaces, and a widow's walk.

In September of that year, Captain Wright married Jesse Orsa Barnes in Christ Church in Cambridge, Massachusetts, and brought her home to Nantucket to live. Because Captain Wright was so wealthy, she had servants and did not have to perform menial tasks, as earlier Nantucket whaling wives had had to. It is reported that because of Jesse Orsa's beauty and refinement and education, she was shunned by the women of the island and considered to be haughty and even arrogant. And although the Quakerism of the island was waning at this time, still she was considered by the island to engage too often in frivolities and improprieties: She had her harmonium brought with her from Boston, and she often played and sang, with the windows open so that the music could drift out onto the streets and be heard by passersby. She had been seen, through those same open windows, dancing by herself to the tunes from her music box. She also drank liquor openly, engaged in smoking in her own house, and ordered books sent to her from the mainland that the librarian would never have allowed in the Atheneum. She rarely socialized with the island women and never attended any of the churches.

Captain Wright's ship, the *Parliament,* was due to leave Nantucket on another whaling cruise in November, but according to accounts, the departure was delayed time and time again due to Jesse Orsa's pleas to her new husband not to leave her so soon. It was said by those who visited the couple that never before had they seen a woman so obviously enamored of and devoted to her husband.

Unfortunately, Jesse Orsa was lucky to have detained her husband for as long as she did, for the *Parliament* left in the spring of 1827 and returned in the summer of 1830 with the tragic news that young Captain Wright was dead. He had not left his young bride with child when he set out, and so she had no child of his for solace. She had no friends on the island and no living relatives in all the world. She lived alone in her elegant, large house on Orange Street, the house her fiancé had promised her if she would be his bride, until she died at the age of eighty-one, a lonely and bitter woman.

Here the account ended at the top of the page so that on the left page and the right two portraits could be shown, in black and white: oils of Jesse Orsa Wright and Captain John Wright. John Constable stared at the figures, transfixed. There was no denying the remarkable resemblance between himself and the young captain. And there was no denying that the picture of "The Widowed Bride" was a picture of the ghost, the beautiful young apparition he had spoken with only the night before.

He was so stunned that he did not think to turn the page, to read on, to see if the account continued.

✖

At dinner that night he could scarcely hear what Willy said, scarcely force himself to respond intelligently. He was obsessed with what he had learned and thought over and over again: I am not mad. I am not hallucinating. She does exist. She does exist.

✖

He went to the attic that night.

The woman was standing by the window, gazing out at the dark harbor. Her hair was loosened and hung in shining waves down to her waist. John thought she was wearing the same cotton dress she had worn the night before, but when she turned, he saw that instead she wore a cotton nightgown. It fell from many tiny pleats at the shoulders, over the small, pronounced bosom, to the floor. Lacework intricately edged the shoulders and collar and cuffs, and while it was a discreet gown, it was also alluring, because its sheerness made obvious the fact that the woman wore no undergarments.

John cleared his throat. He was excited, frightened, aroused.

"You are here," he said, smiling.

The woman returned his smile. "Yes," she said. "I am always here—waiting."

"I know who you are now," John said. "Jesse Orsa Wright." When she did not reply, he continued, "The widowed bride of Captain John Wright, who died at sea during his third command."

He was surprised to see how she lowered her lids at that, and twisted her mouth, so that she looked sardonic, even bitter.

"You are such a gentleman," she said.

John paused, uncertain what she meant by the remark. Then he said, "I should introduce myself. I'm John Constable."

Again that bitter smile.

"I like your name," she said.

"I like yours," he replied. Then, more boldly, "There are so many questions I would like to ask you."

"There are so very few of them I'll be able to answer," she said, still smiling. "But we can talk. I would like to talk with you. I would like that very much. Yet—" She tilted her head, obviously deliberating. "Yet," she continued, "how can we talk? There is not even a place for us to sit. Do you mean for us to remain standing for the rest of our time together?"

"I—I didn't mean, hadn't thought—" John stumbled, surprised and confused at this turn of conversation.

"A chair would be nice," she said. "Two chairs. And perhaps a rug. A table? A crystal decanter of brandy?"

"Oh, well—come downstairs!" John said. "All that is downstairs. It's much more comfortably set up down there."

The woman shook her head impatiently. "I don't *want* to be down there," she said, and again a petulant note entered into the sweet lilt of her voice. "You've already changed all that so much. It's hers. As much as yours, as much as mine. But here—here—" She came closer to him. She came quickly closer, so close he could have reached out and touched her, so close he could smell the agreeable, strangely spicey, unfamiliar smell of his dreams of her. "This could be our place," she said. "Ours."

"Yes, of course," he agreed readily. "It will be. I'll do anything. What would you like?"

"Chairs," she said, smiling, turning slowly to look around at the attic. John stood still, openly staring at her without blinking, as if the strength of his stare could make her disappear if she were not real. But she was real. He could not see through her. He could smell her. He could almost feel her warmth. He could tell how the lace of her nightgown was different in texture from the creamy-smooth surface of her skin. He could see the pulse beating in the side of her throat. He could see the blue veins beneath her white skin.

"And a rug," she continued, turning back. Her smile indicated that she knew he had been studying her. "A table, a crystal decanter of brandy. I like chocolates, too. And . . . of course . . . John . . ." she said, and let the smile drop from her face. They were caught looking at each other with all seriousness then, and John could feel that seriousness deepening inside him like the hue of the evening sky changing from light blue to indigo, so that the darkness stained his blood.

"We'll need a bed," she said.

She continued to gaze at him steadily, seriously, for a few more moments after she had spoken; she kept him spellbound. Then, when he raised his hand to touch her, she vanished, but not before giving him a brief, satisfied smile.

⁂

Now he did not let himself think or question, there were times in life when such blind obedience to a superior force was necessary: as an infant, in the armed services, in school. There was no question of choice. There was no question of values. He had been caught up in something miraculous. If he thought to himself, What kind of man spends his wife's money to furnish a room for an affair with another woman? he pushed the thought aside. He was now beyond turning back.

⁂

Willy's cheeks burned with cold.

"This is crazy!" she shouted, but John was already too far ahead of her to hear. That was how she felt he *always* was recently, going along all on his own, too fast for her to follow, out of the reach of her voice.

She had agreed to come biking with him on this brisk January day simply because she thought the exercise would ease the tension that ran through him these days, making him edgy and impolite. So she had bundled up in long underwear and jeans and sweaters and her parka and gloves, but it was still fiercely cold. And here, by the water, it was painfully so.

She brought her bike to a stop at the end of the street and looked out across the long stretch of sand to the water lapping gently at the Jetties beach. Long grass the color of sand waved stiffly when the wind hit it, and a loose shingle or shutter on the boarded-up concession stand softly thumped like an insistent, irregular heart. The sky and sea were a heathery hue, everything was still, and far out shone a glaze of approaching white, promising that the snow that was now layering the Cape would soon be here.

Willy sighed. It was so lonely here now, it was melancholy. *She* was not lonely, melancholy. She and John had had a fight this morning, not over his buying all the expensive furniture for the attic but over his impatience for its delivery.

"You've gone this long without it—you didn't even want it until we came back from Boston—why get so upset about it, John?" she had asked, trying to be reasonable. But her reasoning, her attempts to calm him, had only infuriated him all the more.

The rug had arrived. It was an antique, different from anything Willy had ever thought John would like. It was a French design of flowers and fleurs-de-lis on creamy wool. Two small armchairs in shiny striped brocades had also been carried up to the attic. And a mahogany side table with scalloped edges and ivory inlay.

What John was waiting for with such impatience was a bed.

He had been waiting for a week now, and it still hadn't arrived from the mainland.

When Willy questioned John, the first time she so much as lightly mentioned all his purchases, he had blown up at her.

"You've repainted your sewing room!" he said, defensive. "Look at it! You've got an armchair, an Oriental rug, and how much did those drapes cost! So you can sit and *sew!* I'm trying to be an artist—do I have to do it in a stark attic? Do I have to try to create beauty in an atmosphere of ugliness?"

"John—" Willy had interrupted. "Hey, John. Wait a minute. What are you so angry about? I was only asking—"

He had bought three electric heaters from Marine Home Center, tan radiator-looking appliances filled with mineral oil, and carried them up the stairs himself. He told Willy they made a huge difference; at last he was comfortable there. He found several old large tables at Island Attic and now had his paints and brushes and pads and pens set out in easy reach.

The last time Willy had been up to the attic, she could see that it was getting shaped up nicely. At one end, by the window looking out at the harbor, were his easels and tables and paints—the working end. At the other end of the attic, the shadowy end, were the rug, the chairs and table, and a crystal decanter filled with cognac set on a silver tray. The relaxing end, Willy supposed.

There were two small, etched, silver-rimmed wineglasses on the silver tray.

"Two glasses," Willy had asked, smiling. "Are you planning to invite me up sometime to view your etchings?"

"No!" John had answered abruptly. Then, seeing the expression on Willy's face, he had apologized. "God, I'm sorry. I'm a maniac. I mean, yes, of course, exactly. Willy, God, I'm sorry."

The apology had come yesterday. Today there had been no apology for his quick temper, his general surliness. The closest he had come to apologizing was to invite her along on this bike ride. "Perhaps I just need the exercise," he had said.

And Willy had bundled up and come along. But he was not with her, not really, not now while he was physically so far off in the distance and not even when he had been pedaling at her side—then his thoughts had clearly been on other things.

What those other things might be he could not seem to tell her. John was more closed off to her now than he had ever been at any point in their life together. She could not even guess what was going on.

Or, rather, she could guess, but it was all so ludicrous, so absurd. So *impossible.* Willy reminded herself of the promise she had made to herself on the trip back from Boston, how she had vowed to leave John alone, to let him have his muse or his ghost or whatever it was in peace and privacy so that he could get on with his work.

Yet in her mind she was constantly troubled. She had to force herself every minute to remain calm, not to bother him about it all, not to question.

Not to ask: John, are you getting a bed up in the attic so you can sleep with that ghost of yours?

Then, in the act of stating the question, even in the silence of her mind, the foolishness of the question amused her, and she would laugh out loud, her common sense returning. It made Willy smile to herself even here on the beach with the wind buffeting her. All this was ridiculous, her fears were ridiculous, people didn't have affairs with *ghosts.* How could she be so silly?

A gust of wind hit her again, and she turned her bike and began to pedal back home. John had already disappeared down the long stretch of road. He had gone off without her. Well, that was all right, that was all right, they were two separate people. And if he was being impatient lately, and rude and preoccupied, well, that would pass. She had never lived with him when he was really working.

Willy was working, too; a church in Boston had commissioned a banner of the seasons for their chancel. It was to be the largest piece she'd ever done and would involve felt and other pieces of material as well as threads. As she biked along, now quite uncomfortable as the cold metal of the handlebars stung through the protection of her gloves and the icy air she breathed seared her lungs, she comforted herself with thoughts of the banner. Trees, fruits, flowers, birds, beasts, a riot of colors would be needed, and she would weave the seasons in a circle so that one would intertwine with the next.

It would be like marriage, Willy thought. There are seasons in marriage, too. Now we are in winter for a while, but spring will come.

Reprinted by permission of the author.

Sena Jeter Naslund

Author Sena Jeter Naslund (b. 1942) is writer-in-residence at the University of Louisville, editor of The Louisville Review, *and director of Spalding University's M.F.A. program in creative writing. A native of Birmingham, Alabama, she began her writing career by publishing short stories in literary magazines. Naslund won her first widespread acclaim with her second novel,* Sherlock in Love *(1993), borrowing Sir Arthur Conan Doyle's immortal character Sherlock Holmes and inventing a romance for the famous detective with a mysterious and flamboyant violinist who turns out to be a woman in disguise. More recently, she has enjoyed considerable success with two historical novels—*Four Spirits *(2003), set during the violent and tumultuous struggle for civil rights during the 1960s in the South, and* Abundance *(2006), a fictional memoir of Marie Antoinette. Naslund has won the Harper Lee Award and grants from numerous organizations, including the National Endowment for the Arts, and she is the Poet Laureate of Kentucky.*

Nantucket readers know her best, however, for her 1999 novel, Ahab's Wife; or, The Star-Gazer. *Written in the style and structure of Herman Melville's* Moby-Dick, *and with many characters and incidents in common, the novel is narrated not by Ishmael, but by a female character of Naslund's own creation—Ahab's wife, Una Spenser. About her inspiration, Naslund has said: "When I read . . . Ahab's references to a wife and child whom he loves (but who are unnamed) I felt he was a character who might have had a very interesting wife, one with her own story to tell. While I loved* Moby-Dick, *I also regretted that no women were included in the microcosm represented on the* Pequod *by men of all colors and creeds. I wanted women to be a part of this grand imaginative picture." Unlike Ahab, Naslund's Una "responds to the tragedies of her life not by striving to destroy what has wounded her but by her effort to go forward and create her life anew." We see the contrast in their spirits in the following excerpt. —SB*

"The Leg," Chapter 115 of *Ahab's Wife; or, The Star-Gazer*

WE SOAKED THE tender flesh of the stub in seawater to help it toughen and callus. My pride when he could bear to be fitted again with the ivory peg! My pain to see it there, more permanent-seeming than any real leg, it and the generations of ivory legs to follow. Ahab could walk again, but how angrily he trod his world! That he had once been whole and competent and now was imperfect and clumsy all but brought despair. Anger, it seemed, was his only antidote to despair, not love. Not even pride in Justice.

As soon as he could, he stalked the beach. "If I see water, I am *there*," he told me. "I am about my business. In the white foam I see the forehead of Moby Dick."

I begged to walk with him.

He replied, "Revenge is ever solitary. Isolating." He looked at me as though I grew strange and remote.

But ten days before the *Pequod* was to sail, he fell on the rocks and was brought home bleeding again.

"Carry him upstairs. To our bedroom," I directed.

Treacherously, my heart rejoiced: now he could not sail. Not on schedule. I could try to calm, distract, dissuade, persuade—beg—him to be content that he was alive.

The bleeding of the stump bloomed like a rose through bandage after bandage.

"Staunch it," he cried, "Staunch it with fire!"

Mrs. Maynard, horrified, backed up against the door.

"Throw wood on the fire," I ordered, and I set the poker in it.

She fluttered about the room, her hand at her throat. Seeing her consternation, Ahab said calmly, "Leave my wife and me alone."

She was glad to flee.

As I pressed a pad to his wound, Ahab and I watched the glow of the metal.

"It's white now," he mused. "White as Moby Dick." I could not move. "Now!" his voice rang. "Now!"

And I grabbed the hot iron and rolled its hot tip over the flesh, searing and sealing the rawness.

That roar—myself, not Ahab.

When he was better, I begged him to wait at least till the New Year, a mere week later, but he would not. He said, "How do ye know I will improve? I may fall again and be utterly wrecked, my vengeance never accomplished." He spoke propped up in bed. I thought his head seemed grateful for the soft pillow behind it. He was beautiful in the white bed, his head framed by the lace of the pillowcase.

"If ye did not try to walk upon irregular rocks or the beach—"

"Ahab will go where Ahab decides to go, Una." He did not speak unkindly, but patiently, for he loved me. I am sure he loved me then. "Note this." He reached in the pocket of his nightshirt and held up a slender glass tube, closed with a cork. "'Tis sand of Nantucket. I scooped it up just before that minion of Moby Dick betrayed me."

"The whale's minion?"

"The leg! the leg!" he pointed to the spare one, a disembodied bone, standing in the corner. "I do not trust the ivory. 'Twas the devil-cousin of this bone that betrayed me. My head dashed against stone? driftwood?—found senseless, brought home senseless."

Stem the tide—the rage of Ahab would not be stemmed. He had no wish to harm me, but I was battered by his raging. Bruised into quietness. His finger shook as he pointed at the new leg standing in the corner.

"'Twas the shaft that bruised the groin—it was my splintered leg has sent me back groaning to bed for these last days before my leaving. It did not pierce the groin, no. But mocks me freshly to incapacity all the same. Yes. That incapacity that so gores my spirit. But here's Nantucket"—he waved the vial again drawn from his pocket—"though Moby Dick send me to the ocean floor, I shall triumph—remember that—for I shall be buried in Nantucket soil."

"Ye could have a wooden leg!" I exclaimed. "Ye could pursue every whale but Moby Dick."

"Nay, nay." He contemplated the vial of sand. "Moby Dick is the King of Dragons, Una. Too many Nantucketeers—he has devoured too many of us."

"Let some younger knight take up the battle." I could have bitten my tongue off to say such a thing. Nights he lay beside me, he had muttered, *Injury or age?* and I had kissed his face slowly and more slowly till he slept.

Now he looked at me. Now his face softened. "My girl-wife," he said quietly.

I stepped toward him, my tears ready to fall.

"Stay." He held up his hand. His gaze moved back to the ivory leg in the corner, a virgin leg, yet untried. "No, it is ivory, bone of his bone, that will carry me to revenge." Suddenly he raged again, "What is revenge but extravagant justice?" He did not look to me for answer. He opened his own jaw, curled down his lip, showed his lower teeth, became what he hated—the sperm whale. His body grotesquely lunged itself upward as far as it could, as leviathan heaves itself from water to air, yet twists its body, eyes its adversary. "Moby Dick! Vanquished! Dead!" Ahab sank back into his bed, his gaze still fastened on the leg standing in the corner.

I stepped between him and the bone.

"Ahab, husband." My voice shook not with fear of him but with fear of failing to persuade him. Only the words of my father came to me, "'Vengeance is mine. I will repay,' thus saith the Lord."

"Yes," Ahab said, exhausted by his passion. He closed his eyes. "I will repay." Something like the smile he had always reserved for me rippled over his lips.

Elin Hilderbrand

Nantucket novelist Elin Hilderbrand (b. 1969) grew up in Collegeville, Pennsylvania, and is a graduate of Johns Hopkins University and the University of Iowa's renowned Writers' Workshop. A director of the Nantucket Preservation Institute, she lives on the island year-round with her husband, Chip Cunningham, and three children. Hilderbrand is the best-selling diva of the summer beach book, the master, as Booklist *puts it, of "fun, stylish, and absorbing vacation reading." Each of her fast-paced novels—* The Beach Club *(2000),* Nantucket Nights *(2002),* Summer People *(2003),* The Blue Bistro *(2005),* The Love Season *(2006), and* Barefoot *(2007)—is set on the twenty-first century island. And each is a page-turner, weaving romance, mystery, island escapades, and loving description of Nantucket places together in a compelling read.*

Our selection is from Hilderbrand's first novel, The Beach Club, *about the trials and tribulations of hotel manager Mack Petersen and an engaging cast of characters—Beach Club employees and guests who are also friends and lovers, coworkers and archrivals, parents and children. These intertwining relationships become especially complicated when a hurricane arrives to menace the resort. Here, Hilderbrand displays a wonderful flair for comedy as an overwhelmed hotel receptionist confronts a parade of bored and whining guests unable to cope with a rainy day. Nantucket readers who understand how the island's maddeningly overcrowded and overscheduled summers can become too much of a good thing will get a smile from Hilderbrand's chapter title alone—"The Eight Weeks of August."* —SB

From "The Eight Weeks of August," Chapter 7 of *The Beach Club*

Because of the weather the lobby looked like a second-grade classroom without a teacher. Guests were eating muffins and bagels and doughnuts, leaving trails of powdered sugar and smears of cream cheese on everything they touched. Someone had spilled coffee on the green carpet, and sections of the newspaper were scattered about as though the whole pile had been dropped from the rafters. Kids ran around screaming, and the phone was ringing. Vance stood behind the desk, his lips puckered.

"You're late," he said.

"Vance, listen, I'm sorry," Love said.

He raised a hand. "I don't want to hear it."

"It wasn't about your story," Love said. "I liked your story."

"Love, the damage is done, okay? Don't insult me further by trying to backpedal."

The phone rang again. Vance made no move to answer it. Love hurried through the office, hanging her wet jacket on the handle of a vacuum. She popped out to the front desk and Vance disappeared. Vanishing Vance. The phone nagged like a crying baby.

"Nantucket Beach Club and Hotel," Love said.

"Do you have any rooms available for this weekend?" a woman asked. "The lady at Visitor Services told us you were located on the beach."

"We're fully booked, ma'am," Love said. "We've been fully booked since early spring."

"Can you check to see if someone has canceled?" the woman said.

"Just a moment, please." Love poked her head into the office. Vance sat at Mack's desk, staring out the window. Why did they have to work together today of all days? Why couldn't he be Jem? "Vance, do you know where Mack is? I have a reservation call."

Vance said nothing.

"Vance?" Love said.

Nothing.

"Okay, *fine*," she said. She picked up the phone. "No cancellations, ma'am. Sorry."

A man with horn-rimmed glasses stood at the desk. He had a muffin crumb in his mustache. "Do you know when the sky is going to clear?" he asked.

"Do I know when the sky is going to clear?" Love said. "No, sir, I don't. You have a TV in your room. You could check the weather channel."

The man wiped the crumb off his lip and Love relaxed a little. "My wife has forbidden me to turn on the TV," he said. "This is a no-TV vacation. Which is going to be really trying if the rain persists, you see what I mean?"

"I'm sorry," Love said.

A line formed at the front desk. This had never happened before—it was as though everyone thought of a question for Love at the same time.

An older woman with two children stepped up. "I'm Ruthie Soldier, room seven," she said. "What is there to do with kids when it rains?"

"There's the Whaling Museum," Love said. "That's only down the street. There's the Peter Foulger Museum. There's the Hadwen House."

"Is there anything to do that will be fun for these kids?" Ruthie Soldier said. "I don't want to bore them with history."

"Thank you, Gramma," the older child, a girl wearing multicolored braces, said. "We have to go back to school in a few weeks anyway."

"You could go out for ice-cream sundaes," Love said.

"We just ate bagels," Mrs. Soldier said. "Is there a movie house with matinees?"

"No," Love said. The phone rang. She eyed the telephone console's blinking light.

"What about bowling?"

"No bowling."

"Do you have any board games?"

Love tried to block out the ringing phone. "Let me check," she said. She thought she'd seen an old, mildewed Parcheesi in one of the closets. In the office, Vance was still lounging at Mack's desk.

"Vance, do we have any board games?" Love asked. "These people want something to do with their kids."

Vance smiled meanly. He was his back-at-work creepy self. Someone whom Love would not date, not sleep with, and certainly never parent with.

The phone continued to ring. Love ran back to the desk to answer it. The people standing in line crossed their arms and shifted their weight. A man still in his pajamas tapped his bony, bare foot impatiently. Where was Mack?

"Nantucket Beach Club and Hotel," Love said.

"This is Mrs. Russo. I'm calling to see if the Beach Club is open today."

Love looked out the window. The peaked roof of the pavilion created a minifalls. "It's raining, Mrs. Russo. No Beach Club today."

"That's a shame," Mrs. Russo said. "We paid so much money."

Love hung up. The line of people swarmed and blurred in front of her hand and then she remembered Mrs. Soldier. "No games," Love said. "Would you like a VCR?"

"That would be lovely," Mrs. Soldier said.

Love went back to Vance. "Room seven wants a VCR."

"They're all signed out," he said.

Love returned to the desk. "The VCRs are all signed out," Love said. The man in the pajamas raised his hand. She was the second-grade teacher.

"Yes?" Love said.

"You're out of coffee," he said.

"You're kidding," Love said. Several people in line sadly shook their heads. Normally, they didn't run out of coffee until midafternoon and by then things were quiet enough that Love could make some more. She poked her head into the back office again. "Vance," she said, in her most pleasant, ass-kissing voice, "We're out of coffee. Could you be a doll and make some more?"

"That's your job," he said.

"I know," she said. "But I have a line of people out here who need help. Really, a line."

Vance smiled at her again. He hated her. "I wouldn't want to *infringe* on your *space*."

"Oh, God," Love said. "Please help me."

Vance had the crossword puzzle from the *Boston Globe* in front of him. Love thought she might cry. She stepped out to the desk. "The coffee is going to be a minute," she said.

The man in the pajamas pointed a bony finger at her. He was a health-class skeleton with skin. "We pay a lot of money for these rooms," he said. He looked to the person behind him in line, as though he wanted to organize some kind of group revolt. "I heard you say there are no more VCRs. Why not? Why doesn't every room have a VCR?"

"I don't know," Love said. "It's not my hotel."

The phone rang. Love's hand itched to answer it, but she was afraid that if she did, the guests would storm the desk. The rain had turned the normally well-heeled guests into a class of emotionally needy students, into a band of ruby red Communists. Where was Mack?

An elegant-looking gentleman in an Armani suit was next in line. Love remembered checking him in: Mr. Juarez, room 12. "I have a flight to New York at ten-thirty this morning. Would you be so kind as to call and see if it's going to be delayed?"

"I'd be happy to," Love said. This man, at least, was pleasant. She liked his tone of voice. She liked his calm demeanor. She wanted to shake his hand. Gold-star student.

Love called the airport and found it was closed temporarily, due to lightning.

"I'm sorry, Mr. Juarez," she said. "The airport is closed. No one is flying."

"I have a lunch meeting at one o'clock that can't be missed," he said.

"The man at the airport said 'temporarily,'" Love said. "So perhaps they'll resume flying in a little while.

"Will you call again when you get a chance?" Mr. Juarez asked. He slid a fifty-dollar bill across the desk. Love hesitated. Everyone behind Mr. Juarez was watching.

"I'm sorry," she said softly. "I can't accept that."

Mr. Juarez slipped the bill into his coat pocket. "It's yours if you get me on a flight."

The honeymooners from room twenty stepped up; behind them, the room was a carnival. "We'd like lunch reservations," the wife said. "Somewhere in town. Where do you suggest?"

Sit in your room and feed each other grapes, Love thought. *There's a big bowl of them over there*—but when Love looked at the breakfast buffet, she saw the grapes were all gone.

"Why don't you go into town and try your luck?" Love said. "I can lend you an umbrella."

"Okay," the husband said.

"We'd like a reservation," the wife said. "We'd rather not waste our time."

The husband nodded along. "That's right."

"The Chanticleer serves lunch," Love said. "So does the Wauwinet. Which would you prefer?"

"I'd prefer coffee," the skeleton in the pajamas called out, "I'd really like a steaming mug of coffee to drink on this dreary day."

Back by the piano, two boys were yelling at each other. Love looked over in time to see them hit the floor. "Whose children are those?" she asked. No one answered. "Well, they must belong to somebody." Still no one. They pulled each other's hair and started slapping and punching. "Boys!" she said. "Stop it!" Her maternal instincts rose in her like a fever. "Boys!" No one in the line made a move to stop them. Love hoisted herself over the desk, and ran to where the boys were rolling around. They were stuck together, one had a death grip on the other's hair. Love physically wedged herself between the two boys. Then, perhaps realizing that there would be no more coffee or lunch reservations until this was taken care of, the honeymooners came to help Love hold the boys away from one another. The honeymooners smiled at each other, as if to say, *Isn't this cute, a fight?* One of the kids started to cry, and the other's nose bled all over the carpet. The husband took out a handkerchief and gave it to Mr. Bleeding.

"Are you two brothers?" Love asked.

Mr. Crying shook his head. He was pudgy and sweet looking, and now he had two raised red scratches under his eye. "No. We're not brothers. We're friends."

"I'm not your friend," Mr. Bleeding said. The handkerchief blossomed with red. "Not anymore."

Love herded both boys toward the office. She didn't make eye contact with anyone in line. At Mack's desk, Vance diligently counted squares on his crossword.

"You can help these two cowboys find their parents," Love said.

"Cowboys?" Mr. Bleeding said. "We are *not* cowboys."

"You're monsters," Vance said. He meant it to be derogatory, of course. Love had never heard Mr. I Want a Child Someday call children anything but monsters, but both boys brightened up.

"We're monsters," Mr. Crying said. He stopped crying, and nudged Mr. Bleeding.

"Yeah, we're monsters," Mr. Bleeding said. "But we're not cowboys."

"Whatever," Love said.

Reluctantly, Vance stood up. Love returned to the desk, and she heard Vance telling the boys a joke as they moved down the hallway.

Back at the desk, Love saw the skeleton in pajamas shaking his head.

"What's your name, sir?" she asked him.

He straightened up and crossed his arms across his chest. "Michael Klutch."

Mr. Klutch! The man who had booked rooms four, five, and six all for himself. He was staying in room five, and the other two rooms were "buffer rooms," so he didn't have to hear his neighbors shutting their dresser drawers or flushing their toilets.

"We're going to make a list," Love said. "Put your name on it and I'll get to you as soon as I can. I am now going to make some coffee." Love walked back into Mack's office, and the phone rang. Love tried to walk past it, but the receiver was a magnet.

"Front desk," Love said.

"This is Audrey Cohn, room seventeen. My son just came in with blood all over his face! I'd like you to call an ambulance right away. There's blood everywhere."

"It's a bloody nose," Love said. "He was out here in the lobby unsupervised and he got into a fight. All he needs is a wet washcloth."

"*Please* call an ambulance," Audrey Cohn said.

Love was glad it had come to this—sirens and flashing lights—maybe *that* would get Mack's attention. When Love stepped out into the hallway, she bumped into Mr. Juarez.

"I didn't sign the list," he said, "because you were helping me before." He removed the fifty-dollar bill from his pocket and wound it through his slender, tan fingers. "I was hoping you'd be so kind as to call the airport again."

"Mr. Juarez," Love said. "I have to make the coffee. Please sign the list." She hurried into the galley kitchen and closed the door. There, taped to the cabinets, was a piece of paper that had been ripped from the front desk notebook, and on it, a note in Tiny's handwriting, "Beware the eight weeks of August."

Love got the coffeemaker chugging and walked back into the lobby. The guests were still standing in a line. Love slowly made her way behind the desk.

"Now," she said, "Who's next?"

Before anyone could answer, Love heard the sirens and saw red lights whip around the lobby walls. A paramedic stormed in the lobby doors, black uniformed, self-important, his walkie-talkie alive with raspy static.

"Who's hurt?" he said.

Love called room seventeen. "Your ambulance is here."

Audrey Cohn laughed. "Jared is fine," she said. "We cleaned him up and it turns out it was just a bloody nose. No ambulance needed."

Love retreated into the office and sat in Mack's chair. She heard a commotion in the lobby, everyone talking at once. Then, Vance walked in.

"What's with the ambulance?" he said.

"Room seventeen had me call it for the kid with the bloody nose. Now she doesn't want it. What should I tell the paramedic?"

"Tell him you're sorry," Vance said.

"I've told everybody I'm sorry this morning," Love said. "I'm sorry it's raining, I'm sorry the airport is closed, I'm sorry we don't have VCRs, nor do we have coffee. I'm very sorry!"

"And don't forget you're sorry you asked me to leave this morning," Vance said. You're sorry you hurt my feelings."

"Of course I am," Love said. She caught his eye. "Vance, I *am*."

"I won't come to Colorado this winter," he said. "Because you only want a summer romance, is that it? No strings attached?"

"Yes," Love said. Was her egg still waiting for a date? For a mate? "Is that okay?"

Vance rubbed the top of his head. Love knew what it felt like, warm and stubbly, alive, growing in. "Sure," he said. He gave her a hug; her feet weren't touching the ground when the paramedic stormed into the office.

"Is there a problem here or *not?*" he asked.

"No, bud, no problem here," Vance said.

The paramedic spun on his heels and left the office, slamming the door behind him.

Love and Vance kissed a long making-up kiss, and then she returned to the desk—but the line had dispersed, all except Mr. Juarez, who stood patiently with his hands folded in front of him.

Love called the airport and found it had opened. "You're all set," Love said. "Let me call you a cab." She thought uneasily of Tracey. *Tell him.*

Mr. Juarez gave Love the fifty, which she tucked into her pocket. Then she poured herself a cup of coffee. Outside, the rain slowed to a drizzle; the clouds were breaking up. Love heard piano music, bright and jangly, a rag tune. Across the lobby, Vance, her summer-romance man, played her a song.

Reprinted by permission of the author.

Frank Conroy

Ernest Hemingway once observed that the best early training for a writer is an unhappy childhood. That was certainly true for Frank Conroy (1936–2005). His father, Philip, was mentally ill and left his wife and two children when Conroy was a boy. His mother, Helga, a Danish immigrant, remarried; the impractical schemes of her second husband, Guy Trudeau, kept the family bouncing between Florida and New York, sometimes living hand to mouth. This childhood was the material for Conroy's first and best-known book, Stop-Time *(1967), a memoir. An* Observer Review *contributor described it as "an autobiography written with the imaginative freedom and variation of a novel . . . clean, witty, surprisingly mature prose, full of insights and sharp moments." Conroy's obituary in* The New York Times *called* Stop-Time *"a model for countless young writers—the sort of book that is passed along like a trade secret." Praised by authors including Norman Mailer and William Styron,* Stop-Time *made Conroy's literary reputation.*

Over the years, other books would follow—a collection of short stories, Midair *(1985); a novel,* Body & Soul *(1994); a collection of essays,* Dogs Bark, But the Caravan Rolls On *(2002); and, finally, Conroy's reflections on island living,* Time and Tide: A Walk Through Nantucket *(2004). But Conroy made an even more vital contribution to literature as an extraordinarily gifted teacher and administrator, nurturing the careers of countless young writers as director of the literature program of the National Endowment for the Arts (1981–87), and, more famously, as director of the prestigious University of Iowa Writers' Workshop from 1987 until his death from cancer in 2005.*

Conroy recalled really connecting with Nantucket when he visited the island on a junket with college friends from Haverford in 1955. Soon he had a summer job exercising his other great talent—playing jazz piano—at the old Ocean House Hotel (today the Jared Coffin House). After the breakup of his first marriage, Conroy moved to the island year-round, where he supported himself by playing the piano at the Roadhouse jazz club, writing magazine articles, and scalloping. Even after his burgeoning career took him away, Conroy continued to summer on Nantucket with his second wife, Maggie, at their home in Polpis. Marianne Stanton, editor of the Inquirer and Mirror, *recalls*

"From the beginning, Frank Conroy was more than a writer who spent summers here. He was one of those people who became part of Nantucket life. He was one of those people who got it, who understood that intrinsic something about this place."

Here, in a selection from Time and Tide, *Conroy describes a situation too familiar to most islanders—a Darwinian moment in the supermarket checkout lane.—SB*

"How About Manners?" from *Time and Tide: A Walk Through Nantucket*

THE MARKETPLACE IS always of special interest to anthropologists, historians, and the like. I suppose the idea it that what goes on in markets reveals the society itself to some extent. That is certainly true for the "Gray Lady of the Sea."

The Cumberland Farms store on the east side of town is a convenience store now—cigarettes, Twinkies, canned soup, Wonder bread, and so on—but it started out a long time ago as a sort of cooperative, organized by some local moms who were fed up with the high price of milk at the supermarket and decided to do something about it. It was true then, and it is true now, that almost everything is marked up in Nantucket. Gasoline, for instance, is quite a lot higher than on the Cape. There is more competition now—more markets (lots of boutique markets, specialty meat markets, a couple of farmer's markets, one of them huge), but prices are still high—no longer due to what you might call captive customers (not so long ago there was only that one place to get the Sunday *New York Times,* the Hub, smack in the middle of downtown at the corner of Main and Federal), but because of the generally "up" market of people who don't have to worry about what a quart of milk might cost. Of course, it is a seasonal economy, and retailers have to survive in February as well as August.

The general priciness perhaps reaches its extremes at the 'Sconset Market, the only grocery store in the village at the eastern end of the island, where the prices of ordinary items like a bag of Oreos or a box of cereal are so astronomical it takes one's breath away. (They do bake some very fine baguettes, in their defense.) But no one does major shopping there. For that one goes to the supermarket—either the rather modestly sized Grand Union built as part of the downtown wharf-development project, or most important the huge Stop and Shop at the edge of town. It was once a Finast, and before that something else, but it has always been the dominant market, and increasingly so as the island has grown to the point where there are more people living out of town (in season, at least) than in town. The Stop and Shop is it, and they must be commended for an honest effort to keep their prices reasonable, not too much more than in their stores on the mainland.

My ex-wife, who lives out West, was struck by the change in atmosphere at the market when she visited the island a couple of summers ago. She remembered a kind of community spirit—high school kids or working college kids at the checkouts, people chatting with friends in the aisles, a certain social cohe-siveness—that wasn't there any more. From the insanely crowded parking lot, with everyone honking horns, jostling for spaces, bumping bumpers, to the jam-packed aisles of people racing inside, eager to get back to the beach or the barbeque, it has a frantic, almost desperate feel in the high season. One rarely recognizes anyone now—to come upon a friend or acquaintance at the deli section is rare indeed, and invariably creates a certain nostalgia for the old days. The checkout staff, the baggers, and the like are mostly Jamaicans now, speak-ing a bewildering patois, unconnected, like migrant workers (which they are), from the culture around them. It is a pressured atmosphere, and not comfort-able or enjoyable. It's a pain in the ass, in fact, for a lot of us.

Four or five years ago my wife was witness to a scene in the supermarket that may be emblematic of the transformation of Nantucket from a small town into something else altogether. A prominent family on the island whom I will call the Smiths—summer people for generations—were involved in various local businesses at a high level; Bob Smith is a big, handsome guy with a thou-sand-watt smile, a lot of charm, and a lot of smarts. His image on the island was carefully cultivated—an honest, thoughtful, family man with good values and a heightened sense of community. And all of this was, and no doubt still is, true. Which makes what my wife saw all the more astonishing.

The Stop and Shop, on a Friday afternoon, was jam-packed with shoppers stocking up for the weekend, anticipating guests, jostling up and down the aisles in a mild frenzy. My wife was waiting in line at one of the checkout lanes. She sees Bob moving forward with a cart filled to the brim, top to bottom, and inserting himself into the express lane. The girl at the cash register protests. "This is for twelve items only," she says. "This is the express lane."

Smiling his warm, knock-'em-dead smile, Bob reaches up and slides the lit-tle placard which says "Express Lane" from its holder and puts it facedown next to the register. "Not anymore, it isn't," he declares, and begins to unload his stuff. Flummoxed, the girl waits a moment, looks around, and then starts the long process of ringing things up. There is some grumbling from the line behind Bob, but no one has the nerve to protest. Bob no longer cares what people think. His assumption is that he'll never see any of the other shoppers again.

I am reminded of a scene in John Cheever's book, *Oh What a Paradise It Seems*. (Cheever was a great fan of the island in its simpler days, but stopped coming when his favorite hotel—an old, rundown place with remarkable views—was demolished to be replaced by a stratospherically expensive luxury establishment.) Although the setting is not Nantucket, the scene is prophetic.

Maybelle was the name of the checkout clerk and she wore a large pin that said so. "Maybelle," said Betsy, "would you kindly explain to this lady that this lane is the express lane for shoppers with nine items only." "If she can't read I'm not going to teach her," said Maybelle. The twelve or so members in the line behind Betsy showed their approval. "It's about time somebody said something" . . . "You tell 'em, lady, you tell 'em," said an old man with a frozen dinner. "I just can't stand to see someone take advantage of other people's kindness. It's like fascism. It isn't that she's breaking the law. It's just that most of us are too nice to do anything about it. Why do you suppose they put up a sign that says nine items? It's to make the store more efficient for everyone. You're just like a shoplifter, only you're not stealing groceries, you're stealing time, you're not stealing from the management, you're stealing from us."

Cheever continues the story until civil behavior breaks down and a minor riot ensues. It's a comic scene with an edge, but an important moment in the text. (Neither my wife nor I have ever felt quite the same way toward old Bob, who has gone on to be a tremendous success in the world of finance.)

Reprinted by permission of Margaret L. Conroy.

David Halberstam

Pulitzer Prize–winning journalist, contemporary historian, and sportswriter David Halberstam (1934–2007), author of twenty-two books (three novels and nineteen works of nonfiction), is among the most prolific and powerful writers to have made land-fall at Nantucket. A resident of Manhattan, Halberstam purchased a modest house on Nantucket in 1969, and for thirty-five summers the island was his escape from the high-pressure, high-profile professional life in the city, as well as a place to relax, fish, and savor the company of family and friends. Above all, Nantucket was a quiet haven for writing; Halberstam once claimed to have written fourteen of his books while on the island.

Born in New York City, the son of an Army surgeon and a schoolteacher, Halberstam attended Harvard University and was managing editor of The Harvard Crimson. *After graduating in 1955, he went south to Mississippi and Tennessee, where he covered the tumultuous early years of the Civil Rights Movement for regional newspapers, an experience underlying two books he would publish much later in life,* The Fifties *(1993) and* The Children *(1998). His reporting brought him to the attention of* The New York Times. *Halberstam joined the newspaper in 1960 and in 1962 went to Vietnam as the Times's war correspondent. Never shy about speaking truth to power, he made his reputation in journalism and rattled both the White House and the Pentagon by insisting that U. S. support for a corrupt South Vietnamese regime would doom the war to failure, and by baldly stating that American generals were lying to the press.*

By 1969, with four books already to his credit, Halberstam was ready to leave the New York Times *and devote himself to his own writing full time. At his new home on Nantucket, he began work on his breakout book,* The Best and the Brightest *(1972), a riveting contemporary history of how the well-educated, privileged, and even brilliant young advisors to the Kennedy administration came to make disastrous decisions about U.S. policy in Vietnam. Passionate, opinionated, copiously researched, and controversial,* The Best and the Brightest *foreshadowed other major works by Halberstam on American power, policy, and war:* The Powers That Be *(1979), examining the dangerous influence of America's media conglomerates;* The Reckoning *(1986), exploring the dueling industrial economies of the U.S. and Japan;* War in a Time of Peace: Bush, Clinton, and the

Generals *(2001); and the posthumously published* The Coldest Winter: America and the Korean War *(2007). Halberstam developed the habit of alternating these larger, more serious projects with books about sports—he has written books on baseball, basketball, and even Olympic rowing. Nantucket readers might especially enjoy his* Summer of '49 *(1989), about the era of Joe DiMaggio and Ted Williams, and an epic pennant race between two teams whose fans often collide on the island—the New York Yankees and the Boston Red Sox. At the time of his tragic death in a 2007 automobile accident, Halberstam was on his way to interview football legend Y. A. Tittle.*

Here we offer a 1999 essay that is nostalgic, affectionate, and characteristically peppered with uncomfortable truths; it is vintage Halberstam.—SB

Nantucket on My Mind

THERE IT WAS last summer, one of the many real estate advertisements in our weekly newspaper, this particular one not even particularly large. It mentioned four houses for sale, all of them said to have great views. I did not doubt that, for one house was listed at $5 million, another at $4 million, a third at $3.5 million, and the fourth, clearly a bargain, a mere $3 million. One would hope they had great views. It was one more sign of the times, of the increased value of property on this strange, semiquaint, once-remote, old-time Quaker island that has now become a target for the young, stunningly wealthy winners of Wall Street. In the past we were more middle class than many of the chicer East Coast watering holes, but now we have become a trophy island where the masters of the universe, as Tom Wolfe called them, can build their magnificent houses for their wives and families—twenty-room houses for four or five people.

I do not remember exactly when it was that the real estate market crossed the magical seven-figure barrier—in Nantucket real estate terms, surely the equivalent of that marvelous moment when aeronautical engineers were able to design jet planes that could break the sound barrier. I think it was two or three years ago, somewhere in that heady period when the Dow was shooting up some three thousand points in under three years. Like many people who have come to Nantucket for years and were drawn here by its simplicity rather than its chicness, I do not think it is a cause for celebration, though clearly in financial terms at least I am a beneficiary, and my wonderful and venerable old house—half-simple and half-gentrified, surely a house with a divided soul (and most assuredly unbeatable)—is certainly worth more now than ever. If, of course, I can continue to afford to live in it.

Because the new wealth is so great, we have lost the one thing that protected us in the past—our inaccessibility. We were thirty miles out to sea, distinctly farther than the Vineyard and much harder to reach. The constant threat of fog made getting here a nightmare: I have several lasting friendships that were fashioned during the long hours of waiting in Logan Airport while the island remained socked in, then finally taking a death-defying late-hour shot at Nantucket—*Well, folks, they say the fog out there's still pretty thick, but what say we give it one little old last try*—followed by a hair-raising approach, the pilot sometimes pulling up at the last second and going back to Boston, where the airline dispensed with us at a less-than-imposing hotel for a few hours, until early morning, when we got on a bus to Hyannis to make the approach by sea. It was the kind of experience that cemented friendships forever. It was also the kind of experience that warned young ambitious Wall Street winners that the island, no matter what its joys, was not worth their time and suffering.

But the newcomers have not let ancient time-honored barriers of geography and low airport ceilings stand in their way. *They come equipped with their own air force.* Private jets—fog-proof, it would seem—have now appeared and are mandatory equipment for these recent arrivals, as fishing rods, tennis rackets, Labrador retrievers, and old jeeps were mandatory to those who came before. Indeed, I have a friend who notes that some of the new people do not even own land on our island but fly in only to play at its new golf course (which initially cost $250,000 to join and filled up in a matter of weeks), and suggests that they are doing it not for the sport, but just to show off their jets. After all, what is the point of having a showcase private plane if there is not some difficult, essentially inaccessible place to fly in to? Be that as it may, the commute, once so hard, is now a piece of cake. One recent Fourth of July, our airport was the busiest in all of Massachusetts, with, it is said, 1,200 takeoffs and landings in a single day, busier than even Logan.

The truth is, I am, almost without knowing it, in the midst of a lover's quarrel with Nantucket; I still love it, but these days I do not always like it. This is therefore something of a cranky piece, and I do not like to write as a crank: I am not in general nostalgic for the past. The Fourth of July, I believe, is not now and never was what it used to be. A few years ago I wrote a book about the fifties, a decade in which I came of age, and it convinced me that for all our myriad contemporary failings, life in America is infinitely better and richer, more diverse and more tolerant than it was at the mid-century mark. But nevertheless I am also uneasy about what happens when so much wealth—wealth to many of us of an incomprehensible nature—strikes an island so small and so fragile.

Long Island, befitting its name, is very big. Nantucket is not. Essentially, the island is a triangle of which the two barrier sides are roughly eight miles and fourteen miles long, depending on how you measure them. Despite the thousands and thousands of vehicles that crowd onto the island in the summer, when the population swells from roughly 7,000 year-round residents to some 40,000 part-time owner residents, we still do not have a single traffic light. Our size therefore is finite, the texture of our daily life oddly delicate because when something goes wrong socially, we feel it immediately.

This is my thirtieth year as an owner here. I bought my house in 1969, the year I began working on *The Best and the Brightest,* the moment when I went over to writing books full time. Over the years I have come to love the island—it has given me sanctuary in a difficult and often volatile professional life, allowing me to work diligently each summer while putting myself back together among people who I know love and care about me. I leave the island in the early fall rested, but with a great deal of work done. I stumbled on it at first—my friend Russell Baker brought me here in 1968 and I thought it was the most beautiful place I had ever seen. It seemed to have more of the good things of life and fewer of the bad than any vacation spot I had ever seen before; it offered an almost-perfect balance between the possibilities for friendship and the right, when I needed to work, to my privacy. Because the happiest part of my peripatetic childhood was spent in a small town in northwest Connecticut, Nantucket—with its strikingly handsome library, the sense of community manifest at high school games—reminded me of the best part of my youth. People knew one another and treated one another with respect. The people who did have money (and it would be considered small money these days), those old Yankee families said to be very wealthy, very consciously did not manifest it. In the great houses along Hulbert Avenue, our showcase street that runs along the harbor, the houses were, as they always had been, a little worn down, with bathroom sinks stained green by the relentless drip of the water—a reminder of plumbers never summoned.

It was still very much a middle-class island in those days. Unlike other East Coast watering holes, we did not have much in the way of a writer's community, and that too appealed to me, because I had spent one summer in the Hamptons and the pace of the social life had been far too intense. My own social circle was eclectic, filled largely with people I would not have been friends with in New York—people I fished with, or, in time, those my wife and I enjoyed cooking with. Not surprisingly, as our daughter grew up, our friends were people who had children who were her friends.

We formed, I think, the squarest of summer communities. Our friends were, it seemed to me, people brought to Nantucket not because it was chic but because it was beautiful and family-oriented, and because they liked the pleasures of the island—the fishing, the sailing, the tennis, and the birding, things that, as they did for me, recalled the happier parts of their own childhoods, even if they now lived in tough, demanding urban environments.

Soon it was the texture of friendships as much as the beauty of the island that held us, friendships that were not work-connected and that near the end of the spring we always looked forward to renewing. Those friendships were based on simple things: fishing with my friend David Fine; going to the beaches with Pam and Foley Vaughan and their children; dinner with Bill Euler and Andy Oates, who ran our best store, Nantucket Looms, a friendship tentative at first because they were so private; rowing in a double scull with Marc Garnick; and, finally, after I sold my fishing boat, fishing with Tom Mleczko, who doubled as a schoolteacher in New Canaan the rest of the year. These were the touchstones of our summer, the friendships sweetened by the many years in grade from the past.

There was over the years, starting in the eighties, a dramatic change in the cast of characters who came here—the rising prices on the tickets of the houses automatically narrowed down the possibilities of who could afford the island. (One summer I called a friend of mine who was a journalist and asked if he was going to rent again. No, he answered, the rent had just tripled, and so he was going to Tuscany for a month—it was cheaper.) In addition, I thought I sensed a change in what people sought from this island—an increase in the importance of status. That has been particularly noticeable in the last few years with the coming of such stupendous wealth, wealth that seems with its vast annual rewards disconnected from the reality of daily life. I realize there is some degree of generalization to what I am going to say, and I am sure that some of the new people are as nice or nicer than the old, and that some of the older people, given half a chance, would be greedier than the new. But I am not sure that the new people are brought to the island by the old and abiding pleasures that drew us.

The new people seem not only very rich, but very young to be that rich; and all too often they seem quite imperious. I suppose that is not too surprising; they have been raised in a modern pressure cooker: starting out in demanding day schools, and then demanding boarding schools, and then making the cut at demanding elite colleges, and then again making the next level, at demanding law or business schools, and then becoming winners in the brutal competition in the world of finance. There, if you are a winner, an annual award of $10 million is thought to be small; it is where people now talk of making a unit—a unit being earnings of $25 million in a year. I think something like that begins to affect a person's sense of proportion.

On our island we are, I think, the worse for it. There is a sharp, indeed an alarming, decline in the requisite courtesy and manners that are so critical to the texture of life in a small town, and that are, comparably, so unimportant in a city like New York. When these people want things—houses to be built, gardens to be made green, rugs to be woven and delivered—they want them right now, with a special immediacy, as if they were back in the city ordering out from a neighborhood Chinese restaurant. If they buy a piece of property for $2.5 million and plan to tear it down and build a new house for $3 million, the money is no longer an object—but the speed of completion is. *By July 1, if you please—otherwise we'll have to go elsewhere.* That has a ripple effect throughout the island—the cost of everything goes up accordingly, and other work orders, small assignments, the repair of a house here, an addition to a house there, tend to be shunted aside. Two summers ago, our gardener fired us because all we wanted was upkeep on our garden, and it was impossible for us to compete with the gargantuan projects offered her by newer arrivals.

The houses being built are different now. The old Nantucket had houses of modest size, and in keeping with the traditional respect for the sheer beauty of the island, they were often nestled in the landscape itself. By contrast, many of the new houses are huge flagships to show that yes, there is a great deal of wealth in the family, and they seem to violate the natural contours of the land as violently as possible. The cars on our island are bigger and fancier, too—they used to be deliberately downscale, and exceptionally well rusted, but these days everyone seems to be driving sport-utility vehicles (SUVs, to use the vernacular) that seem to be like jeeps on steroids.

Worse, the manners of the drivers seem to have declined in inverse proportion to the size of their cars and wealth. Many of our rural roads are paths more than roads, and it was common courtesy, when you were driving down a rural road wide enough for only one car and you spotted a car coming at you, to pull over if at all possible in a niche alongside the road and let the other car go by. Part of that same courtesy was for the driver of the other car to wave as he or she went by signaling some respect for your manners—as if to say, you did it for me this time, I'll do it for you the next. Now you pull over—you had better, because the other car is sure to be twice as big and powerful as yours—and more often than not, there is not the slightest wave of the hand or the beep of a horn. They are telling you that you pulled over because it is your proper place in the universe to pull over for them—and you'd better be prepared to pull over the next time as well.

Somewhere in here is no small amount of money. The island is more crowded than ever, more gentrified than ever, and there is more building going on than ever before, more huge trucks bearing down on our narrow streets and roads. Yet if the island is more crowded, I suspect it manages to remain aloof from many of its most ardent new suitors. I have this theory—that many of the true pleasures of Nantucket are not easily gained and cannot be purchased on demand, that they have to be, like everything else in life, earned, and you have to take time and serve something of an apprenticeship in order to get the full measure of the pleasures available.

For all of the crowding downtown, many of the beaches remain secluded, the nature walks are pleasant and accessible, and there is no line for them. If you want to picnic, and have a boat, there are places in Polpis, the large inner harbor, where, if you know the tides, you can miraculously enough go and picnic in a beautiful spot—more of an idyll than one can imagine on the East Coast—and never see another soul. I am a fairly serious fisherman, and our light-tackle saltwater fishing is arguably the best along the East Coast, perhaps because we are so far into the Gulf Stream. But it takes time and skill to learn how to fish here, and money will not do it all for you—you have to learn to handle a boat in what are daunting waters, going out on days when the weather changes, when the shoals are murderous and when the fog rolls in so suddenly that unless you know what you are doing, it can all be quite terrifying. I know, because I had a boat for ten years, and it was a difficult and exacting apprenticeship, not so much learning where the fish are—that part was easy—but how dangerous the Atlantic Ocean can be. So perhaps it is not surprising that, for all the money being spent on boats, many of them with GPS/Loran guides that should make dealing with fog and shoals virtually idiot-proof, on the July Fourth and Labor Day weekends, the most crowded days of the year, you can be at choice spots for fishing for blues or stripers only thirty minutes from Madaket Harbor and not see another boat.

I realize that what I'm writing reflects not just the change in the economy but the change in the writer himself, the changes in the eye of the beholder: that the adventurousness of a young man come to a new place in his thirties is very different from a man in his sixties, wanting things always to be as they once were, bemoaning, almost unconsciously, the loss of his own youth. And I am aware that one of the critical things I liked about the island remains as true as ever: that it can, in a country as dynamic and volatile as ours, offer you a sense of the seasons of your own life, as life in a city rarely can, the kind of texture and feeling that Thornton Wilder captured in *Our Town*—a sense of the rhythm of your life as it touches those around you. If over the years we have had friends who for various reasons have moved away, and if our list of friends is not exactly what it was two decades ago, there is nonetheless a sense of being rooted here as we are not rooted in New York, and an ability to monitor the seasons of our lives from the changes in the lives of those around us.

In New York our friendships tend to be with peers, more often than not professionally driven, and while we tend to know the children of our friends, by and large, with few exceptions, the friendships bloom in the evening and the children tend to remain in the background, seen but not really known. That is not true of Nantucket: over the past thirty years I have watched the children of my friends grow up, go off to college, and come back and have children of their own. I have fished with my friend David Fine for twenty-eight years now, and our routines aboard the boat—who will catch the first or the biggest fish—have the quality of old vaudeville routines, the sweetness of conversations so oft repeated that they have by now become second nature. Paul and Joan Crowley became our friends because they were friends of David and Sue Fine's, and in time we watched Melissa Crowley grow from a young girl and a superb athlete to a confident, extremely successful magazine editor in New York. Both David Fine and I in time gave up running our own boats, and we have fished for the last few years with Tom Mleczko, who is our best fisherman, and we have had the pleasure of seeing his and Bambi's children, who worked as strikers on his boat, grow up to become strikingly handsome young people, one daughter in

Boston, a son about to start college, and another daughter, whom I wrote about, become a star of the championship U. S. Olympic hockey team, an article that gave me as much pleasure as anything I've ever written. Their cousins, the Gifford kids—how many letters written to directors of admission at different boarding schools and colleges?—have morphed into tall, handsome, confident young men and women. John Burnham Schwartz, who appeared with his parents at my house when he was nine, beautiful and beguiling, and whom I used to take fishing every summer, has remained a friend and the light of my life. We gave his engagement party and the book party for his second novel; he is now a successful novelist, and a peer, someone I count on not merely for friendship but for advice.

The friendship with Bill Euler and Andy Oates, a bit hesitant at first, grew stronger every year, and dinners with them became the evenings we looked forward to with singular pleasure, in time raucous evenings of more wine than normal and world-class gossip. Five years ago I dedicated a book to them (it was a baseball book, and someone, not knowing of our friendship, saw their names and asked "Euler and Oates—which team did they play for?"). This year, Bill, who was my age, died of leukemia, and it was like nothing so much as a death in the family, for he was a shy man who had quietly enhanced many other people's lives, and seemed not to know how much he was cherished and how much he would be missed. We've watched our own child, and those of our friends the Vaughans and the Clapps and the Durkes, grow up together and go off to college. Our daughter on occasion reminds us that she thinks of Nantucket, not New York, as her real home and thinks about living in our old house someday with her own children. And when she talks like that, we are reminded that we have become in some way *of* the island, that it binds us and forms our lives in ways we do not entirely understand, and yet are unconsciously dependent upon.

The places you love will do that to you.

Reprinted by permission of Jean Halberstam.

X

Shipwrecks

Robert F. Mooney

Nantucket native and lifelong resident Robert F. Mooney (b. 1931) grew up on the island during the Great Depression and World War II, when autos were scarce and most year-rounders lived within walking distance of downtown. The only child of Nantucket's police chief, young Robert spent much of his boyhood on Main Street, getting to know the town and its characters well. After graduating from Nantucket High School, Mooney went on to earn degrees from the College of the Holy Cross and from Harvard Law School—and then returned to the island to practice law. Over the years, he has been Nantucket's Representative to the Great and General Court of Massachusetts (when Nantucket had a representative) and Assistant District Attorney. His community service speaks to his love of history and literature. Mooney helped found the Nantucket Lifesaving Museum, and, as president of the Nantucket Atheneum's board of trustees, saw the island's public library through the 1996 renovation of its historic 1846 building and the construction of its new children's wing.

Writing about Nantucket history, both from his fund of personal knowledge and from research in island archives, has long been Mooney's passion and avocation. In addition to numerous articles and monographs on Nantucket history, his books include The Nantucket Way *(with André R. Sigourney, 1980),* Tales of Nantucket *(1990),* The Civil War: The Nantucket Experience *(with Richard F. Miller, 1994),* Nantucket Only Yesterday: An Island View of the Twentieth Century *(2000), and* More Tales of Nantucket *(2005). Mooney brings a lively style and a wicked sense of humor to all of his writing. But to the history that follows, from his monograph on the 1851 shipwreck of the* British Queen *on Nantucket Shoals, he brings something more—a deep sense of family connection. This is the true story of how Mooney's great-grandparents arrived on the island. — SB*

From *The Wreck of the* British Queen

On the cold winter morning of December 18, 1851, the town of Nantucket was awakened by a familiar cry from the watchman in the tower of the South Church on Orange Street.

"Ship in distress! She's a full-master with distress flags a-flying! Big shipwreck off Muskeget!"

For most of the people of Nantucket Island, the news of another ship wrecked along the shore was a grim reminder of their perilous position in the Atlantic Ocean, because the shoals of Nantucket had claimed many ships over the years. During the nineteenth century, all vessels bound for New York and most coastwise traffic were forced to skirt the shoals around Nantucket, where dangerous breakers revealed shallow waters and shifting sand bars. In an era before navigational equipment and wireless radio, the safety of the ship depended upon celestial navigation and skillful seamanship.

Following the decline of the island as a whaling port after the Great Fire of 1846, the waterfront of Nantucket was reduced to a scene of abandoned wharves and empty warehouses, with only a few small ships remaining as reminders of the great old days. Most of the former whalemen were now elderly citizens, spending their days chatting with old friends, playing endless games of checkers and cribbage, dreaming of the past. There still existed a small band of Nantucketers who followed the sea and made their reputations among the dangerous elements which surrounded the Island.

The ablest of these veterans was Captain David G. Patterson, a native of Chatham, whose ship-handling ability had earned him great respect from the Nantucket shipowners. When the Gold Rush of 1849 drew many fortune hunters to California, David Patterson skippered a fifty-foot sloop from Nantucket around Cape Horn to California—a truly remarkable achievement. Returning to find Nantucket marine business in decline, he remained alert to the possibilities of the salvage business as a lucrative sideline for a skillful pilot.

The island was accustomed to salvage operations and the news from the tower brought a hum of life to the sleepy waterfront. Aside from natural feelings of humanity to rescue the passengers and crew in distress, Nantucketers were alert to the potential of a valuable salvage operation, as the prospect of a "full-masted ship" presented a tempting prize to those enterprising and fortunate enough to salvage its cargo. The usual award was one-half of the value of the ship and cargo saved from the sea. There was no monetary award for saving lives.

The prospect was not brightened by the fury of the December gale, which remained unabated. Winter struck early in December of 1851, when freezing weather and high winds had set ice floes surging through Nantucket Sound. The northwest winds were still howling into the harbor and the ice and tides were running against any rescue attempt. Throughout the day of the eighteenth, no vessel was able to leave port. Furthermore, the stricken ship, visible through the long glass from the tower, was caught in a dangerous channel between Nantucket and Martha's Vineyard, a full twelve miles from Nantucket Harbor.

The *British Queen* was an old, full-masted sailing ship, pressed into service to transport the flood of Irish emigrants bound for America to escape the Great Famine of 1846–51. During those years, a deadly disease destroyed the potato crop, which was the staple food of the Irish peasants, one-half of whom depended upon it for their sole sustenance. With the failure of the potato, famine and disease swept the country, and one million people died during the famine years. There was no help forthcoming from the British government, which believed the government should do nothing to interfere with the natural forces of supply and demand. One of these forces was the English demand for Irish produce, and even during the depths of the famine, Ireland continued to export food to Britain. Ironically, the *British Queen* herself, during the summer of 1851, carried a cargo of 688 barrels of wheat and 450 barrels of oats from Limerick to Glasgow.

For many of the surviving Irish, there was only one hope for escape from their misery: emigration to America. Within six years, over two million left their native land. The conditions aboard the emigrant ships were often as miserable and dangerous as those in Ireland, but millions were willing to take their chances on the journey across the Atlantic. Most of them walked the long miles from their cottages to the port cities, carrying their few possessions in a single bag, and paying five pounds for a berth in the steerage of the ship. They were also obliged to purchase their own food for the voyage, a trip that normally took four to five weeks.

On the morning of October 22, 1851, the *British Queen* cast off from the port of Dublin, carrying 226 Irish immigrants bound for New York, with Captain Thomas Conway in command.

The favored vessel available to make the rescue attempt was the paddle-wheel steamer *Telegraph*, which served as the Island's steamboat service to the mainland and occasionally engaged in the rescue business. She was captained by George Russell and the company also employed Captain Thomas Gardner as professional wreck master. The *Telegraph* was moored at Nantucket's Straight Wharf, but her eight-foot draft prevented her leaving the harbor until high tide, and her paddle wheels were in danger of becoming disabled by the ice if she ventured into the shoals near the wreck.

On the evening of the eighteenth, a small group of men met in the brick building of Joseph Macy, the leading merchant and ship-owner of the Island, to plan the rescue. It was agreed that an attempt must be made to reach the ship, for she would not last long under the pounding of the wind and seas. Macy had at the wharf two schooners, the *Hamilton*, with Thomas Bearse in command and Captain David Patterson, a half owner, as pilot and wreck master, and the smaller schooner, *Game Cock,* with his brother, Captain William Patterson, in command. All these men were personal friends, but often professional rivals. Together they devised a plan for the rescue of the *British Queen.* Since the *Telegraph* could not approach the wreck, she would tow the two schooners out of the harbor ice and over the bar and let them get in close to make the rescue. Nothing could be done until the next day, while the passengers of the wrecked ship huddled in darkness and terror, praying for deliverance.

The morning of Friday, December 19, saw the *Telegraph* building up steam at the wharf, while the crews of the *Hamilton* and *Game Cock* prepared for sea. The news of the wreck had spread beyond the waterfront and several churches and charitable organizations had been alerted to the situation, while public halls were made ready to receive any survivors who might be brought ashore. The efforts of the Islanders were all private and voluntary, for there was no Coast Guard, no Red Cross, and no public help to be had.

The departure of the rescue ships depended upon high water over Nantucket bar, the troublesome sandbar which blocked the entrance to the harbor before the construction of the jetties. High tide came at 1:00 in the afternoon when there was nine feet of water over the bar. The *Hamilton* drew eight feet and the *Game Cock* drew seven. At the last minute, Captain David Patterson declined the tow and his *Hamilton* remained at the wharf. He gave no explanation, and the situation did not permit time for discussion. Promptly at noon, the *Telegraph* got under way, paddles churning through the ice floes and towing the *Game Cock* around Brant Point and out to sea. Once over the bar, the *Game Cock* set her sails and plunged through the wind and seas to the west. In the early afternoon, she reached a point a half mile from the wreck where she dropped anchor to survey the situation. The *Telegraph* followed and anchored three quarters of a mile from the wreck.

Aboard the *British Queen,* 226 passengers had endured a night of terror as eleven feet of water drove them out of the steerage decks to the freezing darkness of the main deck. Half frozen and suffering from lack of food and water, they learned that two passengers had died during the night, a grim foreshadowing of what was yet to come. . . .

Captain Thomas Conway, muffled in his greatcoat, stood at the rail, sweeping the ocean with his long glass. The ship had experienced a terrible voyage, eight weeks from Dublin and still far from New York, with headwinds all the way. Conway himself was suffering from illness which prevented him from doing the navigation, and the ship had found itself south of Nantucket, then driven into the dangerous Muskeget Channel, where she had grounded in a snowstorm, north of Muskeget. Unable to free the ship, Conway ordered the foremast and mizzenmast chopped away to prevent the ship from wrenching herself apart, and set the distress signals atop the mainmast. There was not much more he could do but gaze toward the low-lying island on the horizon and pray for help.

The *Hamilton,* with Captain David Patterson aboard, left Nantucket about a half hour after the *Telegraph* and *Game Cock,* but by skillful sailing, soon reached the wreck and anchored. Captain Russell hurriedly conferred with Patterson, and they rowed to the *Game Cock,* where Captain Thomas Gardner shouted: "Whose boat is that?" Russell informed him it was David Patterson's.

"Why, I left him at the wharf!" said Captain Gardner.

"Well, he's here now," called Captain Russell, "and you'd better invite him to join us!"

Patterson's independent action undoubtedly irritated the other captains, but in the emergency, they were glad to have him aboard. The two wreckers now combined their crews in the boats and set off toward the wreck, knowing that time and tide were running against them.

Captain George Russell took the steering oar of the ship's boat with Captain David Patterson on board and started to approach the starboard side of the *British Queen.* Halfway to the wreck, some low breakers showed their white teeth and Gardner said, "Captain Patterson, you'd better take the steering oar— you are more acquainted with these breakers than I."

With Patterson at the helm, the boat passed through the breakers and into the heavy current sweeping between the *Game Cock* and the wreck. Patterson then swung the boat toward a sea ladder hanging from the ship, handed the oar to his mate, and leaped onto the ladder. He then worked his way aft to meet Captain Conway, who was in shock and despair, able only to say that he carried no cargo and his ship was not insured. Captain Gardner then climbed aboard and announced he was the agent for the steamboat and ready to save passengers. He then signaled *Game Cock* to lay alongside, and the frightened passengers began climbing down to the deck of the schooner. It was a perilous procedure, for the smaller boat could not get close aboard, and the surging sea would first lift her high above the rail of the wreck, then drop her into the trough below the ship's counter.

When about sixty passengers had been transferred, Captain Gardner shouted that the *Game Cock* could take no more, as she was striking bottom. By the time he could take the schooner to the *Telegraph* and return, the tide would turn and make the seas too rough for further rescue in this manner. Captain Patterson knew that if he brought the *Hamilton* in to rescue the remaining passengers, he would not only endanger his ship but would leave the salvage of the wreck and its gear to Captain Gardner and the *Game Cock*.

Captain Conway of the *British Queen* said, "We have no cargo and the ship is a total loss. All I want is to get my passengers to safety. The water has been up over the lower deck all night, and they are in horrid condition."

"We get nothing for saving lives," said Captain David Patterson, "but be assured, my schooner will save your people."

Patterson then brought the schooner *Hamilton* alongside as soon as the *Game Cock* got under way. The *British Queen* was now headed north and listed heavily to starboard, with the waves smashing against her stern. The *Hamilton* approached her bow, dropped an anchor, and paid out her anchor cable until she lay across her bow, then slowly worked down her starboard side. Clinging to the wreck with mooring lines, the *Hamilton* was heaved high above the ship with each rising wave, then smashing down on the shoal.

Meanwhile the passengers were jumping or being thrown from the wreck to the schooner, where they were hustled below and wrapped in blankets. As the day darkened and the tide turned, every one of the passengers was rescued without the loss of a single person. When all were aboard, Captain Conway and David Patterson climbed aboard the *Hamilton* and she got under way for Nantucket Harbor.

Shortly after five o' clock, the *Telegraph* and the *Hamilton* reached Straight Wharf, where a large crowd waited in the cold and dark to take charge of the immigrants. Their appearance presented one of the saddest sights the island had ever seen, for in addition to the peril and horror they had endured, they had lost all personal possessions and arrived with only the clothes on their backs. Most of their clothing had to be exchanged, or burned to prevent disease, but the local citizens donated food, clothing, and bedding to them. The unfortunates were housed in Pantheon Hall, two fire houses, and Temperance Hall on Federal Street, now the site of St. Mary's Church. Captain Conway was lodged in the Ocean House to recover from his illness, and the British Consul, William Barney, made arrangements for the crew of the ship. Many women and children were taken into private homes in town. The gratitude of the Irish immigrants was readily apparent, and for several days Nantucketers were stopped on the streets to hear "May God Almighty bless you," from those grateful people.

On Christmas Day, 1851, the old reliable steamer *Telegraph* embarked from Nantucket with most of the immigrants on the first leg of their final voyage to

New York. Several of them elected to stay on Nantucket, unwilling to risk another sea voyage, content to remain on the only piece of America they ever saw. One such couple was Robert C. Mooney, aged twenty-nine, and his twenty-one-year-old bride, Julia (Donegan), who had been married in Ireland shortly before embarking on the *British Queen*. After their experience on the sea, they never went near the water, and settled down as farmers on Nantucket, raising a family of seven children.

The old *British Queen* broke up on the shoals and was sold as she lay for $290. There was little to salvage and no money to be made by the heroic Nantucketers who had risked their lives to save a shipload of strangers from a foreign land. The only remnant of the ship was her quarterboard, which floated ashore and was presented to Robert Mooney as a reminder of his fateful arrival on Nantucket. He kept this last vestige of the ship to the end of his long life, and it has since been preserved by his descendants.

Reprinted by permission of the author.

Edouard A. Stackpole

The author of twenty-eight books on various aspects of Nantucket, maritime, and whaling history, a self-educated man who received honorary degrees from the University of Massachusetts and from Yale University, the indefatigable Edouard Stackpole (1903–93) ranks as the island's preeminent historian. After graduating from Nantucket High School in 1922, Stackpole did a post-graduate year at Roxbury Latin School, and then returned to the island, where from 1924 until 1951 he worked as printer, reporter, and eventually associate editor of the Inquirer and Mirror, *where he published many a newspaper column devoted to educating island readers about Nantucket history. From 1937 until 1952, Stackpole served as president of the Nantucket Historical Association, helping to acquire the 1800 House and the Old Gaol, as well as greatly expanding the organization's library and archives. His first books, published during the Depression, were boys' adventure novels with an historic thrust—*Smuggler's Luck: The Adventures of Timothy Pinkham of Nantucket During the War of the Revolution *(1931) and* Madagascar Jack: The Story of a Nantucket Whaler *(1935) are two fine examples.*

In 1952, Stackpole's expertise on Nantucket's role in America's maritime history earned him a prized Guggenheim Fellowship for historical research. The result was his best-known book, The Sea-Hunters: The New England Whalemen During Two Centuries, 1635–1835 *(1953). From 1951 until 1966, Stackpole would serve as curator of Connecticut's Mystic Seaport, playing a key role in the development of one of the nation's most distinguished maritime museums while continuing to publish books, articles, and monographs. Returning to the island in 1967, Stackpole continued his wide-reaching service to the island. He worked as editor of the* Inquirer and Mirror *and directed the Nantucket Chamber of Commerce. He continued to write and publish, winning a second Guggenheim in 1971 for* Whales and Destiny: The Rivalry Between America, France, and Britain for Control of the Southern Whale Fishery *(1972). Stackpole oversaw the design and construction of the Peter Foulger Museum, and served as its director from its opening in 1972 until his retirement in 1986. Even in retirement, he continued his research and writing—at the time of his death, at age 89, he had just completed a draft of his twenty-ninth book, on Nantucket sealers.*

Somewhere in this astonishingly productive life, Stackpole also found time to be an incorporator of the Nantucket Lifesaving Museum. Our selection comes from Life-Saving Nantucket *(1972), a book that records some of the many shipwrecks on the lethal shoals around the island, and the desperate attempts of Nantucket's lifesavers to rescue passengers and crews. Stackpole's flair for combining well-researched history with gripping story-telling shines to full advantage in this chapter on the 1886 wreck of the* T. B. Witherspoon. — SB

"The Wreck of the *Witherspoon*"
Chapter 14 of *Life-Saving Nantucket*

Whenever a shipwreck on Nantucket was mentioned by islanders of the late nineteenth and early twentieth centuries, one was always certain to be recalled—the loss of the three-masted schooner *T. B. Witherspoon*. The details of that tragic wreck left an indelible memory, never to be forgotten by those who chanced to be on the frozen beach at Mioxes on the Island's southwest shores, standing by helplessly as they watched the men in the rigging of the doomed craft lose their grip in the icy rigging and fall into the sea on that wild day— Sunday, January 10, 1886.

There had been greater loss of life in other shipwrecks. But the horror of the fate of the *Witherspoon*'s crew remained to those who witnessed it the most harrowing of marine disasters. Adding to the sad details were the deaths of the wife and young son of the schooner's Mate Berry. The wreck became the inspiration for the writing of one of the great Protestant hymns of the time— "Throw Out the Life Line"—one that became famed on both sides of the Atlantic.

The year 1886 had been ushered in by unseasonably mild weather. On January 8, however, a northeast blizzard swept in out of the sea, to be followed, twenty-four hours later, by a northwester, with temperatures falling rapidly well below the freezing mark. On the ninth (Saturday) the steamer *Island Home* ventured forth on its scheduled trip across the Sound, but upon reaching Tuckernuck Shoal she wisely turned back, the gale now reaching full strength, and reached her berth at Steamboat Wharf after a battle of an hour and a half.

When the storm first broke on Friday, January 8, the *T. B. Witherspoon* was approaching the New England coast, being on a voyage from Surinam, South America, with a cargo of cocoa, spices, molasses, and pickled limes. Captain Alfred Anderson, in command of the schooner, had a crew of seven men. The mate, Burdick Berry, had with him his wife, Sarah, and their six-year-old son, Sidney.

Well off this section of the coast they had encountered a northeast gale, forcing them off course. Captain Anderson, judging himself as being some twenty miles east of Montauk Point, decided to run before the storm, hoping to make Sandy Hook, and accordingly shaped his course west and west by south. The schooner had been twenty-eight days in coming up from Surinam.

For eleven hours Captain Anderson maintained his course. The snow continued heavily and there was no visibility. To their dismay, the wind began to shift, backing into the northwest and increasing in its intensity. Having been unable to get an observation, Captain Anderson could only estimate his position, and believed he was east of Montauk by some twelve miles. Ice began to form over her bows and rigging. Some hawsers were put out to break the seas and canvas bags, filled with oil, were hung over the bow.

At three o'clock on Sunday morning, January 10, 1886, Mate Burdick Berry, who had the watch on deck, sighted a light between the snow squalls, appearing off the starboard bow. He called the captain, who timed the flash as best he could before the snow closed in again. It was decided that the light was Montauk, and the course was set to run to the east.

It was a decision that cost the lives of all but two on board, and the total loss of the *T. B. Witherspoon*. The light, which had been only briefly sighted through the flights of the snow, was not Montauk but Sankaty on the east coast of Nantucket. Under the circumstances it was not unusual for Captain Anderson to have confused the flash from the lighthouse tower. He had only a short glimpse through the whirling snow, and the reflection in the driving snowflakes at night added to the difficulty of timing the flash.

Not more than half an hour later, heavy rollers came up under her bow, and Captain. Anderson sang out to set the forestaysail and loose the mainsail. But the sails were a mass of ice and the sailors could not clear them—then a break in the snow showed land dead to leeward. It was the south shore of Nantucket.

Desperately, all hands tried to get the *Witherspoon* around, to attempt clawing off-shore, but the schooner began to strike—bringing up on several shoals, staggering and rolling fearfully—then she struck and reared almost upright, fast aground within a hundred yards of the beach at the head of Little Mioxes Pond on Nantucket.

The seas were now making a clean breach over the schooner. All hands were driven below, and as the dawn brought a somber light the hapless men gazed over a waste of foaming white surf to where knots of men had gathered on the beach. The wind still blew at gale force, while the temperature stood at 16° above. The spray, leaping high over the *Witherspoon*, clung to her rigging, sails, and masts in festoons and caked in masses on her decks, as if to get a last grip on the doomed craft.

As news had reached town, hundreds of people braved the severe cold and wind to drive out to Mioxes. The Surfside Lifesaving Station's crew had arrived shortly after daybreak, the schooner having been sighted by Patrolman Jonathan O. Freeman about six o'clock—an hour before—and he had hastened the considerable distance to the station with the report.

The seas soon battered in the skylight of the cabin, and the icy water poured into the craft, flooding the staterooms and main cabin where Mate Berry had placed his wife and little son. In the forecastle the water rose steadily, finally driving the crew to the rigging.

The Surfside life-savers had shot two lines over the vessel, but the crew members, numbed by the cold, were unable to get to them and thus haul aboard the heavy hawser for the breeches buoy. The surf kicked up by the off-shore ground swell, augmented by the gale, was so overpowering that it was impossible to launch the life-boat.

The morning passed, with the hundreds of watchers on the beach forced to witness one of the most heart-rending of sights—the members of the schooner's crew slowly freezing to death in the rigging, one by one—or falling from their perches to drown in the raging sea.

There never was a more pitiless scene than that which took place in the flooded main cabin. Mate Berry had placed his wife and little son on pieces of furniture, but the rising water and the freezing cold gradually had their effect. While he waded about, barricading portholes and trying to keep the seas from washing his loved ones from the cabin, his wife was slowly sinking. She died in his arms as he tried to keep her bruised body from being wedged against a bulkhead and the floating cabin debris.

Overcome with grief, Mate Berry clung to his little boy, attempting to keep his chilled body from freezing. In recounting his story the next day, the mate stated: "He kept asking: 'Oh, Daddy, won't God save us?' I could only answer that He would, and hold on." A short time after his mother had expired, the son also died.

Overwhelmed by the double tragedy, Mate Berry crawled from the cabin and made his way along the sea-swept deck. He spied Captain Anderson in the mizzen rigging on the lee side and called to him: "My wife and boy are gone."

Well, we can do no more for them," shouted the skipper. "Try and save yourself."

The life-savers had succeeded in shooting one line over the schooner's stern, but the sailors could not get along the deck in time to make it fast. A second line went squarely over her amidships, and John Mattis, a strong, active seaman, caught hold of it and proceeded to haul away. He had the attached tail block nearly to the main rigging when the line parted.

Caught off-balance by the sudden break, Mattis staggered along the rail and, before his numbed body could react, he fell over the side into the sea. Helpless to aid him, his shipmates watched him drown within fifty yards of the beach, the current carrying him along parallel to the shore.

Meanwhile, on the beach a dozen men volunteered to attempt launching a life-raft, it being realized that the lifeboat would only capsize in the tremendous surf. The volunteers accepted were Joseph M. Folger, Jr., Benjamin Beekman, Charles Cash, John P. Taber, William Morris, Horace Orpin, Benjamin Fisher, Everett Coffin, and Charles E. Smalley.

A third line had been shot over the *Witherspoon* and made fast, and the crew of the raft attempted to pull the tossing and pitching craft by means of the rope out to the vessel. At a point midway between the shore and the schooner, the line from the wreck parted and two of the raft crew were thrown into the surf. By the quick action of their comrades they were pulled aboard, and the men on shore pulled the raft back to the beach.

The morning had passed and those on shore had watched three figures—Captain Anderson, the ship's boy, Nicholas, and a sailor named Maurice Ryder slump in the icy rigging—and two of them finally succumbed to the cold; Captain Anderson and Ryder dropping into the sea. It was a sight so fascinatingly terrible that an eyewitness, in later years, declared: "I was so horrified by the spectacle—the ship laying over with her masts toward the sea-side—the waves making a clean breach over her—the men in the rigging dropping, one by one, into the sea as they froze to death—that I could not take my eyes from the sight, although I remember I was crying like some of the women to whom I told the story afterwards."

In the late afternoon, a sixth line was shot from the mortar gun by the life-savers, to lay well over the doomed schooner. There were now only two active men on board—Mate Berry and a sailor named Charles Wulff—and the latter ran up the rigging to take the rope's-end and haul it down to the deck. In the procedure, Wulff had his wrist caught by a bight in the line, and only after frantic signaling did the men ashore finally understand and slacken away to allow him to free himself.

Then came the long anxious wait while the men on board pulled out the heavy block with the hawser attached to the breeches-buoy. This was accomplished—but the suspense grew again as the whip-line fouled and the big buoy hung suspended mid-way.

Joseph M. Folger, Jr. volunteered to get into the breeches-buoy and try to pull himself off to the vessel, hand-over-hand along the hawser. Folger tried for several minutes to work the buoy free, but the whip-line running out to the schooner had fouled and it was impossible to free it from the shore-end.

The two men on the wreck worked frantically. As darkness fell they at last managed to free the whip-line and haul the buoy across the raging waters to where the hawser was made fast in the fore-rigging. Darkness had now hidden the schooner. The men on the beach became suddenly hushed, straining their ears to listen. At last a faint hail sounded in the darkness. Carefully, the life-savers took hold of the rope and hauled, keeping a steady strain on the breeches-buoy—hoping that both men on board had gotten into the buoy.

As the buoy came over the hawser through the surf, a dozen men rushed into the sea and, quickly grasping the man in the buoy, carried him to safety up the beach. It was the mate—Burdick Berry—and he was swiftly wrapped in blankets and placed in a waiting carriage, to be driven as fast as the horse could go to the life-saving station.

Again the buoy was hauled out to the night-shrouded schooner. Again came the tense moment of quiet, with the pounding surf and shrieking gale sounding a hundred times more loud in the interim. Finally, a faint hail came winging from the wreck, and once more the anxious pull on the buoy took place. As the lumbering shape of the rescue equipment loomed amidst the white of the breaking surf, men again raced into the water and pulled the occupant to safety.

The sailor was Charles Wulff, whose strong arms had first secured the buoy-rope. He managed to gasp out that there were no more survivors.

Despite the information given by the rescued men, the life-savers stood by their apparatus all night, hoping that there might be someone still on board with life enough to haul the buoy off, or that the sea might subside enough to allow them to board the wreck. But the night passed with only the sound of the schooner's masts rending as they went by the board, and morning found the *Witherspoon*—with only her mizzenmast standing—a complete wreck.

It was not until the following afternoon that the life-saving crew was able to reach the schooner. In the rigging was the lifeless body of the youth Nicholas, literally frozen to the shrouds. He was cut down and taken ashore. The body of Captain Anderson was found by Wallace C. Folger. At 'Sconset on Monday morning the body of John Mattis was sighted and recovered by Charles Norcross. Later in the morning the body of the mate's little son was taken from the water at Surfside by James Terry and John Ayers. Mrs. Berry's body was found during the day by Patrolman Gibbs of Surfside Station. The body of Maurice Ryder was found a short distance west of the station during the day. Thus six of the seven bodies were recovered—that of John Phillips, the colored steward, was never found. Medical Examiner Kite took charge of the bodies, which were placed in the Mass. Humane Society's building on South Water Street, which served as a temporary morgue.

Nothing of great value was ever recovered from the *Witherspoon*'s cargo, except some of the cocoa. The big schooner went to pieces quickly, portions of her hull and some of her spars strewing the beach for miles. What was left of her hull was sold at auction for $55, the purchasers being D. W. and R. E. Burgess, the same parties buying the cargo for $1.

Before Mate Berry left the island, accompanying the bodies of his wife and child, he was asked if he believed a boat could have been launched from the beach in an attempt to reach the vessel.

"No!" was the grief-stricken man's emphatic reply. "What can be done with a boat in the eye of a man is one thing, and what can be done with a boat with a man's hand is another. A boat, perhaps, could have been launched from the beach—but she could never have reached us. The schooner, as she rolled, produced a sort of whirlpool, which, coupled with the great seas, would have dashed the boat to pieces alongside. No, all that could have been possibly done was done."

In its annual report for 1886, the Life-Saving Service described the work of the Surfside crew thus:

No better work under the circumstances could have been done than Veeder and his crew did that memorable day; and when it is related that a vessel was wrecked near the Surfside Station and seven out of nine of her crew perished, it will also be told that the life-saving crew did their whole duty.

The circumstances connected with the loss of schooner *J. H. Eels*, near Nauset life-saving station, on Cape Cod, January 15, 1887, brought forcibly to the minds of the people of Nantucket the sad details connected with the loss of the schooner *T. B. Witherspoon* a little less than a year before. The life-saving crew at Nauset had to contend with difficulties almost identical with those experienced by the Surfside crew on the occasion mentioned. Their lines snapped, lifeboats were useless, and they were compelled to stand on shore and see some of the crew perish, being unable to reach them. The exhausted crew could not pull the lines after they were shot to the vessel. A tug which happened along next morning succeeded in rescuing the two men who were left alive on the wreck. Later in the day the station crew boarded the vessel.

There were two Nantucketers still living in 1946 who formed part of that rescue crew attempting to launch the life-raft. They were Horace Orpin, a well-known figure at the Island Fish Market, at the head of Steamboat Wharf, and Captain Everett Coffin, a retired master mariner, who had made his home in Seattle, Washington, where he was well known as a retired captain of one of the steamboats running to Tacoma. Both declared the wreck of the *Witherspoon* as the most gripping experience of their careers as life-savers.

Reprinted by permission of the Nantucket Shipwreck & Lifesaving Museum.

Ron Winslow

Modern weather-forecasting technologies and aids to navigation have greatly reduced the number of shipwrecks in the dangerous waters around Nantucket, with a consequent reduction in the number of nail-biting nonfiction narratives. Yet wrecks around the island are not simply a tragic phenomenon of the age of sail. The twentieth century, too, had its share of disasters. Nights to remember include May 15, 1934, when the White Star liner R.M.S. Olympic, sister ship of the Titanic, ran down the Nantucket South Shoal lightship in a dense fog, and July 25, 1956, when the passenger liners S.S. Stockholm and S.S. Andrea Doria collided, necessitating the rescue of 1,660 people. But perhaps the archetypal modern shipwreck was the December 15, 1976 grounding of the Liberian-registered oil tanker Argo Merchant, sending 7.6 million gallons of industrial heating oil into the sea and spreading toward Nantucket. No lives were lost, but an entire way of life was at stake—and still is today, as huge oil tankers carrying petroleum products to New England's major cities daily traverse the busy shipping lanes near Nantucket shoals.

Here we offer the opening chapter of Ron Winslow's riveting book, Hard Aground: The Story of the Argo Merchant Oil Spill (1978). Winslow (b. 1949) covered the Argo Merchant disaster for the Providence Journal, conducting firsthand interviews with survivors and other participants. He currently serves as a senior health and science writer and deputy editor of the Wall Street Journal. Nantucket readers will want to read Hard Aground in its entirety to learn about the heroic efforts of the U. S. Coast Guard's Atlantic Strike Team to contain the Argo Merchant's oil as the ship broke up in the fifty-knot winds and huge seas of a winter gale. Hard Aground also tells the story of how Nantucketers mobilized to try and protect the island and its wildlife from a sea of oil. We won't tell you what happened—but everyone who cares about Nantucket should know the Argo Merchant story. —SB

"The Grounding," Chapter 1 of *Hard Aground: The Story of the* Argo Merchant *Oil Spill*

THE TELEPHONE RANG in the captain's quarters at 12:45 A.M., jolting George Papadopoulos awake. The forty-three-year-old master of the *Argo Merchant* had expected the call, but still, coming in the middle of the night, it startled him for an instant as he reached for the telephone near his bed.

"Captain, this is Dedrinos on the bridge," the voice crackled. "It is nearly oh-one-hundred. We are approaching the light."

Papadopoulos, a short man with a black mustache as thick as wire on his long, pointed face, awakened quickly. He was accustomed to having his sleep interrupted at sea since he always came to the bridge when his ship was to make a major course change or approach a port or a light station. He told George Dedrinos, the second officer, he would be right up.

It was December 15, 1976, and the *Argo Merchant,* a 29,870-ton Liberian-registered oil tanker, was plodding through increasingly heavy seas in the North Atlantic Ocean south of Nantucket Island, Massachusetts. Her hull measured six hundred forty-one feet, longer than two football fields. She was bound for the once-famous whaling port of Salem, thirty miles north of Boston, where she was scheduled late that day to discharge 7,677,684 gallons of heavy industrial fuel oil from her white, rust-stained hull. It was enough oil to supply 18,000 New England homes with electricity for one year.

The weight of the cargo, more than 27,500 tons, pulled the hull into the water to a draft of thirty-five feet, so deep that the ship resembled an iceberg; nearly eighty percent of her bulk was beneath the surface as she moved through the water.

The tanker was approaching the Nantucket Lightship, one of the most important navigation sentries in the world. Moored forty-eight miles southeast of Nantucket, at the crossroads of two major shipping lanes, its shining beacon warns mariners of the treacherous and legendary ship's graveyard to its north and west known as Nantucket Shoals.

Dedrinos had begun his watch at midnight and, with the officer of the preceding watch, had estimated the tanker's position as thirty-six miles southwest of the lightship. Though it was just a guess, known as a dead reckoning, Dedrinos was happy with the position because it confirmed an earlier estimate that the tanker would pass just to the southeast of the navigation marker between 3:30 and 4 A.M. He expected to see it about an hour before then.

Papadopoulos came up on the bridge precisely at 1 A.M. and went with Dedrinos into the chartroom. Laid out on a table was a chart showing the waters off the North Atlantic Coast, from Cape Hatteras, where the ship had set its current course two days before, past Nantucket to Cape Sable, Nova Scotia. Using a ruler, they lined up their noon positions of the previous days as they had been plotted on the chart and projected their course northward. They looked at each other quickly and lined it up again.

"It goes right up on the shoals, to the port of the lightship," Dedrinos remarked, without a hint of concern in his voice.

The captain nodded. He was not alarmed. Staring calmly at the chart for a moment, he reviewed the course once again. The wind and seas were coming from the northwest, as they had been for much of the past forty-eight-hours, and would tend to push the vessel to starboard, to the outside of the light, he thought. In fact, he had purposely adjusted his course a few degrees to the north two days before to compensate for those effects, and the ship was on a bearing that pointed directly at the shallow, rocky water of the shoals. But Papadopoulos was certain that the ship had drifted to the east as it headed northeast during the last one hundred miles and was on an actual course that would pass safely to the east of the lightship and the shoals.

Dedrinos pulled out another chart, which showed the direction of natural ocean currents in that area during November. No December chart was on board, so he picked the closest one on hand.

"The currents are offshore," he reported to the captain. "They will carry us to starboard."

"Yes, you're right, I know it," Papadopoulos replied.

What the captain did not know was that the December chart would have shown currents pushing in the opposite direction. If they were having any effect at all, they were pushing the vessel slowly to the west of the light.

He leaned over the table, checking and rechecking the chart on a routine approach to the carefully marked waters and the lightship ahead.

He looked up from the chart at Dedrinos, who, at twenty-seven, was serving on his first ship as an officer.

"We will keep to our present course," the captain said.

Papadopoulos left the chartroom and walked out on the starboard lookout, just off the bridge. He felt the rush of cold December air on his face. Just below him, the bow was rising and falling sluggishly as it surged through the swells, taking a pounding from the seas against her port side. Occasionally a wave broke over the deck and the captain could hear the wind-whipped spray shower the deck's huge cargo pipes with a salty mist.

He peered out over the seas in the likely direction of the lightship. Except for the dim glow of the tanker's running lights and the reflection of the moon off the water, it was black. He saw nothing. But at 1:30 he didn't expect to see it. The beacon beams its light from a perch fifty-five feet above the water. Its range, according to Papadopoulos's chart, was fourteen miles. The captain figured he was about twenty-five miles away. And the visibility was only seven miles that night, so it was unlikely anyone would see the light much before three.

The captain did not cut an imposing figure. He was short, about five feet, eight inches tall and so thin his clothes seemed to hang on him. His black but graying hair was receding at the temples, and his complexion was dark and normal for a man of forty-three, not ruddy or weatherbeaten. Only in his eyes, which were set deep under bushy eyebrows and tired and wrinkled in the corners from long hours of squinting over the waters from the bridge, did he show the wear of his profession. But his appearance was no reflection on his record as a seaman. During much of his twenty-five-year career as a master, he had skippered tankers owned by Aristotle Onassis, the late Greek shipping magnate. And except for a couple of minor oil spills, an affliction common to tankers, he had never had an accident at sea.

When he came off the lookout, Papadopoulos checked the radar. Pressing his face against the rubber eye shield, he peered into the scope for several minutes, watching the relentless sweep of the thin beam of light as it searched for objects on the water. Except for a few blips off to his port side, the screen was blank. Fishing boats, the captain figured. He checked the settings and adjusted the radar up and down its scale from twelve to twenty-four to forty-eight miles. Still, except for the fishing boats, nothing. No stationary spot on the screen that could be the lightship. The captain was surprised. Perhaps the weather had slowed the vessel down and they were behind schedule, he thought.

Out on the lookout, Dedrinos took his turn scanning the blackness as the moonlight flickered on the waters, playing tricks with his vision. More than once he mistook the moonshine for the light of a fishing boat. And shortly after 1:30 he did see a group of boats off to port, the same ones the captain had spotted on the radar. But he knew he had not seen the light. There would be no confusing its bright beacon with the dots from the fishing boats and the reflections from the moon.

Papadopoulos decided to try the radio direction finder, commonly known as the RDF. In addition to its light, the Nantucket Lightship sends out a radio signal, with a range of one hundred miles, that ships equipped with an RDF can pick up to determine their bearing on the light. The Nantucket signal is three dashes followed by a single dash—Morse code for O-T.

The captain clamped the earphones over his head and started working the dials that regulated the volume and turned the antenna on top of the bridge.

He heard nothing. For fifteen minutes he turned the dials, and for fifteen minutes he got nothing but silence. Frustrated, he tore the earphones from his head.

"I don't get anything here, nothing at all," he told Dedrinos, who had come in from the lookout. "There is nothing on the radar either."

"All I've seen is fishing boats," said the second officer. "But it is early. We wouldn't see it yet."

"We must be behind. The weather must have held us back."

Dedrinos nodded and tried to look relaxed. But he was uneasy. He did not understand why neither the radar nor the RDF had picked up the lightship. But he did not mention his concern to the captain.

For the next two hours, Papadopoulos and Dedrinos crisscrossed the bridge, from the lookouts to the radar to the chartroom, searching more urgently at each position than the last. The captain rechecked the RDF every fifteen minutes. Except for the moonlight and the boats, the sea remained black. The radar shows nothing that could possibly be the lightship. The earphones on the RDF remained silent. A knot started to grow in Dedrinos's gut. When he came on the bridge at midnight, he had expected to be alongside the lightship by the end of his watch at 4 A.M. Now it was nearly four and he had not even seen it.

Dedrinos was typical of the three deck officers aboard the *Argo Merchant*. His boyish face looked closer to eighteen than twenty-seven and he was eager for a career at sea. He had gotten his second mate's license only three months ago, and his head was filled with book knowledge of magnetic compasses, radar sets, and ocean currents—knowledge unseasoned by the wind and the sun and long hours on the bridge. And if there was a brashness or a cockiness to the authority he had in his youth, it was suppressed out of respect when the captain was on the bridge. Though Dedrinos was officially in charge of navigating the vessel during his watch—making sure the helmsman kept the vessel on course, checking the instruments, and keeping the charts in order—he yielded his authority when the captain was with him. After all, Dedrinos felt, the captain is in charge of the vessel. He knows what course to choose in charting a voyage and when to deviate from it. Except for the anxiety in his face, Dedrinos kept to himself his doubts about Papadopoulos's insistence on maintaining the present course. But he decided that although his watch was nearly over, he would remain on the bridge until the light was in sight.

At 3:50, George Ypsilantis, the thirty-three-year-old chief mate, climbed out of bed, dressed quickly, and headed for his turn on watch. Before checking with Dedrinos and Papadoupolos, who were inside the glass-paneled bridge, he went out on the starboard lookout to accustom his eyes to the dark and to freshen his sleepy face in the cold, brisk air.

Shortly before 4 A.M. he came in from the lookout. He checked the compass, the helm, and noticed the radar and the depth finder were operating.

"What happened, did you find the light?" he asked in a tone that anticipated an affirmative answer.

"No," the captain replied. "We haven't seen anything."

Ypsilantis was stunned. He looked at the captain, then at Dedrinos. Their faces were stern and drawn and plainly worried. He had never seen them so nervous. The air around him grew taut.

"The lightship. You must have seen the lightship. You should have seen it an hour ago. The light should be alongside right now."

Dedrinos shook his head. "That's what we thought. We haven't seen a thing."

"We must be behind on our course," the captain said.

The chief officer walked quickly back to the starboard lookout. His eyes scanned the horizon. He looked to port. To starboard. Dead ahead. He saw nothing. He stepped back inside.

"Now captain, we should have seen that lightship," he said again, his voice growing sharp.

He went to check the charts. As he studied the ship's course, he wondered aloud whether the heading should be changed a few degrees to the east.

"No. We'll let it go," Papadopoulos said. "We've had the currents and the seas to port, and we are a little behind. The course is okay."

Ypsilantis rarely questioned the captain's judgment. Like Dedrinos, the chief officer relied on the captain to determine the course. And he never had a reason before to challenge him. But this time, he pressed further.

"Look captain, something has to be done. The course is inside the light. We might crash on the rocks and that would be it. We might drown."

"We are in no danger." The captain's voice was impatient. "The fathometer is operating. We are in safe water. We are keeping to this course."

"Okay, captain."

Ypsilantis turned away. He looked again at the fathometer, an electronic depth finder. It was working and the depth was adequate. But that did little to calm him. They should have seen the lightship. He went over to the radar. The sweeping light picked up nothing. For ten minutes he worked at it, adjusting it to different scales. Still, he had no image on the screen.

While Dedrinos returned to the lookout, the captain tried the RDF again. He made a special effort to pick up not only the Nantucket O-T but also the signals from other radio beacons in the area which operate in sequence with the lightship on the same channel. Silence. His confidence in the course he had so insistently kept to for the past three hours began to falter. For the first time, he wondered to himself whether he should change the course. But he didn't consider it for long.

At 4:30, Ypsilantis got his first chance at the RDF. He put the earphones on and twisted dials back and forth. Within a minute, he got a signal. Dah-dah-dah, dah. He turned the dials again and listened carefully. Dah-dah-dah, dah.

"Captain, I've got it! I've got the O-T!"

Papadopoulos nearly sprinted back to the RDF. He took the earphones and listened.

"That's it, you have it! You do have it." For the first time in three hours, Papadopoulos smiled broadly. Ypsilantis could see tension drain out of the muscles in the captain's face.

The chief officer took the earphones back. As he turned the dial slightly, the pitch of the signal grew loud, then soft, then loud again. He stopped the dial at the point where he could barely hear the O-T, then took the bearing. It was nearly dead ahead.

Ypsilantis twisted the headset and put one earphone to his ear. He gave the other one to the captain so they could both listen at the same time. They nearly bumped their heads together.

The dead-ahead bearing indicated that they had not yet passed the lightship. It confirmed Papadopoulos's hunch that the vessel was behind. And it renewed his confidence in the course. Changing it was out of the question now. Both he and the chief officer had found the bit of good news they were looking for and they latched on to it. They felt they were not in danger.

But over the next half hour, none of the other indicators fell in line. The radar screen was still blank. The sea was still black. Not even the loom of the light was visible on the horizon. And the depth-finder was showing increasingly shallow water beneath them. By 5 A.M., the captain noticed readings of twenty fathoms, about one hundred twenty feet. He did not think to check the measurement with the depth readings on his chart.

Ypsilantis went out on the lookout, hoping to see any kind of light. A boat. A ship. Something they could reach by radio to check their course and position. But the fishing vessels that had seemed to dot the waters earlier were gone. The *Argo Merchant* was alone and lost on a vast sea of blackness.

By 5:30, Ypsilantis was desperate. He decided to take an astral fix, an estimate of the vessel's position based on the angle of stars above the horizon. He knew it was too early. To get an accurate reading, he needed to see the stars and the horizon at the same time, a condition that exists only at twilight and just before dawn. He had planned to take a fix between 6:05 and 6:15. But he couldn't wait. Although the horizon was too dark for a good fix, the sky was brightening faintly in the east. He could at least come close, he thought. But he wished he had a Loran set. He could have pinpointed the position electronically, without the stars.

He peered carefully through a sextant, squinting and straining his eyes in an effort to discern the almost invisible line where the black sea and the black sky met. He checked and rechecked the measurements until he was reasonably sure they were correct. Using special navigation tables, he converted his measurements to other numbers and added them up to arrive at the coordinates. At 5:45, he plotted the position on the chart. They were forty miles southeast of the lightship, on a course that would take them to the inside of the marker, toward the shoals.

Neither the captain nor the chief officer were satisfied with the fix. While it reconfirmed the captain's belief that the weather had slowed the ship down, the position indicated they had not even reached the dead reckoning Dedrinos had plotted nearly six hours before. They couldn't be that far behind schedule. Still, they figured the fix was within fifteen miles of accuracy. And everything within that range was safe water.

Ypsilantis was still concerned, however, that the tanker was headed inside the light. He thought the captain would be wise to change the course slightly to the right. But he said nothing. The captain could see the charts as plainly as he could, the chief officer thought. It was Papadopoulos' business to determine the course. Besides, the pressure was off. While the fix was hardly satisfactory, it surely indicated, he felt, that they could wait another half hour. The conditions would be right and he could get another good measurement from the horizon. The ordeal would be over. If necessary, the course could be corrected then.

But under the pressure of the moment, the chief officer in making his calculations had added wrong. His fix was forty miles off. Had he added correctly, he would have come up with coordinates showing that the *Argo Merchant* had already passed to the inside of the Nantucket Lightship and was within fifteen miles of shoal water that was only thirty feet deep.

Five minutes later, Papadopoulos failed to heed the only warning that could have compensated for Ypsilantis's error. The depth finder read fifteen fathoms, ninety feet. The captain raised his eyebrows in disbelief. The chart showed much deeper water in the area around their 5:30 position. A fifteen-fathom reading in the vicinity of the lightship is a clear warning that a vessel is dangerously near the shoals. But the captain didn't trust it. His RDF continued to pick up the lightship's radio signal. The dead ahead bearing had not wavered more than a degree since they had first heard it ninety minutes before. He joined Ypsilantis and Dedrinos, who were out on the starboard lookout, searching the ocean, waiting out the last eight minutes before the chief officer could take another fix.

The captain detected the danger first. He heard a subtle but undeniable change in the sound of the waves, a sign that no electronic instrument would pick up. It was the sound of shallow water. The captain had no time to react. The ship shook lightly, as if a tremor was spreading through it. There was no violent crash. No piercing noise. The officers hardly had to move to keep their balance. The helmsman thought they had plunged into a huge wave. Then they felt a bump.

"Hard aport!" Ypsilantis hollered.

The helmsman put the wheel hard to the left. The bow turned slightly, but the ship's belly was skidding on the bottom. The tanker shuddered to a halt. Papadopoulos, Ypsilantis, and Dedrinos looked at each other. Their wide-eyed faces turned white. Instinctively, all three looked at their watches. It was 6 A.M. From the lookout, they could hear huge crashing waves that sounded like breakers rolling ashore. They had no idea where they were.

Papadopoulos ordered the engines to a dead stop. Then he pushed the emergency alarm. The sound of a siren screeched through the ship. Crewmen bolted upright in their bunks, as if a bomb had gone off beneath them. Engineering officers scampered down narrow walkways to the engine room and waited anxiously for information and instructions. Other crew members grabbed life jackets and headed for the bridge or to lifeboats. No one knew what had happened.

On the bridge, Ypsilantis agreed to go to the main deck and take soundings around the ship, to see how deep the water was and to determine if they could get her off. He told the captain not to do anything until he got back.

As he left the bridge, Ypsilantis could see waves crashing over the deck. He could feel the sway of the ship as it rocked back and forth. Getting soundings would be difficult, he thought.

The captain waited impatiently. He wanted to get the ship off. He was scared. Seven minutes. Ten minutes. Twelve minutes. Ypsilantis had not returned.

"Full astern!" he shouted, pushing a lever that telegraphed the order to the engine room.

The captain had slammed his vessel into reverse. The ship groaned at first, then rumbled as the propeller slowly increased speed and strained against the weight of the oil-laden hull. Thick black smoke belched from the stack. The entire tanker shook in a violent vibration. In the engine room, crew members stumbled and fell. Others grabbed for handrails, ladders, anything they could reach to keep their balance.

Suddenly a pipe connected to one of the tanker's two boilers ruptured. Then a valve that regulated the intake of cooling sea water into the boilers sheared off. The ocean gushed into the engine room.

The officers and crew searched frantically for the source of the leak. They pulled switches, closed valves, and inspected pipes they could see. But the water was swirling around them. They couldn't see the floor. They could hardly stand up. And they could not stop the flow of water into the ship.

When he felt the vibration of the vessel, Ypsilantis was furious. He dashed back to the bridge. The tension and frustration that had been building up for the past two hours during the futile search for the lightship had reached its threshold. When he got back to the captain, it erupted.

"Didn't I tell you to wait?" he hollered. "What the hell are you doing? You were going to wait until I had the soundings. You've lost the ship, goddammit. You lost her!"

"We are stuck aground!" the captain shouted back. "We've got to get her off. I can't wait all morning for the soundings."

"Well, you should have waited. The ship is gone."

Ypsilantis was sure he felt the engine room dip when the captain went into reverse. The move, he thought, had pierced the hull.

At 6:28, the captain ordered all engines stopped, ending what seemed like a thirteen-minute earthquake to the men in the engine room. They worked quickly to survey the damage and close every valve they could find. But water was still coming in. A major intake line had broken.

The chief engineer talked to Papadopoulos by telephone to tell him they were taking on water. The captain decided his only recourse was to try again. He ordered the vessel into reverse once more. Once more, the engine room crew staggered in the vibration as the single propeller tried in vain to pull the tanker from the shoal that had snared her. But she was stuck fast. At 6:55, nearly an hour after the ship hit bottom, Papadopoulos gave up. The engines were shut down. He would have to put out a Mayday. The *Argo Merchant* was hard aground.

Although water was pouring into the engine room, none of the ship's cargo of oil was pouring into the sea. Her thirty cargo tanks, laid out like an ice cube tray in ten rows of three across, were intact. But the water in the engine room at the stern was already putting an unusual strain on the rest of the ship. The seas piled up twelve- and fifteen-foot waves which were battering her portside. She started to list to starboard. She was helpless.

The 7,677,684 gallons of oil that were sloshing around in her tanks had been designated to take the first chill of winter out of hundreds of New England homes, schools, and businesses. Now, encased in a wounded tanker, the oil was trapped atop a shoal somewhere between the sandy beaches and lucra-tive shellfishing areas of Nantucket and Cape Cod and the rich offshore fishing grounds of a section of the Outer Continental Shelf known as Georges Bank. All that restrained the thick, black goo from pouring into the sea was an inch-thick skin of steel. And each surging wave slowly raised the bow, then let it drop with a thud against the hard, sandy shoal.

Reprinted by permission of W. W. Norton.

XI

Finale

Herman Melville

Like the crashing, romantic chords that conclude a Beethoven symphony, the sublime, over-the-top final chapter of Moby-Dick *(1851) seems a fitting place to conclude* The Nantucket Reader. *From the Wampanoag legend of the island's creation to the* Narrative of the Most Extraordinary and Distressing Shipwreck of the Whale-Ship Essex, *Herman Melville (1819–91) managed to incorporate virtually every aspect of Nantucket lore and history that preceded him into a lasting literary classic. And from the high art of Robert Lowell's "The Quaker Graveyard in Nantucket" to the pulp fiction of Peter Benchley's* Jaws, *his* Moby-Dick *has influenced almost every work of Nantucket literature since. But more importantly, the final chapter of* Moby-Dick *reminds us of the one thing about island life that has remained constant since Thomas Macy set sail to avoid persecution by the Puritans in 1659 and the first proprietors began to subdivide the moors, the one thing that will endure after all the traffic jams and trophy houses of today have slipped beneath the waves, the one thing about Nantucket that is truly eternal and an insurmountable challenge to human vanity—the sea. —SB*

"The Chase—Third Day,"
Chapter 135 of *Moby-Dick; or, The Whale*

THE MORNING OF the third day dawned fair and fresh, and once more the solitary night-man at the fore-mast-head was relieved by crowds of the daylight look-outs, who dotted every mast and almost every spar.

"D'ye see him?" cried Ahab; but the whale was not yet in sight.

"In his infallible wake, though; but follow that wake, that's all. Helm there; steady, as thou goest, and hast been going. What a lovely day again! were it a new-made world, and made for a summer-house to the angels, and this morning the first of its throwing open to them, a fairer day could not dawn upon that world. Here's food for thought, had Ahab time to think; but Ahab never thinks; he only feels, feels, feels; THAT'S tingling enough for mortal man! to think's audacity. God only has that right and privilege. Thinking is, or ought to be, a coolness and a calmness; and our poor hearts throb, and our poor brains beat too much for that. And yet, I've sometimes thought my brain was very calm—frozen calm, this old skull cracks so, like a glass in which the contents turned to ice, and shiver it. And still this hair is growing now; this moment growing, and heat must breed it; but no, it's like that sort of common grass that will grow anywhere, between the earthy clefts of Greenland ice or in Vesuvius lava. How the wild winds blow it; they whip it about me as the torn shreds of split sails lash the tossed ship they cling to. A vile wind that has no doubt blown ere this through prison corridors and cells, and wards of hospitals, and ventilated them, and now comes blowing hither as innocent as fleeces. Out upon it!—it's tainted. Were I the wind, I'd blow no more on such a wicked, miserable world. I'd crawl somewhere to a cave, and slink there. And yet, 'tis a noble and heroic thing, the wind! who ever conquered it? In every fight it has the last and bitterest blow. Run tilting at it, and you but run through it. Ha! a coward wind that strikes stark naked men, but will not stand to receive a single blow. Even Ahab is a braver thing—a nobler thing than THAT. Would now the wind but had a body; but all the things that most exasperate and outrage mortal man, all these things are bodiless, but only bodiless as objects, not as agents. There's a most special, a most cunning, oh, a most malicious difference! And yet, I say again, and swear it now, that there's something all glorious and gracious in the wind. These warm Trade Winds, at least, that in the clear heavens blow straight on, in strong and steadfast, vigorous mildness; and veer not from their mark, however the baser currents of the sea may turn and tack, and mightiest Mississippies of the land swift and swerve about, uncertain where to go at last. And by the eternal Poles! these same Trades that so directly blow my good ship on; these Trades, or something like them—something so unchangeable, and full as strong, blow my keeled soul along! To it! Aloft there! What d'ye see?"

"Nothing, sir."

"Nothing! and noon at hand! The doubloon goes a-begging! See the sun! Aye, aye, it must be so. I've oversailed him. How, got the start? Aye, he's chasing ME now; not I, HIM—that's bad; I might have known it, too. Fool! the lines— the harpoons he's towing. Aye, aye, I have run him by last night. About! about! Come down, all of ye, but the regular look outs! Man the braces!"

Steering as she had done, the wind had been somewhat on the Pequod's quarter, so that now being pointed in the reverse direction, the braced ship sailed hard upon the breeze as she rechurned the cream in her own white wake.

"Against the wind he now steers for the open jaw," murmured Starbuck to himself, as he coiled the new-hauled main-brace upon the rail. "God keep us, but already my bones feel damp within me, and from the inside wet my flesh. I misdoubt me that I disobey my God in obeying him!"

"Stand by to sway me up!" cried Ahab, advancing to the hempen basket. "We should meet him soon."

"Aye, aye, sir," and straightway Starbuck did Ahab's bidding, and once more Ahab swung on high.

A whole hour now passed; gold-beaten out to ages. Time itself now held long breaths with keen suspense. But at last, some three points off the weather bow, Ahab descried the spout again, and instantly from the three mast-heads three shrieks went up as if the tongues of fire had voiced it.

"Forehead to forehead I meet thee, this third time, Moby Dick! On deck there!—brace sharper up; crowd her into the wind's eye. He's too far off to lower yet, Mr. Starbuck. The sails shake! Stand over that helmsman with a top-maul! So, so; he travels fast, and I must down. But let me have one more good round look aloft here at the sea; there's time for that. An old, old sight, and yet somehow so young; aye, and not changed a wink since I first saw it, a boy, from the sand-hills of Nantucket! The same!—the same!—the same to Noah as to me. There's a soft shower to leeward. Such lovely leewardings! They must lead somewhere—to something else than common land, more palmy than the palms. Leeward! the white whale goes that way; look to windward, then; the better if the bitterer quarter. But good bye, good bye, old mast-head! What's this?—green? aye, tiny mosses in these warped cracks. No such green weather stains on Ahab's head! There's the difference now between man's old age and matter's. But aye, old mast, we both grow old together; sound in our hulls, though, are we not, my ship? Aye, minus a leg, that's all. By heaven this dead wood has the better of my live flesh every way. I can't compare with it; and I've known some ships made of dead trees outlast the lives of men made of the most vital stuff of vital fathers. What's that he said? he should still go before me, my pilot; and yet to be seen again? But where? Will I have eyes at the bottom of the sea, supposing I descend those endless stairs? and all night I've been sailing from him, wherever he did sink to. Aye, aye, like many more thou told'st direful truth as touching thyself, O Parsee; but, Ahab, there thy shot fell short. Good-bye, mast-head—keep a good eye upon the whale, the while I'm gone. We'll talk to-morrow, nay, to-night, when the white whale lies down there, tied by head and tail."

He gave the word; and still gazing round him, was steadily lowered through the cloven blue air to the deck.

In due time the boats were lowered; but as standing in his shallop's stern, Ahab just hovered upon the point of the descent, he waved to the mate,—who held one of the tackle-ropes on deck—and bade him pause.

"Starbuck!"

"Sir?"

"For the third time my soul's ship starts upon this voyage, Starbuck."

"Aye, sir, thou wilt have it so."

"Some ships sail from their ports, and ever afterwards are missing, Starbuck!"

"Truth, sir: saddest truth."

"Some men die at ebb tide; some at low water; some at the full of the flood;—and I feel now like a billow that's all one crested comb, Starbuck. I am old;—shake hands with me, man."

Their hands met; their eyes fastened; Starbuck's tears the glue.

"Oh, my captain, my captain!—noble heart—go not—go not!—see, it's a brave man that weeps; how great the agony of the persuasion then!"

"Lower away!"—cried Ahab, tossing the mate's arm from him. "Stand by the crew!"

In an instant the boat was pulling round close under the stern.

"The sharks! the sharks!" cried a voice from the low cabin-window there; "O master, my master, come back!"

But Ahab heard nothing; for his own voice was high-lifted then; and the boat leaped on.

Yet the voice spake true; for scarce had he pushed from the ship, when numbers of sharks, seemingly rising from out the dark waters beneath the hull, maliciously snapped at the blades of the oars, every time they dipped in the water; and in this way accompanied the boat with their bites. It is a thing not uncommonly happening to the whale-boats in those swarming seas; the sharks at times apparently following them in the same prescient way that vultures hover over the banners of marching regiments in the east. But these were the first sharks that had been observed by the Pequod since the White Whale had been first descried; and whether it was that Ahab's crew were all such tiger-yellow barbarians, and therefore their flesh more musky to the senses of the sharks—a matter sometimes well known to affect them,—however it was, they seemed to follow that one boat without molesting the others.

"Heart of wrought steel!" murmured Starbuck gazing over the side, and following with his eyes the receding boat—"canst thou yet ring boldly to that sight?—lowering thy keel among ravening sharks, and followed by them, open-mouthed to the chase; and this the critical third day?—For when three days flow together in one continuous intense pursuit; be sure the first is the morning, the second the noon, and the third the evening and the end of that thing—be that end what it may. Oh! my God! what is this that shoots through me, and leaves me so deadly calm, yet expectant,—fixed at the top of a shudder! Future things swim before me, as in empty outlines and skeletons; all the past is somehow grown dim. Mary, girl! thou fadest in pale glories behind me; boy! I seem to see but thy eyes grown wondrous blue. Strangest problems of life seem clearing; but clouds sweep between—Is my journey's end coming? My legs feel faint; like his who has footed it all day. Feel thy heart,—beats it yet? Stir thyself, Starbuck!—stave it off—move, move! speak aloud!—Mast-head there! See ye my boy's hand on the hill?—Crazed;—aloft there!—keep thy keenest eye upon the boats:—mark well the whale!—Ho! again!—drive off that hawk! see! He pecks—he tears the vane"—pointing to the red flag flying at the main-truck—"Ha! he soars away with it!—Where's the old man now? see'st thou that sight, oh Ahab!—shudder, shudder!"

The boats had not gone very far, when by a signal from the mast-heads—a downward pointed arm, Ahab knew that the whale had sounded; but intending to be near him at the next rising, he held on his way a little sideways from the vessel; the becharmed crew maintaining the profoundest silence, as the head-beat waves hammered and hammered against the opposing bow.

"Drive, drive in your nails, oh ye waves! to their uttermost heads drive them in! ye but strike a thing without a lid; and no coffin and no hearse can be mine:—and hemp only can kill me! Ha! ha!"

Suddenly the waters around them slowly swelled in broad circles; then quickly upheaved, as if sideways sliding from a submerged berg of ice, swiftly rising to the surface. A low rumbling sound was heard; a subterraneous hum; and then all held their breaths; as bedraggled with trailing ropes, and harpoons, and lances, a vast form shot lengthwise, but obliquely from the sea. Shrouded in a thin drooping veil of mist, it hovered for a moment in the rainbowed air; and then fell swamping back into the deep. Crushed thirty feet upwards, the waters flashed for an instant like heaps of fountains, then brokenly sank in a shower of flakes, leaving the circling surface creamed like new milk round the marble trunk of the whale.

"Give way!" cried Ahab to the oarsmen, and the boats darted forward to the attack; but maddened by yesterday's fresh irons that corroded in him, Moby Dick seemed combinedly possessed by all the angels that fell from heaven. The wide tiers of welded tendons overspreading his broad white forehead, beneath the transparent skin, looked knitted together; as head on, he came churning his tail among the boats; and once more flailed them apart; spilling out the irons and lances from the two mates' boats, and dashing in one side of the upper part of their bows, but leaving Ahab's almost without a scar.

While Daggoo and Queequeg were stopping the strained planks; and as the whale swimming out from them, turned, and showed one entire flank as he shot by them again; at that moment a quick cry went up. Lashed round and round to the fish's back; pinioned in the turns upon turns in which, during the past night, the whale had reeled the involutions of the lines around him, the half torn body of the Parsee was seen; his sable raiment frayed to shreds; his distended eyes turned full upon old Ahab.

The harpoon dropped from his hand.

"Befooled, befooled!"—drawing in a long lean breath—"Aye, Parsee! I see thee again.—Aye, and thou goest before; and this, THIS then is the hearse that thou didst promise. But I hold thee to the last letter of thy word. Where is the second hearse? Away, mates, to the ship! those boats are useless now; repair them if ye can in time, and return to me; if not, Ahab is enough to die—Down, men! the first thing that but offers to jump from this boat I stand in, that thing I harpoon. Ye are not other men, but my arms and my legs; and so obey me.—Where's the whale? gone down again?"

But he looked too nigh the boat; for as if bent upon escaping with the corpse he bore, and as if the particular place of the last encounter had been but a stage in his leeward voyage, Moby Dick was now again steadily swimming forward; and had almost passed the ship,—which thus far had been sailing in the contrary direction to him, though for the present her headway had been stopped. He seemed swimming with his utmost velocity, and now only intent upon pursuing his own straight path in the sea.

"Oh! Ahab," cried Starbuck, "not too late is it, even now, the third day, to desist. See! Moby Dick seeks thee not. It is thou, thou, that madly seekest him!"

Setting sail to the rising wind, the lonely boat was swiftly impelled to leeward, by both oars and canvas. And at last when Ahab was sliding by the vessel, so near as plainly to distinguish Starbuck's face as he leaned over the rail, he hailed him to turn the vessel about, and follow him, not too swiftly, at a judicious interval. Glancing upwards, he saw Tashtego, Queequeg, and Daggoo, eagerly mounting to the three mast-heads; while the oarsmen were rocking in the two staved boats which had but just been hoisted to the side, and were busily at work in repairing them. One after the other, through the port-holes, as he sped, he also caught flying glimpses of Stubb and Flask, busying themselves on deck among bundles of new irons and lances. As he saw all this; as he heard the hammers in the broken boats; far other hammers seemed driving a nail into his heart. But he rallied. And now marking that the vane or flag was gone from the main-mast-head, he shouted to Tashtego, who had just gained that perch, to descend again for another flag, and a hammer and nails, and so nail it to the mast.

Whether fagged by the three days' running chase, and the resistance to his swimming in the knotted hamper he bore; or whether it was some latent deceitfulness and malice in him: whichever was true, the White Whale's way now began to abate, as it seemed, from the boat so rapidly nearing him once more; though indeed the whale's last start had not been so long a one as before. And still as Ahab glided over the waves the unpitying sharks accompanied him; and so pertinaciously stuck to the boat; and so continually bit at the plying oars, that the blades became jagged and crunched, and left small splinters in the sea, at almost every dip.

"Heed them not! those teeth but give new rowlocks to your oars. Pull on! 'tis the better rest, the shark's jaw than the yielding water."

"But at every bite, sir, the thin blades grow smaller and smaller!"

"They will last long enough! pull on!—But who can tell"—he muttered— "whether these sharks swim to feast on the whale or on Ahab?—But pull on! Aye, all alive, now—we near him. The helm! take the helm! let me pass,"—and so saying two of the oarsmen helped him forward to the bows of the still flying boat.

At length as the craft was cast to one side, and ran ranging along with the White Whale's flank, he seemed strangely oblivious of its advance—as the whale sometimes will—and Ahab was fairly within the smoky mountain mist, which, thrown off from the whale's spout, curled round his great, Monadnock hump; he was even thus close to him; when, with body arched back, and both arms lengthwise high-lifted to the poise, he darted his fierce iron, and his far fiercer curse into the hated whale. As both steel and curse sank to the socket, as if sucked into a morass, Moby Dick sideways writhed; spasmodically rolled his nigh flank against the bow, and, without staving a hole in it, so suddenly canted the boat over, that had it not been for the elevated part of the gunwale to which he then clung, Ahab would once more have been tossed into the sea. As it was, three of the oarsmen—who foreknew not the precise instant of the dart, and were therefore unprepared for its effects—these were flung out; but so fell, that, in an instant two of them clutched the gunwale again, and rising to its level on a combing wave, hurled themselves bodily inboard again; the third man helplessly dropping astern, but still afloat and swimming.

Almost simultaneously, with a mighty volition of ungraduated, instantaneous swiftness, the White Whale darted through the weltering sea. But when Ahab cried out to the steersman to take new turns with the line, and hold it so; and commanded the crew to turn round on their seats, and tow the boat up to the mark; the moment the treacherous line felt that double strain and tug, it snapped in the empty air!

"What breaks in me? Some sinew cracks!—'tis whole again; oars! oars! Burst in upon him!"

Hearing the tremendous rush of the sea-crashing boat, the whale wheeled round to present his blank forehead at bay; but in that evolution, catching sight of the nearing black hull of the ship; seemingly seeing in it the source of all his persecutions; bethinking it—it may be—a larger and nobler foe; of a sudden, he bore down upon its advancing prow, smiting his jaws amid fiery showers of foam.

Ahab staggered; his hand smote his forehead. "I grow blind; hands! stretch out before me that I may yet grope my way. Is't night?"

"The whale! The ship!" cried the cringing oarsmen.

"Oars! oars! Slope downwards to thy depths, O sea, that ere it be for ever too late, Ahab may slide this last, last time upon his mark! I see: the ship! the ship! Dash on, my men! Will ye not save my ship?"

But as the oarsmen violently forced their boat through the sledge-hammering seas, the before whale-smitten bow-ends of two planks burst through, and in an instant almost, the temporarily disabled boat lay nearly level with the waves; its half-wading, splashing crew, trying hard to stop the gap and bale out the pouring water.

Meantime, for that one beholding instant, Tashtego's mast-head hammer remained suspended in his hand; and the red flag, half-wrapping him as with a plaid, then streamed itself straight out from him, as his own forward-flowing heart; while Starbuck and Stubb, standing upon the bowsprit beneath, caught sight of the down-coming monster just as soon as he.

"The whale, the whale! Up helm, up helm! Oh, all ye sweet powers of air, now hug me close! Let not Starbuck die, if die he must, in a woman's fainting fit. Up helm, I say—ye fools, the jaw! the jaw! Is this the end of all my bursting prayers? all my life-long fidelities? Oh, Ahab, Ahab, lo, thy work. Steady! helmsman, steady. Nay, nay! Up helm again! He turns to meet us! Oh, his unappeasable brow drives on towards one, whose duty tells him he cannot depart. My God, stand by me now!"

"Stand not by me, but stand under me, whoever you are that will now help Stubb; for Stubb, too, sticks here. I grin at thee, thou grinning whale! Who ever helped Stubb, or kept Stubb awake, but Stubb's own unwinking eye? And now poor Stubb goes to bed upon a mattress that is all too soft; would it were stuffed with brushwood! I grin at thee, thou grinning whale! Look ye, sun, moon, and stars! I call ye assassins of as good a fellow as ever spouted up his ghost. For all that, I would yet ring glasses with ye, would ye but hand the cup! Oh, oh! oh, oh! thou grinning whale, but there'll be plenty of gulping soon! Why fly ye not, O Ahab! For me, off shoes and jacket to it; let Stubb die in his drawers! A most mouldy and over salted death, though;—cherries! cherries! cherries! Oh, Flask, for one red cherry ere we die!"

"Cherries? I only wish that we were where they grow. Oh, Stubb, I hope my poor mother's drawn my part-pay ere this; if not, few coppers will now come to her, for the voyage is up."

From the ship's bows, nearly all the seamen now hung inactive; hammers, bits of plank, lances, and harpoons, mechanically retained in their hands, just as they had darted from their various employments; all their enchanted eyes intent upon the whale, which from side to side strangely vibrating his predestinating head, sent a broad band of overspreading semicircular foam before him as he rushed. Retribution, swift vengeance, eternal malice were in his whole aspect, and spite of all that mortal man could do, the solid white buttress of his forehead smote the ship's starboard bow, till men and timbers reeled. Some fell flat upon their faces. Like dislodged trucks, the heads of the harpooneers aloft shook on their bull-like necks. Through the breach, they heard the waters pour, as mountain torrents down a flume.

"The ship! The hearse!—the second hearse!" cried Ahab from the boat; "its wood could only be American!"

Diving beneath the settling ship, the whale ran quivering along its keel; but turning under water, swiftly shot to the surface again, far off the other bow, but within a few yards of Ahab's boat, where, for a time, he lay quiescent.

"I turn my body from the sun. What ho, Tashtego! let me hear thy hammer. Oh! ye three unsurrendered spires of mine; thou uncracked keel; and only god-bullied hull; thou firm deck, and haughty helm, and Pole-pointed prow,—death-glorious ship! must ye then perish, and without me? Am I cut off from the last fond pride of meanest shipwrecked captains? Oh, lonely death on lonely life! Oh, now I feel my topmost greatness lies in my topmost grief. Ho, ho! from all your furthest bounds, pour ye now in, ye bold billows of my whole foregone life, and top this one piled comber of my death! Towards thee I roll, thou all-destroying but unconquering whale; to the last I grapple with thee; from hell's heart I stab at thee; for hate's sake I spit my last breath at thee. Sink all coffins and all hearses to one common pool! and since neither can be mine, let me then tow to pieces, while still chasing thee, though tied to thee, thou damned whale! THUS, I give up the spear!"

The harpoon was darted; the stricken whale flew forward; with igniting velocity the line ran through the grooves;—ran foul. Ahab stooped to clear it; he did clear it; but the flying turn caught him round the neck, and voicelessly as Turkish mutes bowstring their victim, he was shot out of the boat, ere the crew knew he was gone. Next instant, the heavy eye-splice in the rope's final end flew out of the stark-empty tub, knocked down an oarsman, and smiting the sea, disappeared in its depths.

For an instant, the tranced boat's crew stood still; then turned. "The ship? Great God, where is the ship?" Soon they through dim, bewildering mediums saw her sidelong fading phantom, as in the gaseous Fata Morgana; only the uppermost masts out of water; while fixed by infatuation, or fidelity, or fate, to their once lofty perches, the pagan harpooneers still maintained their sinking lookouts on the sea. And now, concentric circles seized the lone boat itself, and all its crew, and each floating oar, and every lance-pole, and spinning, animate and inanimate, all round and round in one vortex, carried the smallest chip of the Pequod out of sight.

But as the last whelmings intermixingly poured themselves over the sunken head of the Indian at the mainmast, leaving a few inches of the erect spar yet visible, together with long streaming yards of the flag, which calmly undulated, with ironical coincidings, over the destroying billows they almost touched;—at that instant, a red arm and a hammer hovered backwardly uplifted in the open air, in the act of nailing the flag faster and yet faster to the subsiding spar. A sky-hawk that tauntingly had followed the main-truck downwards from its natural home among the stars, pecking at the flag, and incommoding Tashtego there; this bird now chanced to intercept its broad fluttering wing between the hammer and the wood; and simultaneously feeling that etherial thrill, the submerged savage beneath, in his death-gasp, kept his hammer frozen there; and so the bird of heaven, with archangelic shrieks, and his imperial beak thrust upwards, and his whole captive form folded in the flag of Ahab, went down with his ship, which, like Satan, would not sink to hell till she had dragged a living part of heaven along with her, and helmeted herself with it.

Now small fowls flew screaming over the yet yawning gulf; a sullen white surf beat against its steep sides; then all collapsed, and the great shroud of the sea rolled on as it rolled five thousand years ago.

Select Bibliography

In this bibliography, readers will find both my sources and ideas for further reading. Entries for each of the writers reprinted or discussed in this book are organized alphabetically by the authors' last names. In addition, I have included entries for three subjects—the Atheneum, Nantucket history, and the 'Sconset School of Opinion. I also recommend "Contemporary Authors," *Gale Literary Databases,* http://galenet.galegroup.com, available on-line to cardholders of the Nantucket Atheneum and many other public libraries.

Anonymous

Anon. "Schooner Industry [']s expedition on a Whaling Cruse [*sic*]. A Song Composed On Board of her." Nantucket Historical Association Research Library. Nantucket, MA.

Bolster, W. Jeffrey. *Black Jacks: African American Seamen in the Age of Sail.* Cambridge, MA: Harvard University Press, 1997.

Kaldenbach-Montemayor, Isabel. "Absalom Boston and the Development of Nantucket's African-American Community." In *Nantucket's People of Color: Essays on History, Politics, and Community.* Ed. Robert Johnson Jr. Lanham, MD: University Press of America, 2006. 17–48.

Philbrick, Nathaniel. *Away Offshore: Nantucket Island and Its People, 1602–1890.* Nantucket, MA: Mill Hill Press, 1994.

_____. "'I Will Take to the Water': Frederick Douglass, the Sea, and the Nantucket Whale Fishery." *Historic Nantucket* 40.3 (Fall 1992): 49–51. http://www.nha.org/history/hn-n40n3-douglass.htm

The Atheneum

Beegel, Susan. "The Atheneum's Founders Were Visionaries of Learning and Commerce." *The Nantucket Atheneum: A Commemorative Review.* Nantucket, MA: The Nantucket Atheneum, 1996. 30–31.

_____. "Island Phoenix." *Nantucket Journal* (Summer 1992): 56–61, 63–64, 80.

"Greetings from the Literary Community." *The Nantucket Atheneum: A Commemorative Review.* Nantucket, MA: The Nantucket Atheneum, 1996. 47–50.

Jewett, Sarah Orne. *The Country of the Pointed Firs [1896] and Other Stories.* New York: W. W. Norton, 1994.

Woodward, Hobson. "The Atheneum Is Pleased to Present. . . ." *The Nantucket Atheneum: A Commemorative Review.* Nantucket, MA: The Nantucket Atheneum, 1996. 38–47.

Russell Baker

Baker, Russell. "Nantucket: Sufficient Unto Itself." *The New York Times.* 13 June 1982. A searchable archive of *New York Times* articles published since 1981 is available on-line at *www.newyorktimes.com.*
_____. "Sunday Observer; The Taint of Quaint." *The New York Times.* 7 August 1983.
_____. "Sunday Observer; Quaintness." *The New York Times.* 7 October 1984.

Nathaniel Benchley

Benchley, Nathaniel. *The Off-Islanders.* New York: McGraw-Hill, 1961.
_____. *Sweet Anarchy.* Garden City, NY: Doubleday, 1979.

Peter Benchley

Balling, Joshua. "Peter Benchley, 'Jaws' author, gone at 65." *The Inquirer and Mirror* [Nantucket]. 16 February 2006.
   http://www.ack.net/Benchley021606.html
Benchley, Peter. *Jaws.* Garden City, NY: Doubleday, 1974.
Handwerk, Brian. "*Jaws* Author Peter Benchley Talks Sharks." *National Geographic News.* 7 June 2002.
   http://news.nationalgeographic.com/news/2002/06/0606_shark5.html
"Steven Spielberg." *Wikipedia: The Free Encyclopedia.*
   http://en.wikipedia.org/wiki/Steven_Spielberg
Wyatt, Edward. "Peter Benchley, Author of 'Jaws,' Dies at 65." *The New York Times.* 13 February 2006. *http://www.nytimes.com/2006/02/13/books/13benchley.html?_r=1&oref=slogin*

Robert Benchley

Benchley, Nat (Nathaniel Robert). "'So Sweet a Place.'" *Nantucket Magazine.* Midsummer 1995. 34–39.
Benchley, Nathaniel (Goddard). *Robert Benchley: A Biography.* New York: McGraw-Hill, 1955.
Benchley, Robert. "Abandon Ship!" Ca. 1930–33. In *Benchley Lost and Found: 39 Prodigal Pieces by Robert Benchley.* New York: Dover Publications, 1970. 31–36. [First published in *Liberty Weekly.*]

_____."Why I Am Pale." In *The Benchley Roundup: A Selection by Nathaniel Benchley of His Favorites*. 1954. Repr. Chicago, IL: University of Chicago Press, 1983. 319–21. According to Benchley bibliographer Gordon Ernst, "Why I Am Pale" was written for Robert Benchley's King Features Syndicate column between 1933 and 1936.

Ernst, Gordon E. Jr. *Robert Benchley: An Annotated Bibliography*. Westport, CT: Greenwood Press, 1995.

Eliza Spencer Brock

Brock, Eliza. "Eliza Brock's Journal on the Ship *Lexington*, 21 May 1853–25 June 1856." *http://www.nha.org/digitalexhibits/brocklog/index.htm* [A digital scan of the complete journal offered by the Nantucket Historical Association]

Druett, Joan. "'She Was a Sister Sailor': Mary Brewster, True Woman, Whaling Wife." *The Log of Mystic Seaport* 44.4 (1992): 98–104.

Federbush, Sherri. "The Journal of Eliza Brock: At Sea on the *Lexington*." *Historic Nantucket* 30.1 (July 1982): 13–17. *http://www.nha.org/history/hn/HN-july82-brock.htm*

Edmund Burke

Burke, Edmund. *On Conciliation with America*. 1775. *Project Gutenberg EBook*. http://www.gutenberg.org/dirs/etext04/burke10.txt

Harris, Ian. "Edmund Burke." 23 February 2004. *Stanford Encyclopedia of Philosophy*. http://plato.stanford.edu/entries/burke/#7

Philbrick, Nathaniel. "'Every Wave Is a Fortune': Nantucket Island and the Making of an American Icon." *The New England Quarterly* 66.3 (September 1993): 434–47.

Stackpole, Edouard A. *The Sea-Hunters: The New England Whalemen During Two Centuries, 1635–1835*. New York: J. B. Lippincott, 1953.

Truman Capote

Woodward, Hobson. "American Writers on Nantucket." *The Official 2004 Guide to Nantucket*. Nantucket, MA: Nantucket Island Chamber of Commerce, 2004. 46–49.

Philip Caputo

Caputo, Philip. *In the Shadows of the Morning: Essays on Wild Lands, Wild Waters, and a Few Untamed People*. Guilford, CT: Lyons Press, 2002.

_____. "No Space to Waste." In *Heart of the Land: Essays on Last Great Places*. Ed. Joseph Barbaro and Lisa Weinerman. New York: Pantheon Books, 1994. 161–70.

Owen Chase

Chase, Owen. *Narrative of the Most Extraordinary and Distressing Shipwreck of the Whale-Ship* Essex *of Nantucket*. 1821. In Thomas Nickerson, Owen Chase, et al. *The Loss of the Ship* Essex, *Sunk by a Whale: First-Person Accounts*. Ed. and Introd. Nathaniel Philbrick and Thomas Philbrick. New York: Penguin Books, 2000. 13–73.

Heffernan, Thomas Farel. *Stove by a Whale: Owen Chase and the* Essex. Middletown, CT: Wesleyan University Press, 1981.

Melville, Herman. "Herman Melville's Annotation of Chase's *Narrative*." Ca. 1851–91. In Thomas Nickerson, Owen Chase, et al. *The Loss of the Ship* Essex, *Sunk by a Whale: First-Person Accounts*. Ed. and introd. Nathaniel Philbrick and Thomas Philbrick. New York: Penguin Books, 2000. 75–79.

John Cheever

Cheever, John. "The Seaside Houses." *The Stories of John Cheever*. New York: Ballantine Books, 1985. "The Seaside Houses" was first published in *The New Yorker* 37 (29 July 1961): 19–23.

Donaldson, Scott. John Cheever: A Biography. New York: Random House, 1987.

Tom Congdon

Balling, Joshua. "Peter Benchley, 'Jaws' author, gone at 65." *The Inquirer and Mirror* [Nantucket]. 16 February 2006. *http://www.ack.net/Benchley021606.html*

Congdon, Tom. "FYI; Letter from Nantucket: Mrs. Coffin's Consolation." *Forbes* 160.5 (1 Sept. 1997): S69–76.

_____. "FYI, While You Were Away." *Forbes* 159.9 (5 May 1997): S47–50.

Friedrich, Otto. *Decline and Fall: The Struggle for Power at a Great American Magazine,* The Saturday Evening Post. New York: Harper & Row, 1970.

Frank Conroy

Conroy, Frank. *Time and Tide: A Walk Through Nantucket*. New York: Crown, 2004.

McGrath, Charles. "Frank Conroy Dies at 69; Led Noted Writers' Workshop." *The New York Times.* 7 April 2005. *http://www.nytimes.com/2005/04/07/books/07conroy.html?_r=2&oref=slogin&oref=slogin*

Stanton, Marianne. "Frank Conroy, Writer, Musician, Gone at 69." *The Inquirer and Mirror* [Nantucket]. 7 April 2005. *http://www.ack.net/FrankConroy040705.html*

James Fenimore Cooper

Cooper, James Fenimore. *The Pilot: A Tale of the Sea.* 1823. Project Gutenberg E-Book 2005. *http://www.gutenberg.org/dirs/etext05/8pilt10.txt*

Philbrick, Thomas. "James Fenimore Cooper." *Encyclopedia of American Literature of the Sea and Great Lakes.* Ed. Jill B. Gidmark. Westport, CT: Greenwood Press, 2001. 91–94.

J. Hector St. John de Crèvecoeur

Crèvecoeur, J. Hector St. John de. *Letters from an American Farmer and Sketches of Eighteenth-Century America.* 1782 and 1925. Ed. Albert E. Stone. New York: Penguin Classics, 1988.

Philbrick, Nathaniel. "The Nantucket Sequence in Crèvecoeur's *Letters from an American Farmer.*" *New England Quarterly* 64.3 (September 1991): 414–32.

Philbrick, Thomas. *St. John de Crèvecoeur.* New York: Twayne, 1970.

Frederick Douglass

Beegel, Susan F. "Douglass, Frederick." *Encyclopedia of American Literature of the Sea and Great Lakes.* Ed. Jill B. Gidmark. Westport, CT: Greenwood Press, 2001. 118–20.

Douglass, Frederick. *Life and Times of Frederick Douglass.* 1881. New York: Citadel Press, 1983.

——————. *Narrative of the Life of Frederick Douglass, An American Slave.* 1845. Cambridge, MA: Harvard University Press, 1960.

Garrison, William Lloyd. Preface. *Narrative of the Life of Frederick Douglass, An American Slave.* 1845. Cambridge, MA: Harvard University Press, 1960. 3–15.

Gates, Henry Louis Jr., ed. and introd. *The Classic Slave Narratives.* New York: Mentor, 1987. ix–xviii.

Peters, Pearlie. "Frederick Douglass: The Nantucket Connection." *Nantucket's People of Color: Essays on History, Politics and Community.* Ed. Robert Johnson Jr. Lanham, MD: University Press of America, 2006. 105–29.

Peter Folger

Boyd, Michelle. "Peter Folger and Mary Morrell." 2004. *http://www.boyd-house.com/michelle/swain/peterfolger.html*

"The First New England Poets." *The Beginnings of Verse, 1610–1808.* Vol XV. *Colonial and Revolutionary Literature. The Cambridge History of English and American Literature in 18 Volumes.* http://www.bartleby.com/225/0903.html

Folger, Peter. *A Looking Glass for the Times; or, The Former Spirit of New England Revived in this Generation.* Boston, MA: 1676.

Franklin, Benjamin. *The Autobiography of Benjamin Franklin.* 1793. New Haven, CT: Yale University Press, 1976.

Ralph Waldo Emerson

Emerson, Ralph Waldo. *The Journals and Miscellaneous Notebooks of Ralph Waldo Emerson.* Vol. 10. 1847–1848. Ed. Merton M. Sealts Jr. Cambridge, MA: Belknap Press, 1973.

_____. *Representative Men.* 1850. In *The Collected Works of Ralph Waldo Emerson.* Vol. IV. Ed. Andrew Delbanco. Cambridge, MA: Belknap Press, 1996. Or visit *http://www.rwe.org/pages/representative_men.htm*

Richardson, Robert D. Jr. *Emerson: The Mind on Fire.* Berkeley and Los Angeles: University of California Press, 1995.

Martha Ford

"The Bay of Islands." An Ancestry.com Community. *http://freepages.genealogy.rootsweb.com/~babznz/bayofislands.html*

"Deaths. From the *New Zealand Herald* and Other Papers." 1845–60. *http://www.pearlspad.net.nz/DeathsContinued.htm*

Druett, Joan. *Petticoat Whalers: Whaling Wives at Sea, 1820–1920.* Auckland, NZ: Collins New Zealand, 1991.

"Frequently Asked Questions: What is the Nantucket Girls Song?" *http://www.nha.org/library/faq/nantucketgirlssong.html*

Ford, Martha (?). "Nantucket Girls' Song." In "Eliza Brock's Journal on the Ship *Lexington*, May 21, 1853–June 25, 1856." *http://www.nha.org/digitalexhibits/brocklog/gallery/pages/MS220-136-341.html* [Digital scan of the manuscript original in the collection of the Nantucket Historical Association].

"New Zealand Church and Missionary List: 1800s." *http://www.geocities.com/heartland/park/7572/nzmssnry.htm*

Norling, Lisa. *Captain Ahab Had a Wife: New England Women and the Whalefishery, 1720–1870*. Chapel Hill: University of North Carolina Press, 2000.

Stephen Symonds Foster

Beegel, Susan F. "The Brotherhood of Thieves Riot of 1842." *Historic Nantucket* 40.3 (Fall 1992): 45–48. *http://www.nha.org/history/hn/HN-n40n3-brotherhood.htm*

Foster, Stephen S. *The Brotherhood of Thieves; or, A True Picture of the American Church and Clergy: A Letter to Nathaniel Barney, of Nantucket.* Concord, NH: Parker Pillsbury, 1843. *http://medicolegal.tripod.com/thieves.htm* [copiously annotated on-line edition].

Sterling, Dorothy. *Ahead of Her Time: Abby Kelley and the Politics of Antislavery.* New York: W. W. Norton, 1991. [Abby Kelley was Stephen S. Foster's wife and an important abolitionist and women's rights advocate; her biography is an excellent source of information about Foster.]

William Lloyd Garrison

Garrison, William Lloyd. "Preface." *Narrative of the Life of Frederick Douglass, An American Slave.* 1845. Cambridge, MA: Harvard University Press, 1960. 3–15.

Karttunen, Frances Ruley. *The Other Islanders: People Who Pulled Nantucket's Oars.* New Bedford, MA: Spinner Publications, 2005.

White, Barbara. "Anna Gardner: Teacher of Freedmen, 'A Disturber of Tradition.'" In *Nantucket's People of Color: Essays on History, Politics, and Community.* Ed. Robert Johnson Jr. Lanham, MD: University Press of America, 2006. 71–104.

Frank B. Gilbreth Jr. and Ernestine Gilbreth Carey

Ferguson, David. Comp. "The Gilbreth Network: Books List." *http://gilbreth-network.tripod.com/gbooks.html*

_____. Comp. "The Gilbreth Network: In Memory of Frank B. Gilbreth Jr., 1911–2001." *http://gilbrethnetwork.tripod.com/frankjr.html*

Gilbreth, Frank B. Jr. "'The Gilbreth Bug-lights.'" *Historic Nantucket* 39.2 (Summer 1991): 20–22. *http://www.nha.org/history/hn/HN-summer91-gilbreth.htm*

_____. *Innside Nantucket.* New York: Crowell, 1954.

_____. *Of Whales and Women: One Man's View of Nantucket History.* New York: Crowell, 1956.

Gilbreth, Frank B. Jr. and Ernestine Gilbreth Carey. *Cheaper by the Dozen.* 1948. New York: Perennial Classics, 2002.

Leimbach, Dulcie. "Ernestine Gilbreth Carey, 98, Author of Childhood Memoir, Dies." *The New York Times.* 6 November 2006. *http://www.nytimes.com/2006/11/06/books/06carey.html?_r=1&oref=slogin*

David Halberstam

"David Halberstam Tribute." 22 October 2007. Nantucket Plum TV. *http://nantucket.plumtv.com/archives/topic/27*

Haberman, Clyde. "David Halberstam, 73, Reporter and Author, Dies." 24 April 2007. *The New York Times.* *http://www.nytimes.com/2007/04/24/arts/24halberstam.html?_r=1&page-wanted=print*

Halberstam, David. "Nantucket on My Mind." In *Best American Travel Writing 2000.* Ed. Bill Bryson. Boston, MA: Houghton Mifflin, 2000. 50–58. [Originally published in *Town & Country* magazine, 1 July 1999.]

Sheppard, Steve. "Halberstam Remembered for His Grace, Compassion." 25 April 2007. *The Nantucket Independent On-Line. http://www.nantucketindependent.com/news/2007/0425/Front_Page/002.html*

Joseph C. Hart

Hart, Joseph C. *Miriam Coffin; or, The Whale-Fishermen.* 1834. Nantucket, MA: Mill Hill Press, 1995.

Philbrick, Nathaniel. "Historical Introduction." *Miriam Coffin; or, The Whale-Fishermen.* By Joseph C. Hart. Nantucket, MA: Mill Hill Press, 1995. v–xix.

Ernest Hemingway

Beegel, Susan. "The Young Boy and the Sea: Ernest Hemingway's Visit to Nantucket Island." *Historic Nantucket* 32.3 (January 1985): 18–30. *http://www.nha.org/history/hn/HN-jan85-hemingway.htm*

Hemingway, Ernest. Letter to Mrs. Jenson. 12 January 1961. Hemingway Collection. John F. Kennedy Library. Boston, MA.

_____. *The Old Man and the Sea.* New York: Charles Scribner's Sons, 1952.

Hemingway, Grace Hall. "Tales of Old Nantucket." Ed. and introd. Margaret Moore Booker. *The Hemingway Review* 18.2 (Spring 1999): 46–71.

Elin Hilderbrand

"Elin Hilderbrand." *The Authors.* Hachette Book Group USA.
   http://www.hachettebookgroupusa.com/authors/9/3771/index.html
Hilderbrand, Elin. *The Beach Club.* New York: St. Martin's Press, 2000.
Sheridan, Patricia. "Elin Hilderbrand." *Pittsburgh Post-Gazette.* 28 August 2006.
   Post-Gazette Now. http://www.post-gazette.com/pg/06240/
   716853-129.stm

Christopher Isherwood

Woodward, Hobson. "American Writers on Nantucket." *The Official 2004
   Guide to Nantucket.* Nantucket, MA: Nantucket Island Chamber of
   Commerce, 2004. 46–49.

Thomas Jefferson

Bowman, John S. *The Cambridge Dictionary of American Biography.* Cambridge,
   UK: Cambridge University Press, 1995.
Byers, Edward. *The Nation of Nantucket: Society and Politics in an Early American
   Commercial Center, 1660–1820.* Boston, MA: Northeastern University
   Press, 1987.
Jefferson, Thomas. "Observations on the Whale-Fishery." 1788. *The Avalon
   Project at Yale Law School. http://www.yale.edu/lawweb/avalon/jeffwhal.htm*
Philbrick, Nathaniel. "'Every Wave Is a Fortune': Nantucket Island and the
   Making of an American Icon." *The New England Quarterly* 66.3
   (September 1993): 434–47.

Alice Koller

Koller, Alice. *An Unknown Woman: A Journey to Self-Discovery.* New York:
   Henry Holt, 1982.

Jane Langton

"Jane Langton's Web Page." *http://www.janelangton.com/index.html*
Langton, Jane. *Dark Nantucket Noon.* New York: Harper & Row, 1975.
"Total Solar Eclipse of 1970 Mar 07." NASA Eclipse Home Page. *http://sun-
   earth.gsfc.nasa.gov/eclipse/SEgoogle/SEgoogle1951/SE1970Mar07Tgoogle.html*

William Lay and Cyrus Hussey

Beegel, Susan. "'Mutiny and Atrocious Butchery': The *Globe* Mutiny as a
    Source for *Pym*." In *Poe's* Pym: *Critical Explorations.* Ed. Richard Kopley.
    Durham, NC: Duke University Press, 1992. 7–19, 277–80.

Gibson, Gregory. *Demon of the Waters.* Boston, MA: Little, Brown, 2002.

Heffernan, Thomas Farel. *Mutiny on the* Globe: *The Fatal Voyage of Samuel
    Comstock.* New York: W. W. Norton, 2002.

Hoyt, Edwin P. *The Mutiny on the* Globe. New York: Random House, 1975.

Lay, William and Cyrus Hussey. *Mutiny on Board the Whaleship* Globe. 1828.
    New York: Corinth Books, 1963.

Stackpole, Edouard A. *Mutiny at Midnight.* New York: William Morrow, 1939.

_____. *The Mutiny on the Whaleship* Globe. Nantucket, MA: Edouard A.
    Stackpole, 1981.

Sinclair Lewis

Lewis, Sinclair. *Arrowsmith.* 1925. New York: Signet Classics, 2008.

Goodwin, Donald W., M.D. *Alcohol and the Writer.* New York: Penguin Books,
    1988.

Woodward, Hobson. "American Writers on Nantucket." *The Official 2004
    Guide to Nantucket.* Nantucket, MA: Nantucket Island Chamber of
    Commerce, 2004. 46–49.

Robert Lowell

Freear, Robert. "Survivor Tales of the U.S.S. *Turner* DD648." 2000. Richard
    Angelini and the U.S.S. *Turner* Association. *http://www.geocities.com/usde-
    stroyer/turnersur.html*

Lowell, Robert. *The Letters of Robert Lowell.* Ed. Saskia Hamilton. New York:
    Farrar, Straus, and Giroux, 2005.

_____. "The Quaker Graveyard in Nantucket." 1945. *Selected Poems.*
    Rev. ed. New York: Farrar, Straus, and Giroux, 1977. 6–10.

Woodward, Hobson. "'My Brightest Summer.'" *Nantucket Magazine* (Spring
    2001): 25–35.

Obed Macy

Historical Note: MS96—Macy Family Papers, 1729–1959. *Manuscript
    Collections Held at the Nantucket Historical Association Research Library.*
    Nantucket, MA. *http://www.nha.org/library/ms/msguide.html*

Macy, Obed. *The History of Nantucket: Being a Compendious Account of the First Settlement of the Island by the English Together with the Rise and Progress of the Whale Fishery.* 1835. Second edition, 1880. Clifton, NJ: Augustus M. Kelley, 1972.

Vincent, Howard P. *The Trying—out of Moby-Dick.* 1949. Kent, OH: Kent State University Press, 1980.

Herman Melville

Bloom, Harold. *The Anxiety of Influence: A Theory of Poetry.* Oxford, UK: Oxford University Press, 1973.

Beegel, Susan F. "Herman Melville: Nantucket's First Tourist?" *Historic Nantucket* 39.3 (Fall 1991): 41–44.

_____. "Forever Entwined: *Moby-Dick* and Nantucket." *Nantucket Magazine* (Fall/Holiday 2001): 32–38.

Bercaw, Mary K. *Melville's Sources.* Evanston, IL: Northwestern University Press, 1987.

Carlisle, Henry. *The Jonah Man.* New York: Alfred A. Knopf, 1984.

Eliot, T. S. "The Waste Land." 1922. In *The Complete Poems and Plays, 1909–1950.* New York: Harcourt, Brace & World, 1971. 37–55.

Melville, Herman. "Hawthorne and His Mosses." In *Moby-Dick: A Norton Critical Edition.* Ed. Harrison Hayford and Hershel Parker. New York: W. W. Norton, 1967. 535–51.

_____. *Moby-Dick, or The Whale.* 1851. Ed. Harrison Hayford, Hershel Parker, and G. Thomas Tanselle. Evanston and Chicago, IL: Northwestern University Press and the Newbery Library, 1988. [The definitive edition.]

_____. "The Stone Fleet: An Old Sailor's Lament." 1861. In *Poems of Herman Melville.* Ed. Douglas Robillard. New Haven, CT: College and University Press, 1976. 43–44.

Parker, Hershel. *Herman Melville: A Biography.* Volume 1, 1819–1851. Baltimore, MD: Johns Hopkins University Press, 1996.

Parker, Hershel and Harrison Hayford, eds. *Moby-Dick as Doubloon: Essays and Extracts (1851–1970).* New York: W. W. Norton, 1970.

Sealts, Merton M. Jr. *Melville's Reading.* Columbia: University of South Carolina Press, 1988.

Vincent, Howard P. *The Trying-out of Moby-Dick.* 1949. Kent, OH: Kent State University Press, 1980.

Maria Mitchell

Albers, Henry, ed. *Maria Mitchell: A Life in Journals and Letters.* Clinton Corners, NY: College Avenue Press, 2001.

Booker, Margaret Moore. *Among the Stars: The Life of Maria Mitchell.* Nantucket, MA: Mill Hill Press, 2007.

Mitchell, Maria. *Maria Mitchell: Life, Letters, and Journals.* Compiled by Phebe Mitchell Kendall. 1896. Project Gutenberg E-Book. *http://www.gutenberg.org/dirs/1/0/2/0/10202/10202.txt*

Robert F. Mooney

Mooney, Robert F. *Nantucket Only Yesterday: An Island View of the Twentieth Century.* Nantucket, MA: Wesco Publishing, 2000.

_____. *The Wreck of the* British Queen. Nantucket, MA: Mill Hill Press, 1988.

Lucretia Coffin Mott

Bacon, Margaret Hope. *Valiant Friend: The Life of Lucretia Mott.* New York: Walker and Company, 1980.

Douglass, Frederick. *Life and Times of Frederick Douglass.* 1881. Repr. New York: Citadel Press, 1983.

Mott, Lucretia Coffin. "Discourse on Woman." Speech delivered 17 December 1849. Philadelphia, PA: W.P. Kildare, 1869. *www.infoplease.com/t/hist/discourse-on-woman/*

_____. Letter to Elizabeth Cady Stanton. 1855. In *Selected Letters of Lucretia Coffin Mott.* Ed. Beverly Wilson Palmer. Urbana-Champaign, IL: University of Illinois Press, 2002. 233–34. *http://books.google.com/books?hl=en&lr=&ie=UTF-8&id=5NI5mhy5CR8C&oi=fnd&pg=PR11&dq=lucretia+mott&ots=mBrPl5P6QO&sig=zCsR5FNLBLIDFILteTlaIE5avZQ#PPA233,M1*

_____. Speech to Women's Rights Convention. Cleveland, OH. 1853. In *Lucretia Mott Speaking: Excerpts from the Sermons & Speeches of a Famous Nineteenth-Century Quaker Minister and Reformer.* Comp. Margaret Hope Bacon. Wallingford, PA: Pendle Hill Publications, 1980. 16. *https://www.pendlehill.org/resources/files/pdf%20files/php234b.pdf*

_____, Elizabeth Cady Stanton, Mary Ann McClintock, Martha Coffin Wright, Jane Hunt. "Declaration of Sentiments." 1848. Women's Rights National Historic Park. Seneca Falls, NY. *http://www.nps.gov/archive/wori/declaration.htm*

Women's Rights National Historical Park. http://www.nps.gov/wori/index.htm

Nantucket History

Albion, Robert A., William A. Baker, and Benjamin W. Labaree. *New England and the Sea*. Middletown, CT: Mystic Seaport and Wesleyan University Press, 1972.

Fabrikant, Geraldine. "Old Nantucket Warily Meets the New." *The New York Times* (5 June 2005). *http://www.nytimes.com/2005/06/05/national/class/NANTUCKET-FINAL.html?pagewanted=1&_r=1*

Hoyt, Edwin. *Nantucket: The Life of an Island*. Brattleboro, VT: Stephen Greene Press, 1978.

Miller, Richard F. and Robert F. Mooney. *The Civil War: The Nantucket Experience*. Nantucket, MA: Wesco Publishing, 1994.

Mooney, Robert F. *Nantucket Only Yesterday: An Island View of the Twentieth Century*. Nantucket, MA: Wesco Publishing, 2000.

Morris, Paul C. and Joseph F. Morin. *The Island Steamers*. Nantucket, MA: Nantucket Nautical Publishers, 1977.

Philbrick, Nathaniel. *Away Offshore: Nantucket Island and Its People, 1602–1890*. Nantucket, MA: Mill Hill Press, 1994.

_____. "Nantucket." *Encyclopedia of American Literature of the Sea and Great Lakes*. Ed. Jill B. Gidmark. Westport, CT: Greenwood Press, 2001. 308–11.

Stackpole, Edouard A. *The Sea-Hunters: The New England Whalemen During Two Centuries, 1635–1835*. New York: J. B. Lippincott, 1953.

Starbuck, Alexander. *The History of Nantucket: County, Island, and Town*. 1924. Repr. Rutland, VT: Charles Tuttle, 1969.

Stevens, William O. *Old Nantucket: The Faraway Island*. New York: Dodd, Mead, 1936.

Sena Jeter Naslund

Naslund, Sena Jeter. *Ahab's Wife; or, The Star-Gazer*. New York: William Morrow, 1999.

_____. "Interview." *Page ONE Literary Newsletter Web Site*. *http://www.pageonelit.com/interviews/Naslund.html*.

Eugene O'Neill

O'Neill, Eugene. *Complete Plays: 1920–1931*. Ed. Travis Bogard. New York: Library of America, 1988.

Woodward, Hobson. "American Writers on Nantucket." *The Official 2004 Guide to Nantucket*. Nantucket, MA: Nantucket Island Chamber of Commerce, 2004. 46–49.

Nathaniel Philbrick

"Nathaniel Philbrick Bio." *http://www.nathanielphilbrick.com/about/bio.html*

Philbrick, Nathaniel. *In the Heart of the Sea: The Tragedy of the Whaleship* Essex. New York: Viking, 2000.

Edgar Allan Poe

Baudelaire, Charles, trans. *Aventures d'Arthur Gordon Pym par Edgar Poe.* Paris: Michel Levy Frères, 1858.

Kennedy, J. Gerald. *The Narrative of Arthur Gordon Pym and the Abyss of Interpretation: A Reader's Companion.* New York: Twayne Publishers, 1995.

Poe, Edgar Allan. *The Imaginary Voyages: The Narrative of Arthur Gordon Pym, The Unparalleled Adventure of one Hans Pfaall, The Journal of Julius Rodman.* Ed. Burton R. Pollin. *Collected Writings of Edgar Allan Poe.* Boston: Twayne Publishers, 1981. [While there are many excellent editions of *Pym,* this one is absolutely definitive, with copious notes and comments by the great Poe scholar Burton Pollin. *Pym* appears on pages 1–363. For critical interpretation, see entries for Beegel and Kennedy.]

Verne, Jules. *An Antarctic Mystery; Or, the Sphinx of the Ice Fields: A Sequel to Edgar Allan Poe's The Narrative of Arthur Gordon Pym.* 1897. Trans. Mrs. Cashel Hoey. 1899. Rockville, MD: Wildside Press, 2005.

Edward J. Pompey

"Appendix D: House Bill No. 45, 1845. An Act Concerning Public Schools." In White. 56.

Karttunen, Frances Ruley. *The Other Islanders: People Who Pulled Nantucket's Oars.* New Bedford, MA: Spinner Publications, 2005.

Pompey, Edward J. "Appendix C: Petition of Edward J. Pompey and 104 Others to the Massachusetts State House." 1845. In White. 55.

White, Barbara. *The African School and the Integration of Nantucket Public Schools 1825–1847.* Boston, MA: Boston University Afro-American Studies Center, 1978.

_____. "The Integration of Nantucket Public Schools." *Historic Nantucket* 40.3 (Fall 1992): 59–62.

http://www.nha.org/history/hn/HN-n40n3-white.htm

Jeremiah N. Reynolds

Beegel, Susan. "'Mutiny and Atrocious Butchery': The *Globe* Mutiny as a
Source for *Pym*." In *Poe's Pym: Critical Explorations*. Ed. Richard Kopley.
Durham, NC: Duke University Press, 1992. 7–19, 277–80.

Philbrick, Nathaniel. *Sea of Glory: America's Voyage of Discovery, The U.S.
Exploring Expedition 1838–1842*. New York: Viking, 2003.

Reynolds, Jeremiah N. "Mocha–Dick: Or the White Whale of the Pacific: A
Leaf from a Manuscript Journal." *The Knickerbocker New York Monthly
Magazine* 8 (May 1839): 377–92. Full text available at
http://www.melville.org/reynolds.htm

Stackpole, Edouard A. *The Sea-Hunters: The New England Whalemen During Two
Centuries, 1635–1835*. New York: J. B. Lippincott, 1953.

The 'Sconset School of Opinion

Burne, Lee Rand. "The 'Sconset School of Opinion." *Historic Nantucket* 41.2
(Summer 1993): 27–29. *http://www.nha.org/history/hn/HN-v41n2-
burne.htm*

"The 'Sconset School." *The New York Times*. 20 August 1922.
*http://query.nytimes.com/mem/archive-free/
pdf?_r=1&res=9801E1DB1E3FE432A25753C2A96E9C946395D6CF*

John Steinbeck

Steinbeck, John. *East of Eden*. New York: Viking Penguin, 1952.

_____. *Journal of a Novel: The* East of Eden *Letters*. 1951. New York:
Penguin Books, 1969.

Woodward, Hobson. "The Summer of His Content." *Nantucket Magazine*
(Summer 2001): 24–34.

Edouard A. Stackpole

Akasie, Jay. "Historian Edouard Stackpole Leaves Rich, Scholarly Legacy." *The
Inquirer and Mirror* [Nantucket]. 9 September 1993.

Anon. "In Person." *Nantucket Map & Legend*. 8 September 1993.

Long, Tom. "Edouard Stackpole, 89; Authority on Nantucket, Maritime
History." *The Boston Globe*. 3 September 1993.

Stackpole, Edouard A. *Life Saving Nantucket*. Nantucket, MA: The Nantucket
Life Saving Museum, 1972.

_____. *The Sea-Hunters: The New England Whalemen During Two
Centuries, 1635–1835*. New York: J. B. Lippincott, 1953.

Nancy Thayer

Thayer, Nancy. "About the Author." *http://www.nancythayer.com/about.php*.
_____. *Spirit Lost*. New York: Charles Scribner's Sons, 1988.

Paul Theroux

Theroux, Paul. "Dead Reckoning to Nantucket." *Fresh Air Fiend: Travel Writings 1985–2000*. Boston, MA: Houghton Mifflin, 2000. 70–78.
_____. "Small-Craft Warnings." *Condé Nast Traveler* (August 1989): 66, 68–69, 72–73, 130–31.

Henry David Thoreau

Dean, Bradley P. and Ronald Wesley Hoag. "Thoreau's Lectures After *Walden*: An Annotated Calendar." In *Studies in the American Renaissance, 1996*. Ed. Joel Myerson. Charlottesville: University Press of Virginia, 1996. 241–362. [Their discussion of Thoreau's New Bedford and Nantucket lectures of 1854 is available on-line at *http://www.walden.org/Institute/thoreau/life/Lecturing/47_Lecture.htm* and *http://www.walden.org/Institute/thoreau/life/Lecturing/48_Lecture.htm*]
Thoreau, Henry David. "Life Without Principle." 1863. *The Thoreau Reader: The Annotated Works of Henry David Thoreau*. Ed. Richard Lenat. *http://thoreau.eserver.org/lifewout.html* ["Life Without Principle" was adapted by Thoreau from his 1854 lecture "What Shall It Profit?" and published in *The Atlantic Monthly* the year following his death from tuberculosis in 1862.]
_____. Journal 27–29 December 1854. *The Writings of Henry David Thoreau: On-Line. Journal Transcripts: Manuscript Volume 18*. Eds. Wesley T. Mott and Laura Dasow Wells. *http://www.library.ucsb.edu/thoreau/writings_journals18.html*

John Greenleaf Whittier

Pollard, John A. *John Greenleaf Whittier: Friend of Man*. Boston, MA: Houghton Mifflin, 1949.
Whittier, John Greenleaf. "The Exiles." 1840. In *The Poetical Works of Whittier*. Ed. Hyatt H. Waggoner. Boston, MA: Houghton Mifflin, 1975. 14–17.
Woodwell, Roland H. *John Greenleaf Whittier: A Biography*. Haverhill, MA: Trustees of the John Greenleaf Whittier Homestead, 1985.

Tennessee Williams

Spoto, Donald. *The Kindness of Strangers: The Life of Tennessee Williams.* Boston, MA: Little, Brown, 1985.
Woodward, Hobson. "Summer of '46." *Nantucket Magazine* (Spring 1995): 22–29.

Ron Winslow

"2005 Visiting Journalist: Ron Winslow." University of New Hampshire Journalism Program. *http://www.unh.edu/english/journal/visiting/visitingjournalist_Winslow05.htm*
Winslow, Ron. *Hard Aground: The Story of the* Argo Merchant *Oil Spill.* New York: W.W. Norton, 1978.

Chronology

Acknowledgments

My DEEPEST DEBT IN creating this anthology is to my late husband, Wesley N. Tiffney Jr., founder of the University of Massachusetts Nantucket Field Station and for thirty-five years its director. Wes was an omnivorous, two-fisted reader, who often had three or four books going at once. His Ph.D. was in botany; his specialty was plant ecology; but Wes was passionately interested in just about everything, including literature and history, and especially interested in Nantucket. He wasted no time in persuading me that a literary scholar could find not only connubial felicity on the faraway island, but intellectual fascination, too. Wes was my tutor as well as my husband, and his Nantucket library has been my mainstay throughout this project.

Of course the writing and scholarship of Nantucket historian Nathaniel Philbrick are not only represented in these pages, but lie behind them as well, as my bibliography will attest. To Nat, in his capacity as founding director of the Egan Institute for Maritime Studies, I am also indebted for the very idea of this book. It's been a long time since our original "Wouldn't it be cool if? . . ." conversation, but now the results are in at last. To Jean Grimmer, current executive director of the Egan Institute, I am grateful for unflagging and generous support of that concept. Without Jean, it might never have become reality.

My warmest thanks to the managing editor of Mill Hill Press, Dick Duncan, for his extraordinary patience and sense of humor—both much tried in the course of this project—and to copy editor and Nantucket Historical Association research associate Libby Oldham, for her meticulous attention to detail and expert knowledge of Nantucket history. This book would not have been possible at all without Stacy Fusaro's hard work in obtaining permissions for copyrighted material. My thanks as well to Cecile Kaufman for a book design that gladdens my heart, to Mitchell's Book Corner for permission to use its handsome Kevin Paulsen mural on the jacket, and to Jeffrey Allen for photographing that mural, a very tricky assignment.

Many friends, old and new, helped me with research and selections. My thanks to Mimi Beman, former owner of Mitchell's Book Corner; Margaret Moore Booker, biographer of Maria Mitchell; Anne Derosie, historian of the Women's Rights National Historic Park in Seneca Falls, New York; Scott Donaldson, biographer of John Cheever; Gordon Ernst, director and bibliographer of the Robert Benchley Society; Glenn Gordinier and Richard King, history and literature faculty of the Williams College-Mystic Seaport Maritime

Studies Program; Meg Lamb, of *Condé Nast Traveler;* and Nancy Thayer, Nantucket novelist extraordinaire. Special thanks to author, editor, journalist, archivist, and historian Hobson Woodward for sharing his wealth of published material on Nantucket literature.

There can be no research without great libraries and enthusiastic librarians. My thanks to Sharon Carlee, Ellie Coffin, Mary Macy, Eileen McGrath, and Lincoln Thurber of the Nantucket Atheneum. Now that I'm an off-islander, I'm especially grateful to the Nantucket Historical Association's Research Library and its campaign to make key publications and manuscripts available on-line. Closer to home, Laura Bean, Teeter Bibber, and Leslie Mortimer of the Patten Free Library in Bath, Maine, were tremendously helpful in tracking down hard-to-find publications and information. The reference staff of the Bowdoin College Library deserves kudos as well.

I want to thank my dear friends Bob and Diane Lang, their daughters Jessie and Erica, as well as their dogs Buzz and Rudy for always having a spare bedroom for a visiting researcher and her own canine companions.

A tip of the hat to colleagues Donald Yannella and Mary K. Bercaw Edwards of the Melville Society, Richard Kopley of the Poe Studies Association, Susan Shillinglaw of the National Steinbeck Museum, and Jim Carlton of the Williams College-Mystic Seaport Maritime Studies Program. Each has been instrumental in helping me understand both Nantucket's importance to American literature and the value of interdisciplinary study. And hail and farewell to some of the great Nantucket readers of the past who welcomed and taught me when I first moved to the island as a bride in 1983: historian Edouard Stackpole; archivist Louise Hussey; librarian Barbara Andrews; and her brother, naturalist J. Clinton Andrews.

There are so many friends I should thank—Nantucket readers all—that I would run the risk of leaving someone out if I once began. You know who you are. Warm thanks for your role in the happiest twenty years of my life and many stimulating conversations about books and literature. I miss you.

And finally, my thanks to the staff, trustees, volunteers, and members of the African Meeting House, the Egan Maritime Institute, the Maria Mitchell Association, the Nantucket Atheneum, the Nantucket Conservation Foundation, the Nantucket Historical Association, and the Nantucket Shipwreck & Lifesaving Museum. Each of these organizations has contributed in some way to this book. The role that they play in preserving the island's human and natural history, as well as the artifacts and scenes of Nantucket's literary past, is crucial to the future.